The **SOUND WEAVER SAGA**

Anthem Rising

By

Sterling Stone

To everyone who's faced adversity and came out the other side — and to those still in the thick of it: you've got this.

And to you, the reader — thanks for flipping through these pages and wandering through a small corner of my mind. (Also, full disclosure: this may or may not be Step One in my master plan to get more people to listen to my favorite band, Coldrain.)

A Note About the Soundtrack

The Sound Weaver Saga: Anthem Rising was written with music in mind—not just as a theme, but as a character in the story. To enhance your reading experience, I've created official companion playlists of songs that capture the tone, emotion, and energy of scenes in the story. While entirely optional, listening along can immerse you even deeper in the world of Anthem, Indy, and the Sound Weavers.

How It Works:

- Throughout the book, you'll find music cues that correspond with specific scenes.

- Each song was selected to reflect what the characters are feeling or what the world sounds like in that moment.

- You can listen to the tracks before you turn the first page, while reading; in-between scenes, or after to reflect—it's up to you.

- The playlist lives on Spotify and may be updated over time to reflect new interpretations.

Listen Here:

The Sound Weaver Saga: Anthem Rising — Official Soundtrack

The Sound Weaver Saga Soundtrack

Obsidian Key Set List

Rooftop Set List

Moonlit Grove Set List

Table of Contents

CHAPTER 1

Anthem Fox crouched in the shadow of a rusted dumpster, his breath fogging in the frigid night air. A dense fog rolled through one of the countless narrow maze-like alleyways of Crucible City's Lower District he was now perched in. Overhead, the dull flickering glow of neon signs and billboard projections struggled to cut through the fog's haze. Further above, silent patrol blimps drifted through the sky—massive, looming shadows adorned with spotlights.

The echo of booted footsteps pounding on cobblestone bounced off the narrow walls. A sound that echoed his impending doom. The Silencers were close. A colloquial nickname given to the law enforcers working for the Creative Engagement Authority, governed by the Harmonic Council. One wrong move, one sound too loud, and their lives would be over. The Independent Artists Act had made it clear—any unlicensed performance, any unapproved art, was a crime against The Council's order. For Anthem and his band, Manufacturing Eden, every song was an act of rebellion. Caught without approval, they wouldn't get a trial. Only silence.

Bliss crouched beside him, pulling her hood further over her face. Her sharp green eyes darted to the corner where the Silencer patrolled, the outline of his weapon visible in the low amber light. Geddy, the bassist, shifted uncomfortably behind her, clutching his case like it was a lifeline. Buddy, the drummer, and

Tatum, their keyboardist, kept perfectly still, while Indy, the band's roadie, brought up the rear.

The Silencer stopped. Anthem held his breath. The enforcer's cold, full face mask helmet scanned the alley with an expressionless gaze. He hadn't spotted them yet, but he lingered, his hand twitching toward his weapon.

"Anthem," Indy whispered, barely audible.

"I know," he whispered back, on edge but focused.

A loud clatter broke the silence. A stray cat darted from behind a pile of trash overflowing from a nearby dumpster. The Silencer spun around sharply, watching the cat jump onto a chain-linked fence. From his viewpoint, Anthem got a good look at the Silencer's uniform. It was a stark, intimidating blend of black, white, and gray, designed to symbolize neutrality, quiet, and purity. The base of the uniform was a sleek, matte-black armored bodysuit, segmented at the shoulders, chest, and thighs, with reinforced plates for protection.

Over the bodysuit, he wore a high-collared, double-breasted jacket in sharp gray with white trim that followed the edges of the lapels and cuffs. The jacket, tailored to perfection, extending just past the hips, displayed the insignia of the Creative Engagement Authority—A tuning fork in the center, flanked by two symmetrical wings, encircled by a laurel-like pattern of stylized musical notes, etched in metallic silver on the left breast.

His utility harness carried compartments filled with compact tools and handcuffs. A hand wrapped in black gloves, reinforced at the knuckles, rested on a weapon holstered at his hip. Heavy black boots with reinforced steel toes and soles completed the uniform.

Emerging from behind the Silencer and hovering at his shoulder was a spherical drone. Its surface was a smooth, matte gray broken only by a glowing white band that encircled its middle. About the size of a basketball, the drone emitted a faint hum as it floated effortlessly. The white band occasionally rippled with pulses of light. Apertures dotted its smooth exterior, concealing an array of tools and sensors capable of scanning, recording, and, if necessary, subduing. The tension in Anthem's shoulders eased just slightly as the enforcer and the drone moved on.

"We need to move," Indy whispered sharply.

Anthem nodded, motioning for the others to follow. They crept down the alley in single file, weaving between piles of trash and broken crates until they reached a rusted metal grate set into the ground. Beneath it, the faint thrum of music vibrated through the steel mesh.

Anthem kneeled and pried the grate open, the sharp groan of metal setting everyone's nerves on edge. The others slipped inside one by one, descending into the narrow tunnel beneath the city. It smelled of mildew and damp concrete. Graffiti depicting various social activists over the years covered the walls. Anthem likened it to ancient cave paintings as he ventured deeper into the tunnel.

"*The Club's* packed," Bliss said, running her fingers over the faded outline of a painted phoenix on the wall. "You can feel it already."

"And the Silencers know it too," Indy muttered, her eyes scanning the tunnel behind them. "They're not stupid. We've pushed our luck tonight."

Anthem turned; his expression was grim but determined. "That's why we have to make this count."

At the end of the tunnel, a heavy steel door stood ajar, spilling flashing neon light and the unmistakable pounding bass of the underground music scene. Anthem pushed the door open, and the sound swallowed them whole.

The Club was an eclectic fusion of industrial grit and a bohemian soul. Low, intimate lighting cast shadows on worn leather sofas and velvet armchairs that dotted the venue. Patrons lounged with drinks in hand while their eyes flickered between lively conversation and the stage. Thick, crimson velvet draped the walls, concealing hidden alcoves where whispered rebellions and secret romances flourished. It was a haven for those who dared defy the system. The Council didn't care for it, but that only made the place more vital.

Anthem glanced back at the group. Bliss pulled off her hood, revealing fiery red hair that cascaded over her shoulders, catching the light in waves that shimmered like molten copper. Geddy adjusted his grip on his bass case. Buddy and Tatum exchanged a nod. Indy stood by the entrance, scanning the room for potential threats.

"Let's do this," Anthem yelled over the din of the booming music.

Even amongst the sweat, smoke, color and noise, Anthem possessed an aura of reserved strength, a calm intensity that set him apart. He was a smoking ember just beneath the brush, waiting for the right note to spark an inferno. The strobing lights painted his skin in golds and bronzes, adding a warm glow to his sepia tone.

Sable dreadlocks framed his face, pulled back beneath a blue and gold tie-up headband. His eyes—rich, like fall leaves caught in twilight—swept across the room. No nerves. Just focus. They were the eyes of someone who poured every ounce of himself into his music, someone who didn't just play music but breathed it.

Ripped black jeans clung to his lean frame, and a battered leather jacket hung over a torn graphic tee. Scuffed boots, squared shoulders, unshakable presence—he looked like rebellion in motion. But beneath that edge? To those that really knew him, saw a heart tuned tightly to the world. A heart full of empathy, one that bled with every note he played. His music wasn't just sound. It was survival. His music told the truth. Held people together when the world tried to pull them apart.

Bliss stalked beside him, eyes sharp, movements precise. Even in the Club's chaos, she pulled focus like a spotlight. Sequins shimmered with every step. Her sparkling glamor lit up the space around her like a disco ball. The wide-leg pants and heeled boots gave her height, but her presence did the heavy lifting. She didn't just command a stage—she *owned* it.

Geddy followed, tapping the neck of his bass in time with the pulsing beat. Calm, unreadable, and undeniably cool. Hair in his eyes. Faded tee. Jeans that looked like they'd survived a war. But that bass? It gleamed like it was fresh off the assembly line.

Tatum drifted behind them, fingers dancing over phantom keys. She moved like smoke, silver-blonde hair trailing behind her in soft waves. Layers of gauzy knitted fabrics clung and flowed from her tiny frame, a quiet storm of bohemian grace. Charms at her neck and rings on her fingers shimmered under the lights, but her pale blue eyes never settled on the crowd—they searched some place distant, some place only she could see.

Buddy buzzed at her side, drumsticks twitching in his grip. All curls and ink and restless energy. He bounced on his heels like a spark, looking for something to ignite. Buddy had the kind of enthusiasm that could light up a room—hell, his *presence* was practically enough to set it on fire.

Indy, ever the mama bear, flanked the group, her eyes scanning the crowd as they made their way through. Her movements were subtle but efficient—always observing, always ready. The band could trust her to see everything they missed, especially in a place like this.

They passed the chaotic dance floor, pushing through a soft haze of cigar smoke and more illicit substances that made everything feel like a dream. The stage emerged ahead, hidden behind thick curtains that trembled with the pulse of the crowd. Anthem reached for the curtain and pulled it back just enough for the band to slip behind the velvet drapes. He didn't look at the others—they didn't need to exchange words. This was their rhythm, their routine, the unspoken dance of years spent together.

They set up quickly, each of them falling into place with the precision of a of warriors preparing for battle. Geddy dropped his bass into place, his fingers already resting on the strings, his eyes focused on Anthem. Buddy set his kit with a quiet authority, adjusting his snare drum just the way he liked it. Tatum placed her keyboard with fluid movement, ready to plug into the system. Bliss took the mic and readied herself into a commanding posture.

Anthem made his way to the center of the stage, his guitar plugged in and ready. Buddy walked up behind Anthem and placed a hand on his shoulder before turning back to his kit and settling down on the stool. Anthem nodded at Buddy, then gave the signal to Indy, who stood at the side, just off-stage. She gave him a brief thumbs up and gave the signal to the engineer.

The current music faded into the background, and an eerie hush fell over the crowd. Anthem could feel the weight of it—the silence before this pivotal moment. He strummed a single chord on his guitar, loud enough to snap the silence, but not yet the song. The crowd, sensing the change, hushed further.

Anthem gave a slight nod to Bliss. And then, with a deep breath, he turned to the rest of the band and gave the silent cue.

The curtain dropped.[1]

Their music slammed into the room with a roar, an almost violent intensity. Anthem's fingers flew over the guitar strings, pulling sharp, melodious chords that shattered the stillness like glass.

Bliss's voice hit next, exploding like a grenade through the air with a ferocity that matched the music. *"We were never meant to be caged!"* she screamed into the mic, her words dripping with defiance and fury.

She stomped across the stage, coiling the mic cord around her arm like a whip. Her boots hit the metal riser with a thunderous *boom*, syncing perfectly with the feral growl of Anthem's guitar next to her. The lights flared—red, then gold, then searing white—as the band crashed into the chorus.

"Rip down the walls they built to bind us,"

"Break every chain they wrap around our name!"

She sang like a woman possessed, eyes blazing like a firestorm.

"We are the storm, we are the silence,"

"We are the fire they'll never tame!"

She leaped onto a stack of speakers; her silhouette lit up like the goddess of rebellion.

"You dress your lies up like law..."

---

1. Track 1 - Paramore - Let the Flames Begin

"Your rules carved in rotten awe!"

The crowd roared back, fists punching the air like they were trying to grab hold of Bliss' words.

"This is our reckoning. Our rebirth."

"A symphony born from ash and rage."

"We'll flood this earth—"

"We were NEVER meant to be caged!"

The crowd erupted, bodies swarming, heads bobbing, fists pumping to the beat. For one brief, beautiful moment, Anthem felt like they were all part of something larger—something that the Council's rules could never contain.

The energy in *The Club* swelled as Anthem's guitar shredded through the speakers. The sea of people moved in sync, their bodies pressed together in a writhing mass of noise and sweat, while the more reserved club goers sat on the edge of their seats. Anthem's eyes narrowed, feeling the spirit of the song possessing him. The crowd was his stage now.

Without a second thought, he slid the guitar strap off his shoulder. He shot a look back at Bliss, who was consumed by the rhythm, her voice cutting through the air like a blade. She didn't need him on stage. Not for this.

With a swift motion, he jumped off the edge of the stage, landing in the crowd with a practiced grace. A cheer rose from the front row as people scrambled to make room for him. Anthem didn't hesitate—he dove straight into the mass of bodies, his fingers steadily danced across the strings, the guitar howling as if it was alive. The music wrapped around him, melding with the crowd. They fed off each other, a beautiful cycle of energy.

The crowd went ballistic. People were climbing on shoulders, tears in their eyes, like they'd just seen something holy—or unholy. It didn't matter.

Anthem twisted through the crowd, ducking under raised arms and sidestepping bodies, letting the rhythm of the song guide him. His fingers were alive on the guitar, the music pulling him deeper into the moment, into something primal. He spun, his body a blur of motion, and for a brief second, his eyes met those of a stranger—a face half-hidden behind a scarf, someone who, for that fleeting instant, was connected to him in a way that was more meaningful than he realized.

The crowd roared as Anthem played, their voices and bodies merging into the sound of the song. Every time his guitar screamed a fresh note, they screamed with him, their chants feeding into his intensity. The song was a living thing now, growing with each strum. It was magic; it was liberation; it was everything the Harmonic Council feared and hated.

He moved farther, weaving through the crowd, pushing closer to the center of the pit, where bodies thrashed without care, without rules. He was the music now, and the music was him. Anthem lost himself in it, in the raw intensity of their shared freedom.

His guitar solo stretched out. Anthem's fingers coaxed every ounce of sound out of the instrument as if he were trying to speak through it. Anthem slid and twirled, his feet barely touching the ground as he drifted further into the madness of the crowd. He was surrounded now, the crowd closing in around him, but it felt like the most freeing thing in the world. No longer just a performer anymore. More than just a rebel with a guitar. In this moment, he was *everything.*

Then the doors burst open.

A deafening *boom* swallowed the music as the entrance to *The Club* exploded inward. The lights near the back of the venue flickered, casting jagged shadows as figures in dark, armored uniforms flooded inside. Silencers.

The crowd barely had time to react before the first command was shouted through the air. "Stay where you are! By order of the Creative Engagement Authority, this gathering is unauthorized. Any resistance will be met with force."

The music screeched to a halt, the bass still reverberating through the speakers as silence—true, suffocating silence—descended. Anthem's breath hitched; his fingers frozen on the strings. Every nerve in his body screamed at him to keep playing, to fight against the quiet they were trying to impose.

Bliss turned sharply, her mic still in hand, her expression locked in between disobedience and terror. Tatum's hands hovered over the keys, and Geddy's bass hummed with the ghost of a final note. Buddy gripped his drumsticks tighter, knuckles white.

Indy, stationed near the edge of the stage, reacted first. "We have to move. *Now.*"

The crowd erupted into chaos. Some bolted for the exits, shoving past one another in a desperate attempt to escape. Others hesitated, torn between flight and fight. That moment of indecision would be their downfall.

The first Silencer raised a weapon—sleek, black, and humming with potential energy. A warning shot fired into the ceiling, sent sparks raining down. "Surrender Indie Artists. Now."

Anthem clenched his jaw. Every muscle in his body screamed at him to run, but something inside him rebelled at the thought of leaving *The Club* in silence. Ultimately, his decision was made for him. How Indy managed to maneuver through the pandemonium to get to him is still a mystery to Anthem to this day.

She grabbed Anthem's arm, yanking him back to reality. "We can't fight them. Move!"

After regrouping with the band, they moved as one. Anthem swung his guitar over his back, muscles coiled for action as he followed Indy past the stage. Bliss shot one last defiant glare at the Silencers before following. Geddy was already moving, bass in hand, and Tatum and Buddy abandoned their instruments, focusing instead on escape.

The back exits were their only chance.

The sounds of the raid behind them gradually dampened as Anthem and the band ran through one of the many tunnel openings, replaced by the slow drip of water and the distant hum of generators.

"Keep moving," Indy urged, leading the way through the complex winding tunnel system.

The air was foul. Reeking of stagnant water and waste, but they kept moving, feet splashing through the tunnel. *The Club*'s escape routes—built for nights like this—were the only reason they weren't already dead.

Behind them, a muffled explosion shook the ground.

"They're coming." Geddy panted.

Anthem didn't slow. The passage ahead twisted and narrowed, the dim emergency lights casting eerie reflections in the shallow water.

Figures waited at key turns in the tunnel, half-hidden behind scarves and steel. They didn't flee. They stayed behind to pull switches, seal gates, slow the Silencers however they could. As Anthem and the others passed, an organizer pulled a switch hidden beneath a rusted pipe. A steel gate came crashing down, sealing off a section of the tunnel behind them.

Another steel gate came down. A second explosion rocked the tunnel.

The Silencers were still coming, and they'd have to fight for every inch.

"This way," Indy called, pointing to a passage on the right.

Anthem followed without hesitation. The ground sloped upward slightly, leading them closer to their escape. More detonations echoed behind them—booby traps set to slow pursuit. Metal gates slammed shut, others opened, flooding some passageways, forcing the Silencers to take longer, more treacherous routes.

But the Silencers weren't just hunters. They were executioners. And they didn't stop.

Anthem heard the distant *snap-hiss* of energy weapons discharging. A scream cut through the tunnels.

"Don't stop," Indy barked, sensing his thoughts. "We have to make it out."

A ladder came into view up ahead, lit by a single glowing bulb. Their exit.

Bliss reached it first, scrambling up as the others followed.

Anthem threw one last look over his shoulder. He couldn't see them, but he could *feel* the Silencers closing in. The traps had done their job, but it wouldn't last forever.

He turned and climbed.

As he emerged onto the surface, the cool night air struck him like an electric shock. They were in a back alley, hidden by the looming skeletons of abandoned buildings. The tunnel entrance was concealed beneath a pile of trash bags and random debris—another precaution.

Tatum and Buddy helped Indy shove the covering back into place just as another explosion rocked the sewers beneath them. Anthem's heart hammered in his chest from the chase. But they had made it.

Anthem leaned against the damp brick wall, catching his breath as the others did the same. For a long moment, no one spoke. They just listened—waiting, watching. The city was eerily quiet, but that didn't mean they were safe.

After what felt like an eternity, Anthem exhaled sharply. "That was too close."

"Too close?" Bliss snapped, still winded. "That was a damn disaster."

Anthem straightened. "We got out."

"Barely." Geddy shoved a hand through his sweat-dampened hair. "Do you have any idea what would've happened if we hadn't? What almost *actually* happen?"

Anthem met his gaze, jaw tightening. He knew. They all knew.

Bliss took a step forward, her eyes burning. "We can't keep doing this. Not only for our safety. Did you hear them back there? The people who weren't as lucky as us? Our music can't bring back the dead."

Anthem's fists clenched. He had heard. He had felt every second of it. "They knew the risks."

"Oh, that makes it better?" Her voice rose. "They wouldn't have had to risk anything if we weren't out here, playing revolutionaries with our music."

Anthem's eyes darkened. "We're not playing anything. This is real. This is bigger than us. You think the CEA is just going to stop? That if we keep our heads down, they'll let us live in peace? They *kill* for control. They *silence* anything that doesn't fit their perfect world. And you want to just—what? Walk away?"

"Yes," Bliss shot back, her voice raw. "Because I want to *live*, Anthem. I want to make music, but I don't want to die for it."

Silence hung between them.

Geddy sighed, looking away. "She's right. We're not making a difference. We're just targets."

Buddy shifted uncomfortably. "It's not just about the music anymore. This is survival. And I don't want to spend every night running for my life."

Tatum nodded. "I'm sorry, man. But this... this isn't worth it."

Anthem looked at them, one by one, his chest tightening with every word. They weren't just his band. They were his family. And they were leaving.

Bliss exhaled, her expression softening. "We love you, Anthem. And honestly, this is a long time coming. We've been discussing this for a while now, but we were trying to come up with a way to break it to you. And after tonight, there is no better time than right now. We think it would be best for the band if we got our licenses."

Anthem swallowed hard. He knew what those words in that order meant, but he still had a hard time understanding. He looked at Indy. She hadn't said a word. Just stood there, arms crossed, watching him.

"So that's it, huh?" he asked, voice low. "You're all selling out?"

Buddy pursed his lips. "Selling out is a strong word, man," he said defensively. "We've been flying under the radar so far, but if we want to take things to the next level, maybe we need to consider going mainstream."

Anthem's jaw clenched. "Going mainstream?" he repeated, tasting the bitterness of the words. "That goes against everything we stand for. We didn't start this band to become puppets for the industry." His voice cracked slightly from the mix of frustration and betrayal.

"I get it, Anthem," Bliss said, the edge gone from her voice. "I do. But the reality is, if we want to continue playing without fear of death, we might have to play by their rules. The industry... it doesn't wait for people to figure things out. We have to move or get left behind."

"Sienna...come on, don't do this," Anthem pleaded, one last ditch effort.

"Don't call me that. You know I hate that name." Bliss said through gritted teeth. "Besides, it won't work. We made up our minds long ago. You just have to accept it or not at this point."

Anthem took a deep breath. "Fine." He stepped away from the wall, squaring his shoulders. "Then I'll do it without you."

Bliss shook her head, her expression torn. "Anthem—"

"No." His voice was firm now, resolute. "You chose your path, but I'm not stopping. Not until the system is broken. Not until we can play, create, and exist without fear. If I have to do it alone, so be it."

Then Indy stepped forward.

"You won't be alone," she said simply.

Anthem met her gaze, something unspoken passing between them. She understood. Maybe she always had.

Bliss let out a slow breath and gave a small, sad smile. "Take care of yourselves."

One by one, the others turned and disappeared into the city, leaving Anthem and Indy alone in the alley. And just like that, it was over. Manufacturing Eden was no more.

The city was quiet, save for the distant rhythmic whooshing of traffic and the flickering buzz of neon signs overhead, casting hues of violet and green across the worn cobblestone streets below. Towering buildings, a mix of gothic Victorian spires wrapped in bright lights and sleek, modern skyscrapers loomed overhead like silent sentinels. Their windows glowed faintly in the night. The city felt alive, like a creature breathing in sync with its own heartbeat. Each street moving in tempo with the beast.

Cloaked in shadows, the narrow alleys whistled as the wind snaked its way through them, carrying with it the scent of damp earth and rain-soaked brick. A faint mist clung to this part of the city, giving the streets an ethereal feeling, as if the city existed between two worlds—one rooted in reality and the other dancing just beyond the veil of magic. The wet cobblestones glistened under the faint glow of streetlamps, their light reflecting off the puddles from the evening's rain.

Above it all, the sky was a patchwork of stars barely visible through the thick clouds that lingered like a shroud over the city. The moon hung low, a thin crescent that bathed the streets in pale light, casting ambiguous shadows that danced across the buildings. Crucible City, like many others, was a city that never truly slept; even in the dead of night, it roared with life, a beat that both lured and warned its inhabitants. It was a place of contrasts—where dreams and danger were close bedfellows, where music and magic intertwined, and where, if you listened closely enough, you could hear it singing.

Anthem and Indy walked side by side down the worn, uneven sidewalk, their boots scuffing softly against the cracked pavement as they made their way toward the *Riff Runner*—Anthem's beloved van that now waited like an old friend, parked just down the block. The night's events still gripped him—the heat of the stage lights, the bass of the music, the shooting, the screams. Tension coiled in Anthem's shoulders, but it was the silence that pressed the hardest—heavy, unspoken, unbearable. Not just quiet—absence.

The absence of his band.

His family.

Beside him, Indy was her usual contradiction of tough exterior and caring friend. Her silky, raven-colored hair was swept up into a perfectly imperfect, messy bun, a few stray strands slipping free to frame her face. Her denim jacket was a canvas of character, covered in overlapping patches. Each one stitched with a story—from iconic band logos of punk legends to cryptic indie designs that only a few music aficionados would recognize. It was like a wearable scrapbook of her life spent in the underground scene, where every gig, every wild night, and every impromptu jam session was woven into the fabric.

Underneath the jacket, she sported a fitted black tee that hugged her athletic body, hinting at the strength and agility that came with years of hauling equipment, dodging backstage obstacles, and being the unsung hero of every show. It was clear that while Indy thrived in the world of equipment and cables, she was also ready for anything the rock 'n' roll life could throw at her—no stage too wild, no setup too demanding.

She said nothing at first. She could feel Anthem folding in on himself, could hear the silence behind every scuffed step. So she simply walked with him. Not offering answers. Just being there.

"They really left," he said finally, his voice rough.

Indy adjusted her denim jacket, stuffing her hands into her pockets. "Yeah."

He let out a bitter laugh. "Guess I shouldn't be surprised. Not everyone is meant for this kind of life. I just wish they put a bit more thought into their decision." He shook his head. "We were supposed to change things. Prove that music is more than just *their* approved sound. That it means something." He kicked at a loose piece of concrete, sending it skittering down the alley. "At the first genuine test we faced, they ran."

Indy didn't respond right away, just let him vent.

"They think I'm stupid," he muttered. "That this is just some reckless dream I refuse to let go of. But I *know* what I'm doing. If we give up, the CEA wins. They erase us. Our music, our voices—gone. And people just let it happen because they're scared."

"They *are* scared," Indy said softly. "And they're not wrong to be."

Anthem stopped walking. "Are you saying *I'm* wrong?"

She turned to face him. "I'm saying I get why they left." She held his gaze. "And I also get why you won't."

Anthem resumed walking, but his steps felt heavier with each one he took. The streetlights stretched their glow across the pavement, long and distant, like memories he couldn't quite hold on to. His mind churned. "Maybe they were right to leave." He said, more to himself than Indy. Hearing the words come out of his own mouth made him sick. He quickly realized it was all unraveling. "What if I was the problem this entire time? What if the dream had only ever been mine? The others—they were talented. They could start over, play within the system, maybe even survive. But me? Who am I without the band? Without the stage? Am I just another fool who thought he could change the world with a guitar?" He gritted his teeth, clenching his fist. "Maybe this *is* my fault. Maybe if I had listened more—if I hadn't pushed so hard, if I had been *better*—none of this would've happened." His chest tightened. A part of him wanted to scream, to break something, to *stop feeling like this.* But his thoughts kept circling, dragging him deeper into raw and suffocating despair.

He took a breath.

Anthem barely noticed that the street they had stepped out onto was eerily still. The pressure in his chest grew stronger, like a balloon filled to bursting. His pulse pounded in his ears, too loud, too fast. The streetlights seemed to stretch further away, darkening at the edges of his vision. The world tilted.

A panic attack?

His limbs spasmed. His skin burned.

Something was wrong.

"Anthem?" Indy's concern filled voice was drowned out by static.

He tried to answer, but the words caught in his throat. His vision blurred. The ground swayed. His heartbeat was a frantic, stuttering staccato, out of sync with the world. Panic crawled up his spine, gripping his lungs, squeezing—and then—something deep within him gave way. A wall he hadn't known existed dissolved like mist in sunlight.

A force surged from within him, exploding outward in an unseen pulse. The streetlights flickered violently, windows shattered, cars lined on the street were rocked, setting off their alarms. The air prickled with a staticky charge.

Anthem's knees buckled. His body was no longer his own—his senses were overwhelmed as his mind spiraled into a vast and primordial emptiness.

Indy's panicked shout barely reached him.

"Anthem! *Anthem!*"

His body collapsed. Cold, wet pavement rushed up to meet him. His muscles locked, breath shuddering out in broken gasps. Through the haze, he saw Indy kneeling beside him, her hands gripping his shoulders, fear stark in her eyes.

"Somebody help!" she cried, voice cracking.

Anthem's body lay motionless on the cold pavement, but his consciousness—his soul—his very essence plummeted, yanked away from reality like a note struck so hard it snapped its strings.

He fell—no, he unraveled.

Plunging into a boundless void, an expanse of swirling sound and light, where color had no fixed description, and melody had physical form. He dissolved into a frequency, one of the basic components of a sound wave. His consciousness stretched thin and scattered like a melody played across infinite dimensions. He was more information than man at this point. The surrounding space pulsed and shifted, neither empty nor full, neither dark nor light. It was an existence beyond all of that—an existence simply understood rather than experienced with rudimentary human senses.

Music was not just present here. Music was everything.

The more he unraveled, the more he became part of the symphony. Every vibration resonated against what little remained of his form, weaving through him as if he were made from the same material this place was built from. The harmonies were ancient, limitless.

Suddenly they materialized.

A trio of humanoid shapes, vast yet unfixed, shifting between form and concept, shadow and light, their presence overwhelming—not in mass, not in strength, but in sheer magnitude. Anthem wasn't looking at beings. He was looking at the first notes ever played.

Their movements were like music given shape, their very presence bent the void into crescendos and decrescendos. The air around them quaked with ancient resonance—notes layered upon notes, as if their harmonies carried the memory of every lifeform ever sung into existence. Every sound they made carried echoes of a time before time, before the universe, before the first hands had ever strummed a chord.

They did not speak. They vibrated.

And yet, Anthem understood.

"You have finally heard us," one intoned, its voice rippling through his being, shaking apart the core of what he thought he was. "You have always been connected to the Source, but you were not yet in tune. Now, the melody flows freely through you. Use it wisely."

Anthem tried to answer, to form words, to find his voice in this vast, unknowable chorus—but he had no voice here, no actual body.

He was music. He was frequency. He was part of the resonance.

The beings began to fade, their forms dispersing into shifting sound waves, but their presence still lingered in the air, in the very fabric of existence.

The void shrank, collapsing inward.

Anthem fell again, downward, downward—until—Silence.

A silence so absolute it stretched beyond sound, beyond thought. Then a single note rang out.

Low. Resonant. Pure.

It rippled outward, shaking the void, shaking Anthem, shaking everything.

And then—he woke up.

His chest heaved as his body shuddered against the pavement. His vision now had a golden tint to it. The sight of flickering streetlights and shattered glass was his first indicator that he was back in his body, where he should be. Every nerve in his body hummed, every breath felt like a chord played in harmony with the world.

Indy was there, cradling his head in her arms, her voice thick with panic. "Anthem—Anthem, can you hear me?!"

He could. More than that, actually—he could hear everything. The air sang, the world vibrated, the very atmosphere thrummed with a melody so vast, so infinite, that he could barely contain it.

For the first time—Anthem could hear the song of the universe. He would never be the same.

CHAPTER III

I ndy didn't let go of Anthem right away. Even after he assured her—again—that he was fine, that he wasn't hurt, that he wasn't about to collapse again, her grip on his arm remained firm, her eyes scanning him like she was expecting him to suddenly combust.

"Indy, I promise, I'm fine." Anthem begged, struggling against her grasp. "I will chew this off."

"You literally just blacked out and made the city's power grid have a meltdown," she said flatly. "So no, I don't think 'I'm fine' is gonna cut it this time."

Anthem sighed, rolling his shoulders. He felt... different. Changed. Like his body had been tuned to a frequency he had never noticed before. Other than a few scrapes from hitting the pavement, he was unharmed. No lingering pain. No dizziness. If anything, he felt better than ever.

"Indy, seriously, I—"

She raised a hand, silencing him instantly. "Nope. Not having it. I'm staying with you tonight."

Anthem opened his mouth to argue, but her expression was set, her arms crossed in that way that told him this wasn't up for discussion. He had seen her fend off belligerent musicians twice her size, wrestle with massive sound equipment without breaking a sweat, and talk her way out of trouble with authorities more times than he could count. If she had decided she was staying, then that was that.

He exhaled sharply, shaking his head with a half-smirk. "Fine. But don't expect me to make you breakfast in the morning."

Indy snorted. "Please. Like I'd trust you near a stove."

With that settled, they resumed their walk through the dimly lit streets. The chaos from earlier had mostly faded into the shadows, though the occasional flickering streetlight and the distant whir of emergency sirens were quiet reminders of the night's unraveling. As they turned the last corner, the Riff Runner came into view.

Its two-tone gradient paint job caught the faint light, a vibrant orange at the front melting smoothly into a sleek black toward the back. A thin layer of dirt dulled the shine, and spots of rust bloomed around the fender flares and windows. The entire rear of the vehicle was a collage of countless stickers—cities visited, concerts witnessed, nights survived and immortalized. Each one was a stamp of a story.

It stood out like a sore thumb, and if Anthem was being honest, it wasn't something an illegal performer should roll around in. But what was he if not a rule breaker? Besides, his forged IDs and documents have yet to fail to get him out of a jam.

Anthem slowed his steps, eyes lingering on the van, his lips tugged into the faintest smile. "How you doing ol' girl?" he muttered, patting the hood. "I hope your night has gone better than ours."

Indy rolled her eyes and gave a soft chuckle. "She's still ugly as hell."

"Hey!" Anthem said, stepping up to the driver's side. "I refuse to let you talk bad about the Riff Runner."

"Oh, I'm *so* sorry Riffany." Indy mocked, hopping into the passenger seat. "I didn't mean to hurt your feelings." She said, stroking the dashboard like a purring cat.

"That's better." Anthem said simply before turning the key and awaking the Riff Runner.

They rode in silence for the rest of the ride. Indy didn't press him for details. Not yet. She kept close, though, her concern clear in the way she occasionally stole glances at him when she thought he wasn't looking.

They reached Anthem's apartment, tucked away in one of Crucible City's quieter corners. It was a modest space, not flashy by any means, but cozy and brimming with personality. He unlocked the door, pushing it open and gesturing for her to step inside. As soon as he stepped through the door, he was wrapped in the familiar embrace of soft, golden lamplight and the comforting sound of his vintage stereo. The remnants of an old favorite album gently filled the air, a much-needed relief for his frayed nerves. [1]

The walls were a canvas of inspiration, a vibrant patchwork of soundproofing foam panels, posters, and album covers. To the left, a large, eye-catching poster of Mister Herringbone dominated the space, the legendary guitarist frozen mid-riff, his untamed mane of hair framing a face lit with intensity. To Anthem, Mr. H had always been a symbol of uprising, a beacon of artistic freedom in the stifling world of the country's music scene. Nearby, the minimalistic album cover of Small Town Syndrome's *Bored to Death* glimmered under the

---

1. Track 2 - Alabama Shakes - Dunes

soft light, depicting the band sitting on a worn-out couch on an overgrown, cracked asphalt road. And De La Luna's *Stardust Persona,* featuring the band members in their trademark silver makeup and interstellar attire, representing the avant-garde side of space rock that Anthem admired. It was a reminder of the boundless creativity Anthem pursued, a style of music that challenged the ordinary.

Across the room, directly above his cluttered desk, was a collage of more modern inspirations. A signed poster from The Golden Ratio's *Synthetic Heart* tour hung proudly, a token of Anthem's appreciation for their fusion of electronic symphonies and deep, emotionally resonant lyrics.

Next to it, the sleek cover of Mystery Shopper's *These Scars Won't Define Us* was displayed in a shadow box, the album that had redefined how Anthem thought about the intersection between synthesized sounds and live instruments. These were the sounds that had shaped him, the music that had pushed him to explore new depths in his own art.

Scattered throughout the room were nods to his roots—smaller indie band posters from local concerts and underground gigs he had played or attended. A poster from Pop-Up Powerbomb's gritty debut hung next to a rare vinyl from the Luminous Sound Orchestra. Their orchestral-electronic fusion served as evidence of how far the boundaries of music could be stretched. On another wall, a custom-painted original of Salt of the Earth's *Echoes of Silence* added a touch of abstract beauty. The apartment was a shrine to everything he loved and everything he had poured himself into.

Indy kicked off her boots and flopped onto his couch like she'd been living there for years. "Alright. You good?"

Anthem huffed a laugh, dropping his guitar by the door. "You just forced your way into my place. I think you'd be the better judge of that."

She smirked, but didn't argue. "Damn right."

Anthem shook his head before collapsing into the armchair across from her. Indy sat forward, tucking one leg under the other. She crossed her arms and waited for answers. She had been patient, but Anthem could tell from the look on her face she wasn't letting this go.

The easy banter from earlier had faded. "Alright, spill," she said, firm but not unkind. "What the hell happened back there?"

Anthem exhaled. "I don't know how to explain it, Indy. It was... like I fell into something. Someplace. But not a *place*—not in the way we think of it."

Indy's brows knit together. "You were unconscious, Anthem. You *collapsed.*"

"I know," he responded. "But I wasn't *out*—at least, not like blacking out or sleeping. It was different. It felt *real.*" He hesitated before continuing, the words feeling too big in his mouth. "I was surrounded by... sound. Not just sound—music. But it wasn't *playing*—it *was* the space. It *was* everything. I could *see* it, feel it, like it had substance."

Indy's eyes narrowed. "You're telling me you were just—what? Floating in some musical abyss?"

"Yeah. I think so." He clenched his jaw, frustration gnawing at him. "I know it sounds crazy, but I was *there*, Indy. And I wasn't alone."

Indy sat forward, her interest fully piqued. "Not alone?"

He nodded slowly. "Yeah. Not people, exactly... I don't know what to call them, but the difference in our scale was enormous. They spoke, but not in words—more like they were communicating through the music, like they *were* the music, like they were part of *everything*. They said..." He trailed off. "Damn it. I can't remember."

Indy sat back. "Nothing? Not even a piece of what they said?"

Anthem shut his eyes, trying to force the images back into focus. It was like grasping at fog—there one moment, gone the next. He could still *feel* it—the sensation of being surrounded by vastness and ancient power. But no matter how hard he tried, the details wouldn't come. The more he reached for them, the further they slipped away. He opened his eyes again, looking straight at her. "Nope. Nothing. But this seems *huge*. Bigger than us. Bigger than anything."

A silence stretched between them. Indy wasn't the most spiritual person in the world, and Anthem wasn't either. But this? This had *happened*.

Indy rubbed her temples. "Alright. That's... a lot."

"Agreed," he said.

"But you don't remember *who* they were? What they *wanted*?"

Anthem shook his head. "No. Just... fragments. The void. Their voices. The feeling that I was *supposed* to be there."

Indy exhaled. "I don't know what to say, Anthem. I believe you—I *saw* what happened—but I don't know what any of this means."

Anthem sighed, leaning back against the chair. "Neither do I."

Another silence fell between them, but this time it wasn't heavy. It was thoughtful. Anthem stole a glance at Indy, noting the way she was watching him—not just with concern, but with something else.

A wide grin slowly spread across his face. "You were scared," he blurted.

She blinked. "Uh, yeah. You *collapsed* and made the whole city flicker like a damn horror movie."

"No, I mean—when you saw me on the ground. I could hear it in your voice."

Indy scoffed, rolling her eyes. "Of course I was scared, idiot. You think I just let my friends drop dead in the street without panicking?" Indy sighed, shaking her head. "Look, I just—You scared the hell out of me tonight. And I don't like feeling *helpless* like that."

Anthem tilted his head. "You? Helpless? Never thought I'd hear you say that."

She shot him a glare, but there was no actual heat behind it. "I'm serious, Anthem."

His smirk faded. "I know." He hesitated before continuing, voice softer now. "I don't enjoy seeing you scared, either."

Indy exhaled before leaning back against the armrest. "Man, you're exhausting."

Anthem chuckled. "You're the one who forced me to let you stay over."

"Because I don't *trust* you to not pass out again!" she shot back.

"Which is why," Anthem said, pushing himself up from the armchair, "you're taking the bed, and I'll crash here."

Indy blinked. "What? No. I'm not taking your bed."

Anthem stretched and grabbed the throw blanket draped over the couch. The one Indy was partly sitting on. He gave it a hard tug, dumping her onto the floor. "Too bad. My place, my rules."

Indy narrowed her eyes. "Oh, so *now* you're the stubborn one?"

"For now, yes." He plopped down onto the now vacated couch and folded his arms behind his head, getting comfortable. "Besides, if I face plant again, I'd rather the fall be shorter. You're better off in the bed."

Indy groaned, standing up and pointing at him. "You're lucky I'm too tired to argue."

Anthem grinned. "Wouldn't have worked, anyway."

She grumbled something under her breath, snatched one of Anthem's shirts from the back of a chair, and made her way to the bedroom. But before she disappeared, she lingered in the doorway for a moment.

"Hey, Anthem?"

He turned his head, eyebrows raised. "Yeah?"

Indy hesitated, then shook her head with a small smile. "Good night." She disappeared into the bedroom, the soft click of the door barely louder than the ticking clock on the wall. Anthem lay back on the couch, the blanket pulled up to his chest, staring at the ceiling. Sleep didn't come.

Eventually, he reached for his phone, the cracked screen lighting up with familiar icons and smudged fingerprints. His thumb hovered over a few recent notifications, but he ignored them. Instead, he scrolled down to his music folders. He looked through playlists until his thumb paused over one folder: Manufacturing Eden—*Rehearsals & Demos.*

He tapped it.

A rough recording started playing instantly—tinny, raw, and alive. Buddy's kick drum hit like a heartbeat trying to stay in rhythm. Tatum's voice came in next, deliberately off-key, as she sang a fake operatic scale:

"Meeeee-me-me-muh-MOOO!"

Geddy's groan came in loud and clear over the mic: *"Tatum, I swear, if you start this rehearsal with a musical seizure again—"*

Then someone snorted. Anthem wasn't sure if it was Bliss or himself.

He laughed too, softly. But it caught in his throat and didn't quite make it out whole. He sank deeper into the couch, one arm draped over his eyes. The sound wrapped around him like a memory, refusing to fade.

The track clicked over to the next.

[2] "Ashes & Arsenic"—a frenzied anthem, one of their earlier originals. Anthem remembered screaming that chorus into a half-working mic at a dive bar where the walls bled condensation. That song was chaos and gasoline.

[3] Next was "Heart wired (to Burn)", a track they never got to master. Anthem remembered Bliss's vocals bleeding into his guitar in one perfect moment, like their wavelengths had actually fused. They'd played that one in secret—just the six of them in a warehouse at 2 AM, no crowd, no pressure.

---

2. Track 3 - Lower Than Atlantis - Had Enough

3. Track 4 - Daughter - Youth

4 Then came "Pretty Is a Knife"—Bliss's baby. It opened with Geddy's bass line: low, tense, and mean. Anthem had hated the lyrics at first—too piercing, too harsh. But when she screamed them live, something about it made everyone shut up and listen.

5 The next file was labeled "We Bury the Hook (But It Still Sings)".

That one stopped him cold.

It had been their last group recording. They were tired. Frustrated. Bliss was already pulling away, but that day—just for a few hours—it had felt like the magic was back. Anthem had written the hook during a long walk alone, but when Buddy layered in those unsteady drum fills and Tatum gave the chorus that haunting sound of her keys, it turned into something else.

Something almost... prophetic.

Anthem stared at the waveform on the screen as the track played—unpolished, imperfect, and heartbreakingly real.

He let it play to the end.

With a trembling hand, he backed out of the folder and tapped over to the photos.

There they were.

Manufacturing Eden: laughing on a rooftop with fast food containers, Bliss giving the middle finger to the camera with a toothpick between her teeth. Buddy in a shark costume—he'd lost a bet. Indy with her tongue out, flashing

---

4. Track 5 - Billie Eilish - You should see me in a crown

5. Track 6 - Paramore - All I Wanted

double peace signs behind Tatum's head while Geddy tried to keep a burger intact mid-bite. Anthem had taken it. He remembered the moment clearly.

Anthem smiled.

He stared at it a long time.

His fingers hovered over the message icon. Almost without thinking, he tapped it. Her name was auto filled.

Bliss

He typed:

> Hey. I was just thinking about

He stopped. He stared at the unfinished message.

Then, slowly, he held the screen until the delete prompt appeared.

DELETE THREAD?

He pressed yes.

The message vanished.

But not the emptiness.

Anthem turned the phone off and let it drop to the floor with a quiet thud. He sank back into the couch, letting the songs echo in his mind—songs they'd never finish. Songs they'd never play again.

A nthem ran.

The alleys of Crucible City stretched endlessly before him, twisting and shifting, their walls pressing in like the city itself was trying to trap him. Erratic strobing streetlights cast fractured, dancing shadows like specters. The air was hard to breathe, charged with an energy that made every breath feel like swallowing static.

And behind him—something pursued.

Anthem didn't dare look back. He could hear it—an awful, warped sound, like a revolting, distorted keening. It slithered through the alleys, echoing off the brick walls, surrounding him from every angle. The more he ran, the closer it got.

His lungs burned. His legs ached. But he *knew*—knew with absolute certainty—that stopping meant the end.

Then, the alley ahead twisted in on itself, folding like a piece of crumpled sheet music. The path was gone.

Dead end.

Anthem skidded to a stop, chest heaving, his back pressed against the cold stone as he finally forced himself to turn and *look*.

The shadow loomed. It wasn't a person, not even a creature—just a shifting, amorphous mass in the shape of a nightmare, tendrils writhing as it advanced. It pulsed with unnatural movement, a living accumulation of darkness that swallowed the dim light around it.

The sound it now made was unbearable. Not a growl. Not a voice. It was *wrong*, like an instrument played in reverse through broken speakers, filling the space with a discordant noise that made his skull feel like it was cracking from the inside.

It lunged.

Anthem threw up his hands instinctively, and a golden light *erupted* from him.

It wasn't fire. It wasn't electricity. Solid and unbreakable, it was sound given form. The light expanded outward in waves that shimmered with refracted gold, encasing him in a radiant, translucent golden dome. The dome wasn't a perfect sphere; it was faceted like a crystalline gem.

The shade slammed into it with a violent *thud*, its body splattering into writhing tendrils of darkness before reforming. It recoiled, then struck again, pounding against the barrier with an unnatural fury. The force of its attacks shook the dome, but it couldn't break through.

It howled in frustration, its awful sound growing louder and louder. Anthem's breathing was ragged, his heart hammering as he stared at the thing clawing at his shield. The golden light flickered under the strain, but it held. The sound grew worse. Louder. Higher. A cacophony of screeching distortion. Anthem clamped his hands over his ears, but it didn't help.

Then—through the noise, another sound emerged. A voice. A voice he knew.

"ANTHEM!"

The dome shuddered.

"ANTHEM!"

The sound morphed, shifting from the shade's warped, unnatural scream into something real.

"ANTHEM WAKE UP!"

His eyes *snapped* open.

The golden dome still surrounded him.

For a split second, panic seized his chest. Where was the shade? The warm glow of the shield flickered around him, casting shimmering light across his living room—wait, *his* living room? Reality donned on him as he checked his surroundings. His space looked like it had been caught in a small-scale explosion. The couch had been shoved back, his coffee table flipped on its side. Loose papers, books, and a few unfortunate mugs spun in midair, suspended in the energy pulsing outward from the dome.

But his eyes locked onto *hers.*

Indy was outside the barrier, pounding her fists against it. Her mouth was moving, shouting something, but the dome distorted the sound, turning it into a muffled echo. Her dark eyes were wide, alarmed, darting between him and the chaos spiraling around the room.

A mug flew past her head—she ducked, narrowly avoiding the impact before slamming her hands against the barrier again.

Anthem's breath hitched.

This was *real.*

A surge of panic made the golden energy pulse brighter, humming with a raw power that vibrated through the air. The dome shuddered again, sending another invisible wave outward, knocking over more items. Indy flinched but didn't back away.

She was still calling his name, still fighting to reach him.

Anthem pressed his palms against the shimmering surface of the barrier, his heart hammering. He *needed* to stop this. He *needed* to let her in.

Calm down. Focus.

He squeezed his eyes shut, forcing himself to remember the feeling from the dream. The way the light had come from within him—the way it had answered to his intent.

It's mine. I made it.

He took a slow, shuddering breath. *Then I can unmake it too.*

Anthem exhaled.

The dome flickered—then, with a soft, ringing sound, it *collapsed.*

The moment the energy vanished, everything it had suspended crashed to the ground. Mugs shattered, papers fluttered everywhere, and his furniture groaned as it settled back into place.

Indy stumbled forward with the sudden lack of resistance. Without hesitation, she lunged toward Anthem, gripping his face between her hands.

"What the hell just happened?!"

Anthem barely registered the question. His pulse was racing, his skin tingling where the energy had just been. He glanced at his hands, but the glow had faded, leaving behind only a ghost of warmth in his fingertips.

"I—" His voice cracked. He swallowed hard, still catching up to the moment. "I think... I brought it back with me."

Indy's brows knit together. "*Brought what back? From where?*"

"The dome," Anthem murmured, running a hand through his damp hair. "I—I was dreaming. I was being chased, and I made a shield, and—and then I woke up, and it was *still here.*"

Indy pulled back slightly, scanning his face, trying to piece it together. Her breath was uneven, but her grip on his arms remained firm.

"So, let me get this straight," she said. "You were asleep. And somehow, while unconscious, you created a giant golden *force field* in the middle of your freaking apartment?"

Anthem let out a weak, breathless laugh. "Yeah. Pretty much."

Indy exhaled sharply, running a hand down her face. "You are *so* lucky I didn't get brained by a flying coffee mug."

Despite everything, Anthem smirked. "That would've been a tragic way to go."

She smacked his arm. "*Not funny!*" But there was no actual heat behind it. She sat back on her heels, studying him. "This is getting serious, Anthem."

Anthem stiffened. She was right.

What if he hadn't woken up? What if the dome had expanded—taken over the entire room? The entire *building*? What if Indy had been trapped *inside* instead of outside? Or worse—what if it hadn't been *just* a shield? What if it had been something *deadly?* What happens if the next time it can't be stopped?

His stomach churned violently. "You're right," he admitted, barely above a whisper. "I don't know how to control it."

Indy's jaw tightened. For a long moment, neither of them spoke. Then, finally, she took a breath and squared her shoulders. "Then we *figure it out.*"

Anthem blinked. "What?"

"We figure it out," Indy repeated, her voice firm. "You're not doing this alone. We'll train. We'll test your limits, find out exactly what you can do—and learn how to control it before something like this happens again."

Anthem swallowed, overwhelmed by the hypothetical possibilities. But as he looked at Indy—at the sheer determination in her expression, at the unwavering steadiness of her presence—something in him steadied too.

He wasn't alone in this. And maybe, just maybe, they *could* figure it out.

Indy sighed. "But first, you need to sleep."

Anthem let out a dry laugh. "Yeah, because that's worked *so well* for me tonight."

Indy shot him a pointed look. "You're not sleeping on the couch."

Anthem frowned. "Indy—"

"Nope. Not up for debate." She folded her arms, the no-nonsense look in her eyes daring him to argue. "I don't trust you not to float off into another *golden energy sleep coma,* or whatever the hell that was. We're sharing the bed."

Anthem lay in bed, staring at the ceiling, listening to the soft rhythm of Indy's breathing. She had fallen asleep quickly, exhausted from the chaos of the night, trusting that things would be fine in the morning.

But even now, lying beside her, he could feel it—*that hum*. That quiet, dangerous vibration buried in his bones. It hadn't left him. If anything, it felt stronger in the silence.

He flexed his fingers under the blanket. A faint pulse rippled through his palm. For a second, the small lamp on the far table flickered, casting strange shadows across the room.

Anthem's breath caught.

Indy didn't stir. But Anthem couldn't shake the feeling that things wouldn't be fine. Not now. Not ever. The weight of what had happened—of what he *could* have done—weighed down on him like an anchor, dragging him into a pit of doubt. A deep, gnawing fear took root in his chest.

This isn't a gift. This is a curse.

He clenched his fists. He had spent his life chasing music, pouring his soul into every note, believing that his sound could bring something good into the world. But now...

Now, his music could break things. Now, his music could *hurt* people. He exhaled slowly, trying to suppress the trembling in his hands. More than anything, he refused to put Indy in danger. She had been terrified tonight. He saw it in her eyes, in the way she reached for him, like she wasn't sure if she could still *touch* him. If he stayed, if his powers continued to spiral, she could get caught in the danger.

He would not let that happen.

The decision came quietly. He had to leave. Not just to protect Indy, but to protect *everyone.*

Anthem swung his legs over the side of the bed, moving carefully so as not to wake her. The room was bathed in the soft glow of the city lights filtering through the window. Indy shifted slightly, murmuring something incoherent before settling back into her steady breathing.

His heart ached as he got dressed.

This wasn't how he wanted to say goodbye.

He stood and moved toward the small desk near the window, pulling out a scrap of paper and a pen. His hands shook as he wrote.

Indy,

I'm sorry. I can't stay.

You saw what happened. I don't know what I am anymore, but I know I'm dangerous. Protecting you and others is my only concern; I cannot risk hurting anyone.

I need time to figure this out—somewhere far from here, where I can't hurt the people I care about.

> *Please don't come looking for me.*
>
> *Take care of yourself.*
> *Anthem*

He stared at the letter for a long moment, then reached into a drawer of the desk. From it, he pulled out one of his old picks. With a quiet goodbye, he placed it on the folded letter like a paperweight.

Then, without a sound, Anthem turned, grabbed his keys and jacket, and slipped out the door.

As the late morning sun filtered through graffitied barriers and overgrown brush, Anthem stepped inside Manufacturing Eden's now unused hidden rehearsal space: an old, abandoned metro car nestled on a forgotten track at the edge of the city. They had transformed the car, hidden from prying eyes, into the perfect practice hideaway. It kept a few of its original seats, now draped in vibrant, threadbare tapestries and scattered with mismatched throw pillows, creating a relaxed, lived-in atmosphere. Instruments were squeezed in the narrow aisle. Buddy's drum kit perched at the head of the car, guitars leaned between rows of worn seats, and Tatum's keyboard secured on a series of flipped-down benches. Anthem flipped a switch and the warm glow of string lights intertwined with battery-powered lanterns illuminated the space. They contrasted against the windows papered over with old posters and set lists, diffusing the daylight into a soft, golden hue that gave the car a cozy feel despite its gritty surroundings.

He'd decided to make a pit stop and take a moment to really plan out where he was going. Maybe, if he stayed in a place built on music, built on nostalgia, he could *ground* himself. Maybe he could push all this power back down where it belonged, drown it out with the echoes of the past.

Before he could second-guess himself, he reached for the guitar slung over his back. The idea of playing felt different now, heavier, but not in a bad way. Maybe, just maybe, if he could play here, in the heart of what Manufacturing

Eden used to be, then he could remind himself that the music was still his. That it wasn't just tied to a band or whatever *this* power was.

He barely had time to sling the strap over his shoulder before the sound of the metro car door creaking open cut through the quiet.

Anthem turned, brow furrowing.

And then he froze.

Bliss stepped into the car, a duffle bag slung over her shoulder, her verdant eyes widening the moment she saw him.

For a long second, neither of them spoke.

"What are you doing here?" Bliss finally asked, her voice laced with something between shock and irritation. She shifted her bag, closing the door behind her with a dull *thunk*.

Anthem blinked, still processing the fact that she was here at all. He hadn't seen her since—well, since they threw him out.

"I could ask you the same thing," he shot back, his grip tightening on the neck of his guitar. "Didn't think anyone would come back here."

Bliss exhaled sharply, stepping past him toward the mess of old gear stashed near the back of the car. "I left some of my stuff," she muttered, kneeling down to dig through a crate of cables. "Figured I should grab it before this place rots."

Anthem watched her for a beat, then nodded toward the guitar still resting against his hip. "Was about to practice," he said, the words slipping out before he could overthink them. It wasn't a challenge, just a statement. But saying it out loud felt like admitting he wasn't scared to play.

Bliss paused mid-search, glancing up at him. There was something unreadable in her gaze, a bit of hesitation, before she scoffed. "Well, good for you. At least one of us still thinks music matters."

Anthem frowned. "What's that supposed to mean?"

Bliss stood, crossing her arms. "It means that *this*—" she gestured around the car, at the instruments, at the remnants of their band's dream "—was pointless. We thought we could make a difference. But Manufacturing Eden was just noise. It had no actual power."

Anthem's chest tightened. "That's not true," he argued, stepping forward. "We built something here."

Bliss let out a bitter laugh. "And where did it get us? We played our songs, we rebelled against the system, and what changed? Nothing." She shook her head. "If we had *genuine power—if I* had genuine power—we could have actually *done* something."

Anthem's stomach churned at her words, at the implication behind them.

"Tell me, Anthem—do you actually believe we could've changed anything with Manufacturing Eden? With all your grand speeches and songs about revolution? Because *I don't.* I look at what's happening out there, and all I see is wasted time."

Anthem shook his head, his grip on his guitar so tight his knuckles turned pale. "Then why are you really here, Bliss? If it was all so meaningless, why come back at all?"

Bliss opened her mouth, then hesitated, something shaky behind her expression. For a moment, just a moment, she looked *uncertain.*

Then she scowled, grabbing her bag off the ground. "Like I said, I left something behind," she muttered, her voice quieter now. She turned toward the door. "Guess I shouldn't have bothered."

Anthem took a step forward, half-wanting to stop her. But what could he even say? That she was wrong and Manufacturing Eden *did* matter? That he missed her? He missed *all* of them? The words tangled in his throat, too bitter, too painful to voice.

So, he said nothing.

Bliss gave him one last look before pushing the metro car door open and stepping out into the midday light. The door slammed shut behind her, leaving Anthem alone again in the silence.

Only this time, it felt hollow.

Moments later, the door slammed open, shaking the whole car.

"Anthem Fox, you're a fucking dead man!"

Anthem barely had time to look up before Indy stormed into the room, her eyes blazing with the intensity of a wildfire. She was furious—*rightfully* furious—but he was still surprised by how fast she had found him.

"You *actually* thought this wouldn't be the first place I checked?" she yelled, throwing her arms up. "This is literally the most obvious place you could've gone! You really thought you could just disappear, and I *wouldn't* find you?"

"I thought you'd still be asleep, and I'd have more time?" Anthem proffered, rubbing the back of his neck.

Indy growled.

"I'm sorry, no jokes. I don't know Indy... I thought maybe the energy here would help. Maybe if I—"

"*Energy?*" Indy cut him off. "Anthem, I don't care if this place is built on phoenix feathers and fairy farts! You ran, you *coward!*—without telling me—without even trying to figure this out *with* me!"

Anthem opened his mouth to argue, but she was *not* finished.

"No, *shut up,* I'm not done," Indy steamrolled over him, pacing in front of him with enough frustration to set the entire room on fire. "What, did you think you were being *noble?* That running away was gonna *fix* everything? That just *leaving* was gonna make your powers stop existing? News flash, dumbass, it *doesn't work that way!*"

Anthem kept his mouth shut, letting her words crash over him like waves.

"You *don't* get to decide this alone. You *don't* get to push me away because you're scared! I was *there*, Anthem. I *saw* what happened. And yeah, it freaked me out—but you know what freaks me out *more?* You thinking you have to go through this alone!"

Her words hit him harder than he expected.

The emotion of it—the frustration, the hurt, the raw *fear* in her voice—made his stomach twist.

Anthem sighed. "Indy—"

Before he could say anything else, she surged forward and threw her arms around him, crushing him in a tight hug. The force nearly knocked the breath from his lungs.

For a moment, he hesitated, then slowly wrapped his arms around her.

"I'm *so* mad at you," she muttered into his shoulder.

"I know," he murmured.

"I *hate* that you left."

"I know."

Indy held on tighter, as if she were physically anchoring him in place. Anthem shifted slightly, thinking she was done, but the moment he tried to pull away, she only tightened her grip.

"You're *not* running from this," she whispered fiercely. "We're in this *together*. You hear me?"

Something inside Anthem cracked. A part of him that had been tightly wound, fraying under the stress of everything, finally gave.

He swallowed hard. "Together," he echoed, voice hoarse.

Indy pulled back just enough to look at him, searching his face. Whatever she saw there must have satisfied her, because she gave a small, determined nod. She wasn't going anywhere.

Just as Anthem believed that maybe—*maybe*—he didn't have to do this alone, reality revealed it had other plans.

It hit like a bolt of lightning through his spine.

Pain, unlike anything he had ever known, *ripped* through him. His nerves caught fire. His vision blurred. A violent surge of power erupted from him, seizing his entire body.

Golden spikes erupted from the floor—dozens of them, jagged and brilliant, piercing through the entire metro car like wet tissue paper.

Anthem barely processed the pain of the spikes cutting into his arms and legs—because Indy *screamed.*

His heart stopped.

He turned his head, vision swimming, and saw her—pinned against the wall. Multiple parts of her body were skewered by the golden spikes.

So much blood.

His mind short-circuited.

No. No, no, NO!

His body crumpled, agony slamming into him like a freight train. His breaths came in short, uneven bursts. Unable to move, his fingers clawed at the air as he tried to reach her.

A shadow fell over him.

Through the haze of pain, Anthem's blurry gaze lifted just enough to see a figure in the doorway.

Unknown. Unmoving. Watching.

Then—darkness.

For the next few hours, Anthem drifted in and out of consciousness, his mind trapped in a haze of scattered images. Indy's pale, lifeless face inches from his as he lay slumped in the backseat of a moving vehicle. Buildings blurring pass. The world outside smeared into streaks of color, his body too heavy to move. A strange man lifting him effortlessly, carrying him through a set of double doors with a strange emblem he'd never seen before.

When he finally surfaced from his ocean of unconsciousness, the first thing he felt was the sterile coolness of the air against his skin. His body ached like he'd been wrung out and left to dry. Blinking against the soft, artificial glow above him, he turned his head slightly, taking in the unfamiliar room. He could hear the quiet beeps of monitoring equipment. The walls were a dull, off-white, lined with cabinets and shelves filled with medical supplies. An antiseptic scent lingered in the air, crisp and clinical.

A soft sound drew his attention. Lying in a bed beside him, Indy's chest rose and fell in steady breaths, her face peaceful but pale. Wires traced over her arms, while monitors blinked softly with reassuring signs of life.

Anthem's heart nearly stopped.

He was afraid to move, afraid that if he so much as *blinked,* this would disappear—that this was some cruel dream, and she was still crumpled on the floor, bleeding, screaming. A shudder ripped through him, and before he could stop it, relief crashed over him so forcefully that his vision blurred. His throat tightened as tears surged to the surface, threatening to overwhelm him.

She's alive.

The tight coil of fear that had been strangling his ribs finally loosened, and his body sagged against the pillow. But it wasn't enough. He needed to be *closer.* He needed to see her move, to make sure she was okay.

The moment he tried to push himself up, *lightning* lanced through his ribs. A guttural groan slipped from his lips before he could stop it.

Indy stirred at the noise, blinking blearily as she turned her head toward him. Her gaze was hazy for a second, then sharpened. "Oh, you *moron.*" Her voice, groggy but unmistakably *her,* was the single greatest sound he had ever heard.

Anthem let out a shaky breath as she shifted, wincing slightly, but never took his eyes off her. "You just woke up and your first instinct is to insult me?"

A watery laugh bubbled from her throat.

"You good?" he croaked, his voice hoarse.

Indy lifted an arm weakly and gave him a thumbs-up. "I'll live. Can't say the same for my pants, though. Pretty sure they're ruined. Tragic loss, really."

Anthem huffed a weak laugh, but the movement made him grimace. "You're making jokes?"

"Would you rather I cry and tell you how devastated I am about all of this?" she deadpanned. "Because if you need me to spell it out, you almost killed me, Anthem. And yourself. But mostly me."

His stomach twisted violently. He dropped his gaze. "I—"

"Nope, we're not doing that," Indy interrupted, already seeing where he was headed. "I know what you're thinking, and I will physically fight you if you start with the self-pity—'This I why I left'—crap."

Anthem swallowed hard. "I lost control."

"Yes. Yes, you did," Indy said bluntly. "And you will get a long lecture about it later. But for now, I'd rather not have another emotional heart-to-heart about this being dangerous, because the answer is still the same." Her eyes softened slightly. "I'm okay, Anthem. You're okay. We can figure out the rest later."

Anthem exhaled slowly, nodding. She wasn't letting him fall into guilt—again.

"Where are we?" Indy asked, finally glancing around the room properly. "Because this sure as hell isn't a hospital. Too quiet. And no one's made us fill out paperwork, so that's suspicious."

Anthem frowned, scanning their surroundings. She was right. The equipment was state-of-the-art, the kind that didn't exist in public medical centers. And the beds were more luxurious that any hospital bed he'd ever been in. Before he could process further, the door slid open with a quiet hiss.

Even in his earlier blurry eyed state, Anthem instantly recognized the build of the man that walked in as the person he saw before blacking out. The man confidently stepped into the room. Tall and lean, his wiry frame suggested hidden agility. His unkempt, shoulder-length black hair framed his face in a way that felt intentional, an effortless ruggedness that made him appear like he'd just walked in from a storm. The faint shadow of stubble along his jaw only added to his unrefined charisma.

The man's attire matched his aura: a dark, form-fitting suit with metal accents, gave him a blend of formality with a hint of rock-and-roll edge. A long, flowing scarf was draped over his shoulders, fluttering ever so slightly as if caught by an unseen breeze.

Indy tensed, but didn't move. Anthem felt his muscles tighten on instinct, even as exhaustion pulled at him. The man studied him for a moment, then gave a small nod. "You're awake," he said. His voice was calm, but there was a weight behind it—something deliberate, measured, like he was choosing every word too carefully. "Good. My name is Vale. We should talk." Anthem's eyes narrowed as Vale spoke. There was something familiar about the man. Not clear enough to name—but enough to make him pay attention. "You're in a safe place," Vale said, his eyes sharp and oddly reassuring. "This is a medical facility run by people who understand *what* you are and what happened to you."

Anthem blinked, trying to make sense of the man's words. But he couldn't grasp it yet, not fully. The events that led him here felt like a distant dream, a nightmare almost. His body still ached from his panic, but he tried to steady himself, sitting up straighter.

Indy's eyes pinged nervously between Anthem and Vale. She wasn't saying much—just waiting for some kind of explanation. Vale's gaze softened, his attention shifting to Indy before returning to Anthem. "What you have been going through was your body reallocating resources as you underwent an Octave Shift."

"An Octave what now?" Anthem asked, perplexed.

"Shift, that's what we call it when our powers manifest. The process can be...u nwieldy." Vale replied.

Anthem blinked. "Unwieldy is putting it lightly."

Indy added on, "And who are these 'we' you mentioned?"

Vale didn't blink. His voice dropped—low, steady, dangerous. "Anthem is one of us. A Sound Weaver."

Sound Weaver? The term felt foreign, but familiar, like a name that belonged to someone else.

Indy's face morphed from confusion to disbelief. "A *what?*"

Vale gave her a quick glance, then returned his attention to Anthem. "Sound Weavers are rare. We don't just create music—we shape reality through it. Some of us alter matter. Some influence emotions. Others manipulate forces more...fundamental. We channel the energy woven into the world itself. Fate didn't just call us musicians. She knitted her threads into our souls. And with that, we were given the power to rewrite what's possible."

He paused, sensing Anthem's hesitation.

"This isn't a burden," he added gently. "It's a gift. You're tapping into something ancient, something powerful. And this... this is just the beginning."

Anthem's chest tightened. Sound Weaver? He could feel something inside of him stir at the mention of it, a strange resonance.

Vale said. "Would you like a demonstration?" Following nods from Anthem and Indy, he inhaled through his nose. For a moment, nothing happened. Then the air around Vale rippled, as if invisible currents were folding into him. The ambient noise—the room's subtle symphony of vibrations—funneled inward, drawn into his body like breath.

His body started to change. Muscles thickened beneath his sleeves, broadening his shoulders and arms with deliberate, sculpted density. Veins along his neck stood out stark beneath his skin. As more sound wrapped around him, his skin darkened by a shade, the surface roughening to the texture of stone.

When he opened his eyes again, there was a quiet, controlled power radiating from him.

Without a word, Vale crossed the room in two easy strides.

Anthem tensed instinctively as Vale stopped beside the bed—but before he could say anything, Vale slipped a hand beneath the heavy frame and, with a casual flex of his arm, lifted the entire bed off the floor.

Anthem's body jolted slightly with the sudden shift, the mattress tipping just enough to send a warning wobble through the springs. But Vale's hand stayed steady, supporting the full weight—bed, mattress, and Anthem himself effortlessly.

Indy let out a low whistle from across the room, wide-eyed.

Vale smirked faintly, the low resonance in his body humming against the metal bed frame. Then, just as easily, he lowered it back down with a soft, controlled thud.

The moment his hand withdrew, the ripple of sound he had absorbed seeped away. His bulk relaxed, muscles slimming back into their normal shape. The color and texture returned to his skin, leaving him looking once again like an ordinary man.

Indy exhaled sharply. "What was that?"

Vale lowered his hand, his expression unreadable. "That," he said simply, "was just a taste of what I can do, and a fraction of what is possible."

Anthem swallowed. His fingers twitched as if they remembered something his mind hadn't yet caught up with. He looked at Vale, his throat dry. "And you're saying I can do that?"

Vale met his gaze, unwavering. "Your powers are unique to you, but yes, you've already accomplished similar feats if I'm not mistaken. You just don't know what you are doing."

Anthem exhaled shakily, glancing at Indy, who still looked shell-shocked. Then back at Vale.

This was real.

"A new Sound Weaver's powers can manifest from a variety of stimuli. They normally involve some form of stress that triggers this physical reaction. Yours triggered in a way that was... stronger than normal. You lost control, but there won't be any permanent damage."

"That tracks," Indy interjected. "He was on a bullet train to depression when he collapsed the first time."

His mind was still grappling with the implications. He had sound powers. Was this the reason he'd always felt so different, so disconnected from the world around him? "I... I don't understand," Anthem said, his voice unsteady. "I never asked for any of this."

Vale's gaze softened again, his voice gentler now. "You don't choose to be a Sound Weaver. It is who you are. The sooner you accept that, the better you'll be at controlling your abilities."

Control? He couldn't even control his emotions half the time, let alone some... ability he never asked for.

"Okay, so now we know why all of this is happening. But what now?" Indy asked, glancing at Vale. "Is this going to keep happening?"

"It doesn't have to. He just needs training. You need to learn how to channel it." He paused, letting his words hang for a moment. "I've seen quite a few Sound Weavers who were taught to use their powers without breaking their minds and bodies in the process. It will be difficult. But you're not alone. If you're willing to learn, we can help you."

Anthem exhaled slowly; the importance of the decision was not lost on him. He had no idea what to do, what was even possible anymore. But a glimmer of something—the smallest spark of hope—burned brighter inside him. Maybe, just maybe, this was a way he could still do what he set out to do. Change the world.

But something was nagging at Anthem as he watched Vale. The way he stood, the sharpness in his eyes—familiar. Too familiar. He gasped as the pieces clicked into place.

"*The Club*," he exclaimed, "I saw you there."

Vale arched a brow.

Anthem's pulse quickened. "During my solo. I locked eyes with someone in the crowd right before the Silencers raided the place." He leaned forward, ignoring the dull ache in his body. "That was you? That's how you knew where to find us in that metro car, wasn't it?"

Vale didn't deny it.

Anthem's jaw tightened. "How long have you been watching me?"

Indy's gaze snapped to Vale, her expression shifting from shock to suspicion. "Wait—you were at *The Club*? Before everything went to shit?"

Vale crossed his arms. "Yes."

Anthem's stomach twisted. "Why?"

Vale's gaze flicked to the side. He exhaled through his nose, slow and controlled, then tilted his head a fraction. "You're not just some underground musician, Anthem. You're a Sound Weaver, whether or not you knew it. And people like us? We don't go unnoticed for long."

Anthem's hands clenched into fists. "So, you've been following me?"

"We've been *aware* of you," Vale corrected. "Your performances—your music—it's been pushing at the edges of the supernatural for a while now. I went to *The Club* that night to confirm it myself."

Anthem's stomach churned. His entire life had already been under the heel of the CEA's boot, and now he finds out another organization had been keeping tabs on him as well. He wasn't sure which was worse.

Indy folded her arms, her voice laced with suspicion. "And if the Silencers hadn't shown up? What then?"

Vale met Anthem's gaze directly. "The plan was to approach you alone after your show, but regrettably, I had to abandon that plan."

Anthem scoffed. "Yeah? And you think that makes a difference? You had been spying on me long before that night. How do we know you didn't tip off the Silencers? For all we know, you could have orchestrated that raid."

"You are right. We should have been more straightforward with you, but we couldn't risk our discovery on hunches and speculation." Vale admitted. "But you have earned the truth. And if the Silencers knew I was there, they wouldn't have bothered with the raid. They would have bombed the entire venue, no warning."

That thought sent a shiver down Anthem's spine. He felt like the ground beneath him had shifted. He had been *watched.* Maybe even *targeted.* And now Vale was standing here, waiting for him to just *accept* it.

He exhaled, messing with his hair. "Fine. But why hasn't anyone ever heard of a Sound Weaver before?"

Vale's expression darkened. "Because we were erased."

Anthem narrowed his eyes. "Erased?"

Vale nodded. "Centuries ago, Sound Weavers weren't hiding in the shadows. We were everywhere—musicians, poets, storytellers, artists. Our music didn't just *move* people; it *changed* them. Inspired them. Freed them." His voice hardened. "And that made us dangerous."

Anthem exchanged a glance with Indy, but neither spoke.

"The rulers of the time feared us," Vale said. "Not because we were violent, but because we gave people something they couldn't control—*autonomy.* When a Sound Weaver performed, the audience didn't just *hear* it. They *felt* it. The emotions, the power—it amplified what was already inside them. Joy became ecstasy. Anger became revolution." He leaned forward. "Empires fell because of us."

Anthem swallowed.

Vale's gaze was unwavering. "So, they fought back. We were declared heretics, outlaws, threats to order. They hunted us down, burned our histories, silenced our songs. Over time, Sound Weavers faded into myth, and then, nothing. All while our persecutors thrived, some even migrated here to Musera and formed the Harmonic Council." He exhaled sharply. "But we didn't disappear. Some survived. We went underground, passing our knowledge through whispers, waiting for a time when we could rise again."

Anthem's mind was blown. Not only was the Council tormenting average citizens, but also a secret subset of people no one knew existed.

Indy leaned forward. "So, this is some kind of super-secret society for superpowered musicians. And this place is what...a front?"

Vale chuckled, genuinely amused. "Yes, and no. This building is indeed a cover, Sound Wave Studios. Here, we produce sanctioned music to support our organization financially. But it's also a hub, a sanctuary for our kind. It's a self-sustaining existence—keeping us safe and using our gifts productively. It's also where we eat, sleep, train, where we learn to protect each other, and where we blend in with the world. After all, what better way to hide a 'super-secret society of superpowered musicians' than in plain sight within the music industry?"

"Hmm...how widespread is this community? Are there Sound Weavers in other parts of the world?" Indy asked thoughtfully.

Vale nodded as he acknowledged the question. "Indeed, we are global. While our largest bases are here in Musera, there are smaller cells operating in other countries across the world. Each group functions semi-autonomously but adheres to a core set of principles to ensure our collective safety and anonymity."

Anthem's head spun with the implications before a fierce determination settled over him. "If I join you, what's the catch?" he demanded.

Vale's expression turned quizzical. "Catch? The catch, Anthem, is that the world is bigger and far more dangerous than you know. If you choose to walk this path, you'll face challenges you can't even imagine. There are those who would lock you away or, worse, simply for what you could become. And if they discover you before you're ready, they will take you—by force, if necessary." He paused. "But with us, you'll have allies, resources, training, and the chance to master your power. To become someone not to be trifled with. You could change everything."

Anthem, someone who grappled with his sense of identity before all of this started, was really getting pinned to the mat by all these additional aspects of his newfound identity. Cautiously, he asked. "And these others, the ones you mentioned who aren't as virtuous—what kind of threat do they pose to us and the public?"

Vale's expression sobered. "Not all who discover their powers use them for good. There are those who would exploit their abilities for personal gain, to manipulate, and even destroy. They see this power as a means to gain influence, wealth, or simply to feed their own twisted desires. They are the reason we must remain hidden and vigilant. Our secrecy isn't just to protect us from the public, but also from those who would twist our gifts into something monstrous. So, the threat they pose is a very real and apparent danger."

"That's a lot to take in." Anthem said rhetorically.

"You've been pushing at the deeper meaning of what Sound Weaving used to be—what it *still* is. Every time you perform, it isn't just passion driving your music. It's power. And the CEA doesn't tolerate power they can't control."

Anthem looked away. It made too much sense. He had always felt something *different* when he played—like his music reached past mere sound and pulled from something deeper, something alive. But he'd never put a name to it. Never questioned why it pulled people in the way it did.

"Your power isn't just real. It's rare. Your Octave Shift caused quite the scenes. We did our best to cover your tracks, but it won't be long before the CEA knows just how rare you are. Which means you have two choices."

Anthem forced himself to meet Vale's eyes.

"You can walk away," Vale said. "Pretend none of this ever happened. Hope you didn't make it on the CEA's radar." He let the silence linger. "Or you can fight."

He thought about the band, about his friends walking away. About the dream they shared—the dream he refused to let die. His fingers curled, aching for his guitar. Anthem exhaled slowly, his decision settling over him like the last note of a song. He turned to Indy, searching her face, but she was already watching him—waiting.

"I'm doing this," he said, his voice steady despite the storm still raging inside him. "I can't walk away. Not after everything. Not after what we just learned. If the Council wants to control music, to erase the truth—then I have to fight back. I *have to*."

Indy didn't hesitate. "Then I'm with you."

He blinked. "Indy—"

She rolled her eyes, a smirk tugging at the corner of her lips. "Don't *Indy* me. You think I'd let you do this alone? Please. Besides, someone's gotta make sure you don't get yourself killed before you even figure out what you're doing."

A laugh almost escaped him. Almost. Instead, all he could do was nod. The intensity of her loyalty almost brought tears to his eyes. "Thanks."

Vale watched the exchange with an amused expression, then gave a small nod of approval. "Well, then." He straightened. "Welcome to Sound Weaver Studios. Your training starts now."

CHAPTER VII

After a nurse gave them both a final once over and a quick change of clothes, Vale led Anthem and Indy through the doorway and down a winding staircase. Their footsteps echoed softly in the narrow, dimly lit stairwell. The air grew cooler and slightly damp as they descended. Moving deeper, the stairs gave way to a corridor bathed in a warm amber glow. A faint, upbeat melody drifted through the space, subtle yet persistent.

Vale moved ahead, his footsteps nearly silent against the worn stone floor. Anthem followed, his gaze drawn to the walls, where intricate patterns had been etched into the surface. As they rounded a corner, the music swelled, leading them toward a set of towering double doors at the corridor's end. Anthem slowed, his breath catching as he took in the sight.

Dark, polished wood gleamed under the light, bordered by sleek metallic inlays. At the center, spanning both halves, was the mark of the Sound Weavers—an intricate, symmetrical emblem etched with striking detail. Interlocking paths curved and folded through each other like twisted threads, forming a weave of mirrored lines. The geometry suggested both structure and flow, order and connection. At its core, the lines shaped an "S" while subtlety hidden within the weave, a sharp "W" emerged, almost unseen if you weren't looking closely. The emblem pulsed faintly, alive with an energy Anthem could almost feel.

Vale pressed his hand to a shimmering panel on the wall. The crest split apart, its halves vanishing seamlessly into the frame as the doors slid open with a soft whoosh. Revealing a vast underground complex sprawled out before them, a hidden world beneath their feet.

"This," Vale announced, stretching his arms wide as he turned to face them, "is the heart of our operations. The true Sound Weaver Studios."

The entrance was grander than Anthem had expected, especially for something buried beneath Crucible City's streets. He and Indy stepped forward into an expansive hall teeming with activity. The walls and ceiling were carved from dark stone, threaded with veins of luminescent minerals that shimmered as they passed.

A subtle warmth radiated up through Anthem's shoes, the polished stone floor heated by the planet's natural geothermal currents. Along the hall's perimeter, plush benches lined the walls, and floating digital screens displayed music videos and live performances from artists he had never heard of.

"Impressive, isn't it?" Vale asked, watching their reactions with a knowing smile. As they ventured deeper into the base, an assistant approached and handed Vale a clipboard. Anthem watched Vale silently scan the clipboard before he turned to Anthem. "Oh, by the way, we have your guitar," he revealed. "We have it in an armory, so to speak, and will maintain it while you're here."

Anthem thanked him before Vale reassured him, "Don't worry, your guitar is in excellent hands." He said, handing the clipboard back to the assistant, who promptly disappeared. "Now, I'll give you a quick tour while we're on our way to your training session."

Their first stop was a vast amphitheater-like space. The sheer scale of it caught Anthem off guard. Tiered seating spiraled upward in an elegant curve, designed to create both intimacy and grandeur. Soft ambient lighting bathed the room, reflecting off the smooth, dark stone that lined the floors and walls. At the center, an expansive stage commanded attention, framed by towering speakers and intricate sound-dampening panels.

"This is the Assembly Hall," Vale said with a smile. Despite the size of the space, his voice carried perfectly—no echo, no distortion. The acoustics had been honed to perfection. "We hold performances, demonstrations, and meetings here. This is where we celebrate our craft, where we build our community."

Anthem's gaze swept across the walls, where portraits of past Sound Weavers stood immortalized. Each figure had been captured in the midst of creation—some playing instruments, others wielding their powers in mesmerizing displays of energy and movement. Their passion radiated from the artwork, a silent testament to those who had come before.

Vale allowed them a moment to take it in before leading them onward. Their next stop brought them to the research and development wing. The moment they stepped inside, Anthem felt like he was intruding on a very important job. Scientists and engineers moved with quiet efficiency, testing sound-based technology with careful precision.

From one corner, the low hum of sonic devices resonated through the air, while holographic displays flickered with streams of complex data. Sound wave patterns shifted and reformed in midair, their intricate frequencies visualized in real time.

"Our R&D team is the key to our future," Vale said, pride evident in his voice. "Here, we do more than experiment with sound—we push it further. We're developing tools that can shape the world, not just our own community."

Vale led them onward, through another set of doors and down a corridor. As they approached their next destination, the hallway opened into a vast, brightly lit chamber filled with advanced technology. Large circular lights illuminated the space, casting a crisp glow over the countless monitors and consoles lining the walls.

"This," Vale said, gesturing toward the expansive room, "is the Command Center."

A soft, barely audible hum filled the air, the background noise of dozens of consoles running simultaneously. Operators moved with quiet efficiency, their eyes fixed on streams of data, sound wave analysis, and surveillance feeds from across Musera. Maps, intricate sound charts, and grids of unknown origin flickered on the screens, shifting and updating in real-time.

At the center of the room, the most striking feature dominated the space—a massive, illuminated 3D projection of a planet. Five continents spread across its surface, rendered in vivid detail.

"And this is the keystone of our global operations," he said, gesturing toward the holographic map with the emotion of a proud parent. "From here, we coordinate with Sound Weaver communities across the world. We track everything—sound phenomena, anomalies, potential threats, both terrestrial and...less conventional."

Anthem's gaze lingered on a glowing marker in the northern reaches of the map. He understood now—the reach of the Sound Weavers extended far beyond Crucible City.

"You mentioned sound phenomena?" Anthem asked, tilting his head.

Vale stepped closer to the map. He reached out, grabbing the holographic display and rotated the globe until it centered on a specific continent. "Yes. Take this, for instance," he said, highlighting a sprawling desert. "Lyricor is a land of extremes. It's home to our more adaptive Sound Weaver cousins, who have mastered unique voice manipulation techniques. There, they've studied a natural phenomenon known as the 'Booming Dunes' or 'Drumming Sands.' When the wind shifts the sand in just the right way, it produces a deep, rolling hum—like the beat of a drum echoing across the landscape. It's entirely natural, but strange enough that locals whisper of buried spirits or hidden civilizations."

He rotated the globe again, this time toward the icy polar regions. "Now, up here in Aetherglace, Sound Weavers have developed incredible techniques of their own. They manipulate sound through the ice, using the environment's natural acoustics to communicate and navigate. And under the right conditions, some auroras produce faint, musical tones—almost like chimes."

Anthem nodded, absorbing the information. "I understand. But you also mentioned anomalies. Those don't sound naturally occurring."

Vale smirked. "Right you are. Then let's look closer to home." With a flick of his hand, he zoomed in on Rithmara—their home continent, where Musera occupied nearly two-thirds of the landmass. Anthem studied the terrain—a mix of dense forests, sprawling urban centers, and jagged mountain ranges. The western regions were a tapestry of temperate woodlands, gradually giving way to high-altitude cities nestled in the peaks. Along the eastern coast, vibrant metropolises ran with the rhythm of the ocean, where the tides influenced both culture and music.

"Here," Vale said, tapping on a glowing marker. "Cities like our own Crucible City are where our influence is the strongest. But deep in the forests and mountains, we operate in more secrecy. And if you know where to look, you'll find places where sound doesn't behave the way it should. Ever heard of Echo Wells?"

Anthem raised a brow. "Can't say I have."

"They're deep caves or wells where sound bends in unnatural ways," Vale explained. "Words and noises bounce back, but not immediately—sometimes minutes later, sometimes hours. And sometimes... they repeat things that were never said at all."

A chill ran down Anthem's spine. "That's creepy."

Vale nodded. "We don't have a definitive answer for why it happens. Some believe they're natural sound traps. Others think they're places where time is tangled." He gestured to another marker, this one hovering over a city near Crucible City. "Then, there are the Temporal Echoes. Every so often, sounds from the past—or the future—bleed into the present. A song that hasn't been written yet. A long forgotten secret conversation. They're rare, but when they happen, they make people question reality."

Anthem drummed his fingers on the edge of the console, staring at the glowing marker. "And people don't freak out?"

"Oh, they do," Vale admitted. "We keep them quiet when we can. But not all anomalies are so subtle."

He moved the map south, where a lush tropical expanse stretched across the display. Towering rainforests blanketed the land, crisscrossed by winding rivers. It was a continent teeming with life.

Vale gestured toward a shadowy, unmarked region on the map. "The people of Maridia call this the Screaming Silence. Within these zones, all natural sound ceases—no birdsong, no wind, not even your own voice. Instead, an unbearable pressure fills your ears that sounds like a scream just within hearing range. Those who linger too long have gone insane."

Anthem's expression darkened. "That doesn't sound natural."

"It isn't," Vale confirmed.

He shifted his focus, pointing toward a softly glowing marker on a continent nestled between the southwestern reaches of Rithmara and Maridia. Unlike the others, this land was a patchwork of lush green hills, terraced fields, and sprawling vineyards, its villages pulsing with a rhythmic energy woven into everyday life.

"Cantavera," Vale said, "is a place of harmony, where music, nature, and people move as one. But don't be fooled by its tranquility—the Sound Weavers here are among the most formidable. They have mastered vibrokinesis, attuning themselves to the natural rhythms of the planet. Yet even they face threats." His fingers hovered over a section of the map where faint distortions flickered on the display. "Resonance Wraiths. Entities composed entirely of sound. They have no physical form, but you can see the space they occupy—like a shimmer in the air, just out of focus. They're drawn to places of intense emotion or trauma, and when they communicate, it's through harmonic vibrations. Sometimes it's whispers, sometimes it's screams. Not all are hostile, but when they are...they're nearly impossible to silence."

Anthem's brows knit as he studied the map. Scattered across the oceans between these continents were countless small, isolated islands. Some of these islands were renowned for their mystical properties, where ancient tales told of Siren's Songs and the Sound of Death. Others were home to reclusive communities or exotic wildlife. These island chains formed maritime trade routes connecting the continents.

At both poles, vast ice caps stretched across the planet's surface, gleaming under the glow of distant auroras. Few had ever ventured deep into these frozen lands, and fewer still had returned with stories to tell. But those who did whispered of ruins buried beneath the ice—fragments of an ancient civilization lost to time.

Anthem exhaled, absorbing the sheer scale of it all. "And you're tracking everything? All of it?"

Vale nodded. "We have to. These phenomena aren't just mysteries—they're signs. Of power, of change, of danger. These phenomena are usually a result of Sound Weaver interference, whether through unchecked ambition, gross negligence, or simple inexperience. We make it one of our missions to safeguard these areas." Vale said.

As Anthem's gaze swept across the continents, he noticed a network of small, glowing markers scattered across the land and sea. "And these?" he asked, pointing to the clusters of green lights.

"Our communities," Vale said. His voice held a quiet certainty as he traced the glowing markers, each one representing a hidden enclave of Sound Weavers. "This is our strength. We are all connected—sharing knowledge, resources, and protection. That unity keeps us alive."

An entire world existed beneath the surface of the one he knew—Sound Weavers spread across every continent, each with their own skills, their own traditions, their own battles to fight. This wasn't just a hidden society. It was a global symphony, each piece playing its part in something far greater.

Vale turned away from the map and nodded toward the exit. "There's still more to see."

As they stepped back into the quiet corridors of the facility, Anthem let his fingers drum absently against his thigh, a slow rhythm forming in his mind. With a smirk, he glanced at Vale. "So, what's next? Basketball courts?"

Vale's lips twitched with amusement. "Funny you should say that." He replied smoothly. "Yes, we actually have a couple of professional-quality basketball courts."

Anthem blinked, surprised. "Wait, seriously?"

"Absolutely," Vale said casually. "Sound Weavers need to stay physically sharp as well as mentally and musically. Basketball's a popular way for many of us to unwind and build teamwork. Come on, I'll show you."

Anthem and Indy pushed open the double doors ahead and entered a sprawling indoor sports complex. The room was nothing short of impressive. There were not one but two full-sized basketball courts. Their polished wooden floors gleamed under the bright overhead lights. Electronic scoreboards hung at each end, and a group of Sound Weavers were already deep into an intense game, their sneakers squeaked on the floor as they darted back and forth.

"This place," Anthem said, shaking his head in disbelief, "is incredible."

As they stood watching the game, a missed shot sent the basketball rolling straight toward them. Anthem instinctively bent down and picked it up. The familiar feel of the ball in his hands stirred his competitive nature. As he straightened up, a player came jogging over with a friendly grin.

"Thanks for that!" the man called, slowing to a stop in front of Anthem. His grin was effortless, a flash of white teeth under the bright lights. He was tall and athletic, with long reddish-brown hair pulled back into a loose ponytail, exposing intricate tattoos that spiraled across the shaved sides of his head. The designs were bold yet elegant, snaking down to his neck. He was shirtless, causing the light to catch the sheen of sweat on his chest and arms. Anthem watched droplets beaded on his skin, rolling over the curve of his biceps and along the sharp line of his collarbone before disappearing into the taut muscle of his torso. There was an energy about him, raw and magnetic, that made Anthem linger on the moment longer than he meant to.

"I'm Reed," the player said, extending a hand. His voice had a warmth that matched his grin—easy, open, and with just enough charm to make Anthem take notice. "You new around here?"

Anthem shook his hand, grinning back. "Yeah, just getting the grand tour. I'm Anthem."

"Anthem? Cool name," Reed said, bouncing the ball a few times. "If you ever want to jump in, we're always looking for more players. Keeps things interesting."

Anthem laughed, feeling the friendliness of the group radiate through Reed. "Might take you up on that," he said, a playful gleam in his eyes. "But don't get mad when you end up on a highlight reel."

Reed chuckled, his eyes lighting up. "Oh, shit-talking already? I like it. We can do this right now. There's nothing but space and opportunity." He gestured to the court with an inviting wave.

"Another time," Anthem said with a grin, glancing toward Vale and Indy. "Still got the tour to finish, but don't worry—when I'm back, you're gonna wish you hadn't asked."

Reed shook his head, smiling as he jogged back toward the court. "I'll be waiting. It was nice to meet you, Anthem." With that, Reed rejoined the game, effortlessly weaving through players before throwing down an acrobatic dunk. Anthem watched, impressed by the guy's skill.

Indy nudged Anthem with her elbow, a smirk on her face. "Looks like you might get some court time sooner than you thought."

Anthem chuckled, still buzzing with the energy of the place. "Hey, I'm always ready for a challenge."

"I bet you are," Indy said with an exaggerated wink and a playful smile.

Vale watched the interaction with a pleased expression. "We believe in balance here," he said. "Physical strength, mental acuity, musical mastery—they all feed into each other. You'll find that as you grow as a Sound Weaver, every aspect of your life becomes more connected."

Anthem nodded; his earlier sense of hesitation now replaced with a growing excitement. He hadn't just stumbled into a secret world—he'd discovered a hidden utopia, a place that nurtured every part of him, not just his abilities.

Vale turned to Indy, giving her a parting smile. "There is only one stop left. You're free to continue exploring on your own, but Anthem and I must continue."

Indy nodded, giving Anthem an encouraging look before she wandered off toward the other side of the facility, disappearing into the hallways. Vale led Anthem further into the sprawling complex, moving toward a massive, arena-like space. As they passed through a set of polished doors, Anthem's eyes widened.

"This is the training zone." Vale beamed. Before him stretched a massive space, a blend of modern architecture and leading-edge technology. Sleek, reflective walls rose around him—plexiglass interlaced with sound-dampening panels. A low vibration pulsed through the room.

To the left stood a series of towering, intricate glass-paneled vocal booths with a dazzling array of glowing dials, levers, and screens, each softly lit from within. Inside, Sound Weavers played their instruments—guitars, flutes, hand drums, and strange hybrid creations of wire and wood. The booths pulsed with contained resonance; flickering with waves of iridescent light in sync with each performance. Anthem watched, entranced.

To the right, several Sound Weavers gathered around cylindrical machines that had sleek sensors used to analyze their abilities. As they worked, holographic screens projected before them, displaying every nuance of the sound they created—thresholds, magnitudes, frequencies.

A young woman, her brow furrowed in concentration, played her guitar. The ground beneath her feet vibrated in time with the music, causing the floor to rise, lifting her several feet into the air. She hovered there, bobbing like a leaf caught in a gentle breeze, perfectly in tune with her music's melody.

Above, Anthem could see an array of advanced monitoring systems suspended in midair, sleek devices tracking the movements below. These floating holographic screens displayed complex data in real-time—heart rates, oxygen levels, even emotional intensity. The systems provided immediate feedback, optimizing every action, every breath, every note played. This was not just a training ground—it was a place of total immersion, where every aspect of a Sound Weaver's abilities were meticulously analyzed, refined, and perfected.

Vale nodded toward the various stations. "Every Sound Weaver here is honing a different aspect of their power. Some focus on creating sound and bending it to their will, others study its deeper frequencies, the underlying vibrations that connect everything. The goal is the same: to achieve harmony with yourself, your instruments, and the world around you."

Anthem felt his pulse quicken. The possibilities here were endless. He could feel a stirring within him, an energy that seemed to call out, eager to be unlocked. The potential to become one with the elemental force of sound, to use it in ways he had never even dreamed of—it was all within reach.

Vale turned and began walking further into the arena, gesturing for Anthem to follow. "We're going to start you with some basics. A group session."

As they moved deeper into the training zone, Anthem felt a sudden pang of uncertainty. They entered a side room, and Vale gestured for him to stand by the door. Inside, a small group of children, ranging from no older than six to maybe twelve. Some had instruments: a small harp, a weathered harmonica, a pellet drum, others empty-handed. Vale's voice dropped in volume, but his tone was matter-of-fact. "You'll be joining their class today. They're just beginning to understand the full scope of their powers, but they're already quite talented. It's a good starting point. You'll get a feel for how it works."

Anthem blinked, taken aback. "You want me to train with kids?"

Vale gave a small chuckle. "You'll find their abilities are well beyond what you might expect. You'll learn something from them. Besides, if you don't learn to attune, you can't control your powers. Doesn't matter if you're six or twenty-six." He gave Anthem a push toward the door. "Go on. Don't worry, they bite less than you'd expect."

Anthem, though skeptical, stepped into the training room. The space hummed with a quiet, steady resonance—a meditative pulse that emanated from the floor. The kids were seated in loose circles, instruments in hand, chatting amongst themselves. They barely glanced at Anthem, which somehow made him feel more out of place.

A tall woman with deep-set eyes and dark braids down her back walked to the front of the room. When she spoke, her voice was neither commanding nor soft, but resonated with a clarity that silenced even the most fidgety kids.

"Welcome," she said. "I'm Tessa. Today we begin with something simple: understanding what you are."

Anthem raised an eyebrow. "This a philosophy class?" He muttered to himself.

Tessa turned toward him. "Yes," she said simply. "Because power without understanding is dangerous."

Anthem blinked. The kids giggled.

Tessa faced the group again. "You are not using magic. You are not casting spells. You are aligning with what's already there. The Core Harmonic flows through everything—air, stone, skin, breath. Every living being sings with it.

Sound weaving is the act of aligning yourself to that harmony and using it to resonate with the world."

Anthem raised his hand, hesitating only slightly. "Why *is* it called sound weaving?" he asked, frowning thoughtfully.

Tessa's mouth quirked into a small smile. She turned to the group, hands clasped loosely in front of her. "Good question." She scanned the room. "Anyone know?" A few of the students exchanged uncertain glances. Someone shifted in their seat. No one answered.

"Each note you hear is like a thread," she said. "Alone, it vibrates, simple and pure. But when you layer sounds together—notes, rhythms, resonances—you create something stronger. You interlace them. You weave them." She looked around the room. "Sound weaving isn't just about making noise or playing music. It's about binding different strands of resonance together into patterns—patterns that touch the physical world, the emotional world, and sometimes things even deeper than that. A single sound can move a pebble," she said, her voice soft but certain. "But woven sound—woven intent—can move mountains."

"Now..." She picked up a tuning fork and struck it gently. The sound it made was subtle but sharp, a single note that hummed longer than physics allowed. "This is the Core Harmonic," she said. "Or rather, a representation of it. The Core Harmonic isn't a tone—it's a presence. A frequency that responds to your intent." The fork still vibrated in her hand. "When you awaken, you feel it—briefly. A moment of perfect resonance. A sense of being pulled into something vast."

Anthem flinched. That sentence struck something inside him. The kids listened patiently, but Anthem felt the air shift around him.

He saw that void again. The weightlessness. The eerie calm. That moment—when he thought he was dying, only to be remade with sound from the inside out. "I saw it," he whispered, more to himself than to anyone else.

Tessa raised a brow. "Pardon?"

"The void," he said, louder. "I passed out when my powers awakened. There was this... place. It was made of sound. I was made of sound."

Tessa tilted her head, thoughtful. "Unusual. When most Sound Weavers awaken, there's some discomfort. Very few lose consciousness, even fewer have visions."

"So what does that mean for me?"

She shook her head. "I don't know."

That unsettled him. He was used to being the outlier, but not the unknown. That even someone like her—clearly experienced—had no reference for his experience, made him feel exposed.

Tessa nodded toward the center of the room. "Let's meditate. Everyone, assume attunement posture."

The children shifted, sitting straighter, closing their eyes. Anthem hesitated, then sat down cross-legged and placed the guitar across his lap. The familiarity of the instrument comforted him.

"Breathe in," Tessa said. "And out. Match the rhythm of your breath to the beat of your heart. That's your first frequency. Your internal tempo."

Anthem closed his eyes.

"Inhale... hold... exhale." Tessa instructed.

The room quieted to a stillness so complete it rang in his bones. Anthem shifted uncomfortably on the cushion, his shoulders tense. He inhaled as instructed, held the breath, then exhaled—but nothing came. No sensation. No resonance. Just his own doubt echoing back at him.

He tried again. Breathe in. Breathe out. Match breath to heartbeat, heartbeat to thought. But his thoughts kept scattering like leaves in the wind—frustration, embarrassment, pressure. His fingers hovered over the guitar's strings, whisking them, hoping for a spark. Still nothing.

All around him, the children were already slipping into deep concentration. He could hear their quiet breathing, the occasional shifting of posture. Some of their instruments vibrated faintly, responding to their internal alignment. Meanwhile, his own mind was a wall of static.

"Listen inward. Not to sound—but to vibration. Imagine the space behind your eyes. Feel the flow of blood in your fingers. The Core Harmonic is not heard—it is felt." Tessa said, pacing around the room.

Anthem grit his teeth. Felt? He felt like a fool. Like a man trying to mimic something sacred. Doubt festered in the hollow spaces between his thoughts, making his efforts feel clumsy, off-key.

And that was when it stirred. The void surfaced again—but not like before. It was a reminder that he had touched power once and couldn't find his way back. He chased the memory, reaching mentally for that music, that moment of stillness that had once enveloped him.

Nothing. A hollow beat in his chest. More silence. Dead silence.

He almost gave up. Almost opened his eyes, ready to walk away. But then—he felt that falling sensation. He slowly unraveled. A tremor in his chest. A thread unwinding. Not violent—gentle. Like a pressure valve slowly releasing after being sealed too long. The sensation rushed through him. His fingers jerked on the strings. The guitar vibrated in his lap. The Core Harmonic didn't appear—it *surged.*

A vibration, yes. But no longer subtle. It was like standing in front of a massive speaker during a bass drop. Anthem gasped as the force of it tore through him—not as pain, but as truth. His spine tingled. A tight breath stalled as the space around him expanded. He wasn't floating.

He was *attuning.*

A frequency deep within his being synced with something far older than memory. The void wasn't gone—it had become a vessel, a container for this eruption of alignment. A ripple. A hum that didn't fill the air, but rewrote it.

He was a note, resolved at last.

The hum grew into a chorus that wrapped around his entire being. And then, as suddenly as it came—it quieted. It didn't disappear, only settled. Waiting.

He opened his eyes. He wasn't alone in feeling it. One child gasped. Another giggled softly. Tessa merely smiled.

"Some of you touched it," she said. "That's good. The more you return to it, the clearer it becomes. The Core Harmonic does not hide from you. It waits."

She stepped forward, her eyes briefly resting on Anthem before sweeping the rest of the class. She gave him a quiet, measured look. "You'll need to tread carefully. The deeper the resonance, the more it reveals—and the more it demands."

Anthem said nothing. His body tingled. The resonance hadn't left. It was like a shadow trailing his thoughts, waiting to be heard again.

Tessa softened her tone. "For now, remember this: what you felt wasn't control. It was a connection. And connections, like music, aren't meant to be forced. They're meant to be listened to."

Tessa clapped her hands gently. "Now, we move to the booth."

She gestured toward the far corner of the room, where a cylindrical glass chamber stood. It was tall enough to stand in comfortably and lined with softly pulsing filaments. The glass was thick, reinforced.

"This is the Resonance Booth," Tessa said, her voice calm and deliberate. "It's designed to help us assess your unique connection to the Core Harmonic. The booth measures how deeply your intent aligns with the Core."

She ran her fingers along the outer edge of the glass. "The glowing filaments you see respond to frequency, strength, and structure. The more precise your intent, the clearer the booth reflects it back. You'll see colors, pulses, maybe even shapes. Each reaction gives us insight into how your resonance flows." The booth gave a soft pulse, as if acknowledging her words. "This is not a competition," she added. "This is a reflection. What you see inside is where you are today—not where you'll end up. So step forward, one at a time. Focus not on sound, but on intent. Let your body remember the resonance. Let the Core Harmonic answer. One at a time now."

The children lined up. One by one, they entered the booth, played a few notes on their instruments, and exited. The chamber glowed in different colors, sometimes gently pulsing, other times barely reacting at all.

When Anthem's turn came, the room stilled in anticipation. Even the children quieted, eyes fixed on him as he stepped toward the Resonance Booth. The door hissed shut behind him, sealing him in a cocoon of perfect silence. Even his heartbeat felt muted. The air felt stuffy, almost oppressive. Anthem unslung his guitar, fingers trembling with anticipation. He lowered himself onto the stool, his body taut like a string pulled tight.

He thought of the void. Pulled on the connection he just discovered. The memory of creation rushed through him like wildfire.

He strummed.

A single chord, slow and deliberate.

The reaction was immediate—and violent. The booth exploded with light. Fibers blazed outward in jagged lines of violet lightning, then warped into waves of rich indigo and burning gold. The hum of the Core Harmonic didn't just respond—it roared.

The chamber shuddered, dangerously.

Anthem felt his guitar thrumming against his chest. He didn't play the next chord so much as he channeled it.

The surrounding space warped. From the floor, a ripple of energy rose, coalescing into a faceted sphere of sound—golden, radiant, alive. It pulsed like a heartbeat, expanding, contracting, then hovering mid-air as if held by invisible hands. Sparks of harmonic energy danced off his fingertips. The sphere fractured into crystalline strands of light that twisted around him, forming intricate patterns in the air.

Outside, the children pressed against the glass, wide-eyed. Tessa stepped forward with a similar expression. Inside, Anthem's breath slowed. He wasn't forcing it. His only intent was to shape it, mold it. And when he released the final note, the booth fell still—but the power lingered. Faint. A whisper in the air.

He exhaled and let the silence settle like dust in sunlight. When he exited, the children stared. The pellet-drum girl squinted at him. "Are you sure you've never done this before?"

Anthem shrugged. "Kind of figuring it out as I go."

Tessa tilted her head. "You channeled intent into structure. Not common for a first assessment. Especially with that level of resonance."

"I saw it in my head," Anthem said, still a little dazed. "And it just... responded."

Tessa nodded slowly. "You don't need more power. You need clarity. Control. Balance."

Vale, who had been watching silently since Anthem had entered the booth, stepped away from the back wall and approached Tessa. They spoke in hushed tones, just out of earshot. Tessa gestured briefly toward the booth and then back at Anthem. Vale crossed his arms, nodding slowly, though his expression had grown serious.

After a moment, Vale stepped up to Anthem, his gaze steady. "You know," he said, voice low, "I've seen dozens of first-time assessments. Yours wasn't just strong—it was pure. Like the Core Harmonic was answering *you*, not the other way around."

Anthem blinked. "That good, huh?"

Vale smirked faintly. "Let's just say your potential is limitless."

Anthem scratched the back of his neck. "Felt like the Core... recognized me. Or maybe I remembered it."

Vale's smile faded into something more thoughtful. "That's what worries me."

Before Anthem could respond, his stomach growled—loud, echoing in the quiet room. One kid snorted. Another laughed. Anthem sighed, deadpan. "I guess all that attuning burns calories."

Vale chuckled, then clapped him on the shoulder. "Come on. Let's get you fed before you vibrate into pieces. We'll talk more later."

Anthem didn't argue. He was starving. Slipping his guitar over his shoulder, he followed Vale out of the training zone and into the sleek, well-lit corridors of the facility. As they walked, Anthem glanced around, taking in more of the place. There was still so much he didn't understand, but at least now he knew one thing—he had to work a lot harder if he wanted to see what he was capable of.

As they neared the cafeteria, Anthem's eyes landed on a familiar face in the distance. Indy. She was deep in conversation with another Sound Weaver. The moment she spotted him, she gave a big wave.

"Look who survived training," she called out with a smirk. "Thought I'd find you passed out somewhere."

"Ha-ha," Anthem deadpanned. "I'll have you know I'm a natural."

Indy snorted. "Yeah? Your face says otherwise."

Anthem chuckled, but kept walking. "You coming?" he asked Indy over his shoulder.

She pushed off the wall, said a quick goodbye and fell into step beside Anthem. "Might as well," she said. "I wanna hear all about your 'natural' talent."

Anthem groaned, but a small smile tugged at the corner of his lips as they made their way toward the cafeteria together. Passing a common area, Anthem noticed something unusual. The room, filled with people, was noticeably still. Everyone faced the far wall, where a large television displayed a news broadcast. Urgent commentary reached him from where he stopped.

Anthem frowned, walking closer. "What's going on?" he asked, his voice low as he turned to Vale.

Vale's expression had darkened, his usual calm slipping into a more serious appearance. "Looks like we're about to find out," he said tensely. "Let's sit down."

Seeking a clear view of the screen, the three moved to the center of the room and sat down. The images on the television showed a city skyline—Crucible City. The news ticker flashed with words like "unrest" and "mysterious disturbance."

Indy leaned closer to Anthem. "I've got a bad feeling about this," she whispered, her voice tight with worry.

Anthem's jaw clenched. He didn't respond, but his gut twisted in agreement.

CHAPTER IX

Maestro Virtuoso—better known to the world as MV—sat in the plush chair of the television studio. His every movement, every slight change of his posture, was deliberate, calculated. The stage lights played tricks with his sharply defined features, casting dramatic shadows that only heightened his enigmatic aura. His impeccably tailored suit clung to his muscular frame. A crisp white shirt contrasted starkly against the dark fabric. And a thin, jet-black tie completed the ensemble, giving him the look of someone who demanded absolute obedience.

A thin, perfectly groomed beard framed his jawline, showing the care and attention to detail MV put into his personal appearance. His hair, once an impenetrable black, was now streaked with silver. Evidence of his years of navigating both the glittering highs and the shadowy depths of the music industry. He slicked his hair back, drawing attention to his intense blue eyes. Those eyes, piercing and unreadable, locked onto the camera, holding it in place as if daring it to turn away.

To the public, MV was a legend—an acclaimed music producer and Musera Music Hall of Famer. But, at that moment, he wasn't there to talk about his latest chart-topping hits. No, he was there, prepared to set the world on fire.

The interview began with light banter about his recent successes, ground-breaking production techniques, and iconic status. The interviewer, a seasoned journalist, was good at her job—polite, engaging, and professional. But MV was a master of the game. Slowly, he steered the conversation away from the mundane toward a more shadowy topic of conversation.

"You know," he began, his voice as smooth as silk dipped in chloroform, "it's fascinating what you can achieve with sound these days." His eyes gleamed knowingly, teasing out the secret he was about to share. "The usual beats and melodies are outdated, soon to be replaced by something... more."

The interviewer raised an eyebrow, intrigued. "More? Are you talking about new technology?"

MV chuckled, a low, unsettling sound that sent a shiver through the studio, as though the temperature had just dropped a few degrees. "Not technology," he said, flashing a sharp toothed smile. "Talent. Real, raw talent. Imagine artists who can move you with their music. Not metaphorically. Literally. With an innate power, woven into every note."

The interviewer shifted in her seat. She leaned in, her interest piqued. "You're suggesting there's more to music than we know? That certain artists possess... supernatural abilities?"

MV's smile widened, but his eyes remained cold. "I'm not suggesting it. I'm telling you." He paused for dramatic effect, letting the words hang in the air. "There's a hidden community. Sound Weavers, they're called. People with the power to shape music and reality itself with their sound. I was once one of them."

Stillness fell over the room. The revelation dumbfounded the producers, the camera crew, even the interviewer. The interviewer blinked, trying to keep her composure as she processed this bombshell. "So, you're saying these Sound

Weavers... they have abilities that go beyond music? Abilities that could, in theory, influence people?"

MV's voice turned icy. "That's exactly what I'm saying. They can manipulate sound in ways that can sway emotions, shift perspectives, even control minds—if they wanted to."

A ripple of unease spread through the studio. The interviewer swallowed, her professional mask slipping just slightly. "How widespread is this community? Are they... dangerous?"

MV leaned back in his chair, crossing his legs casually, as though talking to a close friend. "Oh, they're everywhere. In your favorite bands, behind your favorite songs. Hiding in plain sight. And while most of them claim to use their abilities for good, the potential for harm is... significant. Imagine someone with the power to make thousands of concert goers suddenly trample each other in a massive mosh pit."

The interviewer, her skepticism wavering, leaned forward. "You're painting a rather dystopian picture here. Why come forward now? And how do you fit into all of this?"

MV's expression shifted, becoming almost predatory. "I've seen what they're capable of firsthand. I was one of them, but I chose a different path. I believe in using that power responsibly for creation—not control. Which is why I have taken young, talented Sound Weavers under my wing. Unlike the rest of their community, I'm giving them the tools to use their gifts for the betterment of music and humanity—not to hide and deceive. Therefore, we reject the name Sound Weavers." He said the word with disgust. "Our intent is to break the traditions of this antiquated organization. To use our abilities to steal back the unseen control they have over this world. We are Wave Reavers."

The interviewer hesitated as she tried to formulate her next question. Finally, she spoke, her voice firm. "That's quite a claim, MV. But words alone won't convince everyone. Can you show us what you mean? Can we see these abilities in action?"

MV's smile returned, this time sharper, hungrier. "I thought you might ask that," he said in a silky purr. With a snap of his fingers, he summoned one of his proteges—a young woman with a serene expression and a violin cradled delicately in her hands.[1]

She stepped in front of the camera with almost a wraithlike grace, and with a nod from MV, she played. The first note sent a wave of calm rippling through the studio, like a gentle breeze washing over a restless sea. The music had a gentle yet powerful melody. Tranquility and wonder washed over the room, replacing the tension.

Neither the crew nor the interviewer could resist the music's pull. It was as if the sound had reached into their souls and quieted every anxious thought, every fear. For a few minutes, the world outside ceased to exist, and all that remained was the music.

When the violinist finished, the silence that followed was deafening. The performance dazed everyone, subtly but undeniably altering their emotions. MV leaned back with a smile of pure satisfaction. "What you just experienced," he said, barely above a whisper, "is only a glimpse of what's possible."

The camera zoomed in on MV's dark, serious face. "The Sound Weavers are real. They are powerful. And now... you know."

---

1. Track 7 – Ludovico Einaudi - Experience

With that, the interview ended.

Anthem, Indy, and Vale sat frozen, watching the last frames of MV's chilling interview fade to black on the oversized screen. MV's last expression seared itself into their minds. His words hung in the air like smoke from a fire. The shock of seeing MV so publicly reveal and distort the nature of Sound Weavers sent Anthem's mind reeling.

Indy stood beside him, her hand trembling as it covered her mouth. Her eyes, usually filled with curiosity and light, were now wide with disbelief. "Not only did he just expose everything—he's painted Sound Weavers as villains," she whispered, shaking her head slowly. "The world's only going to see monsters."

Vale stood with his arms crossed, his posture as rigid as iron. A cold, dark look set in his eyes. "He's declared war," Vale said bluntly.

Around them, the other Sound Weavers murmured in panicked voices, filled with fear and confusion. Unease replaced the facility's usual mood. At the front of the gathering, an elder of their community stepped forward. Her face, usually serene and inviting, now bore a stern expression. People knew her for her leadership and composure. But now, the gravity of the situation visibly shook even her.

"MV's turned our gifts into a weapon in the public's eyes," she said. "He's distorted everything we've worked for, everything we've stood for, and the world is going to believe him unless we do something." A ripple of agreement spread through the room, but fear lingered in the eyes of many. They knew what this meant. MV drew a line in the sand and dared the Sound Weavers to cross it.

A younger Sound Weaver, known for his environmental work and his creative, unconventional use of sound, took a determined step forward. "We need to show them the truth, show them the good we do, how our abilities can bring beauty and healing, not manipulation," he added, carrying a persuasive earnestness. "It's about transparency, about letting them see the real impact of our work—how we use our powers to create and inspire."

Vale nodded in agreement. "Yes, and we need to do it together. We need to be united in this. MV has challenged the very foundation of our community, and it's up to us to defend it. We'll need to strategize, prepare for the public's reaction, and bolster our security. MV knows too much about us." The room fell silent as the weight of the situation settled on each of them. Vale continued. "Let's use this as a wake-up call. We strengthen our bonds, we improve our outreach, and most importantly, we show the world the real power of Sound Weavers—not through domination, but through the harmony we can create. We've been waiting for a sign when we would have to decide our future. This is it. MV threw down the gauntlet, and now we pick it up."

CHAPTER X

V ale led Anthem and Indy through the winding halls with long, quick strides, the easy hospitality he had shown earlier now replaced by a distant, distracted attitude. They exchanged a glance but said nothing, understanding the shift in his demeanor.

When they reached the cafeteria doors, Vale came to an abrupt stop. "This is where I leave you," he said, his words clipped. His gaze looked past them, already focused elsewhere. Before Anthem or Indy could respond, he turned on his heel and strode off, disappearing into the corridors without another word.

They stood in silence for a beat, the echo of his departure lingering longer than it should have.

Indy glanced at Anthem, her mouth tight with unspoken worry. "I guess he'll figure this out," she muttered.

Anthem nodded grimly, still absorbing everything MV had unleashed into the world.

Finally, Indy nudged him toward the doors with a forced smirk. "Come on. Maybe there's something edible in there. And if not... at least we'll have something else to be angry about."

Before stepping into the cafeteria, Anthem's phone buzzed in his pocket. He glanced at the screen: an unfamiliar number. Usually, he'd let it go to voicemail, but today, something told him to answer.

"Hello?" he answered hesitantly.

"Anthem? This is Mare, formerly from *The Club*."

Anthem stood up straighter, bringing his full attention to the conversation. "Hey, Mare," he replied, trying to keep his voice steady. "What can I do for you?"

"I hope I'm not catching you at a bad time," Mare said warmly but professionally. "Since the unfortunate closure of *The Club*, I've been working for various other venues, and I'd like to book Manufacturing Eden to perform at a few of my shows. You guys killed it last time, and I'd love to get you back on stage."

Anthem's heart sank, the memories of his old band cutting through him like shards of broken glass. He clenched his jaw, searching for the right words. "Uh, yeah. About that..."

Mare waited, sensing something wasn't quite right.

"I'm... I'm not with Manufacturing Eden anymore," he confessed. The words tasted bitter on his tongue, like swallowing a pill. "Things fell apart, and the band is no more."

A pause followed, and when Mare spoke again, her tone was softer, sympathetic. "I'm sorry to hear that, Anthem. I had no idea."

He let out a shaky breath. "Yeah, it's... it's been a rough ride."

"Well," Mare began, a spark of excitement creeping back into her voice, "if you're up for it, I'd still love to have *you*. I know it's not Manufacturing Eden, but you've always had something... special on stage. I think the crowd would be thrilled to see you perform solo."

The offer landed like a punch to the gut and a lifeline all at once. Solo shows? Could he really do that? Could he face the same stage, the same crowd, without his band?

"I... I don't know, Mare," he admitted with a tinge of uncertainty.

"Hey, no pressure," Mare replied, a hint of a smile in her voice. "Just think about it. Open one of my shows and if all goes well, I have two more for you. Who knows? You might surprise yourself."

"Okay," Anthem finally said, his mind stumbling over the possibilities. "Thanks, Mare. I'll think about it."

After hanging up, he stared at the phone, still shocked by the offer. Could he do it? Should he do it? A part of him was screaming to take the chance, to step back into the spotlight and reclaim a piece of what he'd lost. But another part, the part that still nursed wounds from the way Manufacturing Eden imploded, was terrified of what would happen if he failed. Was this a shot at redemption?

Indy, who had been waiting by the door, arched an eyebrow. "You look like you just got propositioned by a ghost. What's up?"

Anthem hesitated, shoving his phone into his pocket. "That was Mare from *The Club*. Well, formerly from *The Club*."

Indy's interest piqued instantly. "Oh yeah? What'd she want?"

He exhaled, massaging his neck. "She wants me to play a show. Just me. Solo."

Indy blinked, then smirked. "Well, damn. That's huge."

"Yeah," Anthem said, shifting his weight. "It's also terrifying."

Indy scoffed, giving him a light punch on the arm. "Anthem, come on. You've played a million shows. You've *commanded* a million shows. Why's this one different?"

"Because it's *not* just another show," he admitted. "It's not Manufacturing Eden. It's just me." He gestured vaguely, like the weight of the words were too much to hold. "What if it's not the same? What if I suck without them?"

Indy rolled her eyes and stepped in front of him, jabbing a finger into his chest. "First of all, you don't suck. Second, you and I both know it was never just about the band. Manufacturing Eden was amazing, sure, but you? You *are* the music. You don't need them to be incredible—you already are."

Anthem let out a half-laugh, half-scoff. "That was dangerously close to a compliment."

"Yeah, well, deal with it," she shot back, folding her arms. "Listen, you can stand here, sulk, and let this pass you by, or you can step up and remind everyone why they know Manufacturing Eden in the first place. Because of *you.*"

Anthem stared at her, her words sinking in. Slowly, the doubt in his chest loosened just a little.

"Think about it," Indy said, nudging him toward the door. "But don't think too hard. You might accidentally talk yourself out of it."

Anthem huffed a small laugh, shaking his head as he pushed open the cafeteria doors. "No promises."

The room was a cacophony of conversation, laughter, and the clinking of utensils. The space was sleek and modern, with its high ceilings, metallic accents, and long communal tables that invited collaboration and casual interactions.

Anthem, still overwhelmed by everything he had seen, looked around absently as they navigated through the sea of Sound Weavers. Just then, his shoulder bumped into someone walking by. The sudden jostle knocked a tray from the stranger's hands, sending food crashing to the floor and splattering across a pair of shiny black boots.

"Hey, watch it!" The man's deep voice cut through the general hum of the dining hall.

Anthem turned, his apology ready on his lips, but it froze as he met the stony gaze of a tall, imposing figure. The man stood before him, anger clear in his stormy gray eyes. His face was clean shaven and unblemished, marked only by a band of freckles that stretched across his brow, traced over his eyes, and scattered down the bridge of his nose and cheeks. His hair was a silvery-white color that transitioned from black at the roots. He wore it in a medium mullet style that fell onto the collar of his form-fitting black jacket. Metallic pins adorned the jacket, gleaming under the soft lights. Strapped to his thigh was a pouch filled with drumsticks, arranged like weapons, ready to be summoned at any moment.

"Sorry," Anthem said, hands up in surrender, though his voice was nonchalant. "Didn't see you there."

The man's eyes narrowed, his posture rigid. "Didn't see me?" he repeated, his voice clipped and dripping with disdain. "Maybe you should pay more attention. Precision is kind of important around here."

Indy stiffened beside Anthem, sensing the eyes of the dining hall shift toward them. The room grew quieter as more and more people turned to watch the scene unfold.

Anthem exhaled through his nose, already tired of whatever this was turning into. "Yeah, well, I'll work on that," he said, glancing down at the ruined food smeared across the guy's boots. "But maybe next time, don't walk like you own the place."

A murmur rippled through the cafeteria. The tension between them was palpable, like two frequencies clashing in an unresolved chord. The man scoffed, tilting his head slightly, eyes flashing with something that wasn't quite anger—more like curiosity masked behind irritation.

"You must be the newcomer," he said, voice edged with dry delight. "I heard they dragged in some wild, untrained recruit. Didn't expect you to be this sloppy in person."

Anthem bristled, but forced himself to keep his expression neutral. "Yeah? And you are?"

The man smirked, and something about it set Anthem's teeth on edge. He lifted his chin slightly, like the answer should have been obvious.

"Solstice," he said, like the name alone should have meant something. And, judging by the whispers and exchanged glances from the surrounding Sound Weavers, it did.

"Try to keep up, newcomer," he said, brushing past Anthem with deliberate force. "Wouldn't want you falling behind before you've even started."

Anthem clenched his jaw, watching as Solstice strode away, his boots still stained with remnants of his ruined meal.

"Wow," Indy said, arms crossed. "You've been here for, what, not even a full day? And you've already pissed someone off?"

Anthem exhaled sharply. "Yeah, well," he muttered, "he started it."

Indy snorted. "You *did* knock his lunch all over him."

"Details."

Shaking her head, Indy clapped him on the shoulder. "Come on, let's eat before you make any more enemies."

Anthem cast one last glance toward where Solstice had disappeared before sighing and following Indy toward the food line. The smell of rich spices filled the air as they tucked into their meals—Anthem savoring a plate of spiced chicken, while Indy enjoyed a fragrant vegetable curry.

"This is exactly what I needed," Indy said between bites, her face glowing with satisfaction. "I could get used to meals like this."

Anthem chuckled, nodding in agreement. "Yeah, definitely beats the mystery chili at some gigs I've played."

They ate in silence for a few moments, but Anthem's mind kept circling back to the possibility of performing again. "Mare's offer... it got me thinking."

Indy tilted her head, watching him. "You thinking of taking her up on it?"

"Kind of, but I'm thinking more about how she was looking for Manufacturing Eden first. Maybe I should use this to start over." He mused.

Indy raised a brow. "Starting over how?"

"A new band," Anthem said quietly. "Something different. Not Manufacturing Eden 2.0. Not a replacement. Just... something that speaks to what's happening now."

Indy sat with that for a moment, chewing slowly. Then she nodded. "I figured that's where your head was going."

"Too obvious?"

"You're you," she said, smiling softly. "You don't know how to stop once you sink your teeth into something."

Anthem smirked just slightly. "You think I'm crazy?"

"I know you are," she replied. "But that doesn't mean you're wrong. And if you're serious about building something new... you know I'm in. Someone's gotta keep your stage from falling apart."

He gave her a look. "You're not in it for the music?"

"I'm in it for the cables, the chaos, and the curry," she said, raising her fork like a toast. "But mostly, I'm in it for you."

If Anthem's face could show it, Indy would have seen him blush. "Thanks, Indy. I'm going to accept her offer as a solo act for now, but keep the new band idea in the back of my mind."

"Sounds like a plan. Don't thank me yet though," she said, grinning. "Wait until you hear my contract demands. I want better snacks this time."

The warmth of the meal helped reset Anthem's mind after the long day he had. But his respite was short-lived. Anthem was about to take another bite when an unknown man approached their table. Anthem looked up to find the man standing before them. He was tall with dark hair, and his eyes were calm and composed, much like his demeanor, hinting at a confidence earned from decades of training and travel. Although Anthem had never seen him before, the air around him felt charged with power. He was clearly someone important.

"Mind if I join you?" the man asked sweetly, but forcefully.

Anthem and Indy exchanged a quick glance, surprised but intrigued. Anthem gestured to an empty chair. "Sure."

The man sat down smoothly. "I've been watching your progress, Anthem," he said, locking eyes with him. "You're doing well, and it's clear you have potential. But there's more to learn, and I think you're ready for the next step."

Anthem straightened in his chair. "Who are you?"

The man leaned forward slightly with an intense gaze. "Please call me Canon. I'm a Mentor here, one of several. We guide Sound Weavers as they develop their abilities. And in three days, we're holding a session for more advanced Sound Weavers. I'd like you to attend."

Indy raised an eyebrow. "Advanced? Anthem's just getting started. Isn't that a bit... soon?"

Canon's gaze shifted to Indy, a faint smile playing on his lips. "Perhaps. But the best way to grow is to face challenges head-on. Anthem's shown resilience. He's ready."

Anthem felt his pulse quicken at the invitation. Excitement and trepidation bubbled within him. "What kind of training are we talking about?"

"Nothing you can't handle," Canon replied with a smirk. "But it will be intense. We'll push you to understand just how much control and discipline you'll need. You've already tapped into your power, but you haven't even scratched the surface."

Anthem's determination flared. "I'll be there."

Canon stood. "Good. More details will be to come, for tonight, get some rest." He paused, glancing at Indy before continuing, "We have assigned rooms to both of you. You'll find them more than adequate for a restful night."

Indy looked surprised, exchanging a glance with Anthem. "Rooms? Really?"

Canon nodded. "That's standard practice for those dedicated to their training. You'll find your rooms prepared when you're ready. You'll be in rooms 198 and 199. Here are your key cards." With that, Canon gave a nod and turned to leave, his presence lingering even after he disappeared out of the dining hall.

Indy leaned back in her chair with a contemplative expression. "Advanced training, huh? You sure you're ready for that?"

Anthem took a deep breath. "I think I have to be. If I'm going to figure out these powers, I need to push myself."

Indy smiled, "Well, at least we've got a place to crash for the time being. Let's get some rest."

Anthem nodded, already mentally preparing for the challenge that awaited him.

After finishing their meal, Anthem and Indy set out on their mission to find the dormitory level, asking a few people for directions. A friendly member of the support team smiled warmly as they approached.

"It's just down that hall. Take a left at the end and you'll see a set of stairs. The dorms are on the second level," the staffer explained kindly.

"Thanks," Anthem said, exchanging a look with Indy as they ventured deeper into the heart of the compound.

As they followed the directions, the atmosphere changed. The usual energy of the main facility faded to quiet, softly lit hallways. It felt like a retreat, as if they had crossed an invisible threshold into somewhere far removed from the chaos of their day. When they reached the heavy wooden doors marking the dormitories, Anthem paused. The doors were elegant and old-fashioned. They seemed out of place in such a modern environment. Brass fixtures gleamed faintly in the dim light, and a small plaque read, simply, "Dormitories."

He pushed the door open, and together they stepped inside.

The space beyond was unexpectedly luxurious. Unlike the stark utilitarian quarters they expected, soft amber light filled the dormitory hall. Sleek, modern artwork lined the walls—abstract sound waves captured in bold, flowing strokes. The faint scent of lavender lingered in the air, instantly calming.

"Wow," Indy whispered, as if scared she'd disturb the tranquility of the space.

Anthem's room was next door to Indy's. They exchanged a glance as they stopped in front of their respective doors.

"Well," Anthem said, his hand resting on the doorknob. "This is it."

Indy smiled. "Yeah. Sleep well, Anthem. We've got a lot ahead of us."

He returned the smile. "You too, Indy. Goodnight."

With that, she disappeared into her room, and Anthem turned the knob on his door, stepping into what felt like a dream.

The room was, simply put, heaven. As he crossed the threshold, plush carpet greeted his feet, causing him to immediately remove his boots and lie face down on the floor. He began making snow angel movements as he rubbed his cheeks on the carpet. Fully enjoying the sensation, it wasn't until he rolled over on his back that he saw the night sky, complete with twinkling stars and a first quarter moon. Confused, he stood up to get a closer look at the ceiling. What he was looking at was a real time simulation of the current sky displayed on advanced screens that generated a soothing glow over the space. He felt as if he'd been transported from the underground facility to a serene mountain retreat. A simulated fire was even crackling away in a corner of the room, enhancing the cozy vibe. When Anthem went to investigate the fireplace, he discovered there was actual heat coming from it. Anthem marveled at the heater before turning and jumping onto the bed. It was large and inviting, draped in soft linens that whispered promises of deep, uninterrupted sleep. Neatly folded pajamas and a change of clothes for the next day also awaited him on the bed.

Anthem let out a low whistle as he ran his fingers over the fabric. The attention to detail was astounding, right down to the toiletries neatly arranged in the spacious modern bathroom. Even the tiles beneath his bare feet were warm as he stepped inside to wash up, a small but significant luxury in a place designed to push people beyond their limits.

He took his time in the shower, letting the hot water soothe the lingering tension in his muscles. His thoughts, however, were anything but still. Images from the day played in his mind—the hidden challenges of this new world, MV, and the growing sense of danger.

Dressed in the soft pajamas provided, Anthem finally crawled into bed. The mattress felt like a cloud beneath him, pulling him into its embrace, while above, the stars twinkled lazily in the simulated sky.

For a moment, Anthem just lay there, staring up at the stars, his mind still buzzing with the day's revelations. He thought about his powers. About Indy, who he had dragged along with him into this insanity and stood by his side without hesitation or failure. And then there was Vale, enigmatic and wise, with secrets Anthem was sure would take a lifetime to unravel.

Anthem sighed, rolling onto his side. It felt like he was standing on the edge of a cliff, and just below his feet was something that had the potential to change his life and the lives of everyone around him. But for now, he was grateful for this moment of peace. As he closed his eyes, the day's events blurred together, and soon, the steady cadence of his breathing was the only sound in the room.

Word of MV's interview spread through the Sound Weaver facility like the flu, carried from hallway to hallway until rumors echoed down every corridor. Within hours, leadership called an emergency briefing. Every Sound Weaver in the complex was summoned. Anthem, Indy, and the rest of the community gathered in the auditorium, their murmurs forming a nervous hum beneath the grand arching ceiling.

As the lights dimmed, the chatter fell silent, all eyes turning toward the podium where Vale stood. Anxiety tinged his usually calm demeanor. He took a deep breath as he swept his gaze over the room. "Thank you all for coming on such short notice," Vale began, his voice laced with an unmistakable edge. The room hung on his every word. "As you know, the recent actions of Maestro Virtuoso, MV, have compromised our community's secrecy, revealing our existence to the world. We now stand at a crossroads. We must act swiftly and decisively, not just to protect ourselves, but to show the world who we really are."

A ripple of murmurs coursed through the audience. Vale allowed it to settle before continuing, undeterred. "The leadership has met, and we've developed a comprehensive plan to counter this crisis. Our first initiative is the Public Outreach Program."

The crowd stirred, intrigued. "This program will involve public performances, demonstrations, and community service projects," Vale explained, gaining momentum. "We must take control of the narrative. Show the world that our powers are not weapons, but tools for good. Many of you will be called upon to take part in these efforts. It will be our chance to counteract the fear and paranoia that MV has sown."

Vale's gaze sharpened as he moved to the next part of the plan. "In addition, we will initiate an Enhanced Training Regimen. This is not just about mastering your powers, but preparing for the dangers ahead. You will learn not only to hone your abilities, but to defend yourselves, and to survive if things take a darker turn."

"Finally," Vale said, his voice dropping a notch as he delivered the most delicate part of the briefing, "we are engaging in negotiations with key figures in the government and media. Our goal is to mitigate the damage caused by MV's betrayal and, where possible, forge alliances to protect our community from further exposure. These conversations will be crucial to our survival."

Silence followed his words, a thick, almost oppressive quiet. Vale concluded, "I know these are difficult times. But we are a powerful community, and we will face this together. I believe in each and every one of you. We will navigate this storm as we always have, by trusting in our powers and in each other."

He paused, letting the words resonate. "I'll now open the floor for questions."

For the next several minutes, the room was a flurry of raised hands, hurried questions, and somber answers. Anthem and Indy listened intently. But just as the crowd started to disperse, Vale raised his hand once more, calling for attention.

"I need the following individuals to remain behind," Vale announced, his voice ringing out clearly. He read off a list of names—Anthem and Indy among them. The two exchanged a glance, uncertainty dancing in their eyes. What now?

As the room cleared, the small group of selected Sound Weavers gathered at the front of the auditorium. Vale's face was even more serious than before, his eyes hard as he addressed them directly.

"We have a deeper problem," he said, lowering his voice. "We need to understand why MV did what he did—why he turned against us. His betrayal is not just personal; it's strategic. He knows our strengths and our vulnerabilities. If we don't uncover his motivations and expose his network of secrets, we'll be fighting in the dark."

Vale handed out dossiers, each thick with documents, reports, and photos. Anthem took his and flipped through the pages—snapshots of MV from years ago, performing with the Sound Weavers, a life that seemed worlds away from his current treachery.

"Your mission," Vale said, his tone grave, "is to dig into MV's past. Find out who he's working with. Follow the leads, connect the dots, and expose whatever network he's built. We need to understand him, to know what drives him, if we're to stop him."

Anthem's eyes narrowed as he studied the information in his hands. This was a hunt for the truth behind a former ally turned enemy. He looked over at Indy, whose expression mirrored his own. They were in this together, and they would uncover the secrets lurking in MV's past.

"We'll sort this out," Anthem said firmly.

Indy nodded with resolve. "We're not letting him tear this community apart."

Vale gave a small nod. The rare smile of gratitude returned to his lips. "I trust you will. Use every resource we have. This is our best chance to stay ahead of whatever he's planning."

They quietly made their way to a sensitive compartmented information facility and got comfortable around a large digital table. Vale grouped many of them into teams, and, much to Anthem's irritation, he assigned Solstice to his team. At the center, a digital screen came to life, casting a bluish glow that illuminated the focused expressions of those gathered. Folders and files appeared on the screen, meticulously organized by dates, events, and personnel as they prepared to dig into the details of MV's past.

Anthem gestured to the screen. "Alright, let's start with the archives. We need to find everything we have on MV—training logs, disciplinary actions, mission reports—anything that can give us insight into his downfall."

Indy, seated beside him, immediately got to work. Her fingers danced over the keyboard, pulling up files and casting them onto the table's surface. The others leaned in, their eyes scanning the displayed information, eager to find the key that would unlock MV's secrets.

Solstice pointed to a specific section of a timeline they putting together. "Look at this log here," he said, pointing at the screen. "About three years ago, there's a sudden shift in MV's assignments. He went from leading important missions to getting sidelined almost overnight."

Indy opened other files, highlighting a series of reports that corresponded with the change. "Looks like Sound Weaver leadership had concerns about his methods—too aggressive, maybe even unethical. They started pulling him back from major operations."

Anthem nodded, absorbing the information. "And not long after, he filed a formal complaint, accusing leadership of holding back the community's potential. He called it a 'stifling of true progress.'"

Indy continued digging, pulling up MV's full profile. "Here's something else. During his time with the Sound Weavers, he went by the name Milton Vikram. And look at his powers—Hypnosis and Mindscape Manipulation." The room fell silent for a moment as everyone processed just how dangerous that combination could be.

Suddenly, Indy froze. Her eyes widened as she pulled up a video file marked as classified. "There's surveillance footage attached here. You guys need to see this." She clicked play, and the group watched as MV appeared on the screen, standing in a public square. At first, the scene seemed normal; people going about their day. But then MV withdrew a conductor's baton from his jacket. He readied his hands and the civilians nearby stopped dead in their tracks. They moved in eerie synchronization, their faces blank, eyes devoid of any emotion.

MV raised his hands, orchestrating their actions with the movements of a conductor. The civilians, completely under his control, walked in unison toward a nearby building. The footage then cut to a rooftop camera, showing them calmly walking to the edge before jumping, one by one, without hesitation.

A stunned silence fell over the group.

Indy added. "Says here that there was no hard evidence that he made those people jump. His defense being that he was just practicing a piece in his head and their actions were completely unrelated. That's the only reason he isn't locked away somewhere now. Instead, leadership excommunicated him."

Solstice leaned back, shaking his head. "If he can influence more than one person at a time, we may be dealing with someone who could sway more sizeable crowds without them even realizing it."

The trio continued combing through MV's file, searching for clues as to the sudden changes in his behavior, hoping to find the moment where his dissatisfaction turned into outright murder.

"Alright," Indy said. "Let's see what our elusive Maestro has left behind in the digital world."

Her fingers clacked across the keyboard, pulling up multiple browser windows with lightning speed. Social media profiles, blog entries, interviews Indy collected every scrap of data available on MV. The screens filled with images, headlines, and video clips of MV's public appearances, each one chronicling his transformation from a musical icon to the controversial figure they were now tracking.

"Here we go," Indy said. Using specialized software, she began analyzing MV's online footprint, cross-referencing it with major events in the Sound Weaver community and music industry. The software was like a digital detective, peeling back layers of sentiment shifts and subtle rhetoric changes over the years.

"Check this out," she said, highlighting a cluster of data points on the screen. "Right after he was pulled from Sound Weaver assignments, his whole vibe shifted—less unity and expression, more isolation and cryptic messaging. Like a switch flipped."

Anthem squinted at the screen, his mind churning as he pieced together the timeline. "That was right after leadership shot down his proposal to push their influence into the mainstream media. He thought it was the future, but they disagreed. He didn't take it well."

Solstice chimed in sarcastically. "As if exploiting our powers for profit would've *really* helped anyone but his ego."

The team studied the screen, watching the puzzle pieces come together. MV wasn't just another disgruntled artist. He had been laying the groundwork for this for a long time.

"It's like he was testing the waters, trying to plant seeds of doubt," Indy speculated. "And when that didn't work, he cranked up the intensity. His posts became more aggressive, more divisive. He'd gone full rogue."

"Classic radicalization trajectory," Solstice added grimly. "Couldn't get his way, so now he's trying to burn it all down from the outside."

Anthem took a step back from the screen. "This is good. It's giving us a clearer picture of when and why MV turned on the community. Leadership denied his ambitions, and now he will do whatever it takes to force his vision on the world."

Indy nodded in agreement. "The real question is, how far will he go? How many people is he willing to take down with him?"

The room fell silent. They had unearthed valuable insights into MV's motivations, but it didn't make the path ahead any less treacherous.

The trio began to gather their papers and packed away their notes. "We need to get this to Vale," Anthem said, stuffing papers into his bag. "If we move fast, we might have a shot at stopping him."

Solstice scoffed under his breath. "Move fast to do *what*, exactly? We don't even know where MV's aiming next. Charging in blind is a good way to get everyone killed."

Anthem straightened sharply. "And doing nothing is better? Sitting on our hands until he burns the rest of us down too?"

Solstice met his glare without flinching. "We act when we have leverage. Otherwise, we're just bodies for him to step over."

Anthem took a step closer, fists clenching at his sides. "You think you're being strategic? You're just afraid."

Solstice's mouth twisted into a half-smirk, half-sneer. "Maybe I'm just not eager to be another dead idealist."

The air between them crackled, the heat of the argument about to boil over—

"Wait... hold on," Indy cut in sharply, her eyes glued to the screen.

Anthem and Solstice both turned toward her.

Her fingers danced across the keyboard, shifting tabs until a muted video feed filled the center screen.

"What is it?" Anthem asked.

Indy's face tightened. "MV. He's live. Right now."

She clicked the volume icon, and the room filled with the sound of MV's smooth, commanding voice—velvet-wrapped steel, honed for performance. Pristine in a dark, high-collared jacket embroidered with gilded resonance patterns. He stood behind a sleek podium stamped with the CEA's insignia, flanked

by two Wave Reavers in ceremonial armor. His expression was calm, composed…
and chillingly confident.

Indy unmuted the feed.

"—And while it brings me no joy to share this with the people I love," MV said,
"it's time we stop ignoring the threat that lives among us. These individuals,
these so-called 'Sound Weavers,' have operated from the shadows for too long."

The screen shifted to a slow-motion replay of a collapsing transit hub. Screaming
civilians, flashing lights, chaos. In the middle of the frame, blurry footage showed
a figure playing what looked like a saxophone—moments before the structure
buckled.

Solstice narrowed his eyes at the screen. "That's edited," he said flatly.

Anthem's jaw tensed. He agreed, but the message was simple.

MV's voice rose with false gravity. "This attack claimed seven lives. Innocent
people. Mothers, children, performers like you and me. And who do we find
at the center of the devastation? A Sound Weaver—with ties to other suspected
Independent Artists."

Another cut. This time to footage of a Wave Reaver unit moving through a
smoky alley, arresting a young woman with tear-streaked cheeks and a fractured
lyre clutched in her arms.

"Let me be clear," MV said. "This is no longer a debate about artistic freedom.
This is about safety. Order. Peace."

Indy's hands slowly curled into fists on the desk. "He's making his move."

MV's tone shifted, as if delivering a benediction. "The Harmonic Council has officially appointed me and the Wave Reavers to locate, detain, and, if necessary, neutralize all active Sound Weavers operating without sanction. We will not tolerate further loss of life. We will not allow unchecked power to destroy what we've worked so hard to build."

The video cut again—to cheering crowds, a public square where people raised their hands and waved posters of MV, painted with words like *Protector* and *Unifier*.

"I implore you—do not fear," MV said. "Stand with me. Stand with harmony. And together, we will silence this uproar."

The broadcast ended with a flash of the CEA's seal.

CHAPTER XII

Anthem tossed and turned, the sheets twisted around his legs. Every time he closed his eyes, fragments of the past few days clawed their way back—his budding powers, MV's betrayal, the unraveling future. His fingers drummed an anxious rhythm against the mattress, and the itch to do *something* gnawed at him until staying still felt unbearable.

By the time the first hints of dawn crept over the horizon, his decision was already made. He threw on yesterday's clothes and made his way next door. He yanked the blankets off Indy's bed, earning a muffled groan of protest.

"C'mon," he said, nudging her shoulder. "We're training."

Indy cracked one eye open, scowling. "Do you *have* to do this at—" she turned her head toward the clock, groaned, and flopped back down—"stupid o'clock in the morning? How did you even get in here?"

Anthem smirked. "I sure do. There's no better time than the present. And you should really lock your door."

Grumbling the entire way, Indy pulled on a jacket and followed him through the still-silent halls toward the training zone.

Indy took up position on a reinforced observation platform. She booted up the monitoring system as Anthem slung his guitar over his shoulder. "Alright," she said through a two-way speaker, rubbing her hands together. "We'll take this step by step. Start slow, something mellow."

Anthem nodded eagerly. He planted his feet, drew a deep breath, and let his fingers glide over the strings. A slow, smooth melody filled the room, rolling through the space like waves on a quiet shore.[1]

Immediately, the connection he drew upon responded, causing the now familiar golden glow to appear. The glow around his fingers deepened, thickening into shimmering faceted orbs of light with each note. As he played, the motes of energy detached from his fingertips, floating in the air like tiny stars. They swayed in time with the music, drifting lazily as if caught in a gentle current.

"They're responding to me," Anthem murmured. He played a piercing, quick riff, and the orbs flared to life, zipping through the air like shooting stars. As he transitioned back to a softer melody, they slowed, orbiting him like planets caught in his gravity.

Indy grinned. "Alright, switch it up. Let's see what happens when you really let loose."

Anthem didn't need to be told twice. He squared his shoulders, took a breath, and launched into a fierce, electrifying riff. The surrounding glow morphed, shifting from soft pulses to molten slags of energy.[2]

Across the room, a training block weighing hundreds of pounds trembled. Anthem's eyes locked onto it. His fingers moved faster, more precisely. The resonance thickened around him, congealing into a shimmering golden mass that

---

1. **Track 8 – John Mayer – Slow Dancing in a Burning Room**

2. Track 9 – Rage Against the Machine – Bulls on Parade

cracked and crumbled midair. From that mass, vaguely humanoid crystalline shapes emerged—hands, roughly formed and unpolished, as if chiseled from sound rather than stone. Its edges weren't perfect, fingers formed incomplete or fused in places.

Indy tensed at the sudden display of power. "Anthem—!"

He ignored her, too caught up in the moment. He played harder. The crystalline hands lurched toward the block, grabbing it with a crack of refracted light. Thin splinters of energy danced across the room from the impact. With brute force, the hands tightened, warping the block under grinding pressure as shards snapped off and reformed midair. Moments later, they collapsed into glittering fragments, the energy vanishing like dust on the wind. In their place remained a crumpled, jagged heap of twisted metal and pulverized concrete.

Indy let out a low whistle. "That's insane, Anthem."

Breathing heavily, Anthem wiped sweat from his brow, a wild grin splitting his face. "It's exhausting but... damn, it feels amazing."

Indy nodded to herself. "Take a break for a minute," she suggested. "I'm thinking we need to explore how different genres affect this. If something fast can create those hands, what could jazz or blues do? There's gotta be more to your abilities—more layers to uncover."

When he was ready, Anthem nodded and exhaled slowly, fingers settling on the fretboard. He started with a slow, deliberate melody, bending the notes with care. The deep, rich tone filled the training zone, resonating off the steel beams.

As the sound thickened in the air, something else emerged—wisps of deep honey colored mist, curled and unfurled around him.[3]

Indy's breath hitched through the speakers. "That's...unexpected."

The mist moved like it had a mind of its own, pouring out from Anthem and spreading outward, coiling around the amplifiers, brushing against the wires and pedals.

"This is incredible," Indy murmured. "The blues seem to draw out a more subtle part of your powers."

Encouraged, Anthem let the melody build, pushing into a groovier rhythm. The mist thickened, hugging the floor, strands swirling like ink in water.

A grin tugged at Anthem's lips. "Let's see what happens when we shake things up."

He transitioned into a heavier rock riff, letting the smooth blues melt into something grittier, more intense. The effect was immediate—the gilded mist evaporated in an instant, replaced by vibrant streaks of red and orange light that crackled and snapped in the air like miniature bolts of lightning. Kinetic energy surged through the space, arcs of light slashing across the air like wild brushstrokes on an invisible canvas.[4]

Indy shielded her face instinctively. "Rock is definitely all about raw energy!" she shouted over the rising sound. "It's like your powers are feeding directly off the music's intensity!"

---

[3] Track 10 – Funkadelic – Maggot Brain

[4] Track 11 – Judas Priest – Painkiller

The surge of power was intoxicating. Anthem leaned into it, driving the chords harder, faster, the rhythm snarling beneath his fingertips. His pulse raced as he slipped into an aggressive metal riff. The moment the first blistering chord struck, the air *buckled.*

Resonance pooled on the ground, thin and glimmering like liquid gold. The puddle trembled—an unstable, swirling pocket of power. And from it, something took shape. This construct wasn't raw like before. It was elegant. Deceptively graceful. A hand formed first—its edges faceted, crystalline, almost delicate. It flexed with a jerky motion that felt... wrong. Like something learning to mimic control without understanding it.

The pool rippled further, and more of the construct pulled itself free—an arm, a shoulder, and then a head emerged, faceted like a living jewel. It rose slowly, as if dragging itself from the grave.

Indy's awe shifted to concern. "Heavy metal is insane! But Anthem—be careful! This doesn't feel safe!"

But he was lost in the sensation. His fingers moved with reckless speed, each chord feeding the storm. The energy twisted around him, spiraling into a vortex of blinding light and distortion. He could *control this.* He could *shape it.*

And then, without warning, the power turned on him.

It hit like a shockwave—too much, too fast. The energy recoiled, slamming into his body like a hammer strike to his chest. His nerves ignited with searing pain, white-hot and all-consuming. His fingers convulsed against the strings, a discordant screech ripping through the air as the swirling light cracked apart.

The crystalline construct shuddered violently. Fractures webbed across its body like lightning in glass. With a groaning wail of stressed energy, the elegant form splintered. First, the arms crumbled into glittering shards, collapsing inward as if pulled by its own body. Finally, the head split clean down the center, a flash of resonance bursting outward in a sharp detonation of sound and light. The pieces dissolved into a flurry of golden dust, sucked back into the floor.

"Anthem!" Indy's voice barely cut through the roaring static in his skull. The world around him deformed, colors smeared together as his limbs turned to lead. A crushing weight bore down on him, as if the air had solidified in his lungs.

His knees buckled.

He hit the ground hard.

The last thing he felt was the raw, unrelenting agony tearing through him—then everything went black.

When Anthem woke, the cold press of concrete against his back sent a dull throb through his aching body. The overhead lights were too harsh. His vision swam as he tried to blink them into focus. A distant ringing in his ears gradually faded, replaced by muffled voices and the distinct beeping of medical equipment.

"Anthem?" Indy's voice cut through the haze, taut with worry.

He turned his head slightly, wincing at the sharp ache in his skull. Indy was crouched beside him, her face pale, eyes rimmed red. Beyond her, a pair of medics hovered nearby, their medical bags open and equipment scattered. Relief flooded her expression the moment their eyes met.

"Thank the Gods," she said, letting out a breath. "You scared me half to death. I don't think I'll ever get used to you passing out."

"Let's hope it doesn't become a habit." Anthem groaned as he tried to sit up, but a firm hand pressed against his shoulder, holding him down. The medic shook his head. "Take it easy. You took quite a hit."

"What... happened?" Anthem's voice was hoarse, his throat dry as sandpaper.

Indy let out a shaky breath. "You pushed yourself too far," she said, her voice raw. "I tried to warn you, but you just kept pushing. And then—" She broke off, looking away. "It all collapsed on you. You hit the ground, hard. I called for help, but... you weren't waking up."

The fragmented memories came rushing back—the raw energy, the thrill, the moment where he had felt unstoppable. And then the pain, the immense pain of his own power turning against him.

"I couldn't stop it," he admitted, flexing his fingers. They ached, his palms scraped and bloodied. "I didn't think... it could turn on me like that."

Indy's fingers twisted into the fabric of her jacket. "I should've stopped you sooner," she murmured. "I didn't realize it was going to get that dangerous."

Anthem shook his head, even though the movement made his vision swim. "No. It's not your fault," he said firmly, though the exhaustion in his voice dulled the impact. "We don't know my limits yet."

Indy grabbed his hand, squeezing it tight. "Well, you hit them, Anthem. Hard. You can't do that again." Her voice wavered, but there was steel beneath it. "You could've—" She swallowed hard. "You could've died, Anthem."

He tried to muster a reassuring smirk, but the lingering tremors in his body made it difficult. "I'll be more careful," he promised, though he wasn't entirely sure how.

The medic checked his vitals once more, then glanced at Indy. "He'll be alright, but he needs to rest. No strenuous activity for a while."

Indy nodded firmly. "Got it."

As the medics began packing up their equipment, Anthem let his head rest against the pillar behind him. His body ached, his limbs felt like lead, but the worst of it had passed. Or so he thought.

Indy lingered beside him, her hands fidgeting, her expression troubled. She hesitated, then took a breath. "Anthem," she started softly, like she was bracing for impact. "There's something else you need to know."

He blinked up at her, noting the way she chewed the inside of her cheek. His stomach tightened. "Just say it."

Indy exhaled, shifting her weight. "Your guitar..." Her voice wavered. "It didn't make it."

The words didn't register at first. "What?"

She swallowed, her eyes darting toward a nearby worktable. Anthem followed her gaze, and the sight knocked the breath from his lungs. His beloved instrument, the medium for all his power—lay in ruin before him.

Anthem looked down at the shattered remains of his guitar and fell to his knees. He had tapped into too much power, more than he was ready for. He had lost control, and it had cost him dearly. The guitar that had been an extension of his soul, his voice, his very identity, was gone—cruelly ripped from his grasp. Its neck lay snapped in two. The body was nothing more than splinters, while the strings dangled limp and broken.

"No..." The word escaped his lungs like a dying breath. He reached out for the headstock with trembling hands—and that's when he saw it. The charm. Still hanging there, against all odds.

It was a small figurine, no longer than his thumb, carved from translucent resin his mother had poured herself—years ago, when he was just a kid dreaming of stages. In the center was a single sapphire stone—his father's birthstone—embedded in the figure's chest like a heart. The figure had no eyes, no mouth, but its silhouette resembled a warrior, a sentinel.

He had never played a single set without it.

He undid the thin leather strap from the broken guitar carefully. It caught the light softly, its edges glowing faintly gold and blue, almost exactly like the crystalline constructs his resonance created.

He hadn't noticed that before. Now he couldn't unsee it.

He curled his fingers around it and pressed it to his chest. His mother's hands had shaped it. His father's spirit lived inside it. And somehow... his powers had echoed its shape, its light. He looped it around his neck, letting the charm fall just below his collarbone.

Turning his attention back to the rest of the guitar, his fingertips grazed the splintered remains as if he could piece it back together. But the harsh reality was that he couldn't. His guitar was beyond repair, and with it, something inside him also felt irreparably destroyed. For long minutes Anthem just stayed there, hunched over the remains of his guitar, his mind a vortex of guilt, anger, and painful, aching sorrow. He had been so consumed by mastering his newfound powers, by the promise of what he could become, that he had forgotten the most crucial thing: patience. He had pushed too hard, too fast, and now he was paying the price. For the first time, Anthem understood.

Power wasn't just a gift to be claimed. It was a burden to be mastered. Without control, it didn't just break the world around you—it broke you first.

With every second that passed, Anthem's mind spiraled deeper into despair. What was he without his guitar? Without the one thing that had always been his voice, his escape, his power. He was just a man, lost and broken, with a force inside him he didn't understand, let alone control. His vision blurred as tears threatened to spill, but he refused to let them fall. He gripped the fragments of his guitar so tightly that his knuckles went pale, the jagged wood bit into his palms. It wasn't until his hands started to bleed that he finally, reluctantly, let go, watching the pieces clatter to the floor.

"I destroyed it, Indy. I destroyed my guitar." Anthem couldn't resist any longer and his tears fell unrestricted.

Her face softened with sympathy, and she placed a warm and steady hand on his shoulder. "It's okay," she whispered, though her voice wavered. "We'll figure this out."

But Anthem shook his head, his body trembling. "You don't understand," he rasped. "I've been pushing myself so hard... trying to control this power, trying to be better... but look what I did. I've lost everything."

Indy's eyes glistened with unshed tears, but she blinked them away, determined to be strong for him. "You haven't lost everything," she insisted. "You've come so far, Anthem. This isn't the end. It's just a setback."

Without another word, Indy pulled him into a tight embrace. "I'm here with you," she whispered fiercely into his ear. "I believe in you. We'll find a way through this. Together." The warmth of her hug was the only thing keeping Anthem tethered to the moment, to reality. He leaned into her, mourning his loss, but also leaning into the strength of their bond. She was always there in his darkest hours, reminding him that not everything was lost.

CHAPTER XIII

The room had shifted to a gray scale winter landscape. The advanced walls and ceiling screens wrapped him in the illusion of a snow-covered forest beneath a pale, overcast sky. Bare trees stretched like skeletal fingers around him. This landscape had spoken to him, it matched the current landscape of his heart. Anthem lay on the narrow bed, half-buried beneath a tangle of blankets. The silence wasn't peaceful. It pressed down on him. Heavy. Suffocating.

His hand twitched toward where his guitar used to rest against the wall—an old habit with no payoff. It was gone. Stolen. Shattered. Lost. That guitar wasn't just wood and strings. It was his anchor. His history. His voice. Now all he had was quiet. He barely noticed the knocking on his door—until it flew open.

"Anthem!"

Indy stood in the doorway, flushed with urgency, hair windblown and eyes blazing. She clutched a tablet to her chest like it might explode.

Anthem barely looked up. "Can you... come yell at me later?"

"No time," she said, already crossing the room and shoving the tablet in his face. "You need to see this. Now."

He groaned and turned away. "Unless it's footage of someone bringing my guitar back from the dead, I really don't—"

"Vale went public."

That got his attention.

"What?"

She handed him the tablet. On-screen was Vale, standing in front of a worn, hand-painted backdrop of the Sound Weaver crest. It wasn't live. The "PRE-RECORDED" tag blinked in the corner, but the energy in Vale's eyes felt fresh, dangerous, and alive.

Anthem sat up slowly, his chest tightening.

Vale's voice came through clearly. "If you're watching this, then you've seen the footage. The one they're using to brand us terrorists, to justify a purge. That video is a lie. The person responsible for that attack was not acting under the guidance—or the blessing—of any Sound Weaver circle. We grieve for the lives lost. But we will not accept guilt for crimes we didn't commit."

The screen shifted to cutaways—scenes of real Sound Weavers: shielding civilians during protests, healing injuries after raids, playing music in shattered neighborhoods. Small glimpses. But enough. "We are not monsters. We are artists. Healers. Protectors. And we will not go quietly."

Anthem's throat tightened as Vale leaned closer to the camera.

"If you come for us, we will defend ourselves. If you try to silence us, we will only speak louder. To the people listening—truly listening—remember: they fear what they cannot control. That's why they come for the music. And to MV—if you're watching—your 'unity' isn't balanced. It's obedience. And it's cracking."

The message ended. The screen faded to black. Anthem stared for a long moment. "Holy shit," he exclaimed. "He actually did it."

Indy was pacing already. "He gave them a target, Anthem. On purpose. No more shadows. No more subtlety. He's daring them to strike."

Anthem ran a hand down his face. "This puts all of us at risk."

"And that video's already gone viral," Indy added. "We're trending under about six hashtags and two different government forums."

He looked up at her. "So, what do we do now?"

She gave him a look that said *you already know the answer.*

"We prepare for battle," she said. "With sound, truth, whatever we've got left."

Anthem's eyes drifted toward the empty space where his guitar used to sit. His hand clenched slowly, as if feeling phantom strings.

"Then I need a new instrument."

Before either of them could speak again, a sharp knock rapped against the door.

Anthem and Indy exchanged a glance.

Indy stepped over and cracked it open.

A young messenger stood there, maybe eighteen, with a buzz cut and an over-sized jacket stitched with resistance patches. He looked winded, like he'd run through half the compound to get here—but his grin was bright and eager.

"Oh wonderful," the courier said, catching his breath. "You're both here."

Indy crossed her arms. "Depends on who's asking."

"Vale," the kid said, holding up a small tablet. "He's requesting your presence. Said it's urgent. Briefing room, fifteen minutes."

Anthem raised an eyebrow. "Did he say why?"

The kid shrugged. "Above my clearance. Just sent me to gather you two."

She gave a half-nod. "Alright. We're on our way."

The messenger gave a brief salute and jogged off down the hall. Anthem swung his legs out of bed, the hole in his chest not gone, but he stood up slowly and pulled on his boots, anyway.

"You good?" Indy asked, her voice softer now.

"No," he said honestly. Then he glanced at her. "But I'm moving."

She offered a faint smile. "Close enough."

They said little as Anthem dressed. There wasn't time, and besides—something had shifted. The feeling Anthem had wasn't mourning anymore. It was momentum. By the time they stepped into the corridor, the compound had changed. Conversations were hushed. Movement faster. The echoes of Vale's message were still bouncing off the walls.

When they reached the briefing room, the door was already open. The space beyond buzzed with energy—strategic maps on the walls, tech flickering, people hunched over consoles, whispering rapid-fire ideas and updates.

Vale stood at the center, arms folded, staring at a projection on the wall. The moment he saw them enter, he nodded.

"Good," he said. "You're just in time."

Anthem and Indy took a seat.

"Well?" he asked, arms spread. "How'd I look on TV? Dashing? Mysterious? Or more like someone's politically unhinged uncle?"

Indy snorted. "You definitely made someone's watchlist."

Anthem offered a smirk but stayed quiet, not understanding the levity despite the gravity of the situation.

Vale's expression dropped back into focus, the humor fading like a quickly struck chord. "All joking aside," he said, "leadership met the moment the message went out. We've had allies and skeptics crawling out of the woodwork all day. But the consensus is clear: the Sound Weaver community can't just keep reacting. We need eyes—and ears—inside MV's headquarters."

A murmur of apprehension swept through the room. Infiltrating MV's headquarters was a step beyond anything they had undertaken before.

Vale turned to Anthem and Indy specifically. "I'm assigning you two, along with a select team, this mission. You'll infiltrate MV's headquarters and plant listening devices in key locations. The most crucial of these will be in MV's personal office."

Anthem and Indy exchanged a look, their resolve hardening. Despite the danger, they understood the necessity.

"We've prepared a detailed plan," Vale said, pulling up schematics of MV's headquarters on the screen behind him. "You'll enter under the guise of contractors hired for technical maintenance. We've secured the credentials and uniforms. This cover should give you access to most of the building, including MV's office." The schematics highlighted various entry points, security checkpoints, and the layout of MV's office. "Our tech team has prepared the listening devices," Vale pointed to the small sophisticated gadgets on the table. "We can activate them remotely, and they are virtually undetectable. Planting these will give us real-time audio surveillance, crucial for anticipating and thwarting MV's plans."

Indy, ever the tactician, raised a hand. "What about security? MV's bound to have countermeasures in place."

Vale nodded, acknowledging the risk. "We've accounted for that. We will equip you with signal jammers to disrupt local alarms while you plant the devices. Additionally, we'll have a cyber team stationed nearby to intercept and delay any security alerts you trigger."

Anthem firmly spoke up. "We understand the risks, Vale. We'll get it done."

Vale surveyed Anthem, Indy, and their team with a mixture of pride and concern. "This mission requires precision and stealth. I trust you all to look out for each other. Remember, the success of this operation is crucial not just for thwarting MV but for safeguarding innocent lives."

CHAPTER XV

Anthem was eager to get the search started for a new guitar, so he was less than enthused as the bus's air brakes hissed, bringing it to a slow stop. The engine grumbled before it shuddered and turned off, leaving only the faint rustle of wind in the towering trees around them. Pre-dawn light barely pierced through the dense canopy, casting long, eerie shadows that danced across the forest floor. Anthem stepped off the bus, the cool air rushing at him like an old friend, crisp with a pine scent.

Anthem glanced around at the others brought there with him. A handful of other Sound Weavers stood nearby, some stretching, others deep in thought, mentally preparing for what was to come. Their expressions mirrored his own—focused, a mix of anticipation and nerves. This was not for the faint of heart. It would push them to their limits, testing not only their powers but their control, their endurance, and their understanding of the deeper connection between sound and the world around them.

Hidden deep within the heart of the forest lay the sacred training grounds; isolated, ancient, and teeming with life. The gnarled trunks and thick canopies of the towering trees that circled the clearing reached skyward, forming a natural cathedral of sorts.

Impressive in itself, the clearing was a large circular space carved from the forest, featuring strategically placed acoustic panels and towering sound-dampening walls around its perimeter. In the center, they set up a series of platforms and training stations, each designed to challenge different aspects of a Sound Weaver's ability. Some platforms had complex arrays of speakers and sound modulation equipment, while others had more rudimentary equipment, having only stones and water where trainees would need to manipulate the natural elements using their powers.

As Anthem continued to gain his bearings, a group of Mentors emerged from the edge of the clearing—a cadre of mysterious figures draped in cloaks that looked like someone had woven them from shadows and sprinkled them with stardust. Their eyes were barely visible under their hoods as they surveyed the trainees, each gaze carrying the wealth of a thousand lessons—and a thousand challenges.

At the front of the group stood a tall bear of a man with a scar that ran across his cheek and an expression that looked like it hadn't cracked a smile in centuries. His eyes swept over the Sound Weavers with a detached, almost amused look of someone about to set a pack of mice loose in a maze.

"Welcome to advanced training," he intoned, his voice low and deep, like thunder rolling in from a distant storm. "Before we begin... we'll start with a short warmup. A simple 10-mile jog through the forest. With your instruments."

A symphony of groans erupted. The tuba players slumped visibly, casting resentful glances at their instruments as if they'd betrayed them. The cellists shifted uncomfortably; their eyes filled with existential dread. Even Anthem had to suppress a grin as he imagined the looks they'd be getting from the deer and squirrels as they trundled through the woods, panting and lugging their instruments along. Then a realization hit Anthem. Slowly, he raised his hand.

The Mentor's gaze swept over the group before settling on Anthem. "You have a question?"

Anthem hesitated for a split second, but figured there was no point in keeping it to himself. "Yeah, uh... I don't have my guitar," he admitted, scratching the back of his head. "There was an accident."

The Mentor tilted his head slightly, eyes narrowing in thought. "No instrument?"

Anthem nodded, already feeling like he'd made a mistake in bringing it up. "That's right."

For a moment, the Mentor said nothing. Then, without warning, he turned, scanned the forest floor, and—with alarming ease—lifted a sizable rock, more of a small boulder than anything else. He carried it toward Anthem as if it were weightless, before dropping it with a resounding *thud* at his feet.

Anthem stared. "...You can't be serious."

The Mentor gave him a deadpan look. "Do I look like the joking type?"

A snicker rippled through the group, and Anthem shot them a glare before looking back at the boulder, his stomach sinking. "How am I supposed to *carry* that?"

The Mentor crossed his arms. "Figure it out. You lost your instrument, so now you train with what you have."

"What I *have* is a rock," Anthem pointed out, gesturing wildly at the boulder.

The Mentor shrugged. "Then make it sing."

More snickers. Someone muttered, *"Rest in peace, Anthem."*

Anthem sighed heavily, rolling his shoulders. With a resigned grunt, he bent down, wrapped his arms around the boulder, and immediately regretted raising his hand. He regretted everything. Every single decision that had led him to this moment.

The Mentor's face remained stone cold, unaffected by the complaints. "While you are out working on your endurance," he said. "Feel the earth beneath you. Listen to the rhythm of the forest. Every breath, every beat, every step—let it harmonize with your energy. A true Sound Weaver becomes part of the world around them. Fail to do so, and..." He shrugged, leaving the consequences ominously unsaid.

With a wave of his hand, he set them off, and the Sound Weavers took off at a reluctant jog, instrument cases clanking and jingling. Anthem, however, was in a world of his own struggle. He hoisted the boulder against his chest. His arms burned instantly, his legs protesting as he struggled to find a rhythm that didn't make him feel like he was about to face plant into the dirt.

The others had it bad—he could hear the wheezing of the tuba players, the occasional string of curses from the cellists trying not to trip over their cases—but at least they could actually *hold* their instruments properly. Anthem gritted his teeth, shifting the rock in his grip as he forced himself to do as he was instructed and connect with the surrounding forest. Leaves rustled overhead, joined by the chirping of birds and the faint babble of a distant stream. It all blended with the dull *thump* of his rock every time he lost grip and dropped it.

It was like the forest was playing along with their own panting and pounding steps, weaving them into its own music. Not that Anthem was in any shape to appreciate it—his arms were on fire, his back ached, and his pride was getting steadily crushed under the sheer absurdity of the situation.

By the time they finally staggered back into the clearing, everyone looked like they'd been dragged backward through a thorn bush. Tuba players collapsed dramatically on the ground, cellists leaned on each other for support, and one poor guy with a massive bass drum gulped down air like a fish out of water.

Anthem, drenched in sweat, barely set his boulder down before face planting beside it, arms shaking. He shot the Mentor a murderous glare. "You're a sick son of a bitch," he panted.

The Mentor smirked, entirely unaffected by the surrounding suffering.

Before Anthem could wipe the sweat from his brow, Canon appeared, his steps silent on the moss-covered ground. He approached without a sound, materializing from the shadows as though he were part of the forest carrying a shoddy acoustic guitar. The guitar was worn, faded, and clearly well-used.

He handed Anthem the old guitar, its neck slightly warped, and the strings thicker than he was used to. "Today, you play this. I suggest finding a new instrument soon."

"I'm working on it." Anthem's fingers closed around the neck of the strange guitar. It felt foreign, awkward, lacking the comfortable weight and balance he knew so well. "How am I supposed to connect with this?" he muttered, more to himself than Canon.

But Canon's ears were sharp. "A Sound Weaver's connection to their instrument is crucial, yes. But a true Sound Weaver understands that it's not the instrument alone that holds the power. It's you," he said, tapping a finger against Anthem's chest. "This attachment, this bond... it's a powerful thing. But if you can only channel your abilities through that one guitar, then your power is limited to it."

Canon gestured to the weathered instrument now in Anthem's hands. "Think of this as a challenge, a trial. Today, you'll need to reach that same place of resonance without the comfort of your own instrument. Push past the surface—the feel of the strings, the shape of the body—and connect to the music itself. And when you can do that, we'll go further, learning to channel your power with no instrument at all."

Anthem glanced at the guitar in his hands, taking a deep breath as he ran his thumb over the frayed edges and worn fretboard. It felt like learning to walk with a limp, a shadow of what he was used to. But he nodded, determination hardening his gaze.

Canon folded his arms and took a step back. "Now, play," he instructed. "Make it yours."

Anthem closed his eyes, feeling the roughness of the unfamiliar strings bite into his fingertips. It took a moment to silence his thoughts, to let go of the frustration, and to stop comparing the instrument to his own. He took a breath, deeper than usual, focusing on the forest around him, on the energy of the earth under his feet, until the guitar in his hands felt a little less foreign and a little more alive.

Slowly, he played, his notes hesitant at first, shaky and uneven, but with each strum, his confidence grew. He imagined his own guitar, the sound he could pull from it, and then... he imagined the music wasn't coming from the guitar at all, but from him.

The music softened, then deepened, flowing out and mingling with the sounds of the forest until the instrument felt almost weightless in his hands. He wasn't fully there yet—he could feel the connection flickering, thin as spider silk, but it was there.

"Great work." Canon said dispassionately. "Now, for the next part, we've assigned you a training partner." Anthem turned, already feeling a knot form in his stomach at the mention of a partner. Canon paused for a moment, as if gauging Anthem's reaction, before delivering the news. "You'll be training with Solstice."

Anthem's face immediately hardened. Of course. Of all people, it had to be *him*. The tension between them had subsided since their last encounter, but the thought of having to spend hours training with him sent a surge of irritation through his veins. He let out a sharp breath, trying to suppress his frustration, but it was clear in the way his jaw clenched and his eyes darkened.

"Great," Anthem said under his breath, unable to keep the sarcasm from slipping into his voice.

Canon, either unaware or uninterested in Anthem's displeasure, continued as if he hadn't noticed. "Solstice finished his run a while ago. You'll be working together to refine your abilities, and perhaps..." the Mentor's eyes glinted with a hint of amusement, "learn to push past whatever friction there is between you."

Anthem shot a glance toward the far end of the clearing where Solstice was already standing. His drumsticks twirled effortlessly between his fingers, fluid and methodical. Solstice was very detail-oriented and meticulous, which showed in many aspects of his life, from his appearance to the use of his powers. The complete opposite of Anthem's more instinctive, raw approach to his powers. Anthem described him to Indy as an anal-retentive checklist warrior. And now they had to work together? He balled his hands into fists at his sides.

He knew there was no getting out of this. If he refused to train with Solstice, it would be a sign of weakness. And if there was one thing Anthem refused to show Solstice, it was weakness.

"Fine," Anthem said, trying to keep his voice steady, though the edge of reluctance was still there. "Let's get this over with."

Canon gave a vacant nod and turned to leave. "Remember, this is about growth. Conflict can be a tool if you use it correctly."

Anthem rolled his eyes as the Mentor walked away, muttering to himself, "Yeah, easy for you to say."

With a sigh of resignation, he made his way toward Solstice, who had been watching him the entire time with a look of mild amusement. The space between them filled with unspoken hostility. Each step brought Anthem closer to the inevitable clash that awaited them.

As he approached, Solstice tilted his head slightly, frowning. "I see you're just as thrilled about this as I am," he said dryly.

Anthem crossed his arms, refusing to rise to the bait. "Let's just get to it."

Solstice grumbled in agreement, the sound low and mocking.

Canon chuckled softly. "I see this will be an interesting session. Follow me, both of you." Canon led them to a separate part of the clearing, where the trees seemed to part even more, creating a natural stage for their training. "Your task is simple," Canon explained calmly. "You will create a sound barrier together. It must be strong enough to withstand the external forces I will generate. This will require synchronization and harmony—two things I suspect you'll find difficult, but necessary."

As the training session began, the difference between Anthem and Solstice became painfully clear.

Anthem, fueled by raw emotion, unleashed his power through his guitar in waves of blazing energy that swelled and crashed like a storm struggling to find its course. His chords reverberated through the air—passionate, fierce, but unfocused.

Solstice, by contrast, stood poised, his drumsticks held lightly in his fingers. With measured precision, he tapped the empty air as if playing an invisible drum kit. At each movement, a flash of violet light shimmered around him, summoning a beat—sharp, deliberate, perfectly timed. rippled outward in perfect rhythm, steady and unshakable—a mechanical heartbeat thrumming with layered hues of deep amethyst and electric lilac. The purple glow twisted and flexed with each note, forming faint, ephemeral shockwaves that anchored the surrounding space, even as Anthem's chaotic energy threatened to tear it apart.

The resulting barrier was unstable, wavering between Anthem's surges and Solstice's steady flow. Anthem's surges of power pushed the barrier outward in brilliant bursts, while Solstice's steady rhythm held it back, trying to keep it under control. It was like trying to combine fire and ice.

Solstice was the first to speak, his voice as clipped as his playing. "You need to control your output," he said, not even glancing at Anthem. "You're all over the place. Focus."

Anthem felt a surge of irritation rising in his chest. *Control?* Sure, Solstice could say that. He played like a robot. "Maybe if you added some feeling to your playing, it wouldn't be so stiff," Anthem shot back, tightening his grip on his guitar. The barrier flickered again, weakening under the strain of their argument. Their voices echoed in the clearing, tension mounting as their attempts continued to falter. In the background, Canon watched with arms crossed, his face unreadable but clearly gauging their every move.

After several failed attempts and increasingly heated exchanges, Anthem finally stepped back, his frustration boiling over. "This isn't working," he said, his breath coming in short bursts. "We're too different."

Solstice, though visibly irritated, remained calm. He met Anthem's gaze with a level stare. "Differences don't have to be weaknesses," he said, surprisingly sage-like. "We just need to figure out how to make them work together."

Anthem blinked. The unexpected insight from Solstice caught him off guard, but he wasn't about to argue with it. Taking a deep breath, he let his anger subside, just enough to try again. "Fine. Let's try it your way."

With a fresh approach, they started once more. Anthem focused on reining in his wild emotions, channeling them into a more controlled and steady rhythm. Solstice, for his part, loosened up—just a little—allowing his rigid control to give way to a more fluid expression. Their music, instead of clashing, intertwined, weaving together like threads of a complex tapestry.

As they played, the barrier shimmered, growing stronger, more cohesive. The energy within it pulsed in harmony. For the first time, they were in sync. The barrier solidified, glowing in hues of gold and violet, crackling with barely contained energy. Anthem barely had time to register their shared success before Canon acted.

BOOM!

A blast of compressed sound, like a cannon of pure energy, shot from his outstretched hand, striking the barrier with devastating force. The barrier shattered instantly, exploding in a flash of light and sound, and the shockwave hurled both him and Solstice off their feet.

He flew backward, crashing through bushes and skidding across the forest floor until he finally came to a stop against the trunk of an ancient pine. A sharp pain jolted through his shoulder, but it was nothing compared to the raw anger bubbling up in his chest. Wincing, Anthem forced himself to his feet, brushing dirt from his clothes and shooting the Mentor a fiery glare.

Solstice staggered upright beside him, equally battered, his usually calm face twisted into an equally incensed expression. But before either of them could voice their outrage, Canon fixed them with an unyielding stare. "Do it again," he commanded, his tone left no room for debate.

Anthem felt his fists clench involuntarily. "Are you kidding?" he barked, his voice tight with frustration. "We finally got it to work, and you just—"

Canon raised a hand, silencing him with a single look. "You think you're here to get it right once? The world will not wait for you to find your rhythm when you're up against something that wants you dead." His gaze shifted between them, stern and unrelenting. "Building a barrier isn't the goal. Making it unbreakable—that's what you're here to learn."

Anthem exchanged a glance with Solstice, both of them still breathing hard, dirt smeared across their faces, resentment simmering beneath the surface. But he saw something different in Solstice's eyes now—a glint of determination, and maybe a flicker of respect.

"Fine," Anthem said, rubbing his shoulder and shifting his stance. "Let's go again."

This time, they didn't waste time bickering. They knew what they had to do. Anthem focused, letting his energy build up, but now he channeled it with more precision, feeling for that elusive balance between his raw intensity and the steady, grounding rhythm Solstice provided. Solstice took his cue, softening his rigid focus just enough to let Anthem's energy flow through without resistance.

The barrier formed again, a translucent wall shimmering with their combined power. But this time, it felt different. Stronger. They poured everything into it, pushing past the ache in their muscles, the sweat in their eyes, the bruises and cuts from their earlier fall. They directed every ounce of focus and strength into making the barrier as solid as steel and as immovable as the ancient trees surrounding them.

Canon watched, then raised his hand once more. Without warning, he unleashed another beam of compressed sound, sharper, faster, and even more powerful than the last.

The barrier held, but just barely. The impact reverberated through the air, straining the shield to its limits. Anthem gritted his teeth, pouring more of his energy into it, feeling Solstice's own strength bolstering his own. Together, they braced against the force. Their barrier trembled but refused to shatter. When the blast finally dissipated, the barrier stood strong. Anthem and Solstice shared an exhausted look of victory.

Canon crossed his arms, nodding approvingly. "Better."

Letting the barrier drop, both were breathing hard. Although they had just proven they could work together, the bad blood wasn't gone, but they discovered a new understanding—a recognition of each other's strengths. They didn't have to like each other, but they couldn't deny the power they'd just created together.

Before they could bask in their achievement, Canon continued. "Your next task is simple: catch a rabbit."

Anthem's eyebrows shot up. "Don't we get a break?" he wheezed.

"Absolutely. Right after you catch the little bunny," the Mentor said with a straight face. "This will again require you to work together if you want any chance of catching it."

Solstice's frown returned as he rolled his drumsticks between his fingers. "Sounds straight-forward enough," he said with a thoughtful look.

Canon didn't respond, simply walking over to a small cage and releasing a sleek, silver-furred rabbit. Before either Anthem or Solstice could react, the rabbit bolted into the forest with a burst of lightning speed, vanishing into the underbrush like a ghost.

"That rabbit is all hopped up on something to be that fast." Anthem said, looking around for someone to appreciate his joke.

Solstice pressed his lips into a tight line, cutting sharply into his cheeks as he shook his head in irritation. "Shut up." Without further warning, he lunged forward into a sprint. Anthem cursed under his breath and followed.

Solstice moved with intense focus, scanning the forest ahead, his movements synced to some internal rhythm Anthem couldn't hear. He would dart closer when he could, throwing up brief domes of energy that bent the trees and stirred the air, working to slow the rabbit's impossible speed.

Anthem tried weaving a net, strumming a construct into shape, but the rabbit zigzagged through the trees with impossible agility.

Anthem and Solstice were moving at full speed, their abilities stretched to the limit, but the rabbit always seemed just out of reach. No matter how fast Anthem moved, no matter how quickly he summoned new barriers, the rabbit always slipped through.

The surrounding forest shifted. The rustling leaves, the sharp bird cries—all slowed, thickening like syrup. Anthem shot a look at Solstice and saw the tension carved into his face, the rapid-fire drumming of his hands in the air growing more frantic and complex.

And then—

Everything stopped.

The rabbit froze mid-leap, suspended mid-leap, frozen in place like a photograph. "Did you just—"

"Yes," Solstice gritted out, his face pale with the strain. "Now hurry!"

Without hesitation, Anthem summoned the last of his energy, creating a shimmering cage of sound that shot forward and wrapped around the rabbit in a burst of light. As time resumed, the rabbit dropped to the ground, safely enclosed in the glowing prison.

They both stood there for a moment, catching their breath, the forest returning to its normal rhythm around them. Anthem turned to Solstice, still wide-eyed, adrenaline burning through his chest. "You—" He shook his head, at a rare loss for words. "You can *stop time.*" There was no disguising the awe in his voice, raw and unfiltered.

Solstice, pale and winded, simply gave a curt nod. "Yeah. Try not to make a big deal out of it."

Anthem let out a breathless laugh, running a hand through his hair. "Too late."

For the first time, genuine admiration—not grudging, not reluctant—flickered behind Anthem's eyes. As much as they clashed, there was no denying it now: Solstice wasn't just talented. He was dangerous. And brilliant.

The rabbit, now safely captured, was a victory that went beyond the task. It was a breakthrough. They had pushed past their rivalry, if only for a moment, and accomplished something neither could have done alone.

As they returned to Canon, rabbit in tow, there was an unspoken understanding between them. Their rivalry was far from over, but now it was a driving force that could push them both to new heights. And for the first time, they both acknowledged that there might be something to learn from each other after all. "Just don't let your emotions get the better of you," Solstice said.

Anthem smirked. "And maybe you should try showing yours once in a while."

With that, they went their separate ways, each with a newfound respect and new challenge in mind, to surpass the other.

CHAPTER XV

They didn't have long to bask in their victory. Canon was waiting at the edge of the woods with a clipboard and a subtle smile. "Your next exercise starts now." Before either could reply, the bus rumbled up the gravel path behind him—its windows dark, curtains pulled tightly shut from the inside. "On board. No questions," Canon said, gesturing them forward.

Anthem and Solstice exchanged a look. Then, wordlessly, climbed aboard.

Inside, the air was cool and stale. The engine hummed low, and the seats were already filled with other trainees from different squads—each looking just as puzzled. The curtains were sealed with magnetic strips, impossible to pull back. One trainee tried. The window buzzed, and a sharp static warning tone filled the cabin.

Solstice raised a brow. "Guess they really don't want us knowing where we're going."

Anthem sat back, hands on his knees. "That's comforting."

No one spoke much after that. Thirty silent minutes passed. Then, without fanfare, the bus jerked to a stop. The doors hissed open, revealing a loading dock in a dim warehouse corridor. Fluorescent lights flickered overhead. The air smelled of old oil and mildew.

Canon's voice came from a speaker at the front of the bus. "You've just been dropped somewhere in the Rustend District. You have one objective. Return to Sound Weaver Studios within eight hours without being captured. Hunters have been dispatched in and around the district. They will use any means at their disposal to find and capture you. If they capture you, you fail. If you return home, you pass. Bring back proof you defeated a hunter? Gain a special reward."

That got people excited. Murmurs snaked through the crowd. "Time starts now." Canon finished. There was no formal starting line. The loading dock doors simply opened, and they stepped off the bus and into the night.

To his left stretched the Narrows—an endless warren of alleyways and overpasses that leaned like collapsing bookshelves. The buildings here had no symmetry, no rhythm. Rusted ladders climbed nowhere. Fire escapes dangled like snapped wires. Narrow walkways above were strung with torn banners and old festival lights that hadn't lit in decades.

Old Iron Row loomed straight ahead—massive factory hulks stacked in long, dead rows like sleeping titans. Their brick faces were cracked and stained, choked by ivy and age. Empty window frames stared down like the eyes of forgotten gods. Inside, he knew it would be worse. Old conveyor belts still clung to the ceilings, machinery groaned in its death throes, and every surface was a trap—metal curled and rusted into thorns. It was a labyrinth of steel and decay. One wrong move and the place would bleed you dry.

Then there was the Belowline.

To his right, just past a collapsed maintenance shed, a staircase led underground into the subway tunnels—its rails long rusted over and half-submerged in water. A warning sign still hung over the entrance: "Transit Suspended. Unsafe Conditions. Do Not Enter."

Perfect.

A single dim light flickered near the mouth of the stairs. Anthem took a step closer and felt the breath of the tunnel wash over him—damp, cool, and old. The smell was worse down there: mold, rust, and something sour he couldn't name.

Somewhere behind him, the bus rumbled shut and pulled away, disappearing like a ghost into the thick haze. Trainees scattered fast. No groups. No calls for teamwork. Every Sound Weaver for themselves.

Anthem took the high road, literally—he climbed a narrow fire escape and dropped down onto the industrial park's crumbling rooftop. Around him, the skeletal remains of Crucible City's industrial age loomed—rusted chimneys and collapsed catwalks, half-swallowed by creeping ivy and twisted steel. In the distance, smokestacks pierced the horizon like broken fingers. Anthem squinted at the crumbling skyline.

Luckily for Anthem, he knew Crucible City like the back of his hand. He may not know where in the Rustend District he was, but he knew the district was southwest of Sound Weaver Studios. He also knew about the ivy. Most of it grew thickest on the northern faces of buildings, reaching toward the morning light. Which meant...he turned slowly, following the angle of the growth. Sound Weaver Studios was northeast.

"All right," he said to himself, taking the wooden guitar off his shoulder. "We have a heading as good as any." He dropped into a crouch and rested the instrument against his thigh, fingers hovering above the strings. His breath steadied. Then he struck a chord—low, clean, resonant. The air shimmered. Vibrations curled from the sound hole and coiled upward into a glowing, thread-thin tether. It hummed faintly as it stretched forward—a luminous filament of gold, pulsing in sync with the guitar's tone. It whipped out ahead like a lazy fishing line, tethering itself to the edge of a skeletal billboard frame a few blocks away. The line held firm for a beat, then vibrated once. Locked securely.

Anthem stood, slinging the guitar across his back. The thread remained—taut, glowing, stretching forward and slightly northeast. "Perfect," he murmured. As he moved, the thread moved with him. It snaked around obstacles, shifting slightly when he turned the wrong direction, shimmering brighter when he was aligned. When he drifted too far from its guidance, the light dulled and distorted, rippling like a mirage. It was simple, but elegant. His music had created a compass—a melody given direction.

He descended from the rooftop, climbing down a sagging fire escape that creaked like an old ship in stormwater. On the ground, he passed burned-out husks of vending kiosks and shattered storefronts. His footfalls echoed quietly through the empty alleys of the Narrows—but the thread glowed on, guiding him through.

Anthem moved with the caution of someone half expecting the city itself to wake up and eat him. He crept along a crumbling corridor between two half-collapsed buildings, his sound-thread compass glowing faintly ahead like a whisper in the dark. The Narrows groaned with age—gutters dripping from forgotten pipes, loose wires swinging like nooses from above. His steps were soft, but every scuffed boot against gravel felt too loud in a place like this.

Then—

CHIK-CHIK-CLICK.

The mechanical snap of tension releasing.

He froze.

A second later, a shrieking alarm tore through the night like a wounded animal—shrill and close. The sound ricocheted off the walls, echoing in loops of rising panic. Anthem's heart lurched. Someone triggered a trap not far away. He dove into a recessed doorway, half-shielded by a stack of caved-in shelves. His breathing slowed to a near stop. Then he heard them. Boots. Heavy. Dozens of them.

Hunters spilled into the zone like wolves drawn to the scent of blood. One hunter landed with a thud directly above Anthem. Another turned down an alley toward his position. He couldn't run. Couldn't fight. And there was no shield strong enough to take this many on without drawing every ear in the district.

So he tried something else.

He played.

Not a song. Not even a note—just a single, muted harmonic plucked gently against the base string. The tone vibrated outward like a ripple on water. Where it spread, it wove light from the sound—a thin, sheet of resonance that spiraled around his body and shimmered like desert heat. Not true invisibility—just the illusion of absence.

The construct masked outlines. Drenched his silhouette in disruption and distortion. Every detail softened into the background, like staring through warped glass. But more than that—it vibrated in a frequency designed to misdirect, pulling perception away, as if this weird blurry spot was a half-forgotten dream.

The hunter dropped from above, his eyes passing over Anthem. They both paused.

Held.

Anthem's heart pounded in his ears. He didn't blink. Didn't breathe. The hunter stepped forward. Another inch and they'd be on him. His eyes flicked away. "False alarm, nothing here." A voice crackled over the comms. "Copy. One confirmed capture. Continue sweep."

Anthem didn't relax—not yet. He stayed perfectly still as the boots retreated. Only when the last sound disappeared did he let the construct drop, its light dissolving in the night. He slumped against the icy wall, every muscle in his body still trembling.

For hours, Anthem slipped through the ruins of the Rustend District like a shadow. He stuck to the edges, followed collapsed scaffold paths, ducked beneath half-buried bus stops, and scaled crumbling walls. His compass thread stretched ever forward, winding him through the Narrows, across the jagged bones of Old Iron Row, and finally toward the concrete perimeter that marked the edge of the zone.

A few more turns, and he saw it: the breach in the city wall. Faded hazard tape flapped in the breeze, barely clinging to rusted fences. Just beyond, the flickering lights of Crucible City proper winked through the haze.

Anthem exhaled—almost smiled. He stepped forward.

"You made good time." The voice stopped him. Smooth. Familiar. A little too satisfied. A figure leaned against a crooked piece of broken signage, half-lit by the city glow. Dark jeans. Hooded jacket.

Reed.

The same guy he'd met on the basketball courts during his orientation tour. Anthem thought back to that day. He fondly remembered the way the sweat rolled off Reed's skin. But now he was an obstacle standing in front of his goal.

Anthem froze, his hand twitching near his guitar. "You're a Hunter?"

Reed shrugged, rolling his neck like he'd just finished warming up. "I prefer 'final boss,' but yeah. Been waiting here a while. Figured you'd show up."

Anthem's eyes narrowed. "Me? Why?"

Reed took a few slow steps forward, hands still in his pockets. "Call it a vibe. Plus, you're the only one who made it this far without setting off half the traps in the district. Kinda hot."

Anthem blinked. "Excuse me?"

"I said it's impressive." Reed's grin deepened.

Anthem adjusted the strap on his shoulder. "That the way home?" he asked, nodding past him.

Reed gestured with a little flourish. "Yup. All yours. Just gotta get past me."

"You're seriously going to stop me?"

Reed tilted his head, still grinning. "That's the job. But hey... if you wanted to buy me dinner first, I might consider a head start."

Anthem stepped forward, expression dry. "You flirting with me or trying to distract me?"

"Why not both?"

Anthem's lips twitched. "We don't have to do this."

"Canon and the Mentors dangled some incentives—rewards for every trainee we take down. Call it a friendly bounty hunt," Reed said with a bright smile.

He stepped in just a little closer, voice dropping with purpose. "You've got the moves, no doubt. But let's see if you hold up when it's not theory anymore. When the pressure's real. When someone's right in your face and not playing nice."

As he spoke, Reed reached to both sides of his waist. Attached to his belt, nestled against his hips, were two sleek, padded holsters. With a flick, he popped both latches and withdrew his weapons of choice.

They were the most dangerous-looking tambourines Anthem had ever seen. Each frame was a sleek matte black, crafted from carbon fiber interlaced with dark-stained hardwood. Instead of traditional jingles, they were fitted with thin, razor-edged, matte discs that shimmered faintly with layered resonances.

The casual air vanished as his eyes sharpened, and the smirk faded. "Let's see if you're ready for what's out there, Anthem..." He raised one tambourine and the air changed. The faint sound of wind disappeared. Anthem's own breath sounded muffled, like cotton was shoved in his ears.

Reed had silenced the world.

Anthem barely had time to react before Reed clashed the edge of one tambourine sharply against his palm, channeling a pulse of compressed sound. It exploded outward—not loud, but concentrated—and slammed into a pillar inches from Anthem's head, blasting off chunks like a frag grenade. Anthem darted behind cover, heart thundering in his chest.

"Come on," Reed's voice echoed from all directions—distorted, layered, playful. "Don't make me chase you, Anthem. Or do. I'll probably like the view."

Anthem didn't respond. He couldn't. Every time he shifted, Reed *heard* it. The creak of his boots. The tension of the strings on his back. Even his breathing.

The moment Anthem leaned against the pillar, another blast shattered the concrete beside him, the force rattling his teeth and sending flecks of debris into the air. Anthem gritted his teeth and pivoted, diving to another patch of cover.

But Reed was relentless.

Every sound Anthem made was met with a concussive burst that left his new hiding spot crumbling. He couldn't stay still. Anthem moved again—another step, another detonation. He rolled behind a crumbling concrete divider just as the tambourine's jingle rang again. It was then that he realized Reed was listening. Not just with ears—with everything. He was using sound as his *radar*.

He dove behind cover again, but this time he laid his guitar flat on the ground. Crouched low, he formed a simple dome—a small one—barely large enough to muffle the surrounding space. Not a shield. Not a weapon. A room.

Inside it, *he was silent.*

Think. Think. He needed to turn the tables. He couldn't hide from Reed—but he could outplay him.

Reed stopped walking. "You hiding, or just playing hard to get?" he called out.

Anthem didn't respond. He had an idea.

He dropped the silence bubble and stepped casually into the open.

"Okay," he said, voice low, almost lazy. "You win."

Reed blinked, clearly caught off guard. His stance didn't change, but his expression softened—just slightly. "You giving up already? I was expecting a little more fireworks."

Anthem shrugged, moving slowly, palms open. "Maybe I've got nothing left. Or maybe I figured if I was gonna lose, it might as well be to someone easy on the eyes."

Reed arched a brow, clearly amused. "Oh? That's your play?"

Anthem took a slow step closer, letting his guitar dangle harmlessly at his side. "Yeah, I gotta admit... you make one hell of a final boss," he said, tone teasing. "You really had me pinned down."

Reed smirked, letting some of the tension in his shoulders unwind. "What can I say? Watching you squirm a little was kind of fun."

Anthem chuckled, smooth as a solo. He closed the last bit of distance between them, slow, relaxed, his body language loose—casual.

Reed watched him, suspicious but not moving.

Anthem's hand drifted up, fingers brushing the front of Reed's hoodie. Like he was admiring the fabric.

Reed tilted his head slightly. "You always this handsy?"

Anthem smiled, eyes glinting. "Only when someone makes it interesting."

Reed smirked.

And then—without warning—Anthem struck.

In a blink, Anthem twisted his grip on the hoodie and dropped low, yanking Reed forward and using his momentum against him. A clean hop toss—Reed hit the ground hard. The wind knocked from his lungs in a stunned gasp.

Before Reed could recover, Anthem strummed a harsh chord, sending sound-formed bands whipping out from his guitar. The constructs slammed into place, crystalline restraints that pinned Reed's arms and legs down like glowing manacles fused to the pavement.

Reed coughed, blinking up at him. "Seriously?" he wheezed. "You flirt your way into a body slam?"

Anthem winked. "You started it. That was me flirting back."

Reed strained against the binds, gritting his teeth. "This is kinda kinky, but don't leave me like this, Anthem."

Anthem stepped back toward the breach in the wall, the city lights spilling across his silhouette. "Relax," he said over his shoulder. "It'll dissolve once I'm out of range."

Reed exhaled, the grin returning to his face despite the restraints. "Okay, so—hear me out...want to grab a drink sometime?"

"Tempting." Anthem said, smiling. "But I've got a full plate these days. Let's see where the next track takes us."

He paused, turned slightly, and eyed the half-moon tambourine lying just beside Reed.

"Nice gear," Anthem said casually, bending to scoop it up. He gave it a small, deliberate shake—just enough for the metallic discs to let out the faintest, defeated jingle. "I'll be sure to give this to Canon. Y'know... as proof." And with that, he vanished through the gap—leaving Reed flat on his back.

The studio's main door whooshed open, and Anthem stumbled through like he'd just crawled out of a war zone. His boots dragged, every joint aching, his lungs burning from the final sprint. The lights inside were low and clinical—too quiet for the hell he'd just crawled out of.

He staggered to a stop in the center of the lobby, chest heaving, eyes scanning.

Empty.

No fanfare. No confetti. Just silence, punctuated by the faint hum of cooling fans and status monitors.

Then a soft chime.

The wall display blinked to life.

"First trainee has returned."

For a heartbeat, Anthem just stared.

Then he threw his fists in the air with a triumphant shout. "YES!" The sound echoed off the high ceilings. "Come on!" He spun in place, laughing breathlessly. "I did it! First one back!" He punched the air again, then dropped to his knees with a wide, almost delirious grin.

His guitar slid forward into his lap, and he cradled it like a medal of honor, tapping the body in a celebratory rhythm. "That's what I'm talking about. Who's the final boss now?"

The studio's main door whooshed open again. Out stepped Solstice—torn sleeve, dirt-smeared face, and three Hunter trophies in hand. He looked like he'd been through the same fire—and maybe set a few along the way.

He saw the screen.

He saw Anthem.

Anthem threw his fists in the air again with another triumphant shout. "YES!" Again, the sound echoed as started his victory celebration over. "Oh man," he laughed, "that look on your face? That's better than any trophy."

Solstice dropped his haul onto the nearest table with a clatter. "You beat me by five minutes. Congrats. Want a cookie with that?"

Anthem sauntered up, proudly holding up a half-moon tambourine. "Don't need a cookie. Got a souvenir."

Solstice eyed the instrument, unimpressed. "Charming," Solstice said. "I fought three of them and had time to stop for snacks."

Anthem shrugged. "Sounds like a personal problem."

"Oh please," Solstice said, crossing his arms. "You got lucky."

"I got smart," Anthem corrected. "And I got here first."

"Barely. And I brought proof times three."

"Still only counts as one."

"You want to compare bruises next?"

"Only if I get to sign yours."

Their bickering echoed through the studio, their voices escalating in volume and intensity. Until—"Ahem."

Both froze.

Canon stood in the entrance, arms behind his back and a raised eyebrow that could cut glass. "Glad to see you two made it back in one piece."

Anthem and Solstice turned slowly, still catching their breath.

Canon walked into the room, eyes scanning the two of them with a mix of disappointment and amusement. "You're loud enough to wake the dead. That was *not* part of the stealth challenge."

Solstice blinked. "Wasn't stealth optional?"

Canon didn't answer—just let the silence stretch, eyes narrowing slightly. From behind his back, he produced two identical boxes embellished with gold and blue swirls. He gave the first one to Solstice.

Inside lay a pair of handcrafted drumsticks—polished ebony, inlaid with faint threads of silver that shimmered like frozen lightning. Each tip was capped with a subtle metallic ring. "A gift," Canon said, "commissioned from our highest-tier craftsman. For skill, control, and precision under pressure."

Solstice let out a low whistle, clearly impressed. "Beautiful." He stepped forward and took the sticks with reverence, testing their weight in his hands. "Balanced," he muttered. "They'll see use."

Canon turned next to Anthem.

"And you," he said, tone shifting—warmer, but still carrying the edge of discipline. He handed Anthem the second box. Inside was a beautiful guitar strap. It was a sleek blend of matte black and deep blue leather, cross-stitched with fine silver thread in a pattern that resembled overlapping sound waves. Along the length ran raised embroidery resembling a constellation chart—subtle, but detailed. The buckle was a smooth, polished piece of black stone, slightly cool to the touch, set in brushed steel. He stared at it for a long beat.

"For when you find a new guitar. This was made by one of our in-house master luthiers—someone who understands both the music and the mechanics. The stitching isn't just decorative. Each pattern was tuned to match resonant frequencies."

Anthem's fingers brushed over the embroidery. For a second, he forgot the ache in his legs, the dried blood on his elbow, the adrenaline that still hadn't fully left his system. The strap wasn't just a reward. It was recognition. It was permission to keep going. But it was also bittersweet as it reminded him of his loss. What good is a guitar strap with no guitar?

He glanced up at Canon. "Thank you."

Canon nodded once. "Earn my respect again tomorrow."

Solstice eyed the strap with the faintest smirk. "Looks fancy. Hope it chafes."

Anthem shot him a crooked grin. "Yeah? Keep talking. I know a place where you can put those new drumsticks."

Solstice twirled one drumstick between his fingers. "Yeah! I just beat three hunters, but I'll still beat your ass right now."

Canon exhaled, already walking away. "Get some rest, both of you. Training resumes at dawn."

CHAPTER XVI

With training over for the next few days, Anthem finally had the time to search for a new guitar and Indy knew of just the place for Anthem to look. The streets were still slick with the remnants of last night's rain, the neon glow of nearby signs reflecting in the puddles as Anthem and Indy made their way down the sidewalk. Anthem kept his hands in his pockets, shoulders hunched against the cold.

"Melody's Music Repair Shop," she read aloud as they stopped in front of a weathered storefront. The sign above the door was faded but charming, the script curling like an old jazz record sleeve. "This is the place."

Anthem exhaled slowly. He wasn't sure if he was ready, but standing still wouldn't bring his guitar back. He followed Indy inside.

A soft chime rang out as they stepped through the door, and immediately, Anthem was hit with the scent of old wood, lacquer, and warm coffee. The walls were lined with instruments in various states of repair; the shelves cluttered with well-loved guitars, amps, and vintage radios. It felt less like a store and more like stepping into a musician's personal sanctuary.

Behind the counter stood a stocky man with a grizzled beard and thick-rimmed glasses, wiping his hands on a stained shop rag. He looked up as they entered, his eyes crinkling with recognition at Indy.

"Indira Jenkins, as I live and breathe," the man greeted, his voice rough but warm. "Been a while."

Indy grinned. "Hey, Gus. Figured you were the best person to talk to." She nodded toward Anthem. "My guy here needs a new guitar."

Gus gave Anthem a once-over, eyes lingering on the way he carried himself—like he was missing something vital. He grunted. "That so?"

Anthem nodded. "Yeah. Lost my old one." The words felt strange in his mouth, like talking behind someone's back.

Gus nodded in understanding. "That's always rough." He tossed the rag over his shoulder and motioned for them to follow. "Got some beauties in today. C'mon, take a look."

As they moved deeper into the shop, Anthem ran his fingers along the rows of guitars, each one whispering its own story. Some were pristine, their finishes gleaming under the warm light. Others bore the marks of time—scratches, dents, evidence of songs played too hard, too often.

Anthem tested a few, strumming absently, listening. He wasn't just looking for a guitar—he was searching for something that felt *right*.

The bell above the door jingled again. Anthem barely noticed, but caught Indy's change in demeanor. He glanced up, surprised to see Buddy and Tatum walk in—two people he hadn't expected to see ever again, let alone in his corner of the world.

Buddy was the first through the door, his wild curls tamed under a beanie that barely contained the mass. He pushed up his long sleeves, showing off the tattoos that snaked up his arms. His bright smile lit up the room as he spotted Anthem. Right behind him was Tatum, as tranquil as ever. An oversized sweater enveloped her, and her silver-blonde hair cascaded in soft waves beneath a wide-brimmed hat.

"Buddy? Tatum?" Anthem blinked at their sudden presence in the shop. It felt like seeing ghosts from another life.

"Hey, man!" Buddy called out; his voice filled the room with its usual infectious enthusiasm. "Didn't expect to find you here! Just out for a stroll with Tatum and thought we'd check out some music shops."

Tatum smiled warmly and stepped forward with her usual elegance and grace. "Hi, Anthem," she said. Her pale blue eyes scanned the shop before settling back on him. "It's been a while."

Anthem set his guitar down. A wave of awkwardness washed over him. The sight of them stirred good memories, mostly, but he hadn't forgotten the memories of recent days, either. "Yeah... it's been a minute."

Buddy chuckled, rubbing the back of his neck. "Look, man, I know things got... messy before. We just wanted to say—no hard feelings, yeah?"

Anthem glanced at Indy, who raised an eyebrow as if to say *your call*. He let out a slow breath, then gave a small nod. "Yeah. No hard feelings."

Indy nodded, her arms still crossed, but the edge in her stance softened. "It was what it was."

Tatum let out a breath, like she'd been waiting for a different answer. "Good," she said, a smirk tugging at her lips. "Because we actually have something to tell you."

Buddy slid an arm around her shoulders, a rare warmth in his usually sharp expression. "We're dating."

There was a beat of silence before Indy snorted. "Oh, finally."

Anthem blinked before laughing. "Yeah, no kidding. Took you long enough."

Tatum rolled her eyes, but grinned. "Okay, *rude.*"

Buddy smirked. "Hey, we had a reputation to maintain."

Indy smirked right back. "Yeah, yeah. Congrats, you two."

Anthem nodded. "Seriously. Hope it works out."

"Thanks," Buddy said, and for the first time, there was no trace of his usual bravado. Just sincerity.

Tatum bumped Anthem's shoulder lightly as they turned to leave. "Don't be a stranger."

Anthem huffed a small laugh. "You either."

With that, Buddy and Tatum headed out, the bell above the door jingling behind them.

Indy let out a low whistle. "Well, that was... unexpected."

Anthem shook his head with a smirk. "In more ways than one."

Indy snorted. "Yeah, one way being a 'will they kill each other or thrive' kind of way."

Anthem chuckled before turning his attention back to the guitars. The exchange with Buddy and Tatum had shaken off some of the unease lingering in his chest, and now he could focus.

He moved through the rows again.

And then he saw it.

Tucked into the farthest corner of the shop, nearly hidden behind a larger cello, was a guitar case he hadn't noticed before. The case was angled just so—half-shadowed, dusty around the edges like it hadn't been moved in a while.

He kneeled in front of it, fingertips brushing across the top. He leaned in and, with a slow swipe of his sleeve, wiped the case clean. The guitar case beneath the dust was striking. Midnight blue with a subtle iridescent finish that shimmered in waves of silver and deep violet, depending on the angle. The handle was made of soft, matte-black leather, stitched in a tight cross weave with silver thread.

Anthem ran his hand along the top edge. No scuffs. No wear. It felt like it had been waiting for someone to wipe away the years and notice it. He pressed the latches. Smooth. Silent.

The guitar inside was stunning. Its surface was sleek and polished. Faint, swirling designs etched into the dark wood, subtle but intricate, like the fingerprints of fate. Anthem's awestruck face was reflected in the chrome frets; while the pearlescent pick guard shimmered like stardust against the black color. The only markings on its otherwise flawless surface were the initials "CVD" elegantly engraved into the back of the body.

Anthem ran his thumb along the neck, and for a split second, he could've sworn it purred in response, like the guitar had longed for his touch. Anthem's breath hitched as he gingerly lifted it out of the box. His fingers trembled slightly as they wrapped around the neck. The moment his skin made contact; a jolt shot through him. Not like a static shock, but a deep, resonant shudder that echoed through the deepest regions of his mind. The swirling designs etched into the body ignited under his touch with a faint glow.

To his surprise, the glow enveloped his hands. Soft threads of light snaked around his fingers, weaving their way through the strings, and as he adjusted his grip, the light latched onto the power within Anthem. His hands glowed brighter as the threads lost its form, melding back into the guitar. It repeated this pattern, blending its power with Anthem's.

Gus's voice snapped him out of his focus. "Find somethin' back there?"

Startled, Anthem whipped his head around to face Gus. He blinked, still holding the guitar, as if it might disappear if he loosened his grip. "Yeah... this. It's incredible." Looking back at it again, he saw the glow had vanished.

Gus lumbered over, wiping his hands on a rag, his eyes narrowed as he took in the instrument. He let out a low whistle. "Well, I'll be damned. That's a beaut'. Must've slipped through the cracks at the auction. Looks almost brand new."

Anthem barely heard him. The guitar's presence consumed him. It felt like more than an instrument. He didn't care how it had ended up here. All that mattered was that it was here now, and it was his. Anthem nodded, his gaze never leaving the guitar. "How much do you want for it?"

Gus scratched his chin, eyeing the guitar thoughtfully. "Tell you what, kid, I'll let it go for a hundred notes. Could charge more, but I got a feelin' this needs to be with you."

Anthem blinked, hardly believing his ears. A hundred notes for this? It was a steal. But more importantly, he felt deep in his bones that he was meant to have this guitar. He didn't hesitate. "Deal," he said, his enthusiasm surprised even him.

Gus grinned, clapping him on the back. "Good choice, kid. Tune it up and see what it can do."

Anthem carried the guitar to the workbench, his heart pounding with a strange mixture of excitement and nervous energy. When he was ready, he plugged it into an old amp and slung the strap over his shoulder. It felt impossibly light, yet solid. As he tuned it, the connection he'd felt earlier grew stronger. Each string he plucked sent a ripple of power through him, as if the guitar's vibrations were syncing with his very soul.

He strummed a chord. The sound that erupted from the amp was unlike anything he had ever heard. The notes were rich, full, and clear, vibrating with a depth that gave him goosebumps. Anthem's fingers moved instinctively, playing a melody that came from somewhere deep within his subconscious. Every note, every chord felt like a revelation, like the guitar had unlocked something inside him that had been waiting to be unleashed. It was magic.

As the last chord rang out and faded into the quiet of the shop, Anthem stood there, breathless. The guitar vibrating in his hands. He knew, without a shadow of a doubt, that this guitar had been waiting for him—waiting for someone who could hear its voice. Whatever that voice was trying to say, Anthem was ready to listen.

Gus let out a low whistle. "Well, I'll be damned," he said in awe. "Kid, I've seen a lot of guitars come through this shop, but I ain't ever seen one *respond* to someone like that."

Anthem ran his fingers over the strings again, letting them hum faintly. "I don't even know where that melody came from," he admitted. "It was just... there."

"That's how you know it's the real deal," Gus said. "It *pulls* the music out of you. And judging by the way it's singing for you, I'd say you've got something big locked up in there, just waiting to come out." Gus stepped back, crossing his arms again, his expression turning serious. "But listen, kid, a guitar like that? It's a partner. Treat it right, and it'll take you places you can't even imagine. But if you're not ready—if you're not *sure*—it'll chew you up and spit you out."

Anthem looked down at the guitar in his hands and tightened his grip on the neck. "I'm ready."

CHAPTER XVII

Anthem's steps echoed as he made his way down the long halls of Sound Weaver Studios toward the training zone, his pulse quickening with every stride. He'd done little else but thinking about the guitar since finding it. And now he finally could really put it through its paces.

The guitar was slung across his back, every inch of it perfect. Mysterious. Heavy with more than craftsmanship. He stepped into the training zone and stopped short. Solstice was already there, sleeves rolled, sweat along his forehead, working through a drill with his drumsticks.

A muted thud followed each strike. Cymbals floated around him, lifted by small purple bubbles. Solstice controlled them, sending them rising, twisting, and slamming into dummies that lit up on contact. The room smelled like sweat, ozone, and heated rubber.

Anthem kept walking, slower now. The guitar case bumped lightly against his back.

Solstice didn't turn around. "You lost, Fox? I don't do live auditions."

Anthem smirked, slinging the guitar case down near the opposite wall, and popped the latches. "Cute. But nah—I was planning on tuning this bad boy somewhere it won't level a wall." He pulled the guitar free and slung it into place. It shimmered beneath the lights—pearlescent pick guard catching the glow.

Solstice finally glanced over, eyebrows raising. "New toy?"

"New partner," Anthem corrected. He moved to an open section just beside Solstice and began adjusting the amp settings. The guitar let out a low, eager hum as he strummed a few quick chords. The sound that emerged wasn't just clean—it was rich, dimensional. Like a melody folded inside a melody.

He glanced sideways. "You mind if I train here?"

Solstice paused mid-strike, rolling his shoulders. "I don't care where you play. Just don't get in my way and don't expect me to clap when you're done."

Anthem grinned. "Wouldn't dream of it." The tension settled between them like dust in spotlight haze. Then, with one foot on the amp and a gleam in his eye, Anthem struck the opening chord to one of his favorite songs, "Dead Chords & Broken Crowns."[1]

The room lit up.

Anthem barely felt the pick in his hand. The moment the first chord rang out, something shifted—not in the air, but *in him*. The sound wasn't just loud. It was layered. Intentional. Like it had been waiting for years to come out of hiding.

His resonance had always felt like reaching into a void—pulling power from somewhere else and trying to shape it with sheer will. The result was always raw, chaotic, *loud*. It worked, but it never felt completely natural.

This was different.

The guitar didn't just channel his energy—it *met it*. Matched it. Merged with it.

---

1. Track 12 – Muse - Stockholm Syndrome

Each string vibrated like a nerve in his own body. Every chord was a muscle flex. Every shift in tone followed the rhythm of his breath without him having to think. He wasn't pulling something out of the void anymore—he was *filling* it. With himself. With all of him.

A jagged construct bloomed from the floor near his feet—a spiraling structure of sound and light that twisted upward like a helix. But instead of the raw, half-formed constructs he used to force into being, this one *flowed.* The angles were sharper, more refined. Balanced. The glow wasn't static anymore—it pulsed in sync with his heartbeat, deep gold layered with thin threads of shimmering blue.

Anthem leaned into the next chord, fingers moving faster. His constructs responded instantly—faster than before. They didn't resist him. They *anticipated* him.

Is this what it was supposed to feel like?

Before, his powers had always felt like an argument—between his intent and the noise inside him. But now? It was a conversation. A duet. He could feel the guitar pulling pieces of his potential into the open, weaving his essence into every sound he made.

No wonder it waited for the right hands.

He twisted into a rising solo, letting his instincts take over. The notes cut sharply across the air, crystal constructs flaring in time, trailing resonance ripples that bled across the floor like ink in water. The studio's sensors flickered and dimmed—unable to process the frequency density he was putting out.

Anthem didn't care.

He was playing for *himself.*

In the corner of his eye, he caught Solstice's routine slow—just slightly. The man was pretending not to be watching, but he'd definitely noticed.

Anthem didn't say a word. He didn't have to. The guitar said it for him.

He hit the final note of the sequence and let it ring. The construct dissolved mid-air in a soft burst of glittering sound, like glass breaking into rain.

Snap.

A pair of drumsticks cracked together in deliberate challenge.

Solstice stepped forward.

No words. No smirk.

He slid into his rig. Around him, thin pulses of violet light blinked into existence, tiny distortions in the air like heat waves caught in strobe light. With a roll of his wrists, Solstice struck the first beat—and time fractured.

A ripple of slowed space bloomed outward, folding the world around him into molasses. The sticks moved in slow arcs, suspended midair—then snapped back into double time with his internal rhythm. It was disorienting to watch, like multiple tempos playing at once. Anthem blinked twice just to keep up.

The air around Solstice bent and flexed with his will. Bubbles of warped time took shape like translucent foam—thin membranes that shimmered and pulsed with each beat. They weren't constructs like Anthem's. They were *stolen seconds,* held in place like glass, ready to reflect or collapse at a moment's notice.

He spun and struck the kick drum pedal. A disc of paused time hovered at his feet, then launched outward, cutting across the floor like a skipping stone. As it passed one of Anthem's lingering golden threads of resonance, the thread froze mid-vibration—*suspended in place* like a note stuck between moments.

Anthem's brow furrowed. "Oh, that's how we're playing it?"

He stepped forward and hit a rising scale. His constructs bloomed again—spirals of sharp, refracted crystal that expanded through the distortion. One slammed into a time bubble, halting instantly as if it hit an invisible wall, its energy trapped mid-crack. Another construct bypassed the dome completely, arcing around it.

Solstice grunted. "You're getting better."

"Wasn't trying to impress you," Anthem shot back. "But if the riff fits."

Solstice struck again—a low rhythmic burst—and a new set of time bubbles spun into the air like orbiting moons. Inside each, bits of debris from the earlier clash rotated in place, caught in slow motion. Then he collapsed all three at once.

BOOM.

Time snapped back violently. The shockwave staggered Anthem, the *temporal recoil* hitting like a reverse echo. But he didn't fall. Instead, he stepped forward into the reverb and played through it. His constructs adjusted mid-air—counter-pulsing with measured dissonance, syncing with the chaotic time waves.

Now *both* of them were building—Anthem from sound and soul, Solstice from rhythm and frozen time. They clashed in rhythm. No fists. Just music and force. Time domes collided with crystalline crescendos. Chords shattered stillness. Tempo against tempo.

The room became a vortex of dueling music—resonance swirling like storm clouds, rhythmic pulses flaring like lightning. Anthem's golden constructs shimmered, fractal and alive, crashing into Solstice's domes of suspended time like ocean waves hitting glass. Each strike triggered a new counterpoint, an extra layer of intensity.

But then—It changed.

Anthem's next chord wasn't an attack—it was *curious*. A rising fifth held just long enough to stretch into something that sounded almost like an invitation.

Solstice answered. A crisp snare hit. Tight. Clean. Then a double-tap of toms with no distortion, no temporal flare. Just *music*.

Anthem raised an eyebrow, lips twitching into something dangerously close to a grin.

He played again. Not a challenge this time—just a groove. Something bluesy at the edges, heavy with undertone. The style of arpeggio that made the air settle differently in your lungs.

Solstice rolled his sticks in his hands, stepped into the beat, and dropped into a pocket so deep it made the walls feel closer.

Crystalline constructs hovered midair but didn't advance. They pulsed gently in time with Solstice's rhythm, rotating softly as if swaying. Anthem shifted his weight, loosened his stance. His fingers moved with instinct now—half jazz, half muscle memory. No power surges, no blasts of energy—just chord after chord, layer after layer, his guitar humming like it was born for this.

Solstice adjusted too. He tapped a cymbal with the edge of his stick, adding shimmer. Then a fill. Then a groove. His foot kept the bass pedal steady as he leaned into the beat, syncing up with Anthem's melody.

The air in the training room softened. The aggression faded.

Time bubbles still drifted in the air, but now they moved slow and steady, orbiting like calm moons around the jam. Anthem's constructs refracted light in slow pulses, almost like stained-glass lanterns dancing to the groove.

A bridge. A swell. A shared glance.[2]

Anthem shifted keys—Solstice followed without missing a beat.

No more rivalry.

Just rhythm.

And suddenly, they weren't training anymore. They weren't fighting. They were *playing.*

Improvised melodies poured out of Anthem like a faucet finally unclogged. Solstice added counter-rhythms that punched clean through, tightening every measure like thread on a spool. The contrast between them—the raw emotion in Anthem's leads and the clinical precision in Solstice's grooves—*worked.*

It shouldn't have.

But it did.

And it sounded *good.*

For several minutes, they forgot why they were even in the room.

By the time the song naturally found its resolution, both men stood in a loose circle of silence—sweat on their brows, breath heavy, and something unspoken hanging in the air.

---

2. Track 13 – Them Crooked Vultures – Elephants

Anthem looked over, still holding his guitar. "So…"

Solstice grabbed a towel off the amp. "That didn't suck."

Anthem grinned. "Yeah. It really didn't."

Anthem slung the guitar behind his back, wiping sweat from his brow with the edge of his shirt. He glanced over at Solstice, who was toweling off his hands and adjusting his wrist wraps.

"Hey," Anthem said, voice low but sincere. "That thing you did earlier—locking my construct in midair? That was sharp. You've got killer control."

Solstice paused, eyebrows lifting slightly—not smug, not surprised. Just… noting it.

"You're not bad yourself," he said after a beat. "Especially now. You've gotten better. Way better."

Anthem raised a brow, letting the guitar slide forward into his hands again. "Yeah?"

Solstice nodded. "Your rhythm used to stumble every time you pushed your power too hard. Now it's like your sound and your strikes are… *synced*. Like it's all finally coming from the same place."

Anthem looked down at the guitar, fingers brushing across the strings. The polished wood gleamed faintly under the training lights, and even idle, it seemed to hum like a living thing.

"I think it's this," Anthem said. "Found it earlier today. Or maybe it found me."

Solstice gave a half-smile. "You naming it?"

Anthem chuckled. "Not yet. Doesn't feel right. Not until I really understand what it can do."

Solstice stepped closer, nodding toward the body of the guitar. "You mind if I take a look?"

Anthem hesitated for just a second—then handed it over.

"Sure," he said. "Just don't try to run off with it."

Solstice chuckled, carefully taking the guitar in his hands. "No promises."

He turned it over, inspecting the craftsmanship. His eyes narrowed slightly at the etching, the initials on the back, and the shimmer of resonance woven into the strap like constellations. "This isn't normal gear," he said. "You can *feel* it."

"Yeah," Anthem said. "First time I held it, it felt like it knew me. Like it'd been waiting."

Solstice handed it back with a quiet nod. "Whatever it is—it suits you. Keep playing like that, and you might actually be dangerous."

Anthem gave a dry grin as he slung the guitar back over his shoulder. "Dangerous, huh? Coming from you, I'll take that as a compliment."

Solstice smirked and turned back to his rig. "Don't let it go to your head, rockstar."

Solstice took one final glance at the guitar before turning back toward his gear. But something made him pause. His eyes flicked back to the instrument—the engraved initials catching a glint of overhead light.

"CVD," he murmured, more to himself than Anthem.

Anthem looked over, slinging the guitar back across his chest. "Yeah. That's the only mark on it."

Solstice tilted his head, brow furrowing. "You know what it stands for?"

Anthem shook his head. "Not a clue. Could be the original owner. Or maybe the luthier. Gus didn't know, and honestly... I didn't care."

Solstice stepped closer again, eyes narrowing slightly as he studied the initials, like a code he hadn't cracked yet. "CVD," he repeated slowly. Then something in his expression shifted. His lips parted—not quite in surprise, but in recognition.

He didn't say anything at first.

Instead, he looked at Anthem, his usual stoicism replaced by something more focused.

"Come with me."

Anthem raised a brow. "What? Why?"

"Just... bring the guitar," Solstice said, already heading toward the training room exit. "I have a hunch."

Anthem watched him for a beat, then followed with a shrug. "If this ends with you selling me out to the CEA, I'm haunting your ass."

"No one would notice," Solstice shot back over his shoulder, smirking as they stepped out into the wide, softly lit corridor that ran through the heart of Sound Weaver Studios.

Their footsteps echoed faintly as they moved—Anthem's with the subtle jingle of his gear, Solstice's fast and certain.

"Where are we going?" Anthem asked.

Solstice didn't slow down. "The archives."

Anthem blinked. "We have *archives?*"

"You think this place runs on vibes and vinyl?" Solstice said, glancing back. "Whole wings of history are buried down here—original scores, resonance journals, recordings no one's touched in decades. A few of the old guard used to keep tabs on all the artifacts with unusual resonance signatures."

Anthem's grip on the guitar tightened slightly. Solstice saw it and nodded. "Yeah. That guitar? If I'm right—someone would've documented it." At the end of the corridor, they found a heavy, ornate door, slightly ajar. Anthem pushed the door open and stepped into a vast, circular library with shelves stretching up to a domed ceiling painted with swirling sound waves and musical symbols. Ladders on rails allowed access to the highest shelves, while on the ground rows upon rows of shelves filled with hundreds of thousands of books dominated the center of the space. Dotted among them also sat reading tables with warm antique lamps that begged for quiet study.

The air had the familiar scent of most libraries—aged paper and leather-bound books. There were scrolls and strange, ancient instruments tucked away on shelves, remnants of an era when Sound Weavers first learned to channel their abilities. It was a treasure trove of knowledge, a sanctuary of music and magic combined.

Anthem stood in place for a moment, overwhelmed by the sheer scale of it all. The weight of history pressed in from every direction. His gaze swept across shelves filled with tomes so old their spines were splitting, maps inked with resonance lines, tuning diagrams etched onto vellum, even stringless instruments that hummed faintly when he passed too close.

"Okay," Anthem said to himself, slinging the guitar across his back. "This is officially cooler than I expected."

Solstice was already moving with purpose, scanning the end caps for something specific. He disappeared between two aisles marked with golden sigils, muttering quietly as his fingers danced over spines and scroll containers.

Left to his own devices, Anthem drifted toward the center of the chamber. As he continued forward, something near the far side of the chamber caught his eye. At the edge of a low dais, surrounded by a velvet rope and standing almost eight feet tall, was a towering totem carved from petrified wood. It was intricately detailed—scored with spirals and angular runes, music bars and waveforms. Around its surface were humanoid figures in dramatic poses, each frozen in mid-performance—singing, conducting, playing.

But the most striking thing about the totem was the way it *radiated.*

Anthem didn't hear a sound, but he *felt* it. Like the surrounding air was charged with static—or vibrating just beyond his range of hearing.

"Anthem."

Solstice's voice rang out from the opposite aisle, snapping him out of the moment. Anthem blinked and turned, casting one last glance at the totem before striding over to join him. Solstice stood beside a table cluttered with scrolls and a massive open tome. Behind him loomed the totem once more—he had unknowingly circled back around to it from the opposite side.

Anthem raised an eyebrow. "So? What'd you find?"

Solstice didn't look up. Instead, he turned the page carefully, revealing an illustrated spread. At the center: a stylized depiction of a deity holding a guitar-shaped instrument inscribed with unfamiliar markings. Swirls of power rose from the strings like spectral dragons.

Anthem's breath caught.

Solstice pointed at the ancient text written beside it. "This section is about the myth of the *Conduits.* Gods or Demi-gods—depends on the version—who were believed to first discover the Core Harmonic in the earliest days."

He tapped the initials. "CVD. *Crowne Vox Dropkain.* This thing wasn't just made by a master luthier. It's a relic."

Anthem stared at the page, mind racing. "So what, this guitar was made by some mythical Sound Weaver god?"

"Or for them," Solstice said, eyes still on the text. "Maybe even *from* them. Some believe the Conduits bled their essence into these instruments—so that when the world needed them again... they'd answer."

Anthem's hand unconsciously found the neck of the guitar strapped to his back.

It felt warmer than usual.

Solstice finally looked up at him, brow furrowed. "If that's what you're carrying—then it didn't just find you by chance. It chose you."

Anthem didn't speak.

The guitar purred softly, like it agreed.

"So, who was this Crowne Vox Dropkain, then?" Anthem asked, eyeing the book.

Solstice kept reading. "Dropkain wasn't just the God of Rock. He was the *Patron of Resistance. The Shatterer of Silence.* He didn't write music to please the divine—he wrote it to challenge them. His solos were defiance. His rhythm was rebellion."

"But there's more. The old texts say Dropkain didn't just fight the outer world—he helped people fight the wars inside themselves."

He pointed to the next panel, a stark and surreal image: Dropkain seated cross-legged in a cavern of mirrors, each one showing a distorted reflection of a different person—young, old, weeping, screaming, laughing. In his lap, his guitar rested silently. The caption beneath read:

*"He who knows every version of himself
cannot be broken by another."*

"Identity," Solstice murmured. "That was one of his domains, too. Not just resistance against the world—but resistance against losing yourself. His music didn't just confront the system. It confronted *you.* Asked: who are you when no one else is listening?"

Anthem's throat tightened.

He traced the next etching—a burning bridge in the shape of a fretboard. Figures walked across it barefoot, their shadows sloughing off as they passed.

"Transformation," Solstice said. "Dropkain believed that music wasn't just sound. It was *alchemy.* If you played it raw enough, real enough, it could strip away who you were and remake you into who you were meant to be."

Anthem stared at the scene—so visceral, so mythic it almost vibrated with truth. Another quote was scrawled near the edge in rougher handwriting, a different writer—maybe a priest, maybe just a fan:

"He taught us to tear off the masks they made us wear. To play until the lies cracked open and bled light."

He turned the page. More artwork sprawled across it—Dropkain mid-performance atop a crumbling spire, his guitar erupting with jagged light as an army of faceless oppressors recoiled in its wake. Beneath him, mortals clutched their hearts and screamed in catharsis.

"He forged a set of instruments," Solstice said, "not just as tools—but as trials. Gateways. They were meant to find those worthy of unlocking the deeper tones of the Core Harmonic. Only the ones whose sound was pure—unfiltered, undiluted—could awaken them."

Anthem's hand drifted to his guitar, fingers brushing the strings. "So this thing… it's not just powerful."

Solstice finally looked up, eyes narrowed, but not unkindly. "It's a piece of a god. And it chose you."

Anthem swallowed.

"One last thing," Solstice said, voice lower now. He gestured to a faded quote etched into the margin beside Dropkain's likeness. The text, read:

"I will not rule you. I will not teach you.
I will only play until the walls fall down.
Follow me if you dare."

Anthem stared at the line. It didn't feel like history. It felt like a challenge.

CHAPTER XVIII

Under the cover of early morning darkness, Anthem and Indy approached the sleek, modern building that housed MV's record label headquarters. Anthem and Indy wore business casual clothes and wigs. Impressively realistic beards completed their disguises. Their ID badges, expertly forged, listed them as contracted IT technicians. It swung lightly from their necks as they walked confidently through the revolving doors.

The reception area was empty, save for a single security guard who glanced up from his desk, a hint of suspicion in his eyes. Anthem stepped forward, his expression loose and casual. "Morning! Scheduled maintenance on the server systems," he said, handing over the forged work order.

The guard scanned the paperwork, brow furrowing for a moment too long. "Server maintenance?"

Anthem offered a sheepish grin. "Yeah. You know how it is—panic mode upstairs."

The guard let out a short, unimpressed grunt, then passed the work order back. "System has been a little slow. Fine. Remember, full sign-in and sign-out."

Indy scratched her fake beard and gave a sharp nod. "Will do." They scribbled fake names into the logbook, clipped on their visitor badges, and headed for the elevators. As they pressed the call button, Anthem felt his nerves ease—until footsteps echoed behind them.

A man in a sharp business suit—mid-40s, badge clipped to his belt—strode up and fell into line beside them with a polite nod.

The elevator dinged open.

All three of them stepped inside.

The doors slid shut with a faint *hiss*—and now they were trapped together.

The man hit the button for the executive floor. Anthem and Indy exchanged the briefest glance. *Same floor. Perfect.*

For a few long seconds, silence ruled.

Then the man turned, giving them an appraising look. "New contractors?"

Anthem forced an easy smile. "Yeah, maintenance. Servers upstairs."

The man chuckled dryly, adjusting the tablet under his arm. "Hope you're ready. Half the network's fried after yesterday's outage."

Indy barked a short laugh, pitching her voice low. "Wouldn't be a proper job without a little pressure."

The man smirked, satisfied.

The elevator dinged again, and Anthem thought he might actually start sweating through his shirt.

Finally—blessedly—the doors slid open.

They stepped out, heartbeats hammering, and headed down the quiet corridor.

Reaching the executive floor, they found it ominously quiet. Anthem used a small electronic device to disable the lock on MV's office door, and they slipped inside. The office was a stark reflection of MV himself, sleek, orderly, and imposing, with large windows that offered a view of the city sprawl.

Indy quickly began scanning for the best spots to plant the bugs while Anthem kept watch. Indy placed one bug under the conference table, another inside a decorative plant, and tucked the final, most crucial device into the underside of MV's desk; all the while, she carefully avoided the room's security cameras, which they temporarily disabled with a localized video loop.

With the bugs in place, Indy turned her attention to MV's computer. It was a risky move—accessing it was not part of the original plan—but the potential to gather immediate, actionable intelligence was too tempting to pass up.

"Cover me," she whispered to Anthem, who nodded and stood by the door, listening for any signs of movement outside.

Indy plugged in a USB drive. Her fingers flew over the keyboard, her eyes scanning the screen as lines of code and data flickered before her as she bypassed the computer's security systems. Within moments, she accessed MV's files. "Who sets their password as 123456789?" Indy remarked, shaking her head. Across the room, Anthem stood as bead a sweat dripped from his forehead, his gaze alternating between the door and Indy, every muscle in his body coiled with anticipation.

"Anything useful?" Anthem whispered, barely audible.

Indy didn't respond immediately, her concentration fully absorbed in navigating the maze of MV's digital files. Suddenly, something caught her eye—an email marked with a high-priority flag. She clicked on it, revealing an invitation and a guest-list for an exclusive party MV was hosting that weekend.

A mischievous smile formed on Indy's face as an idea solidified in her mind. "Interesting," she muttered under her breath.

"What is it?" Anthem leaned in; the change in her demeanor piqued his curiosity.

Indy quickly highlighted the email and added Anthem's name, her own, and Solstice's names to the guest list. "I'm getting us into MV's party," she explained excitedly.

Anthem's eyes widened in alarm. "Are you crazy? It's too risky. MV could spot us the moment we walk in."

Indy shot him a confident look as she typed in their details with a flourish. "We need to get close to MV, and this party is the perfect opportunity. Besides, it's not like we're going in unprepared. We'll have Solstice with us, and we can blend in. Trust me, it's the best shot we've got."

Anthem frowned, "Solstice? Why him? He would never agree to that, and even if he did, what if we get caught? Or worse, what if Solstice blows our cover?"

Indy shrugged, her fingers still moving swiftly across the keys. "Solstice may be unpredictable, but he's not reckless. He knows what's at stake, just like we do. Plus, I doubt MV would suspect we'd be bold enough to crash his party. That might just be our best advantage."

She paused, her hand hovering over the 'Enter' key, then glanced up at Anthem with a reassured smile. "Besides, you know how much Solstice loves a challenge."

Anthem shook his head, exhaling slowly as he tried to push down the knot of anxiety forming in his stomach. "This is a bad idea."

Indy pressed 'Enter,' adding the names to the guest list. "It is a bad idea," she agreed with a grin, "but it's also our best one."

With that settled, she turned her attention back to MV's files, quickly downloading the invitation and the rest of the contents onto a secure drive she had brought for just such a possibility. The process took only a few moments, but to Anthem, it felt like an eternity. He kept his eyes on the door, half-expecting someone to burst in at any second.

Finally, the download was complete. Indy disconnected the hard drive and slipped it into her bag, closing out the files on MV's computer to cover their tracks.

"Got everything we need?" Anthem asked, clearly stressed out.

Indy nodded, shutting down the computer. "We're all set. Let's get out of here."

As they quietly slipped out of the office, re-locking the door behind them, the executive floor was still ominously quiet, but the silence now seemed to echo with the potential consequences of what could happen if they get caught now. "We're really doing this, aren't we?" Anthem muttered as they made their way quickly down the hallway, their steps silent against the plush carpeting, heading back towards the entrance.

Indy glanced at him with a smirk. "Damn right we are. Now let's go tell Solstice the good news."

Just as they were about to turn the corner, a goosebump-inducing command sliced through the quiet: "Stop those two." The sudden command froze them in their tracks. Before they could react, a long arm shot out from someone loitering by an intersection, effectively blocking their path to the exit.

Turning around, their stomachs dropped. MV was striding towards them, a calm, almost eerie composure about him, flanked by three other individuals who looked equally serious. MV stopped at his office door, turning his icy gaze on the person who had blocked Anthem and Indy. "Bring them here," he ordered crisply.

The lackeys corralled Anthem and Indy back into MV's office. The room's sleek, imposing decor felt more menacing now. They stood nervously, watching MV, who appeared unbothered by their presence. MV glanced at them, then did a doubt take. "Don't I know you?" He asked Anthem, his eyes narrowing as he tried to place his face.

His heart skipped a beat, but thinking on his feet, Anthem answered, "I hope so. I've been a contractor here for close to two years. And I'm something of a musician myself—"

"Alright, enough of that." MV cut him off before turning back to his associates. Relief cascaded over Anthem and Indy. Without further acknowledgement, MV continued talking with one of his associates before pivoting his attention back to Indy. He tossed her a hard drive, his instructions clipped and devoid of any warmth. "This drive doesn't work. You have 15 minutes to move the data to another drive and return it to me."

Indy caught the hard drive deftly, exchanging a quick, uncertain glance with Anthem. MV then turned away dismissively, continuing his conversation as if they were merely an inconvenience that had briefly interrupted his day.

As Indy carefully set her laptop on MV's sleek, imposing desk, getting ready to begin the task, MV abruptly halted her actions with a sharp gesture.

"No, not here, you idiot," he snapped, his voice cold and dismissive. He glanced at the laptop with disdain, then sneered at Indy. "You really think I'd let you set up in my office? This is not your workspace. Do it somewhere else."

His insult stung, but it also sparked a realization in both Indy and Anthem. MV had handed them even more data than they had come for, and now they were being unceremoniously dismissed—free to leave with everything they had uncovered.

Hastily, Indy closed her laptop. She met Anthem's eyes, and a silent agreement passed between them. "We're very sorry for the presumption," Anthem said apologetically as he internally thanked his lucky stars for their unexpected freedom.

"Of course, we'll leave immediately," Indy added, keeping her voice steady despite the adrenaline surging through her veins.

MV waved them off, clearly eager to be rid of them. With the hard drive securely tucked away and their laptop in hand, Anthem and Indy quickly exited the office. They moved with purposeful speed, not stopping to speak to anyone as they navigated the quiet hallways of the executive floor.

Once they were out of MV's direct line of sight, they quickened their pace, their hearts pounding as they descended the stairs and made their way through the building's lobby. The weight of the hard drive in Indy's bag felt like a ticking bomb, but every step towards the exit brought them closer to safety and the opportunity to expose MV's plans.

Before they could reach the front door to freedom, another voice called out for them to stop. It was the security guard at the front desk.

"You need to sign out." He called.

"Oh! Right." Indy replied.

"I apologize, we completely forgot." Anthem chimed in, approaching the sign-in sheet. "Have a good day."

They casually walked through the building's doors into the bustling street, disappearing into the morning crowd, the sounds of the city rushing back to greet them. Only when they had put a respectful distance between themselves and the building did they allow themselves to slow down, tearing off their disguises and depositing them in a dumpster along the way.

"We did it," Indy whispered, allowing herself a moment to grasp the full extent of their escape. "We have everything."

Anthem nodded, scanning their surroundings for any sign of pursuit. "Let's get this information to Vale as quickly as possible. MV won't take long to realize what we've got."

With renewed urgency, they hailed a cab and slipped inside, putting even more distance between themselves and MV, unaware of the heist...for now.

CHAPTER XIX

Everyone was on high alert. As Anthem, Indy, and their team entered the main briefing room, all eyes turned towards them. Vale, standing at the head of the conference table surrounded by the community's leaders, signaled for them to step in further. "You're back earlier than expected," he noted with both concern and anticipation. "What have you found?"

Anthem stepped forward with the secure drive containing the copied files in hand. "We've uncovered tons. Everything from blackmail material on key figures across Musera to something even more alarming," he began.

Indy pulled up a specific folder labeled "Priority Threats."

As the contents loaded, the room fell into stunned silence.

It was a hit list.

Organized by region and threat level.

Confirmed Sound Weavers. Suspected Sound Weavers. Known allies.

"Top-priority targets," Indy said, her voice steady but tight. "Every name here has been flagged for capture or elimination. The list includes civilians, families, and even children—anyone showing even a hint of harmonic potential."

A second document opened. It was a series of deployment plans, color-coded and time stamped. The title read: *Community Suppression Directives—Phase One.*

"MV and the Council aren't just targeting individuals," Anthem added grimly. "They're planning raids on entire communities. Disrupt, detain, discredit—those are the marching orders."

Indy tapped one map. "But here's the part that matters: these raids haven't happened yet. Some are scheduled days, even weeks out. We have time to act—move people, secure resources, warn the right cells."

A wave of realization swept through the room. Murmurs turned into strategies. Shock turned into resolve.

Vale's expression hardened. "This isn't just control. It's a purge. He wants to erase us from the inside out."

"We can stop that," Indy said. "This data gives us a head start. If we hurry, we can evacuate the high-risk zones and intercept the first wave of Wave Reavers before they strike."

Vale nodded slowly. "We'll split into teams. Tessa, organize extraction units. Corin, coordinate secure shelters and reroute communication lines. No one on that list goes dark without us knowing why."

Anthem stepped back, letting the leaders work, but his mind was racing. He glanced at Indy, who gave him a curt nod—acknowledging the small win, even if it was only temporary.

"And there's one more thing," Indy added. "While I was in MV's system, I also found an invitation to a party he's throwing this weekend. It's an exclusive event, and I took the liberty of adding our names to the guest list—Anthem, myself, and Solstice."

Anthem shot her a look of surprise, clearly not expecting her to reveal that she'd gone off script, but Indy continued without missing a beat. "This could be our way in. We might be able to gather more intel or even confront MV directly before the festival. It's a long shot, but it might give us the edge we need."

Vale raised an eyebrow, leaning back slightly as he processed the information. His eyes shifted to the other leaders around the table, silently seeking their input. However, the room remained quiet as everyone mulled over the risks and potential rewards.

Vale's closest advisor, Tessa, was the first to speak. "It's bold," she admitted, folding her arms. "Crashing one of MV's events could draw unwanted attention. But if Indy's right, we could learn a lot—maybe enough to stop the attack or at least delay it."

Another leader, Corin, frowned slightly. "But there's a chance MV might suspect something's off. If he's already planning to discredit us, he could be setting this up as a trap. One misstep, and we could end up helping MV to make us the villains in this story."

Vale nodded thoughtfully, weighing both perspectives. "It's certainly a high-risk play," he intoned, his eyes shifting back to Indy. "But it's not without merit. If we can gather more intel, we'd be in a stronger position to act. Confronting MV directly at the party, though... that's dangerous. He'll be surrounded by security and supporters. We'd be walking straight into his territory."

Anthem finally spoke again. "If we're doing this, we'll need to plan for every contingency. We can't go in blind. If MV gets even a hint that we're onto him, we'll lose our only advantage."

Tessa nodded in agreement. "We should treat this as an intel-gathering mission foremost. Get in, observe, and if the opportunity presents itself, we can make a move. But we should be prepared to leave the second things look like they're turning against us."

Vale glanced at the other leaders once more, then back at Indy. "I assume Solstice doesn't know you added him to the guest list?"

Indy shook her head. "Not yet, but I can handle that. Solstice may be a hardass, but he's not a fool. If I explain the stakes, he'll play along."

A thoughtful silence followed as Vale tapped his fingers on the table, eyes narrowing as he weighed the plan. After what felt like an eternity, he finally nodded. "Alright. We'll go with it. But this is an intel-gathering mission, not a confrontation. Indy, you'll brief Solstice. Anthem, you and Indy get in, figure out as much as you can about MV's operation, and report back. If things go south, you leave immediately. Understood?"

Anthem and Indy exchanged a look before nodding in unison.

"Understood," Anthem replied.

Vale stood up. "Good. We have little time. Let's get to work."

The pair left the room and began their search for Solstice. They moved through the quiet corridors of the Sound Weaver complex, neither of them sure how Solstice would react to the news. "Where does this guy even hang out?" Anthem asked, not really expecting Indy to know.

"He's probably in the training hall," she said. "He practically lives there when he's not on a mission."

Anthem raised an eyebrow. "Typical Solstice. Let me guess, brooding while perfecting his *art form*?"

Indy rolled her eyes but didn't disagree. "He's not *that* bad. He just... passionate. About control, about being prepared. I respect it. Yeah, he can be intense, but honestly, you guys are a lot alike."

"I am deeply offended by that," Anthem replied.

They rounded a corner and approached the wide-open training zone. Solstice sat behind an elaborate drum kit, motionless, staring at the drum. The drums glowed brightly with a bluish energy, reacting to his powers. Faint distortions in the air swirled around him, forming a transparent shell.

Anthem and Indy watched in stunned silence as Solstice slowly brought his hands up to strike the drum. Then brought them back down unnaturally slowly. They continued to watch, and his movements sped up. His hands were a blur as he drummed out a beat at superhuman speed. The sound was loud and layered, speeding up and slowing down in sync with Solstice's movement. It also carried a faint echo that was looping back on itself. It was unlike anything Anthem had ever heard before.

"Show-off. Let's just get this over with before he rewinds himself into next week." Anthem muttered, shaking his head.

Indy gave him a sideways look. "Show-off? Well, if that isn't the pot calling the kettle back."

Anthem frowned but didn't argue. Indy stepped forward, and the music cut off abruptly as Solstice stood and holstered his drumsticks. His cool gray eyes flicked between them, lingering on Indy, then hardened after settling on Anthem.

"This can't be good," Solstice said, straightening and grabbing a towel from the bench. "You both showing up together usually means trouble."

"You're not wrong," Indy admitted. She stepped forward, crossing her arms as she leaned against the nearest wall. "We've got a mission, and you're on the team...Surprise." Indy shook her hands sarcastically.

Solstice's brows furrowed, his gaze narrowing. "A mission? Vale sent you two to recruit me? What's the catch?"

Anthem leaned his guitar case against the wall and shrugged. "No catch. Just a party and a chance to rub elbows with celebrities. Sound like fun?"

Solstice's frown deepened. "Sounds vague. Why wasn't I officially briefed?"

"Because I just made the call to add you to the guest list. We need your skill set. And before you start on how you like to be consulted first, let me lay it out for you: This mission could give us critical intel on MV's operations. Vale agreed with me, and you're in. Like it or not."

For a moment, Solstice didn't respond. He ran a hand through his platinum, sweat-dampened hair, his jaw tight. "You know I'm not a fan of being thrown into situations blind."

"I know," Indy said softly. "But you're one of the best we've got. And honestly? I trust you to have our backs."

Solstice was taken aback by the sentiment, though his expression remained guarded. "Fine. What's the plan?"

Anthem stepped forward. "Simple. We sneak into MV's penthouse, figure out what he's up to, and get out before things go sideways."

Solstice's eyes flicked to Anthem. "So, no plan?" He concluded.

Anthem smirked. "Well, this is sort of an on-the-fly operation. Some improvisation will be required. But if that is too much for you to handle, Indy and I can take care of this mission by ourselves."

That earned a faint twitch of amusement from Solstice, though he quickly masked it. "You're lucky I like a challenge," he said finally, tossing the towel over his shoulder. "But if I'm doing this, we're doing it right. No rushing in half-cocked."

"Deal," Indy said, relief flickering across her face. "But fair warning, this mission's going to require us to work... closely."

Solstice raised an eyebrow. "I'm not the problem here. Can *he* handle that?" He nodded toward Anthem, who crossed his arms, feigning offense in response.

"Don't worry about me, Solstice. I'm a team player." Anthem shot back.

"Alright," Indy interjected. "If we're going to pull this off, we need to know how to work together. And that means getting to know each other."

Anthem groaned, sagging his shoulders. "Oh great, team-building exercises. My favorite. Can we at least do this somewhere other than the training area?"

Indy shot him a glare. "I'm serious. But that's a good idea." The trio walked out into the corridor and down the hall, where a sitting nook was currently unoccupied. "Now, we're about to infiltrate MV's operation and trust matters. Solstice," she said, turning to him, "you've always kept your distance, but if we're going to do this, we need to understand what makes you tick. And that goes for you too, Anthem.”

Solstice raised an eyebrow. “You’re really pulling the ‘trust’ card, huh?”

“Yes,” Indy said firmly. “We’re going to be working together a lot, so we might as well start now.”

Anthem sighed dramatically, but waved a hand. “Fine. Let’s hear it, Solstice. What’s your deal? Where are you from?”

Solstice’s expression darkened slightly. “Aetherglace,” he said after a moment, his tone clipped.

Anthem perked up, clearly surprised. “Really? The frozen capital of tradition? Makes sense now.”

Solstice leaned forward, spinning a drumstick in his hand. “My family... they were practically royalty in the Sound Weaver world. Masters of rhythm, discipline, and control.”

Indy tilted her head. “So, how did you wind up here?”

Solstice hesitated, his gaze fixed to the floor. Finally, he sighed. “My powers manifested early. I thought I was special—better than the others. But one mistake proved I was wrong. I was practicing with a group of other trainees. I didn’t realize how fragile time could be until it broke.”

Pain leached into Solstice’s voice as he navigated the memories. “I created a temporal loop. I and everyone else in the room were trapped in that loop. The same day, over and over. At first, it was just disorienting. Then the panic set in. They blamed me. They turned on me. And no matter what I did, no matter how many times I tried to fix it, I failed. For years.”

"Years?" Anthem echoed, his voice unusually soft, pulled into Solstice's story.

"For me, yeah," Solstice said, his gray eyes distant. "For the rest of the world? Weeks. But in that loop, they ostracized me, beat me, even... killed..." He paused, his jaw tightening. "Every reset, I woke up and had to face it all over again. Eventually, I figured out how to break free. But when I got back, I wasn't a hero. I was a problem that needed cleaning up."

Indy's brow furrowed, her voice gentle. "What do you mean?"

"My family covered it up," Solstice said bitterly. "They couldn't have the great Beaumont Clan disgraced by a screw-up. And they never forgave me. My family ultimately disowned and ejected me unceremoniously. Told me I wasn't worthy of the name. So here I am—free, but not exactly whole."

Anthem watched him closely, his own past brushing against Solstice's story like a familiar companion. He could feel the sting of rejection, the pain of being cast out by those you trusted and loved. He shifted, contrasting emotions making him uncomfortable. The contempt he had for his heated rival was losing the war against the empathy and sincere hurt he felt for Solstice. "For what it's worth, I get it. Being kicked out of a group you thought you'd always be a part of? That messes with you."

Solstice glanced at him, a flicker of surprise crossing his face before he masked it. "Didn't think you'd understand."

Anthem shrugged. "Yeah. I've had my fair share of bad times."

Indy, sensing the connection forming, leaned forward with a big smile. "See? This is what I was talking about. We're more alike than we realize. And knowing this about you, Solstice, helps us understand why you're so..."

"Obsessive, moody, rigid?" Anthem interjected, earning a glare from Solstice.

"I call it precision," Solstice shot back, though his tone lacked the usual bite.

"Whatever you call it, it makes sense now," Indy said. "And honestly? I think it makes you stronger. You survived something unimaginable. That's nothing to be ashamed of."

For the first time, Solstice's shoulders seemed to relax. He looked between Anthem and Indy, a faint crack in his guarded demeanor. "Maybe. But don't think this means I'm about to start spilling my guts every time we hang out."

Anthem laughed. "Nah, we'll leave that to Indy. She's great at pulling emotions out of people."

Indy rolled her eyes but grinned. "Alright, Anthem, your turn."

Anthem leaned back, arms folded across his chest. "Yeah... fair."

He glanced at Solstice, then at Indy, then down at the floor. For a second, he looked like he might brush it off with a joke, but then he exhaled through his nose and rubbed the back of his neck.

"I was born into a pair of legends no one remembers," he said finally. "My parents were Independent Artists—real ones. Old school rebels. Underground stars. People believed in them. Hell, *I* believed in them. We were living proof that the CEA didn't own music, and we didn't need their permission to exist."

He paused, fingers tightening around his sleeve.

"My dad... he was the soul of it. Charismatic, brilliant, loud in all the best ways. He called it 'pure resonance'—the way he played. But that kind of defiance doesn't last forever. The CEA caught up with us when I was still a kid. Took him out during a raid. No warning. Just... gone."

Indy's eyes softened. Solstice said nothing.

"My mom and I hit the road after that. Stayed on the move. Hiding in basements, back-alley venues, the underside of cities no one talks about. We lived out of the Riff Runner. That van was our house, our stage, our entire world.

She taught me how to spot Silencer patrols and fool drone scans before I ever learned to read sheet music."

He chuckled softly, a bittersweet sound. "I didn't have a home. Not really. Never stayed in one place long enough to call it that. But we had music. And each other." His voice grew quieter. "Eventually, she got sick. Real bad. Couldn't keep running. We landed in Crucible City, hoping we'd blend in. She passed a few months later."

Anthem didn't look up. His fingers tapped an invisible rhythm on his thigh, a nervous beat.

"I stayed behind. Told myself I could keep playing, maybe do something with what she taught me. But really? I didn't know who I was without her. Without *them.* Without the music we made together. I kept playing like it would bring them back. Like it would make the silence mean something."

He finally looked at them, eyes tired but clear. "I'm not some prodigy with a perfect past or some blueprint for rebellion. I'm just someone who's been running too long... and finally decided to stop."

The silence that followed wasn't awkward—it was heavy, thoughtful. Solstice nodded slowly, his usual frosty edge tempered. "I didn't expect that."

Anthem offered a half-smile. "Neither did I, honestly."

Indy reached out and gave his arm a squeeze. "Thank you."

Anthem let out a breath, finally breaking the tension. "Alright, so we've covered tragic backstories and repressed trauma. Can we do something *useful* now? Like raid a compound or blow something up?"

Indy rolled her eyes with a laugh. "Typical. You bare your soul for five minutes and think you've earned a parade."

"Five minutes?" Anthem smirked. "That's a lifetime in guy-therapy."

Solstice raised a hand, stopping Anthem as he leaned back in his seat. "Wait. Not yet." He turned to Indy, expression unreadable but voice calm. "You've been running along with all of this. Risking everything like the rest of us. But you're not a Sound Weaver. You don't have powers to protect yourself. So why are you here? Why put yourself in so much danger?"

Indy didn't answer right away.

She leaned back slightly, arms crossed, her fingers fidgeting with a frayed thread on one of the patches of her jacket. The moment stretched—long enough for it to feel intentional. Then she exhaled, not quite a sigh, but close. "My dad disappeared when I was ten," she mumbled. "He never came home from work. No call. No text. We never even found his car."

Solstice and Anthem both fell silent.

"My mom and I did everything we could. We reported it. Filed a missing person's claim. Reached out to anyone who might help. But the local officials... they stonewalled us. Said he probably left. That people like him disappear all the time. One of them actually told my mom that we were 'probably better off without him.'"

"They never even *pretended* to care." She paused again, rubbing her fingers together. "After that, the house changed. My mom stopped smiling as much. Stopped singing."

Indy's voice didn't waver, but her gaze was far away now.

"But I remember the music we made before he was gone. I remember him calling me 'Rani'—it means queen. That was his special name for me. Said it fit because I always walked around like I ruled the living room." A ghost of a smile flickered across her lips. "One day he set down his guitar and pulled out a little handheld recorder. Told me and my mom we were going to make our own song, just the three of us."

She glanced at the floor, her voice soft. "He played this mellow, looping melody, and my mom followed him on the tabla. That sound—it filled the room. It felt like magic. Like harmony in its purest form."

A pause.

"After he vanished, the music stopped. The house was too quiet. My mom barely touched the tabla again. I started fixing things around the house. Not because I was good at it—but because something needed to be done. The sound system broke? I'd rewire it. A neighbor's amp blew out? I'd figure it out. My hands were busy, so I didn't have to feel so useless."

She looked over at Anthem, then back at Solstice.

"By the time I was a teen, I'd outgrown our little apartment and the grief hanging over it. So I left. Not to run away—but to find a way forward. Started picking up gigs wherever I could. Wired stages, hauled equipment, patched power from alleyway generators when venues didn't want to pay for permits. I kept things running. That's always been my job." She glanced down at her jacket, fingers brushing a patch stitched near her shoulder.

"Every one of these came from a night I kept the music alive. A venue that didn't fall apart because I was there. A band that got to finish their set because I figured out how to keep their mic working. I don't wear them to show off. I wear them because they're proof I didn't let the silence win."

The vibe in the room now was different—respectful.

"I don't have powers," Indy said softly. "But I have a purpose. And if that means risking my life to keep you two from destroying yourselves or letting the CEA mute one more voice, then so be it."

Solstice nodded slowly. He had nothing clever to say.

Anthem reached across the table and gave her arm a gentle nudge. "You've always been louder than most people I know, Indy."

She smirked faintly. "Don't get sappy on me, Anthem. I only cry when speakers blow."

Solstice leaned back in his seat, one eyebrow arched in that ever-present look of practiced detachment. "So... how *did* you two meet?"

Anthem opened his mouth to answer, but Indy was already leaning forward, a smug little grin pulling at the corner of her mouth. "Oh, that's easy," she said, casually draping one arm over the back of the couch like she was preparing to tell a legend. "I actually *love* this story. Rooftop party in Crucible City. One of those sketchy DIY gigs. You know the type—string lights from the dollar bin, amps half-held together with duct tape and hope, some guy selling mystery tacos out of a guitar case."

Anthem chuckled under his breath.

"Headliner bails last second, and the crowd gets restless. Energy's turning ugly, vibe is dipping fast. Then this guy—" she jerked a thumb at Anthem, "—just strolls up like he owns the city, gets handed a guitar, and begins acting like he's been waiting his whole life for that moment."

Anthem raised an eyebrow. "It wasn't that dramatic."

"You literally stood on the amp like a trashcan prince and told the crowd to scream your name. Keep in mind no one introduced you. You didn't even say who you were."

Anthem laughed. "Okay, *that* might be true."

Solstice looked between them. "So let me guess. You were instantly captivated by his raw talent and dangerous charm."

Indy snorted. "Hardly. I was working tech. The light rig was shorting out, and I had my head elbow-deep in a fried panel when he started playing. But I *heard* it. Loud and clear. The kind of sound that pulls your spine straight. And I thought, *damn, someone up there's actually got something to say.*"

She glanced at Anthem briefly; her smile softening for half a second before snapping back into her usual sarcasm. "Then his set almost imploded."

Anthem threw up his hands. "The board started frying. *Not my fault.*"

"Debatable," Indy shot back, smirking. "Anyway, everyone freaks out, feedback's screaming, the crowd's turning on itself, and I'm like, *great, another dramatic genius crashing the night.* So I run in, reroute the power, slap the limiter, patch in a new ground—all while he's still playing like none of it's happening."

"I seem to remember that night a little different." Anthem injected into the conversation. He leaned forward, mirroring Indy's posture. "One of those nights—I didn't even want to play," he said. "No set time, no warm-up, nothing. I was just there to be a fan, enjoy the music. But then the crowd started unraveling, and the silence hit harder than anything else. So I picked up a guitar and stepped in." He glanced at Indy, a half-smile tugging at the corner of his mouth.

"I play a few notes, not expecting much. Then the whole rooftop just...*settled.* Like something snapped into place. I was killing it up there."

Indy's smirk grew into a bright smile. She remembered the sound.

"Then the board started to die," Anthem said. "I thought I'd lost it—that moment, that connection. But then, through the smoke, I see her." He nodded toward Indy. "She's crouched at the board like she's defusing a bomb. She wasn't panicking. Wasn't yelling. Just working. She patched the board like it was muscle memory. And the sound—*my* sound—leveled out. Smoother than it had ever been." He sat back. "And for a second, the music wasn't mine anymore. It was ours."

Indy snorts. "Still took you twenty minutes to come say hi."

"I had to recover from being awestruck," Anthem said, hand over heart. "Also, I was afraid you'd critique my pedal board."

"I *did* critique your pedal board."

"And I've never recovered," he said solemnly.

Indy rolled her eyes, but her cheeks colored ever so slightly. "I wasn't that magical."

"You were," Anthem said, not missing a beat. "You are."

Solstice groaned softly. "You two gonna write a ballad next?"

Indy elbowed Anthem lightly. "Don't tempt him."

"We already did," Anthem said with a grin. "You just haven't heard it yet."

Solstice blinked slowly. "So basically, you both think you saved the night."

"Exactly," they said in unison—then paused and exchanged a look.

Solstice studied them.

Indy smirked. "That's how we work."

Anthem nodded. "Two sides of the same record."

The laughter between Indy and Anthem was still lingering, soft and warm, like an afterglow. Solstice watched them in silence, arms folded, then cleared his throat pointedly.

"Well," he said, dry as sandpaper. "This little group therapy session has been... surprisingly tolerable."

Anthem snorted. "Careful, Solstice. Your heart might grow a size or two."

"I said *tolerable*," Solstice corrected flatly. "Let's not get ahead of ourselves."

Indy raised an eyebrow. "So what? You're kicking us out of our own bonding circle now?"

"I'm suggesting," Solstice said, standing smoothly, "that while it's touching that we now all vaguely understand each other's childhood trauma and shared existential baggage... we should probably spend *at least* a little time going over how we plan to survive MV's party."

The warmth faded just slightly from the air, replaced by a ripple of tension. Reality was reasserting itself. Anthem stood, the shift in his posture immediate—playtime was over. "Right. The infiltration."

Indy stood and dusted herself off, her voice low but steady. "Let's get to work."

Solstice gave them both a quick nod and started down the hall. "Bring your A-game, kids. We'll need more than nostalgia and charm to get through this one alive."

CHAPTER XXI

The sleek black car glided up to the front entrance of MV's luxurious penthouse, its tinted windows reflecting the soft glow of the streetlights. Anthem, Indy, and Solstice sat inside, dressed to the nines, their nerves hidden behind carefully composed expressions. The driver pulled to a stop, and a valet in a crisp uniform opened the door.

Anthem stepped out first, his tailored charcoal-gray suit fitting him like a glove. His broad shoulders filled the subtly textured herringbone jacket, and a crisp white shirt, fastened with silver cufflinks that gleamed in the low light, was underneath. He had tied back his usually free-flowing locs, giving him a polished but slightly rebellious look. He adjusted his black tie; the knot sitting perfectly at his collar, and took a deep breath as he waited for the others.

Solstice followed, his outfit as sharp and striking as his personality. He wore a midnight blue tuxedo with a black satin lapel, the deep color contrasting against his pale complexion. His bow tie, slightly askew intentionally, added a touch of roguish charm. The pocket square in his breast pocket was a bold splash of red, mirroring the confident smirk on his lips.

Finally, Indy emerged. She struck a captivating visage. Dressed in a deep emerald green gown that shimmered with every movement, the fabric hugging her figure before cascading to the floor in a soft, elegant drape. The dress featured a subtle, off-the-shoulder neckline that highlighted her collarbones and the delicate gold chain around her neck. She pulled her dark, silky hair to one side, revealing intricate gold earrings that complemented her understated, yet sophisticated, makeup.

As they approached the entrance, the security detail, a pair of towering, stone-faced men in black suits, stepped forward to intercept them. One guard, a burly man with a close-cropped beard, held up a hand, signaling them to stop.

"Names?" he asked gruffly, his eyes scanning them with practiced suspicion.

Indy calmly stepped forward with a confident smile. "Indira Jenkins, plus two."

The guard nodded and checked the guest list on his tablet. A tense silence hung in the air as the three of them waited, the seconds stretching into what felt like an eternity. Anthem's hands flexed at his sides, Solstice's smirk faltered ever so slightly, and Indy's smile remained, but her eyes betrayed her nervousness.

Finally, the guard gave a curt nod. "You're on the list. Enjoy the party," he said, stepping aside.

Relief washed over them as they were ushered inside. They made their way to the private elevator that would take them up to the penthouse suite. The ride was as smooth as the jazz softly playing in the background as they exchanged quick, reassuring glances.

The elevator doors opened with a quiet chime, revealing the opulent penthouse beyond. Modern luxury defined the suite, floor-to-ceiling windows showcasing a breathtaking city skyline. The floors were polished marble, gleaming under the soft ambient lighting. Contemporary art pieces adorned the walls, and a huge crystal chandelier hung in the room's center, casting a warm, golden glow on the elegantly dressed guests.[1]

Plush velvet sofas and armchairs in rich colors filled the lavish seating areas scattered throughout the space. A grand piano stood near the windows, its ebony surface gleaming, while a string

quartet played softly in the corner, their music mingling with the murmur of conversation and the clinking of glasses.

Anthem took in the scene, doing his best to appear nonchalant despite the awe that bubbled up inside him. The room held famous actors, musicians, and industry moguls; each was more recognizable than the previous one. He forced himself to stay composed, reminding himself that they were here for a purpose.

They split up, blending into the crowd as best they could. Indy moved gracefully through the room, engaging in polite conversation with the other guests while discreetly observing the surroundings. Solstice was shockingly charming. He slid into a lively discussion with a group of producers, his sharp wit and easygoing confidence masked keen eyes that missed nothing. Anthem drifted from group to group, his nerves slowly settling as he found his rhythm, but he remained vigilant, scanning for any sign of MV.

As Anthem wandered through the suite, he found himself on a secluded balcony overlooking the glittering Crucible City. The air was cooler out here, and for a moment, he allowed himself to relax, taking in the view. That's when he heard the voices—hushed but intense, coming from just inside the open double doors behind him.

---

1. Track 14 - Ludovico Einaudi - Reverie

"...it's all about control," a smooth, authoritative voice said. "We keep them hungry for more, and they'll do whatever we want. And with your influence, Lyric, we can push this even further."

Anthem turned slightly, staying in the shadows as he peered inside. Lyric Rose stood with a group of sharply dressed men, her beauty striking even in the low light. She held a flute of champagne delicately, but her eyes were cold as she listened to the man speak.

"I'm in," she replied smoothly. "But let's keep this between us. The last thing I need is some idealistic nobody thinking they can disrupt my brand."

Anthem's brow furrowed, his fists clenching at his sides. The more he listened, the more it became clear that they were discussing something potentially more impactful than just marketing strategies.

Lost in thought, he didn't notice the sudden silence until it was too late. When he looked up, he saw Lyric Rose's eyes piercing into his, narrowed in suspicion and anger.

"You're not supposed to be here," she said harshly. The men around her shifted uncomfortably.

Anthem stepped forward, holding her gaze. "Neither are you, from the sound of it."

Annoyance flashed across her face before she regained her composure. "You don't know what you're talking about," she said dismissively. "This world isn't for amateurs. You wouldn't last a day in my stilettos."

"I'm not looking for a place in your world," Anthem shot back. "But I will not stand by while you and your cronies tear down everything I believe in."

Lyric took a step closer, intimidatingly despite her smaller stature. "You're in over your head. This industry chews up people like you and spits them out. Stick to your little gigs and keep out of my way, or you'll regret it."

Anthem's jaw tightened. "Maybe it's time someone stood up to you. I won't let you exploit people just because you can."

A bitter smile curved on Lyric's lips. "Then you'd better watch your back. You have no idea how deep this goes."

Before Anthem could respond, one producer placed a hand on Lyric's arm, murmuring something in her ear. She gave Anthem one last, lingering look before turning and walking away, leaving him alone on the balcony, seething with anger and frustration.

As the party continued behind him, Anthem knew his journey had just become much more complicated. Lyric Rose wasn't just a pop star; she was a powerful force in the industry, and now, she was aware of him. The stakes had never been higher, but Anthem was more determined than ever to fight for what was right, no matter the cost.

An hour or so later, the three of them regrouped near the hors d'oeuvres table, their mission in mind but temporarily forgotten as the exquisite spread before them pulled their immediate attention. An array of culinary masterpieces laden the table: delicate canapes topped with caviar, golden puff pastries filled with savory fillings, and tiny crystal spoons cradling single bites of some of the most decadent dishes they had ever tasted.

Anthem reached for a small plate, his eyes widening as he took in the selection. "This is... incredible," he said between mouthfuls.

Indy nodded, equally impressed as she picked up a delicate slice of smoked salmon topped with a dollop of Creme Fraiche. "I've seen nothing like this," she admitted, glancing around to make sure no one was paying them too much attention.

Solstice grinned as he popped a truffle into his mouth. "If nothing else, we'll at least get a good meal out of this."

With plates balanced elegantly in their hands, Anthem, Indy, and Solstice huddled closer together near the expansive hors d'oeuvres table, their voices low amidst the hum of conversation and gentle strains of classical music filling the room. The tantalizing aroma of gourmet dishes mingled with the subtle scents of expensive perfumes and colognes, creating an atmosphere of opulence that almost made them forget the nature of their mission.

Indy took a sip of sparkling champagne before leaning in, her eyes darting around to ensure their conversation remained private. "I've got a pretty good handle on the security layout," she began. "There are four main exits, not including the private service elevators. At least two guards, all armed and communicating via earpieces linked to a central security hub, monitor each."

She discreetly gestured with her glass towards various points in the room. "Hidden cameras cover all the common areas, but there are blind spots near the art gallery section and the outdoor terrace. The security office is on this floor, down a corridor past the main lounge. It's guarded, but traffic in and out seems minimal."

Anthem nodded, absorbing the information as shoved a seared scallop into his mouth. "Any sign of MV yet?" he asked, casually scanning the crowd.

Indy shook her head slightly. "Not yet. Either he's fashionably late to his own party, or he's watching from somewhere unseen."

Solstice smirked, swirling the amber liquid in his crystal tumbler before taking a sip. "While our dear Indy was playing spy, I was mingling with the elites," he said, a hint of playful cockiness in his tone. "Heard quite a few interesting tidbits. Apparently, there's some drama building between a couple of major record labels—could be useful leverage down the line. Also, caught wind that a certain pop star is considering breaking her contract, which could shake things up."

Anthem raised an eyebrow. "Lyric Rose?" He asked.

"Yes," Solstice responded. "Did you hear the same rumor?"

"Not exactly. I ran into her after overhearing her conversation, but wasn't sure what they were referring to." Anthem divulged. "Useful gossip, but does any of that help us tonight?"

Solstice shrugged, undeterred. "Not directly, but information is power, my friend. Never know when these little nuggets could come in handy."

Indy rolled her eyes affectionately before refocusing. "Alright, so here's the plan. We need to find MV or at least get access to the main security console. If we can plant this relay," she produced a small, inconspicuous device from her clutch, "we can monitor his communications and possibly get ahead of any moves he's planning."

Anthem glanced at the device, then back at Indy. "He might recognize me, so I'd prefer to avoid MV if I can."

"Ok. So that leaves the security office," Indy replied. "Which means we'll need a distraction. Something that can pull the guards away long enough for one of us to slip in."

Solstice's eyes gleamed with mischief. "Leave the distraction to me," he volunteered, adjusting his bow tie. "I have a knack for causing a scene when needed."

Anthem looked hesitant. "Just make sure it's not too big of a scene. We don't want to get kicked out before we accomplish anything."

Solstice placed a hand over his heart in mock offense. "Trust me. It'll be just enough to draw attention without raising too many alarms."

Indy nodded, formulating the details rapidly in her mind. "While Solstice is handling that, Anthem, you can position yourself near the security office entrance. Once he diverts the guards, slip inside and plant the relay on their main console."

Anthem took a deep breath. "Got it. What about you?"

"I'll monitor the overall situation and be ready to assist if anything goes sideways," Indy replied. "Plus, I'll try to locate MV. Even a brief interaction could provide useful intel."

They all exchanged resolute glances. The hum of chatter and clinking glasses of their luxurious surroundings faded as they mentally prepared for the tasks ahead.

"Alright then," Anthem said, straightening his jacket and setting his empty plate aside. "Let's do this."

Solstice drained the last of his drink and flashed them a confident grin. "Time to shine."

Indy offered a subtle nod, her eyes sharp and focused. "Be careful, both of you. We only get one shot at this."

With their roles assigned and plans set, the trio dispersed once more into the crowd, each adopting a facade of carefree elegance as they moved with purpose through the lavish penthouse.

Anthem weaved through the clusters of guests; his demeanor composed as he navigated towards the corridor Indy had indicated earlier. The route took him past a series of impressive art displays, abstract paintings and intricate sculptures that likely cost more than he could fathom. He paused occasionally, feigning interest in the artwork while discreetly assessing the security presence.

As he approached the entrance to the corridor leading to the security office, he noted two imposing guards stationed on either side, their watchful eyes scanning the crowd. Anthem maintained a casual posture, positioning himself near a display of a modernist sculpture, waiting for Solstice's distraction to unfold.

Solstice found his way to the center of the main lounge, where a live jazz band was entertaining the guests with smooth, melodic tunes. With a charming smile, he approached the band's lead singer during a brief interlude.

"Pardon me," Solstice began, oozing charisma. "Mind if I join you for a number? I've been known to carry a tune."

The singer, surprised but intrigued by Solstice's audacity, exchanged a glance with the band members before nodding. "Sure, why not? Let's see what you've got."

Solstice's grin widened as he took the microphone, signaling the band to follow his lead. He launched into a soulful rendition of a classic song, his voice rich and captivating. The unexpected performance drew the attention of the entire room, guests turning to watch as Solstice commanded the stage with effortless flair.

Laughter and applause filled the air as he engaged the audience, encouraging them to clap along. The energy in the room shifted, becoming livelier and more animated. Even the security guards joined the spectacle, momentarily forgetting their duties.

Seizing the opportunity, Anthem noted the guards near the corridor had stepped forward, their focus drawn towards the impromptu performance. With ease, he slipped past them, entering the dimly lit hallway unnoticed.

The corridor was quiet, a stark contrast to the lively atmosphere of the main rooms. Anthem moved swiftly yet silently, counting doors as Indy had instructed. Reaching the door to the security office, he paused, listening intently for any sounds from within. Hearing none, he tried the handle—locked, as expected.

From his pocket, he retrieved a slim lock-picking tool, courtesy of Indy's meticulous preparations. His hands steady, he worked the lock carefully; the tumblers clicking into place one by one until the door gave way with a soft click.

Anthem slipped inside, closing the door gently behind him. Monitors throughout the room displayed various camera feeds from around the penthouse. A single workstation sat in the center, the screensaver active, suggesting the guard on duty had likely stepped out, perhaps drawn by Solstice's performance.

Moving quickly, Anthem approached the main console and retrieved the relay device from the inner pocket of his suit. He connected it to an open USB port, watching as a tiny light blinked to life, signifying a successful link. The device would now feed real-time data back to their systems, granting them valuable insight into MV's operations.

Just as he secured the device and prepared to leave, a noise from outside the door made him freeze—a muffled voice and approaching footsteps. Thinking fast, Anthem scanned the room and spotted a small storage closet. He darted inside, pulling the door shut just as the main door opened.

A guard entered, muttering under his breath as he took his seat before the monitors. Anthem held his breath, heart pounding in his chest as he waited, hoping the guard wouldn't notice anything amiss. After a few tense moments, the guard seemed satisfied and resumed watching the feeds on the screens. Out of options, Anthem waited for an opportunity to slip out unnoticed.

Meanwhile, Indy watched Solstice's performance with a mix of amusement and admiration, noting how effectively he had captured everyone's attention. As the song concluded to enthusiastic applause, she noticed movement near one of the previously guarded doors—a figure slipping through quietly.

Her eyes narrowed as she recognized MV himself entering the room. In fact, many people noticed his quick presence despite his attempt at subtlety. He wore a sleek, all-black tie-less suit. Indy's pulse quickened as she considered her next move, understanding that this might be her best chance to get close to him.

Setting down her glass, she smoothed out her dress and made her way through the crowd towards MV, preparing to engage him in conversation and possibly glean more information. As Indy moved toward MV, her phone buzzed in her clutch. With a quick glance, she unlocked it to find a text from Anthem.

Stuck in the security room. Guard's back. Need a way out. ASAP.

Her lips pressed into a thin line. She stole one last glance at MV, who was now conversing with a small group near a gilded bar. This was her shot, her chance to dig deeper into MV's plans—but Anthem's situation was critical. If he got caught, everything they'd worked for would unravel.

With a silent sigh, she turned on her heel and headed back toward Solstice, who was basking in the aftermath of his impromptu performance. He raised an eyebrow as she approached, sensing her urgency.

"Change of plans," she said under her breath, leaning close so only he could hear. "Anthem's stuck in the security room. We need to extract him now."

Solstice nodded, his smile slipping into a more focused expression. "Got it. What's the play?"

"Create another distraction. Bigger this time. Something that'll pull as many guards away as possible," Indy instructed, already scanning the room for potential exits. "I'll handle the rest."

Solstice straightened, his signature smirk returning. "Leave it to me."

Hang tight. Distraction incoming. Be ready to move.

Solstice adjusted his cufflinks and approached the CEOs of two of Musera's biggest record labels. Richard Cane of Vortex Records and Marcus Simons of Apex Industries. Solstice positioned them perfectly, close enough that once the fuse was lit, they would quickly confront each other, but far enough away to give him time to set up and escape. Both men radiated self-importance, their booming voices and dismissive gestures making it clear they were used to being the loudest in any room. Perfect targets.

With a sly smile, Solstice casually positioned himself between the two groups. He feigned a look of surprise, leaning toward the nearest Richard Cane. "Mr. Cane," he said smoothly, just low enough to make it feel like a confidential whisper,

"I didn't realize you'd finally landed Lyric Rose. Congratulations. I heard she's been, uh... less than happy with her current situation."

Richard's brow furrowed. "Lyric Rose? Where did you hear that?"

Solstice raised his hands innocently. "Oh, I must've misunderstood. But you know how these industry rumors go. Everyone's saying she's practically clawing to get out of her contract with Apex. Word is, she's been talking to... well, someone else."

Richard's expression darkened, his eyes darting toward Marcus Simons, who was chatting with a group nearby. Without a word, Richard turned, heading off to somewhere in a hurry. Satisfied, Solstice turned his attention to another cluster of guests, where he spotted a familiar face—Marcus's head of PR. He sidled up to her, adopting a look of quiet concern. "Shame about the drama tonight, huh?" he murmured.

The woman blinked in surprise. "Drama? What drama?"

Solstice tilted his head toward Richard, who was now glaring daggers at Marcus from across the room. "Well, it's none of my business, of course, but I overheard Richard mentioning something about Apex's... let's say, *questionable* business practices with its artists. Something about forcing Lyric Rose into a tour she didn't want?" He shook his head as if disappointed. "No wonder she's about to sign that deal with Vortex, right?"

The woman's eyes widened, her face flushing as she hurried toward Marcus. Once there, she whispered the supposed accusation in his ear. Marcus's expression darkened instantly, and he turned to face Richard. "Cane," Marcus growled, "what lies are you spreading about my artists? She's under contract. She's not going anywhere."

Richard's eyes flashed. "Lies? Maybe you should ask Lyric why she's considering jumping ship. Or maybe she's just tired of being treated like a pawn in your little empire."

The room quieted, all eyes snapping toward the two CEOs as their voices grew louder, escalating into a full-blown shouting match. Solstice leaned casually against the nearest pillar, watching the scene unfold like it was the evening's scheduled entertainment. Guests around them murmured, some stepping back while others leaned in, intrigued by the drama unfolding. Marcus's PR head tried to intervene, but the two men ignored her, too caught up in their egos.

Solstice caught Lyric Rose's attention from across the room with a subtle nod and a pointed glance at the arguing CEOs. She frowned, then started making her way towards him. He gave her an apologetic shrug. "Hate to drag you into this," he said, concerned, pouring on the charm. "But they're tossing your name around like a party favor. Thought you'd want to set the record straight."

Lyric's eyes narrowed. "They're doing *what?*"

She stormed into the fray, her presence like gasoline poured into a roaring fire. "Excuse me?" she snapped, cutting through their shouting match. "Why is my name coming out of *either* of your mouths?"

Richard, Marcus, and Lyric traded accusations, causing their argument to erupt into chaos that could be heard across the penthouse. Guests gathered around, murmuring and snapping photos, while the guards rushed in, their radios crackling as they tried to de-escalate the situation.

Meanwhile, Solstice slipped through the crowd, making his way back toward Indy, who was already moving toward the corridor leading to the security room.

"Effective as ever," Indy said as she passed him, impressed despite herself.

Solstice gave her a mock bow, his grin wide and self-satisfied. "What did I say? Information is power, those little nuggets paid off sooner than we thought." He fell into step behind her, leaving the uproar of furious CEOs, an indignant pop star, and scrambling guards in his wake.

As the guard monitoring the cameras darted out of the security room to assist with the escalating chaos, Indy pulled out her phone discreetly and quickly texted Anthem:

> *Coast is clear. Move now.*

Indy and Solstice lingered near the entrance to the main room, keeping one eye on the corridor and the other on the growing commotion among the guests. Lyric Rose was now demanding answers in a tone that could shatter glass, while Marcus and Richard continued their verbal sparring. Guards were scrambling to restore order, their movements hurried and distracted.

Anthem emerged from the corridor. His expression was tense but focused as he joined them at the edge of the crowd.

"Good timing," Indy whispered, tilting her head toward the chaos. "Let's move before someone realizes Solstice's role."

The three of them slipped out through the front entrance, moving quickly but casually, ensuring they didn't draw attention. Once in the hallway, they broke into a brisk walk, heading straight for the elevators. They chimed softly, and the doors slid open. The trio stepped inside, Anthem leaning against the mirrored wall as he finally allowed himself a small breath of relief.

"Got the data?" Indy whispered.

Anthem nodded. "Everything. His network's ours now. We'll be able to track his movements and access everything."

"Good. Then let's focus on getting out clean," Indy suggested.

As the elevator descended, Solstice couldn't resist breaking the tension. "So, Anthem, what's it like being locked in a closet while we do all the hard work?"

Anthem shot him a dry look. "Better than listening to you perform."

Solstice held a hand to his chest, feigning offense. The elevator doors opened, cutting off the banter. They stepped into the building's lobby, keeping their heads low as they crossed the polished floor toward the exit. Outside, the cool night air greeted them like an old friend. Anthem tugged his jacket collar higher, glancing around as Indy scanned for their car.

It pulled up moments later, and the trio climbed inside, settling into the plush seats as the car pulled away from the building, the city lights blurring past as they drove into the night.

To give Anthem a break from the stress crushing his shoulders, Indy suggested they step out for a bit. She thought they should try out a unique music bar she had heard rumors about.

"Just one night," she said. "There's a spot I heard about. It's called the *Echo Chamber*. Might even make you forget the world's ending."

The city streets were quieter than usual. As they walked, Anthem took in his surroundings. Posters plastered on every corner, lamppost, and kiosk, all bearing the sharp, polished iconography of the CEA. MV's face was everywhere too, frozen in a manufactured half-smile, head crowned by sleek golden text:

"SILENCE IS PURE."

"EVIL WEAVERS ARE AMONG US."

"TRUST THE WAVE REAVERS."

But not all of them were intact.

One had been slashed diagonally with a blade, revealing a jagged graffiti tag beneath:

"IT'S NOT PEACE. IT'S FEAR."

Another poster had been completely blacked out in spray paint except for MV's eyes, which now stared out over freshly stenciled words:

"THE EYES OF A LIAR."

Someone had written **Sound Weavers Saved My Life** in marker directly across MV's chest on one. Another had the CEA insignia altered to look like a muzzle. Anthem slowed his pace, eyes flicking across the layers of ink, paint, and political noise.

Indy caught him staring. "They're trying to control the story," she said. "But the streets know not to believe their lies."

As they approached an unassuming bank, Anthem couldn't help but give Indy a side-eyed glance. The busy scene inside, from the soft whir of ATMs to customers lining up for late-night transactions, didn't exactly scream "secret music bar." Which was kind of the point. Yet, Indy was leading him confidently through the sliding glass doors, a smirk betraying the mystery she had yet to reveal.

"A bank?" Anthem muttered skeptically. "This is your big surprise?"

"Trust me," Indy replied with a mischievous grin.

As they stepped inside, Anthem's phone buzzed in his pocket. He barely noticed it at first, too focused on the absurdity of walking into a *bank* when he'd been expecting something much cooler. But the second buzz made him fish it out, his eyes flicking to the screen.

A new message.

Anthem's pulse jumped. It was one of his leads on MV. The first to actually respond. He quickly scanned for any additional details—nothing. Just the place and time. It could be a setup, sure, but at this point, any information on MV was worth the risk.

Keeping his expression neutral, he subtly angled his phone toward Indy, letting her read the message. She glanced at it quickly; her smirk fading for half a second before she met his gaze again.

Indy gave a tiny, almost imperceptible nod before looking back at the teller. "Good," she said, just loud enough for Anthem to hear. "Now let's hope this surprise adds more to your good news."

They approached the teller, a middle-aged woman in a crisp uniform who greeted them with the standard pleasantries. Without missing a beat, Indy leaned over the counter just slightly and spoke in a low voice, "We'd like to check the contents of safe deposit box 1313."

The teller's face shifted ever so subtly, showing a faint hint of recognition. "Of course," she said with a smile. "Right this way."

As they followed her through a side door and into a long, sterile hallway, Anthem's curiosity piqued. The teller led them into a large room lined with thousands of safe deposit boxes. In the center, a lone table sat under a dim light.

Indy's eyes scanned the room until she found box 1313. She inserted the key given to her by the teller, unlocking the small door with a soft click. Inside, instead of papers or valuables, there was only a bright red button.

With a smirk, Indy pressed it.

The faint whir of machinery filled the air as part of the wall slid open with a soft hiss, revealing a narrow staircase descending into the depths below the bank.

The teller gave a polite nod, gesturing for them to continue down. "Enjoy your evening," she said professionally.

Grinning widely, Anthem exchanged an incredulous glance with Indy. "Okay, now I'm impressed."

As they descended the staircase, the atmosphere transformed entirely. The sterile bank environment above faded as they stepped into a sleek, hidden world that appeared to exist outside the normal rules of reality. The Echo Chamber was a marvel of modern design. Polished chrome gleamed under the shifting glow of LED lights, casting a hypnotic blend of colors throughout the room. Glass walls reflected the hues, amplifying the feeling of stepping into another dimension. The designers built everything here to engage the senses. The low bass of electronic music blended seamlessly with the quiet murmur of conversation, creating an upbeat atmosphere.[1]

A massive backlit wall of bottles dominated the bar, stacked high and glowing like a vibrant mosaic of liquid art. The bar counter, sleek and black as obsidian, stretched invitingly across the room, while clusters of low-slung couches and angular chairs invited patrons to lose themselves in the ambiance.

"Whoa..." Anthem said, taking it all in. Indy watched his reaction, a smug smile plastered on her face.

"Told you it'd be worth it," she teased, leading him to one of the plush booths. As they settled in, the black leather cushions felt amazing under them. When the drinks arrived, expertly crafted cocktails in crystal-clear glassware that sparkled in the shifting light, they raised their glasses, savoring the moment.

---

1. Track 15 – The Midnight – Crystalline

"So?" Indy leaned back. "Worth the suspense?"

Anthem took a slow sip, the smoky flavor of bourbon rolling over his tongue. "Definitely worth it," he said, casting another glance around the room, still a little stunned by the sleek modernity of it all. "How did you even hear about this place?"

Indy's eyes gleamed under the neon lights, a bit of mischief sparkling within them. "I have my ways," she replied, leaning in conspiratorially. "Let's just say word travels fast in the city, if you know who to ask."

Anthem chuckled, taking another sip of his drink. "You always know where to find the best spots."

"I figured we deserved it," Indy said softly. "You've been through hell these past few weeks. I thought a night like this might help you clear your head."

"Yeah," he mumbled, giving her an appreciative look before swirling the amber liquid in his glass. "It's hard to believe places like this have to stay hidden, though. People should celebrate music, not force it underground."

Indy's expression darkened slightly as she glanced around, "You'd think so, but... you know how things are now. Independent Artists, venues like this—they see them as threats. Too much freedom of expression for their taste. They don't want people gathering in large groups unless it's under their thumb, sanctioned, and taxed to the hilt."

Anthem nodded slowly, tracing the rim of his glass with his finger. "It's about more than taxes or regulations. It connects people, opens doors they would prefer to stay closed. And that's dangerous to them."

Indy's eyes flickered with agreement. "Exactly. Every time people come together like this; unsupervised, unregulated, it threatens the structure they've worked so hard to build. They know music has power. It always has. That's why places like this have to stay secret. They serve more of a purpose than just a gathering place for people to have a good time. They are spaces where people can just... be. *It's not music; it's mutiny.*"

As Anthem listened to the upbeat electronic music, he reflected on her words. Music had always been his way of connecting with the world around him. Now, more than ever, that connection felt fragile. But sitting there in the warm, electric glow of the bar, with Indy by his side and a drink in his hand, he felt that connection alive within him. "It's crazy," he murmured. "Music used to be a way to reach something divine, something transcendent. And now, we're sneaking into fake banks just to listen to it freely." Anthem took another sip, letting the moment settle over him.

Indy looked at him curiously. "You mean like religion?"

"Yeah," Anthem replied, nodding. "Think about it—back in ancient times, music was a huge part of religious rituals. They believed it could open a path to the divine, transcend the physical world. Now, we've got the government deciding who gets to play what, where and when. It's like we've traded the spiritual for... I don't even know what."

Indy tilted her head thoughtfully. "That's one way to look at it. Religion's still around, but it's so... structured now. People go to church, to temples, but there's no life anymore, no raw emotion that grabs you by the soul. It's all polished and pre-packaged. There's no room for real, spontaneous, human connection."

"Exactly!" Anthem's voice rose passionately. "Look at the Sanctum of Voices. They're supposed to be the spiritual leaders of Musera, but now they just feel like another arm of the system, keeping everyone in line. There's no humanity in what they do anymore, just rules."

Indy leaned back, staring at the last of her drink in the glass. "Yeah, the Sanctum has lost its way. No wonder people are finding new ways to worship and feel alive. Music, art, underground communities like this—it's where they can finally feel something real."

Anthem's eyes scanned the bar. "Music still has that power," he said. "It's the one thing left that makes us feel something we're not supposed to. It's freedom. Maybe that's why they fear it. They can't control it."

Indy replied. "That's why places like The Echo Chamber matter. Even if we have to hide, even if we have to play in the shadows, it keeps the spirit alive. It's not perfect, but it's a lifeline. A spark that refuses to die out."

Anthem nodded. "Yeah... but how long can we keep this up before someone snuffs that spark out? How long before the system crushes it completely?"

For a long moment, Indy just stared at him. Then she tapped her glass gently against his. "As long as we're still willing to fight for it," she said, unwavering. "As long as we have to."

They fell into another comfortable silence. Then a thought flashed across Indy's eyes. "Do you ever wonder if music is still... spiritual? Even without temples or rituals. Like maybe it's the connection we've been searching for all along."

Anthem drummed his fingers softly against the table, deep in thought. "Honestly, yeah. When I'm playing, it's more than just sound. Sometimes it feels like I'm touching something ancient, something that's been around longer than us, something that doesn't care about rules or structures. It's like... I'm a part of something grand."

Indy smiled. "Maybe you're right. Maybe that's why we keep playing, no matter what. Because deep down, we know it's not just about the music. It's about the connection."

Anthem's eyes softened as he met her gaze, a deep feeling of understanding passing between them. "Yeah... like our connection."

Indy blushed for a moment, thankfully hidden by the bar's low lighting. They allowed the conversation to fade into the background as they sat back and enjoyed the music. Anthem closed his eyes for a moment, bobbing to the beat. But just as he was losing himself in the rhythm, a piercing crash shattered the peaceful night. Glass exploded across the bar, followed by panicked shouts and the blinding glare of flashlights flooding the dim, intimate space.

"This is a raid! Everyone stay where you are!" a harsh authoritative voice bellowed. Masked, faceless CEA Silencers flooded the room like a dark tide, targeting anything that moved. The music cut off abruptly as chaos erupted around them.

Spilling into the room after them, hovering just overhead, were dozens of drones, glowing faintly with a sterile white light. One zipped ahead of the others, rippling with flashes of data as it scanned the room.

Patrons scattered, chairs overturned, and glass shattered on the floor. The CEA swept through the room like wolves through a herd, efficiently subduing anyone too slow to escape.

Indy's hand clamped down on Anthem's arm, her nails digging in as her wide, alarmed eyes locked onto his. "We have to get out of here—*now*," she whispered urgently, her voice barely audible over the chaos.

Anthem's heart kicked into overdrive. They ducked low, sliding out of their booth and dropped behind the bar just as a Silencer wrestled the bartender to the ground on the opposite side. The sounds of glass crunching under boots, barked orders, and the panicked cries of patrons filled the air like a nightmarish hymn.

Then everything got worse.

Two identical feminine figures emerged from the smoke near the entrance, dressed in stylized CEA black, their faces half-obscured by gilded opera-style masks.

Wave Reavers.

Their voices rang out in perfect harmony—smooth, reverberating, and utterly unnatural.

"Find the pulse..."

"Bend it inward..."

The moment their song hit, the air *shifted.*

Anthem's vision tilted violently, like the floor had just slanted beneath him. His balance gave out for half a second—his stomach turned sideways. The room spun. Sounds bled together. Colors ghosted at the edges of his vision.

He gritted his teeth. "What the hell—?"

"They're causing vertigo," Indy gasped beside him, pressing a hand to her temple. Her eyes were watering. "Pitched resonance. It's targeting the inner ear—scrambling our equilibrium."

All around them, others were dropping—some clutching their heads, others vomiting, writhing in disoriented panic.

The twins floated forward in eerie unison, still singing.

"Let them fall..."

"Let them break..."

Anthem and Indy fought through the nausea, stumbling toward the small door Indy had spotted earlier. But another squad of Silencers was already moving to cut them off.

Anthem's eyes landed on the stage.

An old guitar—warped and scratched but still strung—sat abandoned on a stand.

"Cover me," he rasped.

"What?" Indy coughed, blinking through the dizziness.

"I need that guitar." Without waiting, Anthem broke into a sprint—lurching like a drunk, each step a fight against the spinning world. Indy turned and threw herself sideways into a cluster of stacked stools, toppling them in a loud crash that pulled several Silencers toward her instead.

The twins saw Anthem moving. Their song *sharpened.* The resonance doubled.

"Stillness... ends..."

The room warped like heat on the pavement.

Anthem dove onto the stage, the guitar's neck smacking into his palm. He dropped to one knee, strummed once—sloppy, off-key.

Then he inhaled.

And *focused.*

His fingers slid across the strings, not playing a song—*summoning intent.* His will laced through the vibrations, crafting structure, forming function. The air trembled.

Then two sharp chords.

Two gag-like constructs snapped into place—one over each twin's mouth. Semi-solid, wrapped in coiled resonance. Their voices cut off mid-phrase.

The room *lurched* back into normalcy.

The vertigo snapped like a cable pulled taut. People gasped as their balance returned, crawling to their knees, struggling to their feet. The twins reached for their faces, clawing at the harmonic restraints, but the constructs held.

Indy burst through the remaining resistance like a storm, flanking the Silencers who tried to pursue Anthem. She moved fast—slamming a broken chair leg into one Silencer's gut, knocking another aside. Anthem jumped off the stage, grabbed Indy's wrist, and together they sprinted toward the back exit.

Apertures on the drones' surface opened, releasing small barrels. They fired electrified darts that crackled and arced as they flew through the air. One pinned a fleeing patron in place with a paralyzing buzz. Another drone whirred past, scanning overturned tables and the panicked crowd, its glow intensifying as it identified someone noteworthy.

Indy's sharp eyes darted around, looking for an escape route. She spotted it—a small, barely noticeable door tucked into the back corner of the bar. She jabbed her finger toward it, and Anthem nodded, understanding her silent command.

Timing their movements with the frantic energy of the room, they crouched low, crawling through the maze of fallen chairs and spilled drinks. Every sound around them was deafening—the heavy thud of boots, the clang of metal, the muffled grunts of those caught in the Silencer's grip. Anthem's heart pounded in his ears as he maneuvered around bodies and broken glass, his nerves on fire, every sense on high alert. Then, as they neared the door, a Silencer turned the corner, his flashlight cutting through the darkness like a searchlight. Anthem froze, his breath catching in his throat.

But Indy was a quick thinker. She snatched a bottle from the bar and hurled it across the room with precision. It smashed against the Silencer's helmet, momentarily distracting him just long enough for them to make their move. In one fluid motion, Anthem and Indy slipped through the small door and stumbled into the narrow alley behind the bar. The cool night air slammed into them as dozens of other people came spilling out after them. There was no time to catch their breath. Indy grabbed his hand and pulled him into a sprint down the darkened alley. Their footsteps were a frantic echo in the silence of the night.

They ran through the twisted streets as the sounds of the raid gradually faded behind them. Their lungs burned, but they didn't stop until they had put several blocks between themselves and the Echo Chamber. Finally, they collapsed against the wall of a quiet building, panting, adrenaline coursing through their veins.

Indy's breath came in sharp gasps as she pressed a hand to her chest. "That... was...too...close," she said in between gulps of air.

Anthem nodded, still trying to catch his own breath. "We can't go back," he said grimly. "It's not safe anymore. Nowhere is."

Indy agreed; her eyes darted around the empty street, expecting the CEA to reappear at any moment. The Echo Chamber had become just another casualty in the war for freedom.

245

CHAPTER XXIII

The time had come for his first show, agreed upon with Mare. It was at the Obsidian Key. The Obsidian Key was more than just a bar—it was a portal to another world, hidden in the shadows of the city, only accessible to those in the know. Tucked away in a narrow alley behind an unmarked door, the venue carried the kind of mystique that whispered secrets to anyone lucky enough to step inside.

As Anthem approached the old, worn entrance, the door slid open with a groan from its rusted hinges, revealing a small panel at eye level. The doorman's eyes appeared through the slot, scanning Anthem before a gruff voice asked, "Password?"

"Cold Rain," Anthem answered calmly.

The panel slid shut, followed by the metallic click of the lock being undone. Anthem stepped inside as the door swung open, instantly greeted by the sultry ambiance of the underground speakeasy. The space was a throwback to a different era, one draped in deep plum colored velvet, with low-lit chandeliers casting a golden haze over the room. Dark mahogany wood framed the bar, where bottles of rare spirits gleamed like treasures waiting to be uncovered. The scents of incense and aged whiskey mingled in the air, swirling around the slow, rhythmic jazz that resounded through the room like a lover's whisper.

This was no ordinary crowd. The patrons of the Obsidian Key were connoisseurs—sophisticates who craved more than a catchy chorus. They came for the art of the music, to be moved, to be transformed. And tonight, Anthem was here to offer them just that.

Guitar case slung over his shoulder, he strutted to the stage with a subtle swagger. His boots barely made a sound on the plush carpet, but as soon as he stepped into the soft glow of the red velvet lamps, every eye in the room turned toward him, sensing what was to come.

His fingers trembled slightly as he unlatched his guitar case. He had to use a replacement from the Sound Weaver inventory, but was assured he'd be able to perform well, even with an unfamiliar instrument. The crowd—seasoned music lovers, industry insiders, and those who had come not just for entertainment, but to *feel* something—watched in quiet expectation.

Anthem swallowed, adjusting the strap over his shoulder. He nodded toward the bartender, who dimmed the lights just a fraction more. He could feel Indy's eyes on him from the side of the room, unwavering, grounding.

And then—he played.[1]

It was meant to be a slow, haunting blues riff, but the first note came out wrong. The twang of the string sounded brittle, almost hesitant. He winced but pushed forward, transitioning into the next chord. He could recover.

Except his voice cracked.

It wasn't bad. It wasn't catastrophic. But in *this* place, with *this* crowd, any slip was noticeable. A few patrons shifted, exchanging glances. A soft cough echoed

---

1. Obsidian Key Set List Playlist

from somewhere in the back. Someone near the bar leaned forward, as if trying to figure out whether this was nerves or intentional.

Anthem's throat tightened. A whisper of doubt crept in— *What the hell am I doing here?*

He could feel himself slipping, his grip on the song loosening like sand through his fingers. He was moments away from disaster.

But then—something shifted.

Somewhere beneath the nerves, the failure, the doubt—*the music waited.*

He exhaled.

The crowd blurred. The air changed.

Anthem closed his eyes and leaned into the melody, no longer thinking, just *feeling.* His fingers relaxed against the strings, strumming softer now, more deliberate. His voice, still raw with nerves, found a new depth as he let himself sink into the music instead of trying to force it.

And then—power.

At first, the shift was almost imperceptible. The resonance deepened. A low hum vibrated through the room, not just from his guitar, but from the very walls. The glasses on the tables rang softly, harmonizing with the chords.

The crowd hovered at the edge of belief, their skepticism thinning as they leaned in. Anthem's melody spread out across the room, weaving through the haze and golden light, subtle at first, then stronger—like a current pulling them under.

With each chord, his confidence deepened. What started as hesitation became something electric streaking through him. His voice steadied, thick with raw feeling, and the air seemed to tighten with every note, drawing the audience closer.

Anthem caught it—that invisible thread—the one that connected him to the room, to every soul in it.

This wasn't just a performance anymore.

It was a conversation. A communion stitched together by the experience.

He pushed the rhythm harder, letting the music dig deep, pulling out the restless hunger and hope churning inside him. His fingers moved faster, the notes rising and falling like a gathering storm. Around the stage, drinks sat forgotten. No one dared break the spell.

As he surged toward the peak of the song, faint wisps of blue flame shimmered into being, coiling around his boots and guitar. The flames danced with the music—wild but never consuming, shadows and light braided into the melody.

Bathed in that soft, impossible glow, the audience sat frozen.

He had taken them somewhere else—somewhere real and unreachable all at once.

Anthem felt it surge through him: not just music anymore, but something older, deeper. Sound sharpened into light. Emotion given form. He surrendered to it completely, his eyes closed, every part of him stitched into the song as the flames danced around him. The flames flared with the last note, twisting high before petering out. Silence collapsed over the room.

For a long moment, no one moved.

Then, slowly, like a tide returning to the shore, the crowd exhaled. Murmurs filled the air—soft, stunned. He stepped off the stage. The crowd parted for him without a word. Nods, quiet admiration, hands pressed to hearts—It was written in their faces: tonight, he hadn't just played music. He had given them a glimpse of something greater. Something untouchable—and unforgettable.

Venue staff corralled Anthem backstage, straight into chaos. Crew members weaved through the narrow halls, barking orders and hauling gear like their lives depended on it. Managers clustered in tight knots, gesturing over clipboards and phones. Security guards fought to hold back a surging line of fans trying to sweet-talk their way past the velvet rope. Beyond the backstage walls, the crowd's cheers rumbled like thunder.

In the middle of it all, Anthem slumped against a stack of road cases, his breath ragged, sweat cooling on his skin. His heart still hammered from the adrenaline rush—but a slow, unshakable calm had settled in his chest. He'd done it. And for the first time in a long while, it felt right.

A blur of motion barreled toward him—Indy, her grin wide enough to split her face in two. "Anthem!" she squealed, practically bouncing off the floor. "Do you even know what you just did?"

He cracked a relieved smile, letting out a shaky laugh. "I almost tanked, that's what I did."

Indy smacked his shoulder. "No, you started shaky, for sure. But then you turned that whole damn room inside out." She grinned, squeezing his arm. "I mean, did you see their faces? They were *losing* their shit out there!"

Anthem exhaled, the tension in his shoulders melting just a little. "It felt... different. Like I wasn't even in control, like it was just—happening." He wiped the sweat from his forehead. "I don't think I've ever felt anything like that."

"You were unstoppable," Indy beamed, grabbing his arm and squeezing it. "Like, seriously, you had them in the palm of your hand. You were...magnetic."

"Couldn't have done it without you, you know that," Anthem said, sincerity threading through his words. "You kept me on the right track when I felt like I was going to fall apart." There was a raw honesty in his voice, and Indy's excited grin softened into a sincere one.

"Team effort," she replied quieter but no less vibrant. "You might be the one up there playing, but this? *This* is ours."

They shared a moment, a small private instant, just for them in the center of the swirling chaos around them, only for it to be interrupted seconds later by the clatter of falling microphone stands and someone's frantic shouts about missing cables.

"Guess you'd better get used to this," Indy smirked, jerking her thumb at the surrounding pandemonium. "Because something tells me your days of quiet shows are over."

"Bring it on," Anthem grinned, riding the high.

Just then, Anthem's smile faltered. Making his way through the commotion was Geddy, moving with a purpose and grace that seemed to part the sea of crew members around him. He had the same easy-going swagger he'd always had, but now it looked like he'd just stepped off a magazine cover.

Effortlessly cool, dressed in all-black from head to toe, save for a single gold necklace that laid flat on his chest. To Anthem, Geddy's presence felt like an omen, and whether good or bad, he was about to find out. As he approached, Anthem thought to himself, "First Buddy and Tatum, now Geddy...what is going on?"

"Anthem," Geddy greeted smoothly, carrying that old, familiar timbre. "Hell of a show. Seriously, you were on fire out there."

"Geddy," Anthem managed, a cold fury rising in his heart. "Didn't expect to run into you here."

"Neither did I," Geddy admitted with a sly grin. His eyes darted around the room and then back to Anthem. "But imagine my surprise to see you give such a killer performance."

Anthem felt a swirl of emotions and memories flooding back. "Yeah, well, you know...one monkey don't stop no show."

"You're so right and I'm glad our decision didn't derail your dreams," Geddy agreed, much to Anthem's surprise. "You've grown. Your music...it's grown."

"Couldn't have done it without a lot of help," Anthem replied, shooting a glance at Indy. With a steely gaze in her eyes, she gave Geddy a death stare, daring him to dismiss her role in Anthem's journey.

Geddy's gaze shifted to her, and he gave a respectful nod in return. "I can see that. You've got good people around you." He paused, then added, "Hi, Indy."

"Hi Geddy." Indy shot back begrudgingly.

"Well, you're doing a hell of a job," Geddy said sincerely. For a fleeting second, there was something almost nostalgic in his gaze, a glimpse of the old days before everything fell apart.

Then, just as quickly, the moment passed. His expression hardened. "But you know, Anthem... there's always a price."

Anthem narrowed his eyes. "A price for what?"

"For power," Geddy said simply, tilting his head. "For standing out. You think a performance like that goes unnoticed?" He chuckled softly, but there was no humor in it.

He leaned in just slightly, lowering his voice. "The CEA isn't blind, and they sure as hell aren't deaf. It won't be long before they start looking at you—*really* looking."

A thrill of recognition coursed through Anthem, followed almost immediately by unease. He had wanted this—had wanted to be heard, to be seen. But there was something unsettling in the way Geddy said it, like he already knew what came next. Like he'd seen it happen before.

"I know," Anthem said coolly, forcing himself to meet Geddy's gaze. "But I'm not afraid of them."

"And you shouldn't be," Geddy agreed. "But you should be *ready*." He exhaled, shaking his head. "You're making waves, man. You're going to need to decide—are you going to ride them out? Or are you going to get swallowed whole?"

Anthem studied him for a long moment before finally offering a slow nod. "I'll keep that in mind."

Geddy returned the nod, then lifted a hand in a casual mock toast. "Good luck, Anthem," he said, turning to disappear into the shifting crowd. "You're gonna need it."

Anthem watched him go, his words settling deep, a nagging weight pressing into the back of his mind.

Indy finally exhaled beside him, breaking the tension. "Well," she drawled, arms crossed. "That was... cryptic."

Anthem let out a breath, rolling his shoulders like he could shake off the encounter. "Yeah," he muttered. "You could say that again."

Indy studied his face. "Do you think his warning is believable?"

Anthem met her gaze, his stomach tightening with uncertainty. "Maybe."

Indy frowned. "You trust him?"

Anthem let out a dry chuckle, shaking his head. "Of course," he admitted. "Recent events between us aside, it's Geddy. I have no reason not to."

A thoughtful expression crossed Indy's face. "Guess we'll have to wait and see."

Indy's jacket buzzed. She stiffened, fishing out her phone. Her brows pulled together instantly. "It's Vale," she said, already stepping a few paces away to answer. "Yeah?"

Anthem watched her expression sharpen as she listened.

"Now?" she asked. A pause. Then, "Yeah. Got it. We're on our way."

She ended the call and turned back to him, already moving toward the exit. "We've gotta go. Vale wants us back at the Studio. Immediately."

"What happened?"

"They cracked something from the data we pulled off MV's party servers," she said, her voice tense. "Vale said little, just that it's important and we need to see it in person."

Anthem was already following her, weaving through the murmuring crowd, his earlier conversation with Geddy already forgotten.

The doors opened with a heavy groan as Anthem and Indy stepped into the underground briefing room. "You're just in time," Vale said as they approached. "The remote connection we had into MV's system—it's gone. Terminated."

Anthem's pulse ticked upward. "So we lost the feed?"

"Yeah," Vale replied. "But not before we pulled something."

He tapped a control panel, and the central display lit up with a file directory. The heading read: Unity Music Festival—Final Lineup [Encrypted Packet Series 9]. He opened the file. Names cascaded down the screen—dozens of them.

Each one was tagged with a photo. Last known location. Status: *missing, apprehended, unconfirmed, deceased.*

Anthem's heart sank. Some Sound Weavers, some Independent Artists, all gone.

But then his breath caught. There, near the bottom of the list—he recognized names:

Tatum Monk

Sienna "Bliss" Morgan

Buddy Wilde

His fingers curled into fists, knuckles blanching. "No." The word escaped his lips of its own volition.

Vale glanced at him, his expression softening just slightly. "I'm sorry, Anthem. We checked it twice. It's real. They're on the bill."

Anthem's chest tightened. His mouth went dry as his gaze locked onto the screen. The names blurred, but Geddy's absence burned like a hole in the list. "I need to check something," he said, stepping back and fumbling for his phone.

Indy watched him, silent but alert.

He pulled up Geddy's contact, thumb hovering over the call button for only a second before he hit it.

Ring...

It didn't even finish the first cycle. Straight to voicemail.

You've reached Geddy Slate. If this is about a gig—

He ended the call before it finished. Tried again.

Straight to voicemail.

Again.

Same result.

"No, no, no..." Anthem said. His hands clenched around the phone. "Come on, Geddy. Pick up. Say something."

He glanced at Indy, who looked back with worry blooming across her face. "Anthem…"

He shook his head, already dialing again. The screen lit up with *Call Failed*. Anthem's grip slackened, and his arm dropped to his side. "But we literally just saw him, what, twenty minutes ago? They must have grabbed him while he was leaving the Obsidian Key?"

Indy stepped forward, her voice tight. "This isn't a festival. It's a showcase. MV's putting them on stage for a reason."

"A performance," Vale added. "Or a warning. And he wants the entire world to see it."

Anthem stared at the screen, the names blurring as fury built in his chest. "He's going to parade them out like trophies."

Vale gave a grim nod. "Or examples."

Indy's jaw clenched. "We can't let that happen."

"We won't," Vale said. "But now we know the timeline. The Unity Music Festival will stream live to every major public network two weeks from now. Whatever MV's planning, it ends there."

CHAPTER XXIV

Anthem sat at a public bar, waiting for a lead that he had been briefed could have potentially valuable information: Mellow, a marketing specialist who had once designed campaigns for MV. The bar was subdued, the quiet murmur of conversation mixed with the soft clinks of glasses and government sanctioned music playing in the background.

Many minutes passed and Anthem's eyes occasionally flicked to the television behind the bar. As the latest car commercial faded out, the screen shifted to the evening news, catching Anthem's attention with its sudden change in tone. The news anchor appeared; her expression was somber. Closed captions at the bottom of the screen scrolled down as she spoke.

"Good evening. Our top story tonight: the Creative Engagement Authority has conducted a series of high-profile raids across the city," the anchor reported, her voice steady but grave. "These raids targeted the homes of individuals suspected of violating national compliance laws, particularly those related to the creation of unauthorized art and music and unregistered Independent Artists."

The screen cut to footage of CEA officers in tactical gear, moving swiftly into suburban homes, their actions precise and deliberate. Images of distraught families watching their homes being searched, their faces showing confusion and fear, interspersed the scenes, recalling the raid on The Echo Chamber.

"The CEA states these actions are necessary to maintain public safety and order and to ensure proper regulation of all creativity and artists' capabilities," the anchor continued. "However, these raids have sparked significant controversy, with critics arguing that they infringe on personal freedoms and privacy."

As the report showed a CEA spokesperson defending the raids, asserting their legality and the need for strict compliance, Anthem felt a growing discomfort. The implications were clear: the government was becoming increasingly hostile to anyone operating outside the sanctioned norms, especially Sound Weavers like himself.

The news segment faded out, the anchor's voice promising more updates as the situation unfolded. Anthem barely noticed. His mind was still tangled in the implications of what he'd just heard. The ever-growing reach of the CEA was expanding. He exhaled sharply, running a hand through his hair. *How much longer before they tighten their grip even further?*

The screen faded to black for a breathless moment. Then a vibrant swell of orchestral music kicked in, almost violently cheerful after the grim tone of the previous report. Anthem flinched at the shift.

A bright graphic bloomed across the screen—golden hues, gentle flourishes of musical notes spiraling around a rotating logo: The Unity Music Festival.

"In times of discord, we turn to harmony."

The voiceover was warm, authoritative, and oddly soothing. A woman's voice, confident and practiced.

"This year, the Creative Engagement Authority proudly presents the Unity Music Festival—a national celebration of healing, togetherness, and renewal."

Anthem stiffened.

Footage rolled of sweeping crowds, smiling faces, synchronized dancing in the streets—pre-recorded, heavily curated moments designed to sell a single truth: that peace was not only possible, but already here.

"Join Maestro Virtuoso, along with a diverse lineup of state-approved performers, for a one-of-a-kind musical event."

MV's face appeared—glowing, heroic, pristine. He stood on a rooftop overlooking the city, his arms spread wide like a conductor greeting his orchestra. His voice layered over the music.

"This isn't just a festival. It's a declaration. That we are stronger when we sing together—and that true harmony can only be achieved when we silence the noise of fear."

The footage shifted to slow motion shots of Wave Reavers performing on stage, their coordinated movements rhythmic and precise. They didn't look like artists. They looked like a choreographed military unit wrapped in show lights and applause.

"Unity is not about uniformity," MV said. "It's about knowing your part and playing it... in tune with the world."

Anthem's fists clenched.

The camera panned to the crowd—cheering citizens, swaying children, flags bearing the Council's insignia waving high. Then the last image: a glowing marquee with the festival's name etched in gold, surrounded by floating musical holograms.

"The Unity Music Festival—*Broadcast live across all public channels. One sound. One people. One future.*"

The music cut.

The screen went black.

Anthem sat in stunned silence.

He wasn't sure what disturbed him more—the thinly veiled propaganda masquerading as art, or the sheer effectiveness of it. If he hadn't known better, he might have believed it.

He didn't notice Mellow slide into the seat beside him until the familiar voice cut through his thoughts.

"Traffic was a nightmare," Mellow said, taking a slow sip of his drink. His gaze flicked to Anthem, sharp and searching. "You alright?"

Anthem blinked, shaking his head slightly as he refocused. "Just caught the end of a news report. The CEA's stepping things up." He nodded toward the television, where the station had moved on to another segment. "Makes you wonder how thin the line is these days between order and oppression."

Mellow sighed, setting his cup down with a quiet *clink*. "It's getting scary out there."

There was an edge to his voice, a weight beneath the words that Anthem didn't miss. Before he could ask, Mellow shifted gears. "Anyway, what did you want to talk about? Something about MV, right?" His tone was casual, but his gaze was anything but.

Anthem nodded, forcing himself to push his concerns aside. "Yeah. Especially—"

"Look man. I don't know how you found out about it, but I gotta say, I'm impressed." Mellow interrupted.

Anthem blinked.

Mellow let out a short laugh, shaking his head. "Come on, man, no need to play dumb. If you're sniffing around, you already know more than most. But, uh..." He glanced around before lowering his voice. "Look, I don't have all the details yet, but the way they're setting this up? It's gonna be *huge*. Bigger than any gig we've ever seen. Raw, unfiltered talent going head-to-head. Winner gets more than just bragging rights, if you catch my drift."

Anthem leaned forward, intrigued despite himself. "And who exactly is 'they'?"

Mellow grinned. "Now *that's* the real question, isn't it?" He shot Anthem a knowing look. "Some people don't like the direction the CEA is taking things. Maybe this is their way of fighting back."

Anthem's frown deepened. "The CEA? What do they have to do with—"

Mellow's expression froze. Slowly, his grin faded.

"...Wait." His eyes narrowed. "You *weren't* here to talk about the Battle of the Bands, were you?"

Anthem shook his head. "Nope."

Mellow groaned, rubbing his temples. "Dammit. I said too much. What was it you wanted to talk about?"

Anthem hid a grin. "What can you tell me about the Unity Music Festival?"

"Right," Mellow said, cracking his knuckles one at a time. "Okay. Look—I came across it by accident. Was freelancing some low-level branding revisions for a CEA-adjacent entertainment firm, cleaning metadata off old asset files. I found a series of hidden entries marked U.M.F.—Unity Music Festival. No campaign slogans, no target audiences. Just logistics. Stage schematics. Travel permissions. Suppression tech requisitions."

Anthem's brow furrowed. "Suppression tech?"

Mellow nodded grimly. "The kind they don't use for crowd control. This stuff was military-grade harmonic dampening. Not for show. For containment."

He glanced around, then lowered his voice. "It's a trap, man. I don't know the whole layout, but I know bait when I see it. They're building this thing up as some grand national gesture—music, healing, unity... but underneath it all, it reeks."

Anthem leaned back in his seat, his pulse quickening. His mind flashed back to the lineup they'd recovered from MV's penthouse. A trap...it was starting to make sense.

Before Anthem could probe for more details, the bar's door flew open, and a squad of CEA Silencers stormed in. The room instantly fell into stunned silence. Anthem's pulse quickened as the Silencers searched through the bar. One turned to face him and froze for a moment. Even through their faceless helmets, the Silencer's body language conveyed recognition and Anthem cursed.

"Anthem Fox," a different one barked, yanking him out of his seat by the arm. "You're coming with us."

CHAPTER XXV

P atrons froze, their faces flashing with shock and fear as the scene unfolded. The capture happened so fast it barely felt real—one moment Anthem was standing there, the next he was being hauled toward the door, his boots scraping uselessly against the floor.

They dragged him into the night before he could even think, let alone resist. Panic flared—he needed a plan, now.

But the second they shoved him into the back of a waiting van and the city lights began slipping away into the shadows, Anthem knew this wasn't a ride to any prison.

The van screeched to a halt outside a drab, featureless building—a place so ordinary it was invisible, the kind of structure people passed without ever seeing.

A Silencer ripped the door open and yanked him out.

The heavy steel door ahead groaned open. And as Anthem stumbled inside, the noise of the outside world cut off sharply, swallowed by the stark, blinding brightness beyond.

MV didn't even look up at first. He idly shuffled a stack of papers, as if Anthem's capture were no more exciting than rearranging his desk. "Welcome, Anthem," MV said with false hospitality. "I've been expecting you." Sitting behind a polished wooden desk, MV radiated an unsettling calm, his presence dominating the room. "The infamous independent artist. I've heard quite a bit about you. You also broke into my office and crashed my party, if I'm not mistaken."

Anthem said nothing. He wouldn't give him the satisfaction. Wouldn't let the crack show—no matter how loud the fear clawed at his ribs.

"Oh, spare me the silent defiance," MV said, locking eyes with Anthem. His lips twisted into a thin sneer. "The CEA has taken quite an interest in you. But luckily for you, I pulled a few strings. The CEA so graciously allowed me to use one of their black sites. If I hadn't, you'd be rotting in a much less... pleasant place right now." His voice dropped, almost playful, cruel amusement flickering in his eyes. "You should thank me."

Anthem's blood boiled. He took a step forward, eyes blazing. "I don't need favors from you, MV. And I'm not playing your twisted games."

With a slow, deliberate grace, MV rose from his chair like a predator sizing up prey. He circled the desk, hands clasped behind his back, his voice a velvet whisper lined with menace. "You really don't understand the situation you're in, do you?" He stopped inches from Anthem, his gaze drilling into him. "The CEA would love nothing more than to lock you away for good. You're not just some renegade artist anymore. You're a target. And without me? You won't last long. They'll come for you, Anthem. But there is another option..."

Anthem's suspicion flared, and he narrowed his eyes. "What are you getting at?"

MV leaned in, his voice a dark, silky promise. "Join me." His words hung in the air, thick with temptation. "You've barely scratched the surface of your abilities. With my guidance, you could become something far greater than you ever imagined. You could be... unstoppable."

Anthem scoffed, stepping back with a defiant glare. "You think I'd ever side with you? You're nothing but a power-hungry murderer."

For the first time, MV's smile faded. His eyes darkened, cold and calculating. "You think you're special? Just because you can strum a few chords and make the lights flicker?" His voice dropped, venomous and sharp. "You're naïve. The world doesn't care about talent unless you can wield it like a weapon. And that's what I'm offering. Real power. Real control."

Anthem's fists clenched at his sides. "Control for what?" he said, his voice rising. "So, you can destroy everything that doesn't fit your perfect tiny vision of the world?"

"No, you sound like those imbeciles in the community." MV replied, his voice now a low, dangerous growl. He took another step closer until Anthem could feel the ice in his words. "Control to reshape it."

For a moment, the room was deathly silent, the air between them charged with a white-hot tension. Anthem's breath came fast, his chest tight with anger. He knew what MV was capable of. Knew that with the CEA watching his every move, this wasn't just a threat—it was a calculated trap.

"You think you can scare me into siding with you?" Anthem asked defiantly, despite the fear in his bones. "I don't need your help. I'll figure this out on my own."

A slow, chilling smile spread across MV's face, as if he'd been expecting those exact words. "So full of pride," he said, a distant gleam of satisfaction in his eyes. With a nonchalant wave, he gestured toward the guards stationed at the door. "Put him with the others. We'll see if a little... persuasion changes his mind."

Anthem's heart raced as the guards grabbed his arms, their grip unyielding as they hauled him toward the door. His mind whirled with a mix of fear and fury, not for his own sake, but for Indy and the mission. He couldn't afford to be captured now, not with everything he had to lose.

The cold, sterile hallway stretched out before them, lit by harsh fluorescent lights overhead. Anthem's boots squeaked against the linoleum floor as the guards dragged him forward, their grips like steel vices. They stopped in front of a thick, reinforced door with no markings—only a solid red light overhead. A loud buzz echoed as it unlocked, and the door slid open with a hiss. The guards shoved him inside without ceremony.

Anthem stumbled into the dimly lit cell. It was sterile, silent, and suffocating in its design—an oblong box of reinforced concrete and dull silver plating, engineered more for psychological pressure than comfort. A single overhead light buzzed faintly, casting a sickly green light that failed to reach the corners, leaving shadows to fester like mildew in the seams. No clocks, no sounds beyond distant footsteps and the occasional echo of someone screaming.

There were no beds, only low, hard platforms built into the walls, lined with thin mats that felt more like industrial padding than anything meant for rest. The air was chilly, filtered and recirculated, and carried the faintest trace of antiseptic.

But the worst part—the most haunting element—was the window.

Set into the far wall, a large, reinforced pane of observation glass overlooked an adjacent room. At first glance, it might have passed for a medical chamber: gleaming floors, clinical lighting, stainless steel tables. But a closer look told another story.

The room was a study in cold, calculated horror—surgical in design, sadistic in execution. Its walls were lined with matte-gray soundproofing panels, stained with faint splatters no amount of sterilization could completely scrub away. Dried, copper-colored specks clung stubbornly to the lower corners like bruises that refused to fade. Floor drains marked the corners of the room and another in the middle of the room.

The main interrogation chair stood in the center like a throne of suffering—bolted steel with leather restraints that had long since lost their softness. Straps lined the arms, chest, legs, and even the throat. Their edges were frayed, crusted in places with something dark that had dried into the threads.

Nearby, a tall, wheeled tray held instruments—needles of varying gauges, contact probes with blackened tips, and scalpels that gleamed under the surgical light hanging overhead. A rack of audio torture tools stood to the left; cables curled like serpents. Frequency modulators, pitch enhancers, a sub-harmonic disruptor built into a helmet-like cage. It looked almost absurd—until you imagined it fitted to a human head, flooding their skull with waves of nauseating resonance until their eardrums bled. Most people never survive it with their minds intact.

The floor was tiled, streaked and scuffed from years of dragging feet and struggling bodies. In the far corner sat a small drain-fed basin, stained with rust, accompanied by a crusted sponge and a stack of course, blood streaked towels that had never truly been clean.

There were no cameras and no guards in sight.

A voice broke through the quiet like a match striking in the dark.

"First time seeing the butcher's box?"

Anthem blinked, flinching slightly as the voice pulled him from the tunnel vision that had locked him in place. He hadn't even heard the rustle of movement behind him. His eyes were still fixed on the torture room beyond the glass, but now he noticed the faint reflection of someone standing beside him.

The woman had ink-stained fingers, and a mess of paint-speckled dreads tied back in a low, haphazard knot. She leaned against the cell wall with her arms crossed, watching the torture room with a blank expression that somehow made the whole thing more unnerving.

"Takes a minute, doesn't it?" she said, not unkindly. "They make us watch."

Anthem turned to fully face her. "They actually use that?" he asked, his voice low, his throat tight.

"They don't build rooms like that for decoration," she replied. "And you don't bring out the instruments unless you're planning a concert."

Anthem's stomach churned. He took a step back and finally took in the others.

"The name's Isa, but I go by my graffiti tag, Spectra. Welcome to the cage, Rockstar," the graffiti artist said, pushing off the wall and walking back toward the bench where she'd been sketching something on the side of her boot with a dull nail. "Try not to stare too long. That room eats people."

"Name's Quinn. You might know me as Null. Or, uh, Public Enemy #3, depending on who you ask," said the tall and wiry man with long dark hair.

Anthem didn't respond, still cataloging the room. A woman near the back gave Null a look before standing. She stepped forward with quiet authority, her eyes scanning Anthem like a file she was updating in her head.

"Marisol Chen," she said. "Journalist. Or I was. Most people just call me Mari. I wrote the piece that exposed the CEA experiments in one of their private prisons."

A deep chuckle rolled from the corner where a broad-shouldered man sat against the wall, arms crossed.

"Didn't help much," he rumbled. "They just moved their experiments to another prison, and they still caught her."

He pushed himself up, stepping into the light. Scars across his knuckles, and a military calm that screamed "former operative."

"Desmond Rourke. Breaker, if you want to be informal. I submitted my resignation from the CEA to my supervisor by way of a high-power round through his skull. Been here ever since."

Anthem nodded, still silent, still measuring them.

"I'm Anthem—" The heavy door on the other side of the window groaned open, cutting Anthem off.

Two guards dragged a bruised, bloodied man into the chamber. MV followed behind, immaculate in his tailored uniform, dark hair slicked back, gloves pristine. MV didn't speak to the man shackled to the chair. He didn't ask questions. He simply began his grim task.

Surveying the tools available, he settled on a scalpel. Then a torch lighter. Then something electrical. The others looked away.

But MV didn't want the others.

He wanted Anthem.

With deliberate pacing, he walked toward the glass, locking eyes with him. Then he smiled. Cold. Delighted.

Anthem tried to look away.

"Don't you dare," MV shouted, banging on the glass.

Anthem held for another second.

Two.

Three.

Then turned his face toward the wall.

The screams didn't stop.

MV's voice came over the intercom, smooth as silk:

"Aw, come now, Anthem."

"Where's that fire? That fury? Or are you only brave when your audience is cheering?"

"You want to change the world? You can't even watch it bleed."

Satisfied, MV and the guards exited the room, leaving the man there for the others to watch as he slowly bled to death. Anthem stared at the wall long after the intercom clicked off. The screams had stopped. But the silence was louder.

Something had shifted.

His breathing slowed. Focus sharpened. Not rage—purpose.

He turned back to the group. They were each tucked into corners again. But they were watching him now. Measuring. Waiting.

Anthem's voice came low but firm.

"How do we get out of here?"

That got their attention.

Null leaned forward first, fingers steepled. "We've got fragments of a plan. Security loops, signal blind spots, patterns in the guards' rotations. Problem is, there are too many variables. Too many ways it can go wrong."

"Wrong means dead," Desmond added flatly. "Or worse. You've seen what they do when they don't even want answers."

Anthem didn't flinch. "Then we don't get this wrong."

Marisol tilted her head, eyes narrowing, taking a moment to study him. "What changed?"

"I did," Anthem said. No bravado. Just truth.

Spectra gave a short, bitter laugh. "You sound like every prisoner before they try something dumb."

"Maybe," Anthem replied. "But none of them were me."

That gave her pause.

Marisol looked at Desmond. "You still know the lower levels? Utility routes, sub-grid pathways?"

"If they haven't changed the core layout," he confirmed. "And I've got two access codes left that might still open a few doors."

"That's a lot of 'ifs'," Isa said.

"Let's not concern ourselves with 'ifs'," Anthem said.

"A man of action. I like your style." Desmond said, crouching in the far corner of the cell. He stood slowly, deliberately, walking to the center of the cell like it was a war room. "We don't have tools. We don't have weapons. But we've got the schedule." Everyone's attention fully snapped to him. "Sanitation cycle hits at 0300," he said. "They clean the cells from the outside—vents cycle air, bots scrub surfaces. That's our opening."

Isa arched a brow. "You planning to choke the bot with your winning personality?"

Desmond didn't flinch. "The system runs a pre-scan ten to fifteen minutes before the cycle. If there's an obstruction in a vent—something blocking airflow—it flags it. It won't skip it. Doesn't trust the bots to fix it. So, it sends a human."

"A guard?" Mari asked.

"Sometimes. More often, a maintenance tech with a wrench and a short fuse. But someone has to open the door to let them in." He looked around at them all. "That's all we need."

Anthem leaned forward. "So, we jam the vent, trip the alert, and wait."

Desmond nodded. "One guard stays in the hall. One comes in with the tech. If they follow routine, the inside man watches us while the tech fixes the vent. That's our window."

Null was already thinking ahead. "Best case, it's the two of them. Worst case—"

"They smell something off," Desmond finished. "And bring backup. That's why the strike has to be clean. Fast. No noise. We don't get a second chance."

A beat passed. Then Isa exhaled through her nose and stood. "Alright," she said. "Let's break something." She gripped the bottom of her sleeve and tore it with her teeth, then again with her hands, peeling off a strip of fabric. Another followed. She twisted them together roughly, walked to the vent, and crouched.

"Don't pack it too tight," Desmond warned. "You want to trip the alert, not snap the fan."

"I got it," she said, reaching into the vent and stuffing the cloth deep inside. "Little pressure. Just enough to say, 'this is broken,' not 'this is sabotage.'"

Anthem watched her work, quiet and still. He didn't blink. "Get ready," he said. "We have to make this count."

They waited.

No one spoke.

Then a faint mechanical alert chirped from the hallway. Followed by another.

Null looked up. "That's the pre-check failing."

Heavy boots echoed down the corridor.

"They're coming." Null whispered.

The group scattered into position. Isa crouched by the far corner. Desmond stood near the door, still and unreadable. Mari sat with her back against the wall, legs folded, hands out of sight. Anthem stood near the center, perfectly calm.

The door hissed open.

Two guards entered—one stepped just inside the cell, baton already in hand. The other remained in the hall. Between them, a maintenance tech clutched a small toolkit and looked like he wanted to be anywhere else.

"Against the wall. Now," barked the first guard.

They moved, slow but compliant. One by one, they dropped to their knees, backs to the far wall, fingers laced behind their heads.

The tech hesitated at the vent, frowning. "Yeah... blockage confirmed," he said. "System flagged it as a mechanical obstruction. I'll need a few minutes."

The guard inside the cell turned to acknowledge him, and that was enough.

Desmond moved.

A clean step. A turn of the hips. Then arms locked around the guard's throat from behind in a flash. No sound but a brief, strained grunt before the body sagged to the floor.

Mari lunged, catching the tech as he startled, holding a hand gently over his mouth.

"You don't scream," she whispered. "You don't die."

He nodded quickly, frozen in place.

Isa pounced, grabbing the downed guard's baton and access card in one fluid motion. She slid the card across the floor to Desmond without a word.

Null was already watching the hallway, eyes locked on the other guard.

"Three... two..."

Anthem was already moving.

He charged through the open doorway like a blast beat, slamming into the guard outside with full force. They crashed into the wall, Anthem delivering a quick chop into the man's only exposed area, his throat, before wrestling the baton from his grip. One sharp strike across the jaw dropped the guard. Anthem bent down, snatching the guards' key card and communication device. He pressed the comm to his ear, adjusting the frequency until he intercepted the static-laced chatter of the security network.

A camera blinked red above them.

An alert pinged.

Lights flickered.

Then came the klaxons.

Searing red spilled into the corridor. Sirens screamed. The sound of shouting voices and boots thundered from deeper within the block.

"MOVE!" Anthem shouted.

They did. At a junction, they split up.

Mari and Null veered left, sprinting toward the control room. Desmond and Isa turned right, slipping through a side door toward the utility corridor. Anthem bolted straight ahead—slamming doors open, kicking panels loose, creating noise wherever he went.

Anthem reached a T-junction. Guards shouted behind him. No time to think—he pivoted and sprinted down the corridor. From his stolen radio came MV's irate voice. "Seal every exit. Let the others run. I only want Anthem."

Anthem smiled at his MV's frustration, but that humor was short-lived as, to his horror, he skidded into a dead-end hallway. Having no other choice, he ran to the far wall and prepared for the fight of his life. Heavy footsteps and voices grew louder, closer. Then he saw it. A panel. Slightly crooked because of missing screws. Not luck. Neglect. This place was falling apart. Must be hard to find good help for secret prisons.

It wouldn't take much to remove it. He jammed the tip of his liberated baton into the seam. The metal shrieked as it gave way. He winced. Too loud.

A shout rang out.

He yanked harder. The panel clanged loose, revealing a crawlspace just wide enough. He squeezed in, scraping his arm against protruding metal, and replaced the grate as best he could. Footsteps thundered past. One paused. A beam of light skimmed the corner...

Then moved on.

Anthem crawled forward, elbows grinding against the metal floor. The air was scorching and choked with dust. Pipes throbbed overhead, echoing with hollow clangs that made it feel like the tunnel was groaning in pain. The walls closed in the deeper he went; the ceiling brushing his back in places

The shaft twisted abruptly, dropping into a steep angle that forced him to slide. His shoulder scraped raw against a jagged bolt. He pressed on, pulse thudding in his ears. The tunnel grew narrower, a ribcage of rusted grates and snarled wiring hemming him in from all sides. Sweat stung his eyes. The only light came from a flickering glow ahead, just beyond the last bend.

There it was.

The maintenance corridor and hopefully the service lift.

Adrenaline surged through his veins as he kicked open another grate and stumbled into the dim corridor. He quickly ducked into shadows, avoiding the main path. His training with the Sound Weavers had prepared him for more than music; it had taught him stealth, how to move unseen when needed. He had to hurry; every second here was a second closer to whatever horror MV or the CEA had imagined.

Reaching the lift, he stepped in and slammed the button. As the cage rattled upward, he exhaled through clenched teeth. Finally, he reached an emergency exit, an imposing door marked with faded letters. Anthem swiped the stolen key card, holding his breath as he waited. For a moment, nothing happened. Then, with a soft beep, the door clicked open, revealing the cool, crisp night air beyond.

He stepped out into a darkened alley, the heavy door shutting behind him. Anthem paused, his breath visible in the cold air. He had done it. He was outside.

Without wasting another moment, he crouched low, his body tense as he moved swiftly through the narrow alleyways. Crucible City towered around him, its tall buildings cast jagged shadows for him to stick close to. The distant buzz of nightlife floated in the air, but it felt a world away from the dread gripping him. The CEA was relentless. They wouldn't give up easily.

He darted between the shadows, calculating each move. For a brief, fleeting moment, he thought he was free. He turned a corner, the sounds of the city masking his footsteps when he heard it.

The unmistakable clatter of boots. They'd spotted him.

"Stop! We have you surrounded!" a voice echoed through the night, cutting through the distant city sounds.

Without hesitation, he broke into a full sprint, his boots pounding against the pavement as he zigzagged through the narrow streets. The city, once a place of familiarity, now felt like a labyrinth of danger. He could feel the Silencers closing in, their heavy footsteps echoing behind him.

"Stop now, or we'll bring you down!" another voice yelled. Anthem didn't slow. He couldn't. There was too much at stake.

He burst out into a busy street, startling the pedestrians enjoying their evening strolls. Anthem wove through the crowd, his breath coming in ragged bursts as he moved like water through the masses. The Silencers weren't far behind. He could see them in the distance, their gray uniforms unmistakable against the neon-lit night.

Desperate, Anthem pushed deeper into the city, his breath ragged, pulse hammering in his ears. The hum of traffic, the muffled bass lines from nearby bars, and the fragmented chatter of people on the sidewalks all blurred into white noise as he ran.

Anthem spotted a construction site up ahead and bolted toward it. The scaffolding rattled as he leaped onto a pile of discarded sheet metal and kicked it over behind him. The crash echoed like a cymbal—loud enough to make the Silencers flinch, giving him just enough of a lead.

He spun, his boots skidding over slick concrete, and ducked back into a narrow side street. The flickering neon signs above threw mismatched colors across the walls, casting the world in flashes of blue, red, and green.

He tore past a stack of trash bins, shouldering one over with a crash to slow his pursuers. The sudden noise startled a couple nearby, but Anthem barely registered them—his mind was too focused, too wired.

At the next turn, he skidded around a corner—and ran straight into another Silencer.

The enforcer lunged.

Anthem reacted purely on instinct. He dropped low, grabbing a loose trash bin lid from the ground, and swung it up like a shield. It collided with the center of the Silencer's facemask with a hollow *clang*, sending him stumbling back into the wall with a grunt.

Anthem didn't wait to see if the Silencer stayed down. He could still hear the others shouting behind him, closer now. His legs burned from the effort, his lungs screamed for air, but he pressed on, knowing this could be his only chance. His pulse quickened as he spotted a figure ahead. For a split second, panic surged through him. Was it another Silencer? No, this was someone else. Ragged clothes, a crazed look in their eyes, like someone who had seen the underside of the world.

The stranger motioned for Anthem to run towards him, his gesture frantic but silent. Without thinking, Anthem darted toward them, trusting his instincts. The stranger, a homeless sympathizer, nodded quickly, pulling back a tattered sheet draped over a stack of crates, revealing a hiding spot beneath.

Anthem ducked under the cover, the space cramped and musty. He held his breath for multiple reasons, listening as the CEA agents stormed past the alley, their heavy boots pounding against the pavement.

"He couldn't have gone far!" a Silencer barked.

Their footsteps faded into the distance, frustration clear in their voices.

Only when the last echo of the Silencers vanished did the figure pull back the sheet, revealing Anthem's wide-eyed, breathless face.

"You're safe for now," the stranger said in a low, raspy voice. "But you'd better keep moving. They'll be back."

Anthem nodded, the stress in his body finally easing as he stepped out of the hiding spot. Gratitude and adrenaline flooded through him, but he knew it wasn't over. He had escaped—for now—but the CEA wouldn't stop hunting him.

"Thank you," Anthem said, glancing back down the alley. The stranger gave a small nod, disappearing back into the shadows as silently as he had appeared.

Anthem stepped into the night. He had to find Indy.

CHAPTER XXVI

After what felt like an eternity of weaving through Crucible City's maze of alleyways, avoiding the CEA's patrols and keeping to the shadows, Anthem finally approached one of the many hidden entrances to Sound Weaver Studios. His clothes were damp with sweat, the grime of the city's alleys clinging to him like a second skin. The night's intensity overwhelmed his mind; his muscles ached from running, and exhaustion wracked his body. As he slipped into the building, the familiar feeling of the studio's energy felt like a refuge, a sanctuary from the chaos outside.

Eventually, he found Indy in one of the lounge areas, casually reclining on a plush couch, her eyes glued to her laptop screen. When she looked up, her eyes widened slightly at the sight of him, her nose wrinkling slightly. "What happened to you? You look like hell," she said with a teasing grin. "And, uh, not gonna lie, you smell like a walking dumpster fire."

Anthem couldn't help but let out a tired laugh, shaking his head. "Hilarious. It's been a long night." He said, dismissing her comment.

She raised an eyebrow, leaning back in her chair. "Clearly. You smell like it's been a long week."

Ignoring her, he said, "We need to focus. The CEA nearly caught me tonight. It's getting bad, Indy. They know who I am. And MV, he was behind it. He pulled some strings to keep me from landing in a CEA cell."

The light humor quickly faded from Indy's face. She sat up straighter, her eyes widening even more with concern. "What? How did they find you? What happened?"

"The CEA got to me before I even realized what was happening. I barely got away." Anthem ran a hand through his grimy hair. "I'll explain everything, but we need to gather the team and get Vale up to speed. Can you do that for me while I grab a shower and try to wash off this entire ordeal? Meet me in the briefing room in thirty?"

Indy smirked, standing up and stretching. "Make it an hour. You smell like you've been living in the sewers."

Anthem chuckled and shook his head, pushing himself up off the couch. "Yeah, yeah, you're hilarious. I'll see you in an hour." As Indy disappeared down the hallway to gather the others, Anthem made his way toward his room.

Once under the warm spray of water, Anthem closed his eyes and attempted to get the tension in his body to release. But try as he might, his mind wouldn't allow it. It kept replaying the night's events and the narrow escape. Then realization dawned on him that terrified him—he couldn't go back to his apartment. The CEA knew who he was now, and there was no telling how close they'd be watching him.

There was no turning back now. His world had upended. He was a fugitive in his own city, and there was no telling what would come next. Drying off, he took a deep breath, steeling himself for the fight ahead. For the time being, Sound

Weaver Studios was now his home, and the people inside it were his allies. He had to trust that Vale, Indy, and the others would stand by him when the time came. Pulling on a fresh set of clothes, Anthem stepped out of the bathroom, his mind clearer, but still muddled with the reality of his situation.

Anthem's boots echoed softly as he made his way through the quiet halls of Sound Weaver Studios. By the time he reached the briefing room, the others were already there—Indy, Solstice, Vale, and a handful of the senior Sound Weavers seated around the central table. Indy gave him a subtle nod as he entered, and Vale motioned for him to speak.

Anthem didn't waste time.

"The Unity Music Festival," he began, voice low but steady, "it's a trap."

The words settled over the room like a thunderclap. Even those who had been leaning back in their seats suddenly sat upright.

Vale's jaw tightened, though he didn't look surprised. "Go on."

Anthem took a deep breath. "It's a staged event—designed to look like a peace offering. A public gesture of unity and healing. MV is organizing it with the Council's full backing. But what it really is... is a showcase. A lie. They're using our missing people—Sound Weavers, Indie Artists, people we care about—as *acts*. Some are alive. Some... maybe not. And the worst part?" He looked around the table, locking eyes with each of them. "They're putting them onstage to control the narrative. To show that we've been neutralized. That we've bent the knee."

Solstice cursed under his breath. Indy's fingers curled tightly against the edge of the table.

"And I think it's bait." Anthem said. "They want us to come. They *expect* us to come. This whole thing is one big loaded mousetrap."

Vale leaned forward, his expression unreadable. "We've suspected something was wrong for a while," he admitted. "Encrypted transmissions. Sudden disappearances. Disrupted comm lines. But this? This confirms it."

"So we cancel?" Indy asked, her voice tight.

"No," Vale said. "We go."

Anthem blinked. "What?"

"We *have* to go," Vale said, louder this time, addressing everyone in the room. "If they've got our people, this is our best shot to free them. This will be their one and likely only time away from a CEA prison—this is it. No matter how tight the trap is, it will be easier than breaking into one of their compounds."

He stood and turned toward the wall of screens. "We'll operate in cells. Infiltrate as attendees, stagehands, musicians—whatever gets us inside. Teams will be assigned to extraction, sabotage, and contingency. But the primary mission is the safe retrieval of the captives."

Indy stood too, arms crossed. "And if it all goes sideways?"

Vale turned to her. "Then we improvise. But we do *not* leave our people behind."

The planning began immediately.

CHAPTER XXVII

For his second show, Anthem found himself on the rooftop of a high-rise, the glittering city of Crucible City sprawled out beneath him like a sea of jewels. The air was cool and crisp, the perfect weather for a night show. A small crowd had gathered for the midnight concert, lit by the stark glow of the skyscraper's obstruction lighting. They stood in tight clusters, the murmur of conversation hushed with anticipation. Some leaned against the ledge, peering down at the twinkling world below, while others clutched drinks or were occupied by their phones, ready to capture whatever was about to unfold. The stars above were faint, lost in the light pollution of the city. Up there, the rooftop stretched into infinity, perched above Crucible City like a stage made for gods.

Anthem took his place at the center of it all, framed against the glittering backdrop of the city like a figure carved out of myth. His guitar, strapped across his body, shimmered with its own gentle power, ready to channel whatever magic he was about to unleash. He had a simple setup—just a guitar, amp, and a few speakers—but in the night air, even the smallest sound carried for blocks. He took a deep breath and as the clock struck midnight, his fingers strummed the first chord.[1]

---

1. Rooftop Set List Playlist

The sound was soft at first, a gentle ripple that stirred the silence. The notes echoed in the air, blending seamlessly with the distant sounds of the city below. Anthem's fingers moved with graceful precision, each strum deliberate, as though he wasn't just playing for the small crowd in front of him but for the entire city spread out beneath him. The surrounding air hummed in response, alight with a faint glow that flashed in time with his rhythm. At first, it was just a soft

aura, barely noticeable, but as the music deepened, so did the light, growing stronger, more vivid.

Indy watched from the edge of the rooftop; her eyes were wide as the glow took form. Small trails of light swirled around Anthem, as if the music were weaving a spell. The spectacle mesmerized the crowd. Their faces illuminated by the growing aura, they leaned forward, drawn into the spectacle like moths to a flame.

As the tempo shifted, the aura surrounding Anthem exploded into a dazzling spectrum of colors—vibrant blues, deep purples, fiery reds—each note sent a fresh wave of brilliance into the air. The lights didn't just trail around Anthem; they danced. Sparks leaped from his guitar and cascaded across the rooftop before falling over the edge of the building and transforming into ribbons of neon that weaved through the surrounding buildings. Anthem's eyes were closed, lost in the music, his entire being flowing into the strings beneath his fingers. The energy surged through him, a living, breathing force that wrapped itself around his audience and pulled them into his world. Each strum sent shockwaves of color rippling across the sky, that transformed the rooftop into a kaleidoscope of shifting hues.

The audience was enthralled. Some gasped aloud as the strands of light curled around them, brushing against their skin with a gentle caress, while others stood frozen in awe as the music filled their ears, hearts, and souls. The colors reflected in the windows of the towering buildings around them, turning the entire city into a canvas for Anthem's performance.

As the music reached its peak, the lights flared brighter, bolder, painting the night sky with their brilliance. To those watching, it was as if the stars had descended to become part of the performance. Anthem's fingers flew across the strings as his body moved with the rhythm. The lights surged out from him in every direction, intertwining with the steel and glass of the skyscrapers, wrapping Crucible City in a glowing embrace.

And then, as suddenly as it had begun, it faded. Anthem played the final chord, holding it in the air for a heartbeat longer, letting it linger like the memory of a dream. The glowing coils of light dimmed as they retreated into Anthem, leaving behind only the soft glow of the city's lights. The rooftop fell into a breathless silence while the energy dissipated, but the magic still hung in the air.

For a long moment, no one moved. Anthem's music held the audience suspended in a fragile space between reality and the world he had created. And then, as if on cue, they erupted into applause—cheers, whistles, and shouts of admiration rang out loudly over Crucible City. Anthem, exhausted but exhilarated, gave a small nod of acknowledgement as he soaked in the moment.

As the crowd dispersed, Anthem stood for a moment longer, gazing out over the glittering skyline. For that brief, extraordinary moment, he had not only played for Crucible City—he had become a part of it.

The cheers were still echoing in Anthem's ears as he and Indy made their way toward the staircase leading back into the building.

Indy nudged him playfully with her elbow. I told you you'd kill it.

Anthem smirked, adjusting the strap of his guitar case. "Yeah, yeah, let's just get back inside before someone reports me to the CEA for turning the skyline into a damn light show."

They were almost at the door when the heavy thud of boots on metal stairs made them both freeze. A moment later, three figures emerged from the stairwell, stepping onto the rooftop—Wave Reavers.

The one in the middle, tall with slicked-back hair and a silver chain glinting against his hoodie, was clearly the leader. He cocked his head, his sharp grin cutting through the dim light. "Well, well. We saw the pretty lights from the street. Thought we'd see what all the fuss was about," he drawled, his voice laced with a cocky tone. He glanced at Anthem, then at Indy. "Didn't expect a private show from exactly who we were looking for. And here we thought you were lying low. Not very subtle."

The second, a woman with a half-shaved head and tattoos that snaked down her neck, tilted her head at Anthem, eyes narrowing with amusement. "You put some serious juice in that performance, Fox. No wonder MV wants you found."

Anthem's stomach turned cold. "What did you just say?"

The Wave Reaver's smirk widened. He gestured vaguely to the city below. "Oh, you didn't know? MV's got us scouring the streets for you. Guess he didn't appreciate you turning down his *generous* offer. Took it kinda personally, actually. Now here you are, putting on rooftop concerts like you're untouchable."

Indy's eyes darkened. "And you're stupid enough to tell us that?"

The third, a blond-haired Wave Reaver, rolled his shoulders lazily. "Does it matter? Not like you're walking away from this chat, anyway."

The tall guy cracked his knuckles, distorting the air around his fists like water rippling before a storm. Nearby, the woman raised her hands, fingers twitching, sending unseen tremors dancing through the rooftop. She was tuning the entire structure like an instrument about to be played. A slow exhale escaped the blond one, and suddenly a sharp pressure filled the air—subtle, but dense, like an invisible weight pressing against Anthem's ribs.

Indy shot Anthem a look.

The look.

The "You got a plan?" look.

Anthem *did not* have a plan.

But he did have an idea. A reckless, stupid, beautifully bold idea.

He took a deep breath, straightened his shoulders, and raised his hands in surrender. Then he stepped slightly behind Indy, nudging her forward as if guiding her.

"MV wants me, huh?" Anthem said, voice cool and even. "Well, let's go. Come on. I don't need to keep looking over my shoulder for assholes like you. Take me to your boss right now."

Silence.

The Wave Reavers froze.

The sheer audacity of Anthem surrendering so easily was not something they had accounted for. It was so unexpected, so effortlessly confident, that for a few precious seconds, they simply stood there, blinking, watching as Anthem and Indy brushed past them and walked straight into the stairwell.

Anthem smirked.

The moment they stepped through the doorway, a thick, golden wall of energy surged up behind them, sealing the Wave Reavers off from the exit. The barrier glowed like the embers of a dying campfire.

Anthem turned back, grinning as the trio slammed into the wall, fists pounding uselessly against it. Their shouts of anger were muffled behind the vibrating energy field.

"Oops," Anthem called over his shoulder. "Looks like we'll have to reschedule."

He grabbed the stairwell door and slammed it shut, locking it behind them for good measure.

CHAPTER XXVIII

M are set the last show at The Moonlit Grove, an enchanting open-air venue nestled deep within a forest clearing, where towering trees stretched their ancient limbs toward the sky, cradling the stars in a canopy of leaves. It felt like the place had come out of a fairytale. The smell of pine and blooming jasmine hung thick in the air. The ground felt soft beneath their feet, carpeted with moss and fallen petals. As Anthem and Indy arrived, he felt a jolt of excitement mixed with respect. This place was magic waiting to happen.

Lanterns, strung high among the branches, bathed the grove in a dreamy, golden glow, casting shifting patterns of light and shadow that danced across the faces of those gathered. People sprawled on picnic blankets, snuggling in couples or huddling in small groups, sipping mulled wine and cider.

"Wow," Indy whispered, her breath curling in the cool night air as she took in the sight. "It's like we've stepped into another world."

Anthem nodded, his heart swelling. "Feels like the kind of place where anything could happen, doesn't it?"

He made his way to the simple wooden platform that served as a stage, surrounded by clusters of ferns and ivy, as if nature framed this moment. The stage was unadorned, but it didn't need to be—every branch, every leaf, every star above was already part of the performance. Anthem's fingers brushed across the strings of his guitar like a painter tracing the outline of a masterpiece.

He glanced at Indy one last time, catching her encouraging smile, and it anchored him. Taking a deep breath, he played and in a moment of serendipity the clouds parted, bathing Anthem in a column of moonlight that fell perfectly through the canopy.[1]

The first notes drifted into the air, light as mist, and the grove stirred, a low whisper rustling through the trees. Anthem's fingers glided across the strings, drawing out a melody that felt both like a lullaby and lament. The music wasn't just heard—it soaked into the ground, into the branches, into the breath between every heartbeat. It became the forest's pulse.

From the earth, thousands of tiny motes of light rose like fireflies waking from a long slumber. They shimmered with every chord, swirling into patterns that danced and broke apart, drawn to the music as if it were the only gravity they knew.

A gasp rippled through the crowd—but then silence, reverent and awestruck, as the lights spun around Anthem, sketching trails of blue and gold in the darkness.

The energy surged through him—stronger, wilder than ever—and Anthem surrendered to it completely. Fear, hope, regret, dreams: he wove them all into the song until it no longer belonged to him, but to everyone listening.

The motes thickened into ribbons of living light, coiling around the ancient branches overhead, turning the grove into a glowing cathedral. Colors burst

---

1. Moonlit Grove Set List Playlist

forth—prismatic, radiant—twisting through the crowd, wrapping them in the music, in each other, in the stars overhead.

Gasps of wonder rippled through the crowd as tiny motes of light rose into the air, lifting fallen leaves in a slow, swirling dance. The grove bloomed with magic—leaves spinning in a living vortex of sound, caught in a melody only Anthem could weave.

Children squealed with laughter, chasing the glowing orbs with outstretched hands. Couples leaned closer, pulled into the quiet awe threading through the night. Anthem played with them, not for them—tuning every note to the pulse of the crowd. He caught them all, threading them into a tapestry of sound and light that shimmered across the grove.

He caught Indy's smile through the whirl of motion—a wide, brilliant thing that punched straight through him. She stood swaying to the beat, her worries shed like a second skin, her hands carving lazy arcs through the air.

The final chords rang out, hanging in the air like a held breath.

For a moment, no one moved.

Then applause broke loose—hesitant at first, then swelling into a storm of cheers that filled the night.

From her place in the crowd, Indy clapped until her hands stung, pride swelling in her chest until she thought it might break her in two. Anthem caught her gaze as he stepped off the stage. He caught her eye, and they exchanged a look that needed no words. This performance had been an experience, a moment that felt almost sacred.

But before he could dwell on it, a small tug at his sleeve made him pause.

He looked down.

A little girl, no older than six, stood there, her brown eyes wide and shimmering in the glow of the lanterns. Her tiny hands gripped the edge of his jacket like she was afraid he might disappear if she let go.

Anthem kneeled instinctively, bringing himself to her level. "Hey there," he said, offering a warm smile. "You okay?"

The girl nodded, then hesitated, glancing at the open space where his performance had just taken place. "Did you make the lights?" she asked in a whisper, like she was sharing a secret only he could hear. "With your music?"

Anthem blinked, caught off guard. He glanced toward the stage, where the last remnants of golden motes still drifted lazily through the air before fading into the night.

He could tell her no. Tell her it was just some fancy trick, some cool visual effect. But he shook his head instead, his voice soft when he answered, "Sort of. It's just a part of the song."

The little girl's face broke into a beaming smile, one so pure and unfiltered that it sent an unexpected warmth surging through his chest.

"Then that means you're magic."

Anthem opened his mouth, unsure what to say, but before he could, the girl's mother approached, placing a gentle hand on her daughter's shoulder.

"Sorry, I hope she's not bothering you," the woman said with an apologetic smile. "She's just... mesmerized. We all are."

"She's not bothering me," Anthem assured, still processing the moment.

The woman glanced back toward the clearing, where people were still murmuring about what they had just witnessed, their voices full of something close to wonder. "Whatever it is you're doing... whatever this gift is—you're giving people hope."

Anthem felt the weight of her words settle deep in his bones.

Not just music. Not just a show.

Hope.

He had spent his entire life believing his music was meant to be a release, a way to express the things words couldn't. But this was something else. This wasn't just about making people feel something—it was about changing their lives.

And that scared him.

Because if music was this powerful... if *he* was this powerful...

What did that mean?

Anthem swallowed, glancing at the little girl's expectant expression, her belief in him unshaken, unquestioning.

He managed a soft chuckle, reaching out and ruffling her hair. "Well, if I'm magic," he said, "then that makes you part of the spell, huh?"

She giggled, nodding eagerly.

The mother gave Anthem a final, knowing smile before leading her daughter away. The little girl waved as they disappeared into the crowd, and Anthem still kneeled, watching them go.

He had little time to process the interaction before a small group had gathered around him, some hesitant, others eager, their eyes alight with something between admiration and awe. It took him a second to realize what was happening. Then came the first tentative voice:

"Anthem—can I get a picture?"

Another chimed in, overlapping the first:

"Dude, that was insane—I've never seen anything like that! Can you sign my notebook?"

"Man, I used to go to all of Manufacturing Eden's shows—I always knew you had something special!"

"Glad to see you're still making music. Honestly, you were always the best part of the band."

Anthem blinked, surprised. Autographs? Pictures? That had never been a *thing* for him before. Sure, he and the band had their die-hard fans back in the day, but this felt... different.

Indy nudged him with an amused smirk. "Well, you gonna leave them hanging, rockstar?"

Shaking off his initial shock, Anthem forced a grin and rubbed the back of his neck. "Uh, yeah—of course!"

He took the outstretched notepad, signing his name with quick, practiced strokes, then posed for a few impromptu photos. One guy, still breathless from the performance, shook his hand firmly.

"Man, I can't tell you how much it means that you're still out here making music. When word got out that Manufacturing Eden was no more, I thought we'd lost something great—but seeing you tonight? This? *This* was next level."

Anthem's chest tightened at that.

He had spent so much time concerned about Manufacturing Eden's implosion that he hadn't considered how many people had been missing him. Not waiting for him to fall. Waiting for him to *rise*.

"Thanks," he said, shaking the fan's hand. "That means a lot."

Another fan, a woman wearing a faded Manufacturing Eden t-shirt, stepped forward next. "I've been following your music since *Dead Air Revival.* I always thought you had the most soul in the band. It's good to see you stepping into your own."

Anthem let out a soft, breathless chuckle. "*Dead Air Revival?* Wow, that's a deep cut. That was one of our first live recordings." He remembered the late nights recording it in an abandoned warehouse, the echo, the sweat, the laughs. "And where did you get this shirt? I want one."

He took the pen from her, adding his signature to the sleeve of the worn-out shirt, feeling the moment cement itself into history.

The requests kept coming; the admiration pouring in waves, and Anthem did his best to give each person the attention they deserved—to show them that their belief in him wasn't misplaced.

As the surrounding crowd thinned, Anthem felt a light tap on his shoulder. He turned to see a young man, probably in his early twenties, standing a few feet away. He looked nervous, shifting from foot to foot, his hands gripping a battered notebook. His clothes were worn but clean, and there was a hesitance in his eyes, like he wasn't sure if he belonged in this moment.

Anthem offered him a small nod. "Hey, man. What's up?"

The fan took a deep breath, his fingers tightening around the notebook. "I—I don't want to take up too much of your time," he started, voice a little shaky. "I just... I needed to tell you something."

Anthem gestured for him to go ahead. "Take your time."

The young man swallowed hard, then exhaled. "A couple of years ago, I lost my mom. It was sudden. One day she was fine, and the next she was just... gone." He glanced down at the notebook in his hands before looking back up. "I didn't handle it well. I stopped going to school. I barely left my room. I didn't talk to anyone. It felt like the world had just—closed in."

Anthem's chest tightened. He knew that kind of pain. He knew what it was like to feel like the world had collapsed around you, leaving you buried under the weight of something too heavy to carry.

The fan continued, "One night, I was just lying in bed, staring at the ceiling, feeling like nothing mattered anymore. And then, I don't know why, but I hit play on one of your old songs—'City Lights Fade.'"

Anthem inhaled sharply.

"I listened to it over and over again," the young man said, his voice steadier now. "The way you sang about feeling lost, about trying to hold on to something real when everything feels like it's slipping away... it was the first time I felt like someone *got it*. Like I wasn't alone."

He looked Anthem in the eye then, his expression raw but grateful. "Your music got me through that. It gave me something to hold on to when I felt like I had nothing left. And I know I'm probably just another face in the crowd to you, but to me... your music mattered. It saved me."

For a moment, Anthem didn't know what to say. The weight of those words settled into his bones, heavy and humbling. He had spent so much time running, doubting himself, wondering if what he was doing even *mattered.*

But here, standing in front of him, was proof that it did.

"You're not just another face in the crowd," Anthem finally said, his voice quieter but firm. "And I don't think I'll ever forget what you just told me. In fact, only Manufacturing Eden knows this...but I lost my parents too. I wrote that song at one of my lowest points. I had really been missing them and I felt like nothing was certain, like the world was moving on without me."

The young man let out a shaky gasp at their shared connection.

Anthem reached out, gripping his shoulder. "I'm glad you're still here."

The fan smiled, genuinely. "Me too."

Anthem took the notebook from his hands and flipped to a blank page. He didn't just sign his name—he wrote a message, something personal, something real.

For the nights that feel impossible—keep going. The world is better with you in it.

He handed it back, and the young man looked down at the words, his fingers brushing over them like they were something fragile and precious.

"Thank you," he said.

Anthem smiled, but it wasn't just a performance smile, not the one he gave for pictures or polite conversation. It was real.

And as the fan walked away, disappearing into the night, Anthem realized something.

This—*this*—was why he played.

CHAPTER XXIX

The briefing room was darker than usual, dimmed not by power issues but by choice. The walls hummed with quiet energy, screens displaying a rotating series of maps, schematics, and surveillance footage. At the center of it all stood Vale, arms crossed, his gaze as sharp as the angular projections surrounding him.

Anthem, Indy, and Solstice entered side by side. Vale didn't waste time. He nodded as they approached. "We've locked in our strategy. Everyone's moving into position tonight."

A three-dimensional blueprint of the Unity Music Festival bloomed above the table: a massive, open-air venue with multiple stages, layered security zones, and thousands of expected attendees. In the center, a spire-like structure marked as the Council Broadcast Tower pulsed faintly.

"The broadcast goes live tomorrow night," Vale said, circling part of the hologram with a gesture. "Our window's tight. Anthem, Indy, Solstice—your objective is to infiltrate the lower compound beneath the main stage. That's where they're holding the captives. We've confirmed the presence of at least six Sound Weavers—maybe more."

Indy leaned over the table, examining the subterranean pathways lit in dull red beneath the stage. "How do we get down there?"

Vale tapped a section of the blueprint. "This service tunnel. It's restricted, but you'll have clearance badges, disguised as festival staff. We're feeding in identities tonight. Indy, you'll spoof the network from the outside using your uplink patch to keep their internal scans from flagging you. Once you're in, it's stealth only. If you get caught, we won't be able to pull you out."

Anthem stepped forward slightly. "What do we know about security? How tight are they locking down the inner ring?"

Vale met his gaze. "Tighter than we've ever seen. The perimeter's guarded by CEA Silencers. Internal checkpoints will be manned by Wave Reaver support units. Facial scans, random ID checks, and patrol rotations every fifteen minutes. It's built to be impenetrable—except for where we're slipping you through."

He brought up another layer on the display, highlighting several routes in yellow. "There are blind spots—small ones—where security coverage overlaps without full visibility. That's where you'll move. But if something goes wrong, you improvise and vanish. The CEA won't hesitate to turn the crowd against you if you're exposed."

Anthem nodded slowly, processing. "And if we're spotted before we reach the holding area?"

"You abort," Vale said flatly. "You get out. No heroics. We can't afford to lose anyone else."

"Next," Vale said, pulling up a list of coded phrases on the side display. "If comms go down, or anything goes sideways, these are how we keep coordination. Memorize them. There won't be time to second guess."

Solstice nodded once. "Got it."

Indy added, "We'll keep them close."

Anthem said nothing, but his jaw tightened in quiet focus.

Anthem nodded. "What about extraction?"

"Other teams will handle the distraction and cover your exit. They'll initiate a decoy fire drill in the north compound. That'll reroute crowd control and open an emergency corridor through the vendor lot. You'll exit there, blend with evacuees, and rendezvous at the safe house in District Six."

"Any intel on the captives' condition?" Solstice asked.

Vale's mouth tightened. "Some are confirmed as intact. Others... unknown. But they're alive. That much we're sure of. And they've been moved into uniforms, possibly drugged or sound-suppressed. You'll need to get them stable enough to move."

Anthem nodded, sealing it back up. "Understood."

For the next few minutes, Vale answered any lingering questions until he gave one last look at all three of them. "Go check your gear. Get sleep if you can. Tomorrow, the world gets a different kind of show."

Later, in their shared prep room, Anthem, Indy, and Solstice checked over their gear in silence. Micro comms. A collapsible grappling hook with magnetic anchors. Flash pulse grenades tucked into discreet pouches. Rations and a compact water purifier. A half-dozen disguises—hooded jackets, visors, festival lanyards—for when the captives needed to vanish into the crowd.

Indy hunched over a battered workbench, running diagnostics on the forged ID bands, her brow furrowed in concentration. Solstice leaned against the opposite wall, methodically checked the signal flares. Anthem sorted through the medical kits.

When the last checklist faded into silence, Anthem reached up and unclasped the leather cord around his neck. He rolled it between his fingers, feeling the figurine's edges, the tiny imperfections from a lifetime of movement and music. A piece of history he couldn't leave behind.

Crossing the room, Anthem picked up his new guitar from its stand. The strings caught the dim light, gleaming like steel wire strung across a battlefield. With steady hands, he tied the charm just below the headstock, letting it dangle above the frets, exactly where it belonged.

Indy glanced up. "You ready for this?"

Anthem paused, then gave a quick nod. "I am."

Then Indy reached into her bag and pulled out a compact, oblong device about the size and shape of a fanny pack. The surface was matte black with faint resonance lines etched along its casing.

"Here," she said, handing it to Anthem. "Something I've been tinkering with. It's a portable amplifier-speaker combo. You can strap it on, plug your guitar straight into it, and project your sound with no need for a full setup."

Anthem turned the device over in his hands, blinking. "You built this?"

"More like cobbled it together from scraps, but yeah. It should help you project farther than normal—especially in close quarters." She paused. "I haven't had time to test it, though, so... if it explodes, I call not it."

Anthem laughed softly, shaking his head. "You never stop surprising me."

"Well," she said, smirking, "it's not a legendary sword, but it should get the job done."

He met her eyes, his voice quieter. "Thank you. Really."

Solstice cleared his throat dramatically. "Not to ruin the moment, but... Indy, you got any gadgets for the rest of us, or is Anthem just the favorite?"

Indy rolled her eyes with a grin. "Sorry, Sol. You don't shred like he does."

The tension broke with shared laughter. For a moment, the looming weight of the mission lifted. They stood together—not just teammates, but a trio forged by rhythm, risk, and resilience.

That moment shattered as Vale appeared in the doorway, urgency written across his face. "Plans changed," he said without preamble. "MV is now headlining the closing act. That means more security. More surveillance. Expect heavy resistance near the stage."

The room fell silent. Indy exchanged a glance with Anthem, while Solstice's smirk faded into a grim line.

Vale continued. "That stage will be the most secure zone on-site. Proceed with caution. This complicates our timing—but it also means we're getting closer to the truth. We move as planned, but adjust on the fly."

Anthem gave a single nod. "Understood."

They returned to their prep, the ease of the moment gone. Then, as if struck by a sudden idea, Solstice snapped his fingers and turned on his heel. "Wait here. Don't move." Without another word, he jogged out of the room.

Anthem and Indy exchanged a puzzled glance, but said nothing. A few minutes passed in silence—just the soft rustle of gear being packed, straps tightened, checks re-checked.

When Solstice returned, he carried a small, slender bottle filled with clear liquid and three mismatched glasses stacked in one hand. He set them down with a soft clink and flashed a crooked grin. "Aetherglace spirits," he said with a grin. "Was saving it for something worthwhile. Think this counts." He uncorked it with a pop and poured three uneven measures.

They each took one. Indy raised hers first. "To tomorrow."

Solstice tipped his glass with a smirk. "To raising hell."

Anthem looked between them—his family, for better or worse—and lifted his own glass high. "To freedom."

The glasses met with a soft *chime* that rang louder than it should have in the quiet room. And for a moment, hope tasted sharper than the burn of the spirits.

CHAPTER
XXX

The day of the music festival dawned clear and bright, the early morning sun cast a golden glow over the sprawling festival grounds. The venue was a state-of-the-art open-air stadium on the outskirts of the city, transformed into a vibrant tableau of colorful banners, towering stages, and bustling vendor stalls. Everywhere Anthem looked, there were people busy at work setting up. Sound technicians efficiently erected the massive speaker systems. Vendors stationed at booths eagerly preparing for the waves of festival goers to arrive.

As the early-bird festival goers began trickling in, they embraced the event's spirit of freedom and self-expression, donning bold, vibrant outfits that were as much a part of the experience as the music itself. Some wore flowing, bohemian garments in rich jewel tones. Long skirts and billowy shirts paired with layered jewelry and hand-dyed scarves that fluttered in the light breeze. They adorned their hair with intricate braids, beads, and feathers, creating a look as fluid and free as the music they celebrated.

Others embraced a more futuristic style, their clothing a mix of neon colors and sleek metallics that shimmered in the sunlight. Some wore tight-fitting jumpsuits in electric blues, greens, and pinks, accented with glowing accessories, LED wristbands, fiber optic hair extensions, and sunglasses with holographic lenses.

Here and there, a few individuals opted for minimalistic attire, simple but stylish plain white shirts, vintage denim, and leather boots. Yet, even in their simplicity, these festival goers made a statement, choosing to let their body art do the talking. Tattoos of intricate symbols, geometric patterns, recognizable characters, and swirling constellations covered almost every inch of exposed skin.

Groups of friends wore coordinated outfits, bright, patterned outfits, a mix of florals, tie-dye, and geometric prints, each member complementing the others in a display of unity. Some wore matching flower crowns, while others painted their faces with glitter or marked them with tribal designs.

As Anthem moved through the growing crowd, he noticed a few costumed attendees—festival goers dressed as mythical creatures or cosmic beings, covered in shimmering body paint and dramatic makeup. Wings crafted from translucent fabric sparkled under the sunlight, while others sported headpieces made of crystals and elaborate masks. These festival goers seemed almost alien, walking through the grounds as if they had stepped out of a fever dream.

Despite the festive atmosphere, Anthem wasn't here for a good time. His eyes scanned the perimeter, picking up details others missed. Screens mounted to towers pulsed with swirling visuals—golden light, synchronized dancers, serene faces all moving in perfect rhythm. A clean-cut narrator's voice played on loop over ambient synth chords:

"Unity through harmony. Peace through purpose."

MV's face appeared next, larger than life, projected above the main gates like a deity watching his congregation. He wore a sharp, white suit embroidered with gold thread, smiling with practiced warmth as he walked through a mass-produced montage: shaking hands with children, conducting an orchestra, placing a hand over his heart.

"In a time of uncertainty, we choose structure."

"Faced with chaos, we choose balance."

"True unity must be *earned*—not given."

Beneath the screen, sleek banners swayed in the breeze along fences and railings. The Creative Engagement Authority's crest was stamped on everything: security checkpoints, vendor stalls, even the water bottles being passed around.

Anthem nudged Indy, nodding toward a security drone hovering overhead. Its camera lens gleamed as it scanned faces in the crowd.

"Facial tracking." He muttered. "They're not just watching—they're *cataloging*."

Indy followed his gaze and made a quiet, displeased sound in her throat. "This whole place feels contradictory."

Even the performers warming up on side stages wore uniform looks—flowing neutral tones, carefully choreographed movements. There was no rawness, no improvisation. Just curated "expression" under tight direction.

A group of young attendees near the east wing wore silver lanyards stamped with "Unity Guides"—CEA-sponsored volunteers trained to maintain crowd order, distribute flyers, and report "disruptions." They handed out pamphlets with smiling slogans like:

"Art belongs in safe hands."

"Protect our purity. Get licensed today."

Anthem crumpled one into his pocket without reading further. He could feel the bullshit hidden beneath the surface. The crowd didn't see it. Not yet.

As he and his fellow Sound Weavers made their way through the grounds, he had to remind himself of the responsibility that brought him there that day. The knowledge of what could unfold here dampened his usual enjoyment of such events. Anxiety drummed loudly in his heart, but a steely resolve kept it from completely taking over.

They dressed inconspicuously, blending in with the various crews and staff moving about. Carefully crafted prosthetics had been applied to their faces. They had more than enough run-ins with MV and the CEA to require some way to conceal their identities. Anthem's eyes swept over the venue, noting the key locations they had memorized during their planning: the main stage where the headlining acts would perform, the secondary stages for up-and-coming artists, and the central sound control booth.

Soon Anthem had reached their designated covert command post, a nondescript tent set up near the production area. Inside, monitors displayed feeds from cameras discreetly placed around the venue in areas where they suspected would be suitable areas of egress or where potential threats could originate from.

Anthem adjusted the strap on his guitar and leaned over the table to study the map. Beside him, Indy methodically checked their equipment. Solstice stood near the entrance, observing the monitors with his arms crossed, his stony eyes flicking between the screens, analyzing every pixel.

"Ready?" Indy's voice broke through his concentration.

Anthem nodded, meeting her gaze. "Ready as I'll ever be," he replied.

Indy gestured toward Solstice. "What about you? Got any of your time tricks ready if things go sideways?"

Solstice's lips twitched in what might have been a smirk. "I'm always ready. Question is, can you two keep up?"

Anthem rolled his eyes, muttering under his breath, "Always with the ego."

Solstice's smirk widened slightly. "Says the guy who thinks he can save the world with a power chord."

"Alright, boys," Indy interjected, holding up a hand to forestall further banter. "Focus. We've got a mission, remember?"

The first chords of live music drifted through the tent from a distant stage, a reminder of what they were there to protect. Anthem took a deep breath, trying to steady his nerves. With the Sound Weavers all gathered in the covert command post and the sound of the festival outside getting underway, the crowd blissfully unaware of the peril looming over them, everyone stood with bated breath as Vale called for attention. Despite the seemingly apocalyptic situation that gathered them under that tent, Vale's voice was powerful as he spoke.

"Today, we stand on the brink of a moment that will define not just our futures, but the future of the entire world," Vale's voice boomed in the close quarters. "We have been painted as villains, misunderstood, and feared for the gifts that should have made us heralds of progress and harmony. Today, that changes."

He paused, locking eyes with every single person as he let his words sink in. "This festival, a celebration of music and unity, is under threat because one of our own has forgotten what it means to be a Sound Weaver. MV has chosen fear and destruction as his instruments. But we choose courage. We choose to protect, to heal, to unite."

Passion leached into Vale's voice. "We know the challenge ahead. We know the dangers. But remember, we also know each other, and there is no team I trust more to handle this crisis. You have each been trained in the use of your powers and in the ethics that guide them. Today, your actions will speak louder than any words could. They will tell the true story of who we are."

He took a moment to look at each person again, this time with a softer expression. "Spread out, keep your communications open, and stay alert. Watch for any signs of MV, his associates, or any suspicious activity. Use your judgment, stay safe, and protect each other."

With one final nod of encouragement, Vale concluded, "Let's show them that our powers are not to be feared, but to be celebrated. Go now and may fortune favor us."

Bolstered by Vale's words, the team gave nods and murmurs of agreement. As they dispersed headed towards their designated areas, Anthem felt energized, Vale's rallying speech having done wonders for his morale. Stepping out from the tent, the juxtaposition of the music and cheers of the crowd that greeted them as they exited the tent was a stark contrast to the dark nature of their mission, yet a poignant reminder of what they were fighting to protect.

CHAPTER XXI

Anthem, Indy, and Solstice slipped out of the tent and began navigating the festival grounds in search of their objective. Anthem adjusted his hood and made sure his festival lanyard was secure around his neck. The forged badge clipped to it bore a false name and clearance level, printed to match the formatting used by the festival's operations crew. Beside him, Indy and Solstice wore similar maintenance tech uniforms, matching his own.

They kept an eye out for anything unusual, but with so much happening and so many distractions, it was an arduous task. The Unity Music Festival was a sensory overload of sights, sounds, and smells. Brightly colored tents and booths lined the pathways beneath towering banners emblazoned with the CEA's crest. Festival goers wandered through crowds where soft drones buzzed overhead, broadcasting curated playlists interrupted occasionally by propaganda messages.

Food vendors offered a dizzying array of culinary delights from around Musera. There were towering food trucks selling sizzling skewers of grilled meats, spicy street noodles, and hand-rolled sushi, alongside artisanal stalls offering gourmet pizzas baked in portable wood-fired ovens. Sweet treats, too, were everywhere—creamy gelato, freshly spun cotton candy in vibrant hues, and decadent pastries that wafted sugary aromas through the air. One stall even offered festival-exclusive confections: candies shaped like musical notes, each flavor inspired by different artists set to perform later that day.

Farther down, a row of interactive games attracted a growing crowd. Carnival-style booths enticed festival goers with challenges that ranged from the simple to the elaborate. There were ring toss games where winners earned branded Unity Music Festival pins and novelty flags, and high-striker machines where participants could test their strength by hammering a lever that sent a glowing ball rocketing toward a bell. In one corner, a digital rhythm game drew in large groups, who tapped to beats that synced with the live music. The game projected their performance onto a massive screen.

Merchandise stalls were everywhere, selling everything from official festival gear to handcrafted jewelry and clothing. T-shirts, jackets, and hats adorned with logos and the names of performing artists filled racks, while limited-edition vinyl records and posters lined the display walls—each stamped with a small, unobtrusive seal: "Certified by the Creative Engagement Authority." Some vendors offered personalized gear—festival goers could have their names embroidered on hats or create custom tie-dye shirts right on the spot. Indie artists and local craftspeople showcased their creations under the watchful eye of CEA-assigned booth monitors, selling everything from intricate handmade bracelets to glowing LED accessories, perfect for lighting up the night as the sun set.

What made this festival truly unique were the immersive experiences scattered throughout the grounds. At the heart of the festival was a giant interactive art installation—a towering sculpture made of old musical instruments visitors could touch, strike, or play, creating a cacophony of sounds. The installation symbolized the power of music and creativity, drawing crowds who took turns experimenting with the sounds they could make. A nearby area, the "Sound Lab," invited festival goers to take part in workshops where they could try out instruments or create their own beats using touch-sensitive walls that emitted sound when tapped.

Roaming performers added to the magic, walking through the crowd on stilts, dressed in elaborate costumes made of flowing fabric and lights. Some of these performers embodied characters from Musera's mythical past—ethereal beings representing the essence of sound—but even these figures wore sashes bearing the Council's insignia. Others played spontaneous acoustic sets or juggled glowing orbs, drawing small crowds that cheered and clapped, as auto-drones hovered just above, capturing the moments for official festival feeds.

Between all the activities scattered throughout the grounds were relaxation areas. Massive canopies shaded these quiet zones, filled with comfortable seating, hammocks, and oversized cushions where people could take a break from the excitement and soak in the atmosphere.

The music thumped around them, beats and melodies blending together from various stages, creating a potpourri of sound. Anthem, Indy, and Solstice moved carefully, scanning the crowd while doing their best to blend in. Solstice's eyes darted from one group of festival goers to the next, his body tense.

"Try to relax," Anthem muttered as he adjusted his event staff lanyard. "You're making people nervous."

"Noted," Solstice replied dryly.

"Yeah, play it cool. It's just another day at work. Nothing to see," Indy added.

Anthem fell into step beside Indy and Solstice as they rounded a corner. The festive glow from the central plaza dimmed behind them, swallowed by the shadows of stadium's corridors as they ventured towards their first test. Here, the banners didn't display smiling artists or colorful slogans.

Indy checked the map on her tablet, voice low. "Checkpoint Alpha is just ahead. We're approaching from the northeast utility path. Two guards. One scanner post."

Solstice's eyes scanned the area. "These badges had better work. I doubt they stand up too much scrutiny."

"We just need thirty seconds of doubt," Anthem murmured. "Long enough to walk through like we belong."

Anthem shifted the weight of the hard case slung across his shoulder. From the outside, it looked like a standard sub-audio calibration unit—gray panels, a fake cooling vent bolted to one side, and a battered inspection tag reading *Pre-Cleared: Tower One—Handle with Care.*Inside was no piece of tech—just his guitar, tucked beneath layers of forged credentials.

Indy adjusted the maintenance bag at her hip, a coil of fiberoptic cable peeking out of the side pouch for appearances. Solstice slung a duffel marked with faded hazard stripes, the outer layer packed with diagnostic readers and bundled cords.

They didn't need to look invisible.

They just needed to look boring.

The gate came into view. Two CEA officers manned a reinforced booth—one seated, bored, flipping through a tablet; the other alert, watching them approach. A drone hovered nearby, its optical sensor rotating to lock onto them.

Anthem's throat went dry. He didn't let it show.

Indy strode up first, her forged staff badge held at a slight angle for the drone to scan. "Level 4 Tech Services," she said evenly. "Rerouted from Sector Six. Cabling interference flagged a sub-audio fault."

Beep. **Green.**

The seated officer barely glanced up. The standing one gave her a once-over, then nodded.

Solstice stepped forward. His badge gleamed under the scanner's lens.

Beep. **Yellow.**

The drone let out a flat chirp and paused, the lens flaring red for a heartbeat before settling on amber.

The standing guard straightened. "Hold up."

Anthem froze mid-breath. Solstice kept his smirk in place, but his jaw twitched—just once.

The guard gestured to the tablet mounted on the booth wall. "Badge isn't confirming clearance."

"His badge was reprinted this morning." Indy said immediately, stepping forward. Calm. Controlled. "Tech glitch from Sector Six's scanner."

The guard narrowed his eyes and tapped through a few layers of clearance data. The silence stretched.

Finally—after what felt like a full measure of silence—the standing guard grunted. "Yeah. I see it."

He tapped the screen again. The yellow light on the drone blinked green.

Solstice gave a small, easy nod, then stepped through.

Anthem was last. He stepped forward and held out his badge. The drone scanned him with a soft electronic whine.

Beep. **Green.**

The standing guard furrowed his brow. "You with them?"

"Stage logistics," Anthem said smoothly. "Sub-audio load balancing. Special request from Tower One."

The seated officer finally stirred, tapping at his pad. After a beat, he nodded slowly. "Yeah, I saw something about that earlier. They're doing redundant sweeps tonight."

Another silence.

Then: "You're good. Go."

They moved through the checkpoint with practiced calm, boots echoing against the concrete floor. No one spoke until they'd turned two corners and left the checkpoint behind.

Solstice exhaled, tension leaking from his shoulders. "That drone glitched. Hard."

"I don't think it flagged us," Indy said, checking over her shoulder. "But that yellow flash? That'll sit in the system log. We've got a clock now."

The further they moved from the checkpoint, the more the festival's pulse faded behind them. The tunnel narrowed, the concrete floor clinking softly beneath their boots. They passed an empty break station—a steel bench bolted to the wall, a vending unit humming with nutrient bars and caffeine shots stamped with CEA seals.

Anthem glanced at the walls. Embedded into the smooth surfaces were sound-dampening panels that looked brand new and out of place. A gentle but constant pressure began building behind his eyes.

A low-frequency hum throbbed in the background—inaudible to most, but Anthem could feel it like a presence. His own internal rhythm was off. His thoughts didn't echo the way they normally did. Even breathing felt difficult.

Anthem watched Solstice crouch low at the hallway corner, his eyes narrowing. "Motion camera."

He leaned back and exhaled. "There's a lot of ground to cover without getting spotted. I could just..." From the holster at his thigh, Solstice pulled a pair of sleek, battered drumsticks. The wood shimmered faintly with purple undertones as he turned them in his fingers and then cracked the sticks together.

A sharp *crack* echoed down the corridor—and a ripple of violet light pulsed outward, forming the outline of a temporal dome.

But it didn't hold.

The shimmer convulsed—edges fraying like static on an old screen. For a moment, the bubble split, collapsing in on itself with a distorted hiss before vanishing entirely.

Solstice staggered back a half step, brow furrowing. "That's not—"

"Try again," Indy said quickly, glancing behind them. "We're out of time."

Solstice grit his teeth and struck the sticks again. The shimmer returned—but this time it flickered. Pulsed. Faded. Reappeared. It wasn't stable.

Anthem stared at it. Every few seconds, the dome blinked out—briefly exposing the hallway, the motion camera, the team—before snapping back on. "You sure this is masking us?"

"...It's cycling," Solstice muttered. "A rhythmic instability. There's something interfering with my powers, but as long as the dome's up, we're moving faster than their eyes can track. Cameras too. All they'll catch is a blur—if anything. But if it flickers off at the wrong moment..."

Indy finished his sentence: "We're caught."

"We'll have to move with it," Anthem said, eyes locked on the rotating motion camera. "Match the motion. Time our steps. Like a beat."

Solstice's lips curled. "Ain't that poetic."

He nodded once, then struck the sticks together again, syncing the dome's rhythm into a more predictable pattern: three seconds on, two seconds off.

The shimmering bubble flowed down the hallway in slow waves, washing over the camera—but only in bursts. The timing had to be perfect.

Anthem counted under his breath. "Three... two... one—go."

They moved.

Through the pulsing field, every step had to fall in rhythm. In the "on" beat, they glided forward, invisible to the sweeping lens. When the dome flickered off, they froze—mid-stride, breath held—as the world snapped back to real time.

Then the shimmer returned. Another few steps. Another pause. The hallway stretched like a metronome's pendulum—forward, hold, forward.

Indy reached the stack of crates first, sliding into cover just as the dome blinked out again. Anthem followed next, pulse pounding to the rhythm of flickering magic. Solstice was last—jaw clenched, sweat already dotting his brow.

He barely made it into the shadow before the dome vanished completely, the final pulse sputtering out like a broken note.

Solstice leaned against the wall, panting. "That's all I've got for now."

Anthem peeked around the crates, checking the camera. "Appears to be fine. No alert lights."

"They probably didn't see us," Indy said. "But whatever's messing with your powers is only getting stronger the deeper we go."

Anthem scanned the hallway above them—eyes settling on faint silver coils running along the base of the camera and deeper into the walls. "They're damping our abilities. Probably built it into the infrastructure." Anthem whispered, "They're definitely keeping Sound Weavers down here."

Indy nodded grimly. "We're close. Next hallway takes us to the freight lift. From there, we drop to Sub-Level Two."

Solstice fell into step beside them, glancing behind. "Still clear."

The freight lift groaned as it descended, the hum of its old mechanisms masking the trio's shallow breathing. The lights overhead cast a sickly yellow that grated against the tension already crawling up Anthem's spine.

"Sub-Level Two incoming," Indy whispered, her eyes fixed on the control panel. "No second chances after this."

Anthem nodded, his fingers tightening around the strap of his gear bag. Solstice rolled his shoulders in silence, flexing tension from his neck.

With a final shudder, the lift halted. A soft chime announced their arrival.

Then the doors opened.

Two guards stood just outside—startled, but trained. One reached for his comm, the other for a weapon.

They never got the chance.

Anthem lunged first, slamming his shoulder into the nearest guard and driving him into the wall with brutal force. The comm device clattered to the ground. Solstice pivoted smoothly, sweeping the second guard's legs out from under him and striking his throat with the heel of his hand before he could shout. Indy was already sliding in, snatching up their restraint cables and using them to bind the wrists of both of them.

In less than ten seconds, it was over.

"Check their tags," Indy said, crouching beside the unconscious bodies. "We can spoof a code from these if we need to."

Anthem gave a tight nod and turned to take in the room beyond.

The hallway opened into a vast chamber—roughly half the size of a football field. It was dim, lit only by rows of red-glowing dampeners embedded into the ceiling and walls. The suppressors gave off a constant low-frequency hum that settled like pressure behind the eyes.

Cells dotted the open floor in symmetrical rows—metal cages lined with dull acoustic foam, spaced ten feet apart. Some were dark and empty, silent. Others weren't.

Anthem's breath caught.

Found them.

Figures slumped on narrow cots or curled against the far corners of their cages. Each one clad in the same gray jumpsuits. Some blinked slowly. Others didn't move at all. A few stirred at the sound of the lift, eyes heavy and disoriented. One man pressed himself against the bars, mouth moving, but no sound escaped. The dampeners were working well.

"This is Solstice. We found them," Solstice muttered into his comm. "How long have they been like this?" He asked the group.

"Doesn't matter," Indy said, already stepping into the rows, eyes scanning. "We're getting them out."

At the far end of the room stood a single set of double doors, completely unmarked. No signage. No windows. "Guessing that's the funhouse entrance," Solstice said, nodding toward the doors. Anthem nodded grimly.

Cells hissed open one by one as Solstice worked the control panels. Each sharp click of a locking mechanism seemed louder than the last in the suffocating, red-tinted chamber.

Indy moved quickly, crouching beside a dazed prisoner and helping him to his feet. He was unresponsive at first, just blinking, lips parted but saying nothing. A glazed stare.

"Hey—hey, look at me," she whispered. "You're going to walk with me, alright?"

The man nodded, slow and uneven.

Anthem moved to another cell, arms open to a frail girl slumped against the wall. She looked no older than sixteen, shaved head patchy, wrists wrapped in faded medical tape. Her eyes twitched at the sound of his voice, then darted past him. Her breath hitched.

"No, no, no, no—this isn't real!" she screamed.

Her voice shattered the still air, echoing off the concrete walls like a crack of lightning.

Anthem flinched. "Easy! It's okay—"

She scrambled backward, kicking and thrashing. Her limbs flailed wildly. Indy dove in, grabbing the girl's wrists before she could hit her own head on the cot frame. "Shh—listen to me! Breathe. You're going to be fine. Look at my eyes." She rocked the girl gently, whispering into her ear until the trembling slowed. The prisoner sobbed against her shoulder.

Anthem turned; breath ragged. But then his stomach dropped. A slumped figure just inside one of the last open cages. The prisoner was still. Unbreathing. Blood trickled faintly from his nose, pooling beneath his ear. Anthem crouched beside the man. "We should've been faster," he whispered. He said a silent prayer. Then a nod. Time to move.

One of the last cells opened with a metallic hiss—and the figure inside didn't hesitate. A man, mid-thirties, wild-eyed and barefoot, ran.

Straight for the double doors at the far end of the chamber.

"Wait!" Indy shouted.

Too late. He was through.

Solstice swore and took off without a word, drumsticks still in one hand. The doors slammed closed behind him.

Anthem turned to Indy. "I guess that's our exit." Anthem and Indy guided the dazed prisoners toward the back of the room—toward the double doors. Some could walk on their own, limbs shaky but responsive. Others leaned on fellow prisoners, murmuring softly, confusion and fear thick in their eyes.

They handed out hastily packed disguises—hooded jackets, visors, and festival lanyards that matched the civilian gear worn above ground at the festival.

"You're safe now," Anthem repeated, again and again. "We're getting you out. Just follow our lead."

A woman with short-cropped hair, damp with sweat, pointed a trembling finger toward the double doors. "That door," she rasped. "It goes straight to the stage. The main one. They bring us through there when they want us to... perform."

Anthem felt a chill snake down his spine.

"For the cameras?" he asked.

She nodded. "For everyone. It's their show. They drug us, clean us up. Then we go on. Like dolls."

Indy's jaw tightened, and she gently helped the woman slip into a jacket and visor.

"We have to go after Solstice," Anthem said grimly. "And it sounds like our fast way top-side." Anthem tapped the comm in his ear. "Anthem, reporting—Captives secured and en route."

A long pause.

Nothing.

He frowned and tried again.

Still nothing.

"Damn it," Anthem said. "They're jamming the signal down here. We'll have to hit the surface before we can call it in. We should get moving. Quiet and fast."

Indy appeared beside him, nodding once. "Everyone's ready."

Anthem dropped the hard case and slung his guitar before pushing open the heavy doors with a quiet hiss. Beyond the final threshold was a wide corridor sloping upward, glowing faintly with the promise of freedom. Light poured in from the far end—bright, searing, almost holy after so much darkness. The sound of the Unity Festival filtered down in warped echoes: pounding bass lines, distant cheers, melodies stretched thin by the structure overhead.

The air had changed.

Cooler. Thinner.

They crept forward, ducking past open alcoves and unused prep rooms. Anthem soon found Solstice in a narrow corridor, halfway between the chamber and the sloped service route leading to the stage access.

Solstice stood pressed against the wall with one arm braced in front of the runaway. The man was pinned, panting, eyes wild, fists clenched but shaking.

Solstice didn't move aggressively—just blocked the way. Quiet. Unmoving. Like a dam holding back a flood.

"Easy," Solstice said. "You're not being chased. There's no show. No lights. You're safe."

Anthem stepped closer, slowly.

The man looked between them, eyes watering. "They said we were done. That we'd get out. That I could sing again. I just wanted to—" He choked on the last word, voice cracking like glass.

Anthem gently took his arm. "You still can. But not by running blind. We're going together. Stay with us, yeah?"

The man nodded, folding in on himself.

They turned back toward their escape route. The group moved silently, darting between cover, following Solstice's hand signals. The further they rose, the louder the music became. Indy scouted ahead, confirming which corners and open doorways were clear.

With every step, the music grew louder. Closer. Then at the end of the narrow hallway, a single service door, left slightly ajar, just wide enough to let bright daylight pour in.

Beyond it: freedom. A sliver of the real world.

Anthem squinted through the gap and saw a sea of distracted festival-goers dancing under a haze of lights and sound.

"This is it," Indy whispered. "Once we're through, we blend in, stick to the outer rings. Evac team's waiting near the vendor corridor."

Anthem turned back to the captives. "One at a time. Quiet. Keep your heads down. Move quickly."

One by one, he ushered them through the threshold—slipping from shadows into light, into a crowd that didn't even know they were there.

Then—"Anthem?"

He froze mid-step.

Three figures approached just behind him, the last three of the captives. Geddy. Tatum. Buddy.

His friends. His bandmates.

They looked wrecked—clothes torn, faces drawn. Tatum's lip was split, eyes rimmed with exhaustion. Geddy sported a sizable black eye. Buddy had a gash on the bridge of his nose and half his head shaved unevenly, like someone had started and never finished.

Anthem blinked. "There you guys are…"

Tatum surged forward and threw her arms around him. "We thought you were dead."

He held her tightly for a long moment. Releasing their embrace, he stepped back, looking at each of them with disbelief and growing relief. "You made it out. I can't believe—wait…"

A knot formed in his throat.

His voice dropped. "Where's Bliss?"

"Behind you."

Anthem turned sharply.

Bliss stood in the corridor's shadow, untouched by the light spilling through the door. Flanked on either side stood two Silencers, weapons at the ready—but not raised. She was dressed in a matching modified gray uniform, a sleek, gray armor reinforced at the shoulders and ribs.

She looked at Anthem with a frosty gleam in her bright green eyes.

"Did you miss you me?"

CHAPTER XXII

B liss' silhouette was unmistakable, her posture as imposing as it was familiar. She stood in the corridor's shadow, framed by red emergency light. Bliss carried herself with the same confidence that electrified their performances together. But this time, she wasn't leading a band—she was leading the enemy. For a moment, Anthem froze. Memories of their shared history crashed over him like a rockslide. The way they used to create together, the music, the passion—it felt like another lifetime.

Bliss didn't flinch. She watched him with the same cool detachment, like none of it mattered. Like it was already over. Anthem's chest tightened, but he forced the emotion down. Now wasn't the time. He spun to the three stunned faces still behind him—Geddy, Tatum, Buddy—their relief already curdling into panic.

"Get out of here," he ordered. "Find Indy."

Tatum hesitated. "What about you—"

"GO!" Anthem barked, louder than he meant to.

Buddy grabbed her hand and pulled her back toward the door. Geddy lingered for half a heartbeat longer, then nodded and followed.

Bliss gave a sharp glance to either side and gave a crisp command. "Go after them. Don't let them escape."

The two Silencers broke formation and dashed past Anthem like wolves smelling blood. He tore his eyes away and turned to Solstice, who had already drawn his drumsticks. "Solstice," Anthem snapped. "Protect them. Do whatever it takes."

Solstice blinked, nodded once, and bolted through the door. "On it."

Anthem didn't watch them leave.

His eyes were locked on Bliss.

And Bliss... was smiling.

She stopped a few feet from him. "You look surprised."

Shock and betrayal, emotions all too familiar between the two, were written across Anthem's face. "What are you doing here?" he demanded, his voice thick with emotion. "Why are you *doing* this?" His words carried disbelief, hurt, and anger in equal measure.

Bliss's lips curved into a small, venomous smile. "Why?" she echoed. "I told you why. That day at the rehearsal space. I told you the only way to make a difference is if I had power. Now I finally have it. I have outgrown you, Anthem. I have outgrown you all! When we kicked you out...got rid of that dead weight...it felt so good. It was almost orgasmic." A fanatical look flashed in her eyes. "Like I was dying of thirst and didn't know it. And the look on your face was the most refreshing glass of water I'd ever had. My powers awakened that same night. We played one gig without you, Anthem. Just one. MV saw us—saw *me*. And the rest is history."

"Is that really what you believe?" he asked, his voice low, measured, barely containing the storm brewing inside him. "That power is the only way? That all we built together meant nothing?"

Bliss let out a sharp laugh, her eyes flashing with something raw and ugly. "We? We built?" she sneered, stepping closer, venom lacing every syllable. "That's the thing, Anthem. It was never *we*. It was always *you*."

Anthem felt the words hit like a slap, but Bliss wasn't done. She prowled forward. "Do you know what it was like standing next to you all those years? Always second best, always just *supporting* Anthem Fox? You walked into every room like you *belonged*, like the world was *yours* to take, and everyone—*everyone*—just *gave* it to you." Her breath was heavy, her voice shaking with a fury she had kept buried for years. "You weren't the most talented, you weren't the smartest, but somehow, you were the *favorite*."

Anthem's throat tightened, his mind flashing back to the countless gigs, the endless rehearsals—had she felt like this the whole time? "That's not—"

She cut him off with a bitter scoff. "Do you remember when we were kids? The first time we played together at the talent show?" Her eyes darkened with memory. "I was the one who pushed for that. I was the one who signed us up, made the set list, convinced Buddy and Geddy that we could actually *do* something. But who did they talk about afterward?" She jabbed a finger at his chest. "*You*."

Anthem's gut twisted. He *had* been the one people noticed that night, the one the teachers praised, the one who got the biggest cheers. But he had thought—no, he had *hoped*—that it had never been a competition between them.

Bliss let out a shaky breath, her mask slipping just enough for the bitterness beneath to show. "It never changed. Every song, every show, every deal we chased, *you* were the center. I was just the *girl singing next to Anthem*." Her voice cracked, raw with old wounds. "I wanted to be more. I *deserved* to be more."

Her expression twisted into something almost gleeful, manic with vindication. "And the moment you were out of the picture. The moment I stepped into the spotlight. *I felt it.* The power. The *freedom.* You were the ball and chain keeping me from my true potential. And I've never looked back." Her voice took on an almost evangelical fervor as she stepped closer. "You *were* holding us back, Anthem. Without you, we soared. Signed on the spot. And now, I'm not just some singer in a bar band—I'm a force. I have power beyond music, beyond the stage. I'm shaping the world."

Anthem's pulse pounded in his ears. "I never held you back, Bliss," he said, his voice softer now, almost pleading. "I never wanted that. If I had known—"

"What?" she snapped. "You *would've stepped aside*? Don't insult me, Anthem. You were born to lead, weren't you? Born to shine? You *never* would've stepped aside for me."

His heart ached at the truth in her words. Would he have? Could he have?

Bliss exhaled sharply, shaking her head as if shaking off the weight of old memories. "It doesn't matter anymore. You can't *undo* the past. You had your time. Now this is *mine.*"

Anthem felt a chill as he listened to her, the realization dawning on him that Bliss had fully embraced her new path, one that justified her actions, devoid of any guilt. "You think causing pain, spreading fear, tearing people apart—that's making a difference?"

Bliss's eyes narrowed, her expression hardening. "If it brings order, if it creates opportunity, then yes. The world doesn't change without a little nudge, Anthem. You never got the bigger picture, but I do. And I'm exactly where I need to be."

This wasn't the Bliss he remembered—the fiery singer who used to pour her soul into their music. This Bliss was colder, sharper, and terrifyingly skilled. She wasn't just taking part in MV's plan—she was thriving in it.

And then his heart sank further.

A familiar voice called out from the doorway. "Bliss?" Indy's shocked voice matched the look on her face at Anthem's side, her wide eyes flicking between the two of them.

Bliss's smirk deepened; her disdain on full display. "Well, if it isn't Anthem's little pet sidekick. Come to play hero too?"

Indy's face flushed with anger, her hands balled into fists. "I'm nobody's pet or sidekick," she fired back. "And I'm sure as hell not someone for you to mock. You're a *traitor*. You sold out your friends, your ideals—everything you used to stand for. For what? Power? Is that all you care about?"

Bliss's laugh was bitter, devoid of humor. "Oh, Indy," she said mockingly. "Still so small-minded. This isn't about your quaint little 'ideals.' This is about playing on a scale you'll never understand. You're out of your depth."

Indy's eyes narrowed. "I understand plenty, *Sienna*. You abandoned everything good about yourself to chase something empty. And all you're doing now is proving how far you've fallen."

Bliss let out a sinister chuckle before her smile twisted into a snarl. "Oh, I'm going to tear your head off," she vowed. "Keep talking, Jenkins. It'll make it all the sweeter when I rip your head off."

Anthem barely had time to register the venom in Bliss's voice before she moved. She tilted her head back slightly, lips parting just enough—then fired a focused, concussive blast from her mouth. The sound shot through the air, tightly compressed and violently fast, like a laser forged from pure sound.

It was aimed with pinpoint precision—straight at Indy.

Anthem was faster.

Moving strictly on instinct, he whipped his guitar forward, striking a sharp, reactive chord that flared into a barrier of golden sound between them. Bliss' blast collided with it midair, exploding into a ring of vibrating force that sent a deep tremor through the shield.

The impact hit hard, shaking Anthem to his core. The surrounding air crackled with the dissipation of the energy, his barrier flashing with strain as the blast reverberated off the corridor walls. Across from him, Bliss lowered her chin, eyes glinting with challenge.

Indy didn't flinch, standing her ground as Bliss's attack fizzled against Anthem's barrier. "That's the difference between us," Indy said, her voice steady despite the tension in her body. "You think power is about domination? But real strength? It comes from your desire to protect those that can't protect themselves."

Bliss sneered, circling them like a predator toying with its prey. "Spare me the self-righteous speech. You think you're some beacon of virtue? That you're on the 'right' side?" She scoffed. "Wake up. The world doesn't care about your ideals. Power doesn't ask for permission—it takes."

Anthem swallowed hard, still reeling from the sheer *wrongness* of this moment. This wasn't just Bliss making a selfish decision—this was *Bliss reveling* in her choices. It felt like looking at a reflection in a warped fun-house mirror.

"You sound just like MV," Anthem said, his voice quiet but cutting. "Like you're reading straight from his manifesto."

Bliss's expression darkened. "MV gave me clarity. He showed me what I was capable of. What *we* were capable of, if we had the will to take what we deserved." Her hands twitched at her sides. "And I'll tell you what, Anthem—you were never *meant* to be part of that. You're soft. You always were."

Anthem's jaw clenched. He had seen many sides of Bliss over the years—passionate, headstrong, fiery—but never this. Never *cold.* Never *cruel.*

"So what now?" Anthem asked, forcing his voice to stay even. "You want to prove something? You want to take us out to show MV how loyal you are?"

Bliss's lips curled into a slow, deliberate smile, a cruel mockery of the grin she used to flash him before a show. "I don't need to prove anything," she said smoothly. "But I *do* need to send a message." She took a deliberate step backward, drawing in a breath. Anthem and Indy flinched reflexively in anticipation for another blast.

Instead, her lips parted, and she released a short pulsing tone—low and dense, like thunder folded into a whisper. The sound wasn't meant to be heard. It was meant to travel. The vibration thrummed beneath their feet, rolling outward through the structure itself—a private signal woven into the bones of the building.

Thin strips of lighting embedded in the upper walls flickered from neutral white to **a** deep, pulsing red. No sirens. No announcements. No crowd-wide panic.

Just silence.

And then Bliss smiled.

"Security's already en route," she said smoothly, her voice barely above a murmur.

Anthem's pulse pounded in his ears. This wasn't just a fight—it was a battle of ideologies, of paths that had once run parallel but had now violently diverged.

"Bliss, don't do this," he tried once more, though his voice had lost some of its hope. "This isn't you."

Bliss's green eyes flashed with something unreadable—maybe anger, maybe amusement. "That's where you're wrong," she said. Her voice developed an echo. As if there were more than one Bliss speaking at the same time. "This has always been me."

Bliss surged forward, her mouth opening slightly as she unleashed a rapid barrage of concussive sound blasts. One blast shattered the floor panel where Anthem had stood just a second earlier, forcing him into a rough dive as a second blast tore past his shoulder and cracked into the wall behind him. The corridor echoed with the aftershock—walls groaning; the floor vibrating with the pressure left in her wake. Indy ducked behind a thick support beam, narrowly avoiding a third blast that chipped concrete just above her head. "She's driving us into a trap!" Indy shouted, shielding her ears. "We're too exposed here!"

Anthem strummed a dissonant chord to throw off Bliss's aim, sending his own blast of solid sound. It gave him just enough space to move—he darted across the hallway, placing himself between Bliss and Indy.

Bliss answered with another blast, this one wide and rolling, forcing Anthem and Indy to stagger into the side hallway. The ceiling groaned above them from the strain, dust cascading in fine sheets.

They ran.

Bliss followed unhurriedly, stalking the pair like a villain from a slasher horror movie.

They spilled into a half-finished section of the venue, a blocked-off area shielded from festivalgoers by privacy panels and hanging tarps. Scaffolding towered overhead. Tools lay scattered across the floor. The distant music was muffled now, replaced by the hum of industrial lighting and the rumble of generators.

Here, they had more room to move.

And nowhere to hide.

Anthem spun around, guitar in hand, fingers flying across the strings as he summoned a wave of harmonic force that bent the scaffolding between them. Bliss skidded to a halt, her own resonance flaring like wildfire in response. Her hair danced around her face, lifted by the charge of power.

And then the real fight began.

CHAPTER XXIII

B liss laughed. "Oh, come on. Is that's the best you've GOT?" She used the natural shape her mouth made, saying the last word to let loose another cannon like blast of sonic energy, forcing Anthem into a rough dive. Barely managing to roll aside in time. The blast slammed into the concrete, pulverizing the floor where he'd just stood. Dust and jagged chunks exploded outward.

Indy dove for cover behind a leaning scaffold, but Bliss flicked her head slightly—redirecting a smaller, thinner burst of concussive sound directly at her. It struck Indy's left shoulder with shocking precision.

The impact threw her sideways, slamming her against a pile of coiled cabling. A strangled cry escaped as the blast scorched her flesh.

Anthem's eyes widened. "Indy!"

"Hiding already?" Bliss taunted, her voice cutting through the air like a serrated blade. "Pathetic."

Indy crouched low behind a half-assembled truss rig, forcing herself to stay conscious. Her fingers scrambled through the debris until they closed around a length of rebar.

Nearby, Bliss stretched her neck slowly, making a show of how she was relaxed—unhurried. "You're just delaying the inevitable," she said.

Anthem caught the shift in the air—Bliss was gearing up for another attack. She opened her mouth wide—and fired. Anthem lunged, throwing himself toward Indy just as another beam of sonic force erupted from Bliss's mouth. Anthem deflected it with a well-timed shield. It tore through the scaffolding with explosive power, shattering metal joints and sending debris spiraling. A stack of speakers behind them exploded into splinters, shards spraying through the air. One caught Anthem across the ribs. He hissed, clutching the wound.

Indy rolled away from a falling beam, her wounded arm now bleeding. The moment she regained her footing, she swung the rebar hard, catching Bliss just as she advanced. The metal cracked against Bliss's shoulder and jaw, knocking her off-balance.

Bliss staggered back with a snarl, one hand going to her face. She glared at Indy, her green eyes burning with fury.

"Not so pathetic now, huh?" Indy said, panting through the pain.

Bliss wiped a line of blood from the corner of her mouth with the back of her hand. "I'll admit, I underestimated you," she hissed, her tone dropping into a dangerous hiss. "But it won't save you."[1]

Then she stepped back, exhaled slowly—and sang.

Her voice floated low and melodic, deceptively soft against the clamor of the ruined construction zone. The air seemed to hush in awe, like every person in the stadium stopped to listen. Anthem froze, the first note catching in his chest like a breath he couldn't release.

---

[1]. Track 16 – Billie Eilish – Bury a Friend

Bliss's tone darkened into a resonant hum, then rose into a siren's verse—haunting, layered, threaded with harmonic overtones that caused her to shimmer like light caught in smoke.

"Wanderer, come, lay your burdens down,"

"Your war is done, your silence drowns."

"Follow the voice that calls from below."

"Come to the sound, come to the echo..."

The melody wrapped around him like silk soaked in memory. Anthem's thoughts slowed, limbs heavy. His grip loosened on his guitar. He saw her—not here, not now—but years ago, in the backroom of a rundown venue, humming that same tone under her breath while he tuned his strings. He blinked, confused, caught between two timelines.

Indy shouted something—he couldn't hear her.

Bliss took a step closer.

"No need to fight, no need to flee,"

"I am the shore, the sun, the sea."

"Give in, drift down—let your pulse rest..."

"Come home to me, come be my guest."

His pulse slowed to match the rhythm of her words. His breath synced with her melody.

He didn't notice he was crying.

A part of him, buried under shock and song, whispered that something was wrong—very wrong—but her voice lulled it quiet. Each note stirred a longing in him, not for love or forgiveness, but for stillness. Oblivion. Peace.

He took a step forward.

"Anthem, NO!" Indy's voice cracked, raw and desperate.

Bliss smiled, extending her hand.

"Your fire fades, your war unwinds."

"So rest your hands and close your mind..."

Anthem's fingers twitched, reaching, then a sharp sting cut across his temple. Reality snapped back like a coiled spring. Indy, bleeding and shaking, had hurled a metal clamp at him. It struck him hard enough to jolt the spell. His knees buckled, breath ragged, as he dropped to the ground.

Bliss's song choked off mid-verse, her voice warping into a discordant growl. She stepped back, fury twisting her features. And without warning, she reared back and unleashed a scream—raw and primal. The sound warped the air itself, a sonic shockwave that tore through the area like a hurricane.

Anthem barely raised a protective shield in time. The edges cracked and flickered—but held.

Indy didn't have a shield.

The blast struck her like a wrecking ball, flinging her backward. She hit the floor hard, her body sliding across concrete and coming to rest beside a broken lighting rig. Blood streaked beneath her as she tried, trembling, to push herself up.

Anthem's heart lurched. Taking off at a full sprint, he ran to reach her. But slowed when he got within arm's reach. Seeing her stir caused relief to flood his chest. She rolled onto her side; her wounded arm shaking. Her face was pale but defiant. She locked eyes with Bliss, who was advancing again, her boots crunching over glass and gravel. Bliss was glowing now—resonance crackling faintly along her throat and chest, heat radiating off her body. She was preparing another strike. One that could finish it.

Bliss lunged after Anthem and Indy, her boots striking the concrete like war drums. Anthem ducked under a collapsing scaffold, dragging Indy with him as they emerged into the crowded edge of the Unity Festival.

Color, sound, and light exploded around them—thousands of people dancing, cheering, unaware of the battle crashing toward them.

That changed in an instant.

Bliss tore through the temporary curtain behind them, unleashing a concussive blast into the air. The force of it shattered the festival's ambiance. Nearby festival-goers screamed, objects flying from their hands as the shockwave knocked over speakers and display stands. The music faltered, stuttering like a skipped record.

Panic spread like fire.

People shoved past each other in waves, scattering in every direction. The crowd dissolved into shrieking chaos. "Too many civilians," Indy gasped, ducking behind a merch booth. "Be careful using your powers here!"

Anthem nodded grimly. Bliss was thinking the same thing—which is why she didn't stop.

She came at them fast. Bliss swung first with a jumping elbow strike. Anthem caught her elbow, twisting it. She countered with a vicious knee to his ribs. He stumbled back, then ducked under a sweeping kick, slamming his palm into her sternum to create space.

Indy circled behind, swinging a broken tent pole. Bliss caught it mid-swing, yanked it away, and jabbed with its broken end. Indy dodged barely in time.

It was brutal. Close. Dangerous.

And Bliss was growing increasingly frustrated.

Her voice snarled over the chaos. "I'm tired of the games!"

She turned.

A young girl, no older than fourteen, stood frozen a few feet away, paralyzed by in fear.

Bliss's mouth opened—a blast charging on her tongue.

"NO!" Anthem roared, already moving.

There was no time to raise a proper shield. No time to think. He poured all he had into a thin, vibrating layer of resonance—not a wall, but a second skin, stretching across his body as he dove between Bliss and the girl.

The blast hit him point-blank.

It sounded like thunder shot out of a cannon and Anthem was lifted off his feet like a rag doll caught in a storm surge. The world spun. He crashed through a row of festival lights, shattered signage, and finally—straight through the main stage wall.

The performance above screeched to a halt as debris exploded across the platform.

Dancers scattered. The lights froze.

MV stood at center stage, bathed in golden light, holding a microphone mid-verse.

He stared at Anthem, who groaned, looking up from amidst the wreckage at his feet. The protective layer around Anthem faded as they made eye contact for a long moment. The crowd, momentarily stunned, watched in silence as dust settled around the two men. MV lowered the mic slightly, a smirk curling at the edge of his lips. "Well," he said, voice smooth and amplified across the plaza. "Look who decided to crash the main stage."

CHAPTER XXXIV

Anthem groaned, pushing himself to one knee amid the wreckage of the stage—smoke curling around him, spotlights wobbling in fractured beams.

MV stood above him, radiant in his tailored stage costume, a gilded mic still in hand. The crowd hushed out of uncertainty. Eyes squinted past the haze. Cameras focused. Drones hovered like curious birds.

And then, MV smiled. Not a friendly smile. A predator's smile.

"Ah, there he is," he said into the mic, tone velvet-smooth and soaked in satisfaction. "The underground legend himself. The martyr. The myth. The man who couldn't stay off my stage if he tried."

A few in the crowd chuckled nervously. MV turned, slowly, theatrically, to address them.

"People of Musera," he said, sweeping an arm wide. "What you see before you is not a hero. He's not a savior. He's not a freedom fighter."

MV leaned down toward Anthem, mock concern in his voice. "You're just noise, Anthem. Static. An untuned instrument in a world that craves harmony."

Anthem glared up at him, breathing hard, blood trickling from his nose.

"You don't belong here," MV said, turning back to the crowd. "And lucky for all of you—I came prepared."

He raised one gloved hand. A chorus of boots thundered onto the stage. Silencers emerged from the wings in perfect formation, weapons trained on Anthem. MV took a step back, giving the illusion of nobility, like a ruler showing mercy. "Take him," he ordered, voice smooth but cold. "Let's show the world what justice sounds like. Show everyone that we are harmony. And we will—"

BOOM.

An explosion tore through the festival grounds with concussive force, a deep, resonant thunder that drowned out MV's voice and shook the stage rigging above. Fire erupted at the northern wall, sending up a column of smoke that caught the spotlight like a stage effect gone rogue.

The crowd screamed, panic rolling like a shockwave through the bodies pressed against the stage. MV stumbled backward. "What—?"

Another blast followed. One to the east this time, somewhere near the security compound. Controlled detonations, *timed like percussion hits.*

MV spun to face Anthem, fury in his eyes. "What was that—?"

A third explosion hit with earth-shaking force, deep and guttural, like a bass line dropped into the core of the planet itself. The entire stage lurched beneath them, tremors rattling through the stage.

Lights above swayed wildly, scaffolding groaned, and one of the enormous LED panels behind MV crashed to the ground with a blinding spark of electricity.

The stage pitched violently, and one by one, Silencers lost their footing. MV stumbled with them, his arms pinwheeling for balance as he was bucked from the stage. Two Silencers tumbled clean off the edge, vanishing into the sea of bodies below.

MV hit the ground hard, his polished uniform now streaked with dirt. "No—get him!" he roared, scrambling to rise, but—Anthem was already gone.

He had recognized his chance and seized the moment. His body surging with adrenaline, he turned, sprinted across the fractured stage, and without hesitation, dove off the platform. He landed and rolled across the festival grounds, allowing his momentum to bring him back to his feet. Then bolted back through the thinning smoke and crumbling light structures. He ran like a madman. He sprinted across the wreckage, but he didn't just *run*.

Anthem *played* his body into motion. A chord struck beneath his skin—un-heard—and his resonance kicked in. The world warped at the edges of his vision as his internal tempo exploded.

The Doppler effect flared around him. To anyone nearby, the sound of his footsteps didn't follow his motion—it *chased* it. A strange echo trailed him, warped and stretched like a synth bending into a scream, each pulse of sound lagging behind the blur of his body.

Canvas banners snapped as he passed. The ground underfoot seemed to stagger, unprepared for the frequency pouring off him in waves. As he ran, he spotted a teenage girl pinned beneath a lighting truss, its jagged metal arm teetering on collapsed scaffolding. Anthem saw it fall—and so did she, eyes wide with paralyzed fear.

He was at her side in a flash of gold. He skidded to his knees and extended his hand. A crystalline construct bloomed instantly—a sheet of golden resonance that caught the rigging mid-collapse, just inches above her chest.

Anthem grunted and created another construct wedged under the metal pinning her. "Can you run?" he asked.

She nodded, tears streaking down her face, and took off into the crowd. Anthem took off as well, but it didn't take long until he was being chased by a pair of drones. Without slowing, he stomped hard and struck a single power chord across his strings—*BOOM*—wall of stalagmites erupted from the earth. The drones were impaled mid-charge, their husks peeling back like metal petals of a flower.

He rounded a collapsed speaker tower and saw a man clutching his leg, pinned against a support beam. Worse—flames from a vendor stall were licking closer, sparks catching on plastic tarps and paper signage.

Anthem didn't hesitate. He sprinted past a stampede of retreating festival goers and skidded to a stop beside the man.

"Hold on," he said, planting his hand on the beam.

The guitar pulsed against his back, and a crystalline construct erupted beneath his palm. Golden shards exploded outward, fracturing the beam cleanly. Anthem pulled the man out just as the flames reached the edge of the stall.

Trembling, the man asked. "How—how did you—"

But Anthem was already up again, moving. He didn't stop. Not until he finally rounded the far edge of the staging zone, where temporary walls shielded a half-built side structure from the crowd's view.

And then he saw Indy.

Fighting like hell.

She wielded a length of twisted rebar like a quarterstaff, deflecting sonic blasts that shook the air with every impact. Her wounded arm was streaked with blood, her face set in determined fury. Across from her, Bliss loomed like a dark crescendo, her voice tuned to devastation.

But it wasn't just them. Behind broken barricades and scattered debris crouched Geddy, Tatum, and Buddy.

And shielding them—Solstice.

His arms were outstretched, a shimmering dome of violet resonance holding back debris and stray blasts. He gritted his teeth, bracing with everything he had as tremors rippled through the ground and the air sizzled with volatile frequency.

Something must have gone wrong if Solstice was back *with* them.

Bliss turned toward Anthem upon spotting him, and her lips curled into a smile that promised violence.

"You're back," she called sweetly.

Anthem's eyes locked with Indy's. She was hurting—bad—but she didn't back down.

"Yeah," Anthem said, reaching for his guitar. "And I brought the remix." He tightened his grip on his guitar and took a step toward Bliss—

Click. Click. Click.

The unmistakable sound of rifles being armed echoed around them.

He froze.

From every shadow, from behind scaffolding, speaker towers, and smoke-wreathed walkways, Silencers emerged like phantoms—weapons raised, visors glowing faintly. A perfect circle, like a closing noose, surrounded Anthem, Indy, Solstice, and the others.

Even Bliss stepped back slightly, letting the Silencers take formation. She didn't look pleased—but she didn't interfere. Reluctantly, everyone stood down. The silence was broken only by the dull roar of the festival in chaos behind them—sirens, screaming, crying.

And then—footsteps.

Slow. Deliberate. The rhythm of a man who believed the world moved at his tempo.

MV appeared.

He walked between the ranks of Silencers like a conductor through his orchestra pit—casual, almost amused, his baton now visible in his gloved hand, its silver tip glinting in the dim light.

"Well, well…" he said, drawing out the words like silk through fingers. "Is this the start of the Manufacturing Eden reunion tour?"

He stopped in front of Anthem, studying him like an unfinished verse.

"You really don't know when to quit, do you?"

Anthem met his gaze, saying nothing.

MV sighed theatrically, raising the baton. "Let me show you what real harmony looks like."

He turned slowly, facing the outer edge of the compound where a group of panicked civilians—vendors, tech crew, scattered festival-goers—had taken cover behind a stack of crates.

MV raised his baton—and conducted.

Not a performance. A possession.

The civilians' eyes glazed over. Their postures went slack—then rigid. As if strings had been attached to their limbs.

MV's hand moved in a slow upward sweep, and the civilians stood.

Another flourish, and they charged.

Straight at Anthem.

"No!" Indy cried out.

Anthem reacted instinctively, summoning a crystalline sphere of resonance that pulsed around him. The civilians struck the surface, flailing like marionettes gone mad. He wasn't protecting himself from enemies. He was separating himself from innocents. They pounded on the shield. He could feel their hands, their confusion, their terror—beating against the bubble he dared not drop.

MV grinned, his voice smooth and venomous. "You see, Anthem? You're still thinking this is a performance. A battle of sound. But this..." He gestured to the civilians outside the shield. "This is conducting. The world doesn't follow musicians. It follows power."

Anthem's jaw clenched. "Stop this. How can hurting so many innocent people come so easy to you?"

"Practice." MV replied simply. He turned back toward the others. Geddy, Tatum, and Buddy stood huddled behind Solstice, fear plain on their faces. Solstice took a step forward, planting himself in front of them, arms spread. MV barely glanced his way. "Remove him."

Two Silencers advanced. Solstice prepared to strike, but four more trained their weapons on him. Solstice froze. His hands trembled with restrained rage.

Anthem's shield wavered, but he was confident it would hold despite their relentless pounding—He was trapped. Forced to watch.

"Please. Don't do this," Anthem begged.

MV gave a nod.

Three Silencers moved behind the trio.

Three rifles were raised.

Three triggers pulled.

CRACK—CRACK—CRACK.

Anthem screamed, the sound rattling his barrier, shaking the very air around him as Geddy, Tatum, and Buddy's lifeless bodies collapsed.

Indy turned away with a stifled cry, fists clenched.

Solstice just stood there, eyes wide in shock.

The civilians MV was puppeteering, finally stopped their beating at Anthem's shield, as MV released his control of them. Upon which, they immediately ran off screaming in different directions. MV looked back at Anthem with quiet satisfaction.

[1] Anthem dropped to his knees inside the shield, hands shaking, head bowed. The world outside raged in sound and fury, but inside the barrier, everything was eerily still. His eyes were void of expression, hollowed by shock and sorrow. With a slow breath, he lifted his hand—barely—and the dome expanded. It moved like the tide coming in. Smooth, inevitable. A shimmering veil of golden resonance progressing outward in a concentric wave. As it grew, it encompassed Indy first, slumped behind a pile of debris, blood-soaked and tear stained. She gasped as the silence swept over her. At the same time, the bubble pushed Bliss away from Indy. Her boots skidded across the gravel as the barrier forced her further away. It did the same for every Silencer nearby.

Next, Solstice—who had collapsed to one knee beside the bodies of their fallen friends—was caught in the growing field. His eyes widened as the wall of resonance washed over him, the noise of the world dropping away in an instant, replaced by pure stillness.

Then, finally, his fallen friends.

The moment the field covered them, the light within the dome shifted—softer, like sunlight filtered through stained glass. The resonance curled protectively around their forms, preserving their stillness like statues in a temple.

Outside the barrier, MV paced back and forth, baton raised, barking orders—but his voice didn't penetrate. Bliss, lips curled in a sneer, attempted another sonic blast—but the energy splashed harmlessly against the defensive bubble, muted instantly. Silencers aimed and fired, but their rounds evaporated on contact.

The dome held firm.

---

[1] Track 17 - Radiohead – Exit Music (For a Film)

Everything inside it was untouched. Everything outside was shut out.

Anthem stood slowly, his body heavy with exhaustion, rage, and heartache. Each step was painful, like every step forward cost a piece of him he'd never get back. As he walked toward the bodies of his friends, the surrounding air shifted. It began quietly—barely audible at first. A low vibration thrummed through the air, resonating with his heartbeat, stirring particles of golden light like dust caught in sunlight. Overhead, the shimmer intensified, blooming into a slow-turning cloud of crystalline shards, suspended in an invisible current.

The fragments weren't uniform—they spun in lazy spirals and jagged arcs, their shapes asymmetrical, like broken glass made of sound and light. Each shard pulsed with a faint glow, refracting the broken hues of the surrounding world into brilliant flares of amber, rose gold, and spectral white. The cloud of golden shards thickened as Anthem approached.

The fragments above him multiplied, spinning faster, tighter—a literal storm of bereavement held just barely in check. The sky above the ruined festival area took on a gilded glow. By the time he reached them, the cloud had grown to fully encompass Anthem's surrounding area, a glittering cyclone of sorrow.

Anthem dropped to his knees.

He couldn't breathe.

His fingers hovered over Geddy's chest, hoping—praying—for a heartbeat that wasn't there.

"Tatum..." he whispered.

Anthem's shoulders trembled. He pressed his hand to his mouth, trying to hold it in, but the dam had already cracked. The tears came—hot and furious, tracking down his dirt-streaked face. He bent forward until his forehead touched the earth between them.

"I'm sorry," he said again. "I'm so sorry."

He didn't hear the footsteps behind him at first. Registered nothing but the crippling silence of loss.

Then—a hand on his back.

Gentle. Steady.

Indy.

She kneeled beside him, her own face streaked with dirt and tears. She didn't speak. Solstice joined them, slower, stiffer, but there all the same. He stood there for a beat before lowering himself into a crouch at Anthem's other side. He looked like he didn't know what to do with his hands—so he just rested them on his knees, his jaw clenched against everything he didn't know how to say.

The three of them kneeled together in silence.

Around them, the golden cloud of resonance continued to churn—swirling tighter, louder now. The shards vibrated with increasing intensity, resonating with Anthem's pulse, his pain.

He wailed.

It was pure heartbreak, a sound that didn't come from his throat but from the core of his being—a cry of everything that had been taken, broken, lost.

And the cloud responded.

In a sudden flash, the gilded storm of jagged resonance exploded outward in every direction. The crystalline storm sent razor-sharp fragments raining across the battlefield, striking down scattered drones, detonating fuel tanks, slicing through everything in its area of effect.

The crystalline shards fell like judgment, singing a dirge Anthem hadn't consciously composed—but which had erupted from the deepest, most broken place in his soul.

The golden storm struck everything surrounding them and obliterated it. Silencers were hurled like rag dolls, their weapons torn from their hands and scattered among the debris. Towering pylons collapsed like brittle reeds. Sections of the main stage splintered and caved, the LED screens warping under the pressure of Anthem's unleashed power.

And yet—at the center of the chaos, he and his friends remained untouched. Not one shard touched Indy, Solstice, or the three fallen bandmates beside him. They kneeled together; the shards continued to strike the dome and dissolved on contact, absorbed without resistance, turned into quiet ripples that danced across its surface like a soft lullaby.

Inside, Indy watched the storm rain down around them and placed her hand gently on Anthem's arm, her expression a mix of heartbreak and awe. Solstice watched the storm from under furrowed brows, saying nothing, but the tension in his shoulders eased. Anthem didn't move. He sat hunched forward between his friends and his fallen family, chest heaving from the scream that had torn the world open.

The light from the last few falling shards dimmed, drifting like ash on the wind.

And then—it was over.

All around them, the world lay in tatters—rubble, twisted steel, broken bodies. Thousands of golden shards now littered the wide area, the wreckage of a festival turned war zone. Anthem remained still, his shoulders slumped beneath the weight of grief. His hand rested on Tatum's, fingers brushing over the cooling skin, unwilling to let go.

Then—Indy's hand, firm but gentle, squeezed his shoulder. "Anthem," she said, her voice hoarse. "We can't stay."

Her eyes were glassy, rimmed with red—but resolute. Not because she wasn't grieving. That would come later, but because survival meant something now. Someone had to carry their memory forward, but more immediately, someone needed to be strong for Anthem.

Anthem's jaw clenched. He nodded slowly, as if each vertebra in his neck had to give permission first. With trembling hands, he traced one last circle across Geddy's chest—his symbol for closure, for goodbye. Then to Tatum. Then Buddy. "I'm sorry," he whispered again. "I won't let this be for nothing. I swear it."

He rose, slowly, painfully.

The golden barrier that had protected them sputtered once, then dissolved. He turned, and with Indy and Solstice beside him, they walked away from the battlefield.

And then—a slow clap echoed across the wreckage.

Anthem froze.

From the far side of the destruction, a heap of armored bodies shifted, and something moved—uncoiling from the wreckage like a serpent shedding its skin.

MV.

Blood streaked one side of his face, dripping onto his once perfect uniform. Around him lay the broken remains of a dozen Silencers, their blank visors shattered. At the last possible moment, he had conducted several Silencers to shield him from the raining shards. As Anthem turned, MV stood tall, brushing ash from his shoulders like an insult. "Touching," he said, his voice hoarse but smug. "Tragic, really. But you have no one to blame but yourself."

His boots crunched over broken crystal and concrete as he took a step forward.

"Let me make something clear, Anthem," MV said, raising his baton. "This symphony isn't over. It's barely begun. You want to protect what's left of your minor rebellion? Your friends? Your music?"

He pointed the tip of the baton at Anthem like a dagger.

"I'm going to shatter everything you love," he snarled. "And I'll make you watch as I conduct the finale."

Anthem's fingers twitched toward his guitar—but Indy's hand was already tugging him back.

"Leave it," she said.

MV took one last mocking bow. "So run, Anthem. Run like the rest of your kind. But remember—when the final verse plays... it'll be in my key."

CHAPTER XXV

Everywhere Anthem looked, chaos reigned. Sirens screamed from every direction. Flashing lights bathed the crumbling festival grounds in red and blue. The once-ecstatic crowd had become consumed by a tidal wave of fear, stampeding toward exits, leaping over barricades, and ducking under fallen structures as armed responders tried—and failed—to regain control.

Anthem, Indy, and Solstice ran with them, swallowed by the chaos.

Their faces were lowered, heads buried under hoods. They didn't speak, didn't slow down. Solstice pushed through the crowd like a man possessed, glancing back only to make sure Anthem and Indy were still with him.

They burst through one of the exit gates with the surge of panicked civilians. Out on the open street, the flood of bodies poured in every direction—sirens, shouts, and rumors bleeding into the air like static. They ran for blocks, weaving between alleys and back streets, clinging to the crowd until the noise thinned as the footsteps behind them dwindled.

Finally, they ducked into a narrow alley between two shuttered storefronts, their footsteps splashing through a puddle of runoff as they slipped behind a bulky recycling unit, humming faintly with power. The moment they were out of sight, they collapsed into a crouch, panting hard. Solstice ripped off his disguise and threw it behind the dumpster.

"Off," he snapped. "All of it. Now."

Anthem's fingers fumbled with the zipper of his outer layer. His hands quivered from fatigue. He pulled the garment over his head with a grunt and tossed it into the open slot of the recycling unit, where it was sucked in with a hiss of compressed air. Indy stripped off her disguise and tossed them into the unit without hesitation. Beneath, she wore a black, close-fitting sweatshirt and utility pants. From her belt pack, she produced simple hats and sunglasses, distributing them wordlessly.

Once changed, they moved quickly at a brisk walk, trying not to make too much eye contact with others passing by. The city blocks grew quieter the further they moved from the festival grounds. By the time they reached the industrial district, only the occasional patrol drone passed overhead, scanning the shadows with a bored hum.

Indy led them through a quiet side street until they reached a nondescript building tucked between a closed gallery and a courier depot. They walked through the door and Indy stopped in front of a steel service lift. Without a word, she pressed a sequence of buttons on the adjacent keypad.

The lift dinged softly before its doors slid open with a whisper. They stepped inside and the doors sealed behind them. As the lift ascended, the dim metal walls were briefly illuminated by strips of soft golden light.

No one spoke.

When the lift stopped, the doors opened into a spacious loft, quietly elegant and dimly lit. The floors were matte black tile, and the high ceilings revealed exposed beams with hanging acoustic panels. A small kitchenette glowed warmly in one corner. The furniture was sleek and low-slung—designed for utility, but far from uncomfortable. Cedar and lavender scents perfumed the space—a sharp contrast to the smoke and ozone of the chaos they'd just escaped.

Solstice stepped in first. Followed by Anthem, his gaze sweeping the room like a man still expecting danger. Indy followed last, locking the control panel behind her. "We're clear," she murmured.

The moment it did, Anthem spun on his heel.

Before either Indy or Solstice could react, he grabbed Solstice by the collar and slammed him against the wall so hard it knocked a few acoustic panels loose.

"WHY WERE THEY STILL THERE?!"

His scream carried throughout the room. The walls of the sleek loft caught the sound and threw it back in echoes.

Indy flinched.

Solstice didn't move. He gasped from the impact, but he didn't resist—he just stared straight into Anthem's eyes.

"I told you to protect them," Anthem seethed. His fists trembled as he held Solstice pinned. "To do whatever it takes. You let them—you let them—"

"I KNOW!" Solstice shouted back, the words sharp and jagged.

Anthem paused. His grip loosened slightly.

Solstice's voice cracked as he continued. "They... they thought they could get through to her. Bliss! Tatum kept saying she saw something in her eyes—that there was still time, that she'd come around."

He swallowed hard, blinking fast. "And I didn't stop them."

Anthem's breathing was ragged. His fingers curled tighter again, eyes filled with fury and grief.

"I didn't stop them," Solstice repeated, softer now. "Short of hurting them myself, I couldn't. I—I thought if we just had a second more…" His voice trailed off. The gravity of it hit him then, and he let his head slump back against the wall. "I got them killed," he said. "And I will carry that for the rest of my life."

Anthem's hands dropped away from Solstice's jacket. He took a step back, staggering like he'd just been hit. Solstice looked at him, and there was no bravado left in his eyes—only the same hollow rage and unbearable guilt.

"But hear me, Anthem." His voice steadied, hardening like tempered steel. "This is on me. But MV will answer for it. I swear to you—I'm with you until the end. Until that bastard pays in full."

Anthem's breath shook. Indy stepped up beside him, gently pressing a hand to his arm. The air between the three of them vibrated with a shared vow. Solstice lingered for a moment, staring at the place where Anthem had shoved him, at the dent his body had left in the wall. Then, with a breath that seemed to carry the weight of the world, Solstice looked away. "I'll… go see if there's anything to eat," he muttered. "Or maybe some tea. Something warm."

No one stopped him.

Solstice turned and walked away, his footsteps soft but distant, like a man moving through ash. Anthem remained standing, but only for a breath longer. Then his knees gave out. He leaned back against the nearest wall and slid down until he was seated on the cold tile. He sat heavily, his hands resting uselessly in his lap. Indy sank down next to him without a word, knees pulled close to her chest.

Anthem finally broke the silence, a voice barely above a whisper. "Tatum always hummed under her breath. Even when no one else could hear it."

Indy nodded slowly. "And Geddy... he used to warm his hands on the back of the amp before sets. Said it helped him find his tone."

Anthem's throat worked around a knot. "Buddy... he'd stand behind me before we went onstage. Just rest his hand on my shoulder. That one gesture made it all okay."

He swallowed hard.

None of it was okay now.

"It's not fair," Indy murmured, her voice cracking. "We were so close. They were right there."

"I should've done more," Anthem said. "I should've—"

"Don't," she said, turning her head to him. "Don't you do that. You did everything you could. You threw yourself in front of a sonic blast to protect a stranger. You held all of us together."

Anthem's eyes burned. "I failed them," he said, barely audible. "They trusted me. And I led them into that."

Indy's voice was quieter still. "We all did."

Anthem leaned forward, pressing his forehead to his knees, his shoulders tight. Indy shifted beside him, and slowly, gently, she leaned against him—her head resting on his arm. Not to comfort him, not to be comforted, but because grief had no place for solitude.

Together, they stayed like that for some time. Minutes passed like hours. Solstice returned a few minutes later, a chipped ceramic pot in his hands, steam curling from the top. He didn't interrupt them. Just set it down quietly on the counter, sat across the room, and let the moment unfold.

Later that night, after long, silent showers and a brief check-in with Vale—just enough to confirm they were alive and off the grid—the loft felt still again.

Exhausted but unwilling to sleep, Anthem drifted to the modest kitchenette. The cupboards held little, but there were just enough ingredients to scrape together a meal: rice, canned vegetables, a few spices, and a dented tin of beef stew.

He moved slowly, not because of fatigue, but because it felt good to focus on something normal—something that didn't involve running or shielding or screaming.

By the time everything was ready, the others had gathered at the table. Solstice sat slouched in one chair, arms folded. Indy leaned on her elbow, her wet hair tied back with a spare cable tie, her eyes watching Anthem in quiet gratitude.

They ate without ceremony, the only sound the clink of spoons and quiet chewing. No one said it, but the warmth of the food seemed to anchor them, even for just a few breaths. Anthem took a slow bite. It tasted like crap, but he was grateful.

Then he looked down at his bowl—and paused.

His voice, when it came, was soft. "I keep thinking about the last time I saw them."

Indy glanced up, her spoon halfway to her mouth.

"Not just at the cells," he said. "I mean before that. Before this whole thing spiraled."

Solstice shifted slightly, watching him from beneath hooded eyes.

Anthem stared down at his food, barely seeing it. "Indy, do you remember when we ran into Buddy and Tatum at Melody's Music Repair Shop?" A faint breath escaped him.

"Yeah. I was there when Geddy popped up at your show too," she said.

"I thought those moments were random," he mumbled. "But what if they weren't? What if The Conductors or some other part of this universe gave me two chances to say goodbye... and I missed them both?"

The silence that followed was deeper than anything they'd carried since walking through the door. Indy looked at him with a quiet, breaking softness. "You didn't miss them," she said. "You had no way of knowing what those moments were?"

Anthem let out a shaky breath. "If I'd known... if I'd known that was the last time—I would've said something. I would've done something. I would've told them—"

He stopped himself; the words clinging to his throat.

Indy reached across the table and took his hand.

"They knew," she said.

Solstice didn't speak. But he nodded—once, firm and slow.

Even later into the night, long after the last bite had gone cold, one by one, the three of them drifted toward the loft's wide, curtainless windows. They gathered on the couch. None of them said it out loud, but none of them wanted to be alone.

Anthem sat in the center, his posture heavy, hands resting on his knees. Indy dropped beside him, curling her legs beneath her and leaning gently into his side. Solstice took the far end, arms folded, head tilted back, eyes flicking occasionally to the moonlight pouring through the glass.

Outside, the city murmured softly in its sleep. From up here, the chaos of the festival felt far away, like a dream that had already dissolved. They sat in silence, shoulder to shoulder, staring out at the world that kept spinning, indifferent to their losses.

Above, the full moon hung quiet and watchful, casting pale light across the loft's dark tile floor, silvering their skin and softening the edges of the grief still clinging to them. A patrol blimp floated by lazily, cutting a path in front of the moon.

They sat like that for a long time.

No one spoke. There was nothing left to say.

Anthem's breathing slowed first, his head gently tipping back against the cushions. Indy followed, her eyes blinking slower and slower until they finally closed, her head falling to rest on Anthem's shoulder.

Solstice was the last to surrender.

He stayed upright for a while longer, watching the stars just barely visible beyond the skyline, before his chin dipped to his chest and sleep quietly claimed him too.

The three of them, scarred and silent, fell asleep together beneath the windows' glow.

And the moon—bright and full—kept its vigil.

Above them, the sky never changed.

But inside that loft, something had.

They had survived.

For now.

CHAPTER XXXVI

T he team staggered into Sound Weaver Studios in the early morning hours, just as the faint blush of dawn stretched across the horizon. The underground headquarters—once buzzing with laughter, music, and creative chaos—felt hollow. Instruments sat untouched in their stands.

The usual rhythm of the base had been replaced by silence.

Exhausted, bruised, and emotionally gutted Sound Weavers filled the briefing room, some slumped against the walls, others curled in chairs, staring through the floor. The only sound came from the low hum of the air system and the distant murmur of a newsfeed loop—an endless stream of polished lies and half-truths.

Vale stood at the front of the room; his expression carved from stone. He scanned the room, taking in the slumped figures and vacant expressions. He cleared his throat to get their attention. "We averted disaster." He began, voice hoarse. "Lives were saved because of your efforts. Families were reunited. Indie Artists and Sound Weavers who were missing for months. Some thought lost forever. For that, I thank you." His words drifted through the air like vapor. No one clapped. No one smiled. They knew what was coming. "But let's not fool ourselves—this wasn't a victory. MV got exactly what he wanted. We made costly mistakes, and we need to address these issues—internally—if we're going to stand a chance against what MV had planned next or anyone like him, for that matter."

For a moment, silence reigned. Then Keen stood from where he'd been sitting. "Let's talk about those internal issues, Vale. Starting with you." The room stirred, and all eyes turned to Keen. Vale didn't interrupt, but the storm behind his eyes raged. Anthem remembered seeing the bold Mentor before. He was there during his training session in the forest.

Keen stepped forward, unyielding. "You talk about principles and patience, but look at where that's gotten us. Patience didn't stop MV from turning an entire festival into a war zone. While we debated ethics, he made weapons. While we held back, he struck. You keep preaching these niceties, but all I see is hesitation disguised as wisdom."

Anthem's chest tightened. The room felt like it was shrinking from every word.

"Keen—" Vale started, but Keen didn't let him finish.

"No, Vale," Keen snapped. "We shouldn't have kept playing it safe while MV was out there plotting his next move. You held back intel. You vetoed strike plans. You refused to deploy early recon. Your reluctance to take bold action cost us dearly. Every second we hesitated, people suffered. We could have prevented tonight's disaster before it ever started if we'd taken the fight to him instead of waiting for him to come to us."

Murmurs swelled. Several team members nodded; their expressions conflicted but supportive. Kayla, one of the older teenage Sound Weavers, hesitated before speaking up. "Keen's not wrong. I lost a friend last night. He died because we weren't prepared. Waiting cost us people, people we *loved*."

Vale's jaw tightened, his knuckles going pale as he gripped the podium. "What you're talking about isn't strategy—it's recklessness. If we abandon our principles, we're no better than MV. Recklessness isn't bravery; it's a path to ruin."

The room tensed as more voices joined in. A Sound Weaver, sitting with his arms crossed, leaned forward. "Maybe playing it safe is just another way of saying we're scared."

Vale's voice rose, his usual calm cracking under the weight of the argument. "We're not scared. We're careful. And that care keeps us from becoming the very thing we're fighting against. If you think throwing caution to the wind is the answer, you're not just wrong—you're dangerous."

Keen stepped forward. "Then consider me the most dangerous man in the world."

The room erupted into overlapping voices; the argument spiraling out of control. Accusations flew, frustration boiling over into personal grievances and past resentments. Anthem remained quiet, his eyes darting between the arguing factions, his expression unreadable. Indy, standing near the back, looked like she wanted to intervene, but wasn't sure how.

Finally, Keen raised his voice above the fray. "That's enough!" The room fell silent, all eyes on him. His face was taut with frustration, his voice hard with conviction. "I can't keep doing this, Vale. I can't be part of a team that doesn't have the guts to act. I won't follow a leader who clings to broken ideals while the world burns. You're holding us back, and I'm done watching us falter. I'm leaving."

The words hit like a sledgehammer. For a moment, no one moved. Then Keen turned to the rest of the room, his gaze sweeping over the team. "Those of you who are ready to make a real difference come with me. We'll take the fight to MV and anyone else who threatens what we stand for."

The anxiety in the room shifted as several members glanced at one another.

Kayla stepped forward. "I'm in," she said, her voice firm despite the tears welling in her eyes.

Then two more. Five. Seven. Eleven. Each step they took toward Keen felt like a wedge being driven into the team's unity.

Anthem watched the divide grow—not just physically, but philosophically. Friends looked at one another across the widening gap, no longer sure who stood on what side. Some looked down, ashamed. Others looked straight ahead, defiant.

Indy grabbed Anthem's sleeve gently, her voice low. "He's splitting us down the middle."

Anthem couldn't answer. He was too busy watching everything he'd fought for fracture right before his eyes.

Vale watched them leave. His expression was stoic, but his eyes betrayed the unspoken emotion. "I hope you find the answers you're looking for," he said. "Just remember, we're all fighting for the same future."

Keen didn't respond. He turned and walked toward the exit; the others trailing behind him. The door closed behind them with a finality that echoed in the silence left behind.

After a long moment, Vale exhaled through his nose and turned back to what remained of the team. "They made their choice," he mumbled, his voice more tired than angry. "Let's end our debrief there. You all have earned some much-deserved rest."

The room slowly emptied as the remaining team members dispersed, their exhaustion now laced with uncertainty. Shadows clung to the corners of Sound Weaver Studios, no longer a sanctuary—just a bunker barely holding against the storm. Only Anthem, Indy, and Solstice remained, unmoving, as they stared at the screens that lined the far wall.

Footage from the Unity Music Festival looped relentlessly—panic-stricken crowds pushing against toppled barriers, emergency lights cutting through smoke, stretchers vanishing into swarms of fleeing bodies. The sound was muted, but the images said enough.

The headlines scrolling beneath the footage weren't any better.

"Unity Music Festival Descends into Terror."

"Superpowered Musicians Revealed to the World."

"Heroes or Havoc?"

Death Toll: 23

Anthem exhaled sharply, running a hand through his hair. Festivals are supposed to be a celebration of music. Instead, it had become exactly what MV wanted: a catastrophe. In the corner, Solstice stood, arms crossed as he leaned against the wall, his gaze still fixed on the monitors. Across the room, Indy sat hunched over her laptop, her fingers striking the keys like she was typing through fire. "It's bad," she said, the glow of the screen highlighting her furrowed brow. "Social media's gone nuclear."

She turned the laptop toward them, showing a deluge of trending hashtags.

#SoundWeaverDanger

#FestivalFail

#MusicalMenace

But interspersed with the hate were sparks of support: **#Support-SoundWeavers** and **#ThankYouAnthem** were gaining traction. Shaky cell phone footage of Anthem playing his guitar to calm a panicking crowd had gone viral, captioned with things like, *"This guy saved my life last night,"* and **"Music isn't the problem—it's the solution."**

Anthem let out a hollow laugh, shaking his head. "Great. I'm a meme now."

"Better than being a terrorist," Indy said dryly, though the edge in her voice betrayed how little comfort that really offered.

She clicked into a new tab.

MV's face filled the screen—pristine, composed, and framed by a carefully neutral backdrop. His statement had already been distributed across every major news outlet and social platform. The caption below read:

"MV SURVIVES TERROR ATTACK. SOUND WEAVERS ATTACK."

The video played:

"The chaos at the Unity Festival was not spontaneous," MV's voice rang with faux solemnity. "It was orchestrated by radicalized elements from within the Sound Weaver community—led by Anthem Fox, whose destructive influence endangered thousands. This... wasn't art. This was terrorism. And Musera will not be held hostage by dissonance."

The screen cut to heavily edited clips—Anthem mid-strike, smoke and fire in the background. No footage of the civilian attacks MV orchestrated. No evidence of the hostages. No Bliss. No truth.

"Let this be a turning point," MV said. "Let it mark the beginning of account-ability."

Indy's voice cracked. "He's already being awarded a civic honor. They're calling him a symbol of unity. A survivor."

Anthem tensed, but said nothing. His face—his own face—was plastered across the news reel below:

WANTED: ANTHEM FOX.

DO NOT APPROACH–EXTREMELY DANGEROUS.

IF SEEN, REPORT TO CEA IMMEDIATELY.

His name, his face, his worst fears—all twisted into a weapon he couldn't control. Indy opened another stream. A news panel debate, four speakers in tiny boxes arguing over the footage.

"These so-called musicians wield weapons of mass destruction," a woman said. "What else do you call this kind of power?""They saved lives," someone countered. "There's footage—raw, unedited—of one shielding people from debris.""We need stricter control," said another. "We can't let them hide anymore."

"Hide?" the last one scoffed. "He was on stage. Not hiding. He was fighting back."

Anthem turned away, the pit in his stomach growing heavier. The noise from the screens, the arguments, the hashtags—it all felt like a relentless tide threatening to drown him. He pressed his hands to his face, wishing for a moment of silence, a second to think.

Indy's voice snapped him back. "This is exactly what MV wants."

He looked at her, his hands dropping. "What?"

"Division," she said, gesturing at the screens. "Doubt. He wants the public to hate us. If they see us as a threat, as reckless or dangerous, then everything we've worked for falls apart. And it's not just the public—he's trying to divide us from the inside, too. Look at what happened with Keen."

"So, what do we do?" he asked, his voice low but laced with frustration. "How do we fight back when he's got everyone eating out of his hand?"

Solstice turned away from the monitors. "We don't fight back with powers. We fight with the truth. We need to show people who we really are—not just through words, but through action. Let them see what we stand for."

"And if they don't want to see it?" Anthem's voice cracked slightly.

Solstice's gaze locked on his, fierce and unyielding. "Then we keep showing them until they do. Because if we don't, there will be no place for us, and I will not lose *another* family."

The conviction in his voice lit a spark in him, a flicker of determination that he thought had burned out. "You're right," he said, his voice firmer now. "We can't let him take this from us."

Indy nodded, her shoulders relaxing slightly, though the tension in her eyes remained. "Good. Because the fight's not over. Not even close."

The weeks following MV's attack cast a long, trembling shadow across Musera. A country once known for its vibrant rhythm and cultural soul now carried an uneasy stillness. The music had faltered. The aftermath shattered any lingering illusion of normalcy, dragging the Sound Weavers out of the underground and forcing their existence into the unrelenting light of public scrutiny. While the nation slowly tried to piece itself back together, the Sound Weavers faced a new, uncharted path.

In the immediate aftermath, the Museran government responded with swift and decisive action. But instead of cracking down on artists, as many had feared, they did something unexpected: they lifted the restrictions. Not out of generosity, but necessity. With national attention turned toward the dangers that Sound Weavers posed, the government needed every available resource to maintain order.

Citing the incident as proof of the destruction Sound Weavers could unleash, the Harmonic Council declared them a threat to public safety. The Council also enlisted the help of MV's Wave Reavers into their ranks. They now wore the Silencer insignia, their destructive abilities rebranded as instruments of "order." Their loyalty, secured through fear, ideology, or promises of power, made them the Council's most volatile and effective weapons.

For the first time in generations, Sound Weavers were no longer living in secret—but they were still living in hiding.

The attack had brought the Sound Weavers into the public consciousness in a way no one had expected, and now they were everywhere in the media. News reports discussed the implications of their powers, while debates raged about whether or not they should be allowed to live without government oversight. Headlines splashed across the front pages. *"Sound Weavers: A New Age of Art or a Dangerous Threat?"* read one, while another proclaimed, *"City Divided: Should Sound Weavers Be Regulated?"* The divide between fear and fascination was palpable, with some citizens curious about the Sound Weavers' abilities, while others eyed them with suspicion.

As news of the attack and its aftermath rippled beyond Musera's borders, the world responded. Some neighboring nations hailed the Harmonic Council's actions as a necessary measure to protect their nation. Other's reactions were ones of horror, opening their borders to fleeing Sound Weavers.

Some governments and private corporations saw the unfolding chaos as a rare opportunity to seize powerful assets. Sound Weavers with unique abilities were targeted for extraction, either for experimentation or recruitment,

No matter how many ripples and causalities these events have caused, one thing was for certain: for the first time in years, artists were free to create wholeheartedly. No permits to apply for, no inspections to pass, no government-mandated themes to adhere to. The chains that had bound their creativity for so long had been cast aside. What once required bureaucratic navigation and constant fear of censorship could now be shared openly, loudly, and unapologetic.

Across Musera, the streets stirred with new life. Sidewalks turned into makeshift stages. Alley walls transformed into murals overnight. The hush of fear was slowly being replaced by the hum of music, the thrum of poetry, the bold colors of rebellion painted across the city's bones. Rooftop concerts popped up like wildflowers, and underground art galleries spilled out into public parks. What had been silenced for too long now surged forth with unrelenting force—raw, chaotic, beautiful.

It was as if Musera itself had remembered how to breathe.

The people responded. Not just the artists, but the citizens who had always hungered for something more—something real. Crowds gathered in forgotten plazas to dance again. Strangers stood shoulder-to-shoulder under string lights and impromptu performances, swaying not just to the beat, but to the promise of a new beginning. For the first time in a long while, art felt dangerous again. And powerful. And sacred.

Even the old venues—those that hadn't seen life in years—threw open their doors. Places like The Obsidian Key, The Echo Chamber and The Moonlit Grove were filled to bursting. Stories were told. Ballads were born. People cried, laughed, remembered—and hoped.

But for Anthem, a strange quiet settled over his life. The chaos and intensity of the confrontation with MV had left him drained, but also reflective. He had retreated to his sanctuary, the *Riff Runner,* which now sat parked outside the wrought-iron gates of the cemetery where his parents were buried.

The graveyard sat on the outskirts of Crucible City, nestled between rows of cypress trees that swayed gently in the breeze. It wasn't grand—just a quiet, humble place tucked away with a beautiful view of the city below.

Anthem strolled the winding path. He spotted the three graves before he reached them—Geddy, Tatum, Buddy—side by side, marked with polished stone that caught the late afternoon light just enough to sting. Dozens of bouquets laid at the base. He stopped, exhaled, and dropped to one knee.

"I... don't even know what to say anymore," he began, voice hoarse. He placed his hand gently on the ground between the three markers, fingertips brushing the cool grass. "I've already said I was sorry. But it doesn't feel like enough." He looked up, eyes scanning the names carved in granite.

Tatum Monk. Geddy Slate. Buddy Wilde.

"They gave you the nice script. The 'beloved artist, cherished friend' stuff. But you weren't just that. You were chaos and courage and cracked jokes at the worst times. You were *loud.* And now it's so damn quiet." The breeze blew through the cypress again, rustling leaves like pages in a book he didn't want to finish.

"I know it's not the same, but I'll keep playing. I'll carry your sound with me every time I touch a string. I'll make sure people remember you—your music, your hearts. Not just how you died."

His fingers curled into the earth.

"And Bliss..."

The air shifted as he said her name.

"She was one of us. She stood on the same stage. She knew you. She *loved* you. And she still let it happen."

His eyes darkened as he stared into the horizon, his voice low and heavy.

"I don't know what happened to her. What MV twisted in her head. But what she did to you... that's on her."

A breeze stirred the leaves, whispering between the trees like a lost harmony.

"I'm going to make sure she answers for it. I don't know how. I don't know when. But I swear to you she will."

He stood slowly, wiping the back of his hand across his eyes, then pressed his palm to each headstone in turn. Tatum. Geddy. Buddy.

"I'll carry you with me," he said. "Always."

Then he turned and walked away.

Next, he stopped in front of another pair of small, side-by-side headstones. Weatherworn, but lovingly maintained. His mother's favorite flowers—blue aster and trumpet vine—had been placed there by someone else recently.

He just stood there for a long moment, staring at the names etched in stone, waiting for the quiet to settle inside him.

"I... don't even know where to start," Anthem said softly, dropping to one knee. He placed a hand on the ground between the two graves, as if trying to feel them through the soil.

"I thought stopping MV would feel like a victory. I thought the moment we ended him, the world would breathe again. That I would breathe again. But it doesn't feel like that. Not really."

His voice wavered as he looked down.

"I didn't save everyone. I couldn't. People got hurt. People died. And I—I keep thinking there's something else I could've done. Some power I didn't use right. Some sign I missed."

He swallowed, his eyes stinging.

"I keep asking myself... if you were here, would you be proud? Or would you see what I've become and wonder if this was what you raised me for? Music was always supposed to bring people together. But lately... it feels like it just tears the world apart."

The silence that followed didn't answer him. But it didn't scold him either.

Anthem wiped his eyes and exhaled through a tight chest. "I'm trying," he murmured. "I really am. But I don't know what kind of leader I'm supposed to be. Everyone's looking at me like I've got this figured out, like I'm some... symbol. But I'm just a guy with a guitar. And powers I barely understand."

He reached into his jacket, pulling out a worn photo of the two of them—his parents standing beside the Riff Runner, arms slung around teenage Anthem's shoulders, all three of them beaming.

"I miss you," he said. "And I wish I knew how to carry this. Because the fight's not over. And I'm tired. I'm so damn tired."

A breeze rustled through the trees, lifting a few petals from the nearby flowers. They danced briefly in the air before settling again, quiet and soft.

Anthem closed his eyes, just letting the moment be what it was—unresolved, raw, but real.

After a while, he stood, his movements stiff but steady.

He didn't have all the answers. He probably never would. But for now, this was enough to keep going.

He gave the headstones one last glance.

"I'll come back soon," he promised, turning away.

The sun had dipped low by the time Anthem made it back to the Riff Runner. Bathing the cityscape below in a soft amber glow, painting its gleaming towers and wide streets in shades of gold and orange.

Inside, string lights softly. Indy sat in the passenger seat with a blanket around her shoulders, her feet outstretched, resting on the dash, cradling a mug between her hands. Solstice relaxed in the back, one knee pulled up, absently tapping a slow, steady rhythm on it with his drumsticks. From the radio, a low, mournful song drifted through the van — heavy drums, distant guitar, and a raw melodious voice.

They both looked up as Anthem stepped in and closed the door behind him.

"Hey," Indy said softly, her voice like a song that had traded melody for understanding.

Solstice didn't smirk or offer a sarcastic quip this time. He just gave a small nod. "How are they?"

Anthem paused. The compassion in the question settled into the van like a fourth passenger. He didn't answer right away. Just sat there, resting his head back against the headrest.

"Quiet," he finally said. "Peaceful."

Indy watched him closely, her expression softening. "You don't have to say more."

He nodded, grateful. The silence between them was surprisingly comfortable, a quiet understanding shared by those who had faced the seemingly insurmountable together. Occasionally, a faint rustle of leaves or the muted noise of the distant city interrupted the stillness, but it only emphasized the moment's calm.

"They would've been proud of what you did," Indy said, breaking the silence. "What you're doing."

Anthem gave a short laugh, dry and tight in his throat. "Would they? I don't know. MV destroyed half a festival. We nearly died on multiple occasions. And nothing has gotten better. I could argue we made things worse."

"But you stopped MV before things could really spiral out of control," Indy said, leaning forward. "You saved lives. You saved *me.* That matters, Anthem. More than you realize."

"You were where you needed to be," Solstice added. "You always are. That kind of instinct? That doesn't just come from talent. It comes from the heart. You've got more of that than anyone I've ever met."

Anthem looked between them—two of the only people who'd stood beside him in the fire and refused to leave.

Indy changed the subject. "You know, this view almost makes everything feel... manageable."

Anthem glanced at her and smirked faintly. "Almost."

"Managing isn't really my thing," Solstice said from the back, laced with dry humor as he twirled a drumstick between his fingers. "But I'll take the quiet while it lasts."

Anthem chuckled. "Quiet's rare these days. Might as well enjoy it."

Indy nodded, her gaze still fixed on the city. "It's nice to know we can still have moments like this. Even if they're few and far between."

"Yeah, even if everything's changing," he said. "The world's cracking open and I don't know what comes next. But I know I don't want to face it alone."

Indy smiled. "Good. Because you're not."

Then Anthem looked toward the front of the Riff Runner, toward the horizon that was waiting just beyond the glass. "We should make something out of this," he said. "Something new. Bigger than us. A sound that fights back."

Indy turned her head to look at him, her dark eyes full of understanding, as though she had been waiting for this conversation. "Go on." She prompted gently, taking a sip from the mug.

Anthem sighed, his fingers absentmindedly drumming on the steering wheel. "I'm grateful for the Sound Weavers, for what they've done for us. They gave us a community when I felt lost, helped me understand my powers when I didn't know what was happening. But..." He paused, finally turning to meet her gaze. "My heart is in the music. And with recent developments, I feel like that's where I can make the most difference."

Indy nodded slowly, a small, knowing smile playing at her lips. "I figured you'd say something like that. You've always been more about creating than destroying. It's part of what makes you who you are."

Anthem chuckled softly. "Yeah, well, sometimes I wonder if I'm just running from the responsibility of it all. But the truth is, I can't keep fighting battles that tear things apart. I want to build something, something that lasts."

He leaned back in his seat, eyes fixed on the ceiling of the Riff Runner. The ghost of *Manufacturing Eden* still played in his mind like a song that wouldn't fade. "Manufacturing Eden was... special. We had something, but it feels like a lifetime ago. Things are different now. I'm different. I want to move forward, to create something new."

Indy set her mug down on the dashboard and shifted to face him fully. "And what about the Sound Weavers? Do you still believe in their mission?"

Anthem nodded slowly, his gaze drifting back out to the city. "More than ever. But the way we've been doing things—hiding underground, acting like ghosts—it's not sustainable. We're not in complete secrecy anymore, but we're still running. Still flinching every time the CEA gets too close." He exhaled. "We shouldn't have to be rebels forever."

Indy studied him for a long beat before reaching out and resting her hand over his. "This could be it. The moment. We have a chance to show the world what we really are. Not fugitives. Not freaks. Artists. Leaders. A renaissance for real this time."

Anthem let her words sink in, feeling them resonate deep within him. *Renaissance.* Rebirth. Reinvention. The idea of a Renaissance for the Sound Weavers—of rebuilding their identity from the ground up—wasn't just hopeful. It was necessary.

He turned to her, a slow grin spreading across his face. "A Renaissance, huh?"

Indy laughed softly, the sound light and filled with optimism. "Why not? It's time for something new. Something bold. I mean, look at the world out there," she gestured to the glowing city below them. "It's ready for a change. We just have to be the ones to lead it."

[1] Anthem's mind churned with possibilities. The idea of starting fresh, of taking everything they had learned, everything they had been forced to hide, and unleashing it for the world to see—stirred something deep within him. For a long time he had felt untethered, a string of potential with no melody to ground it. But now, a new idea took shape, building into something undeniable.

As if on cue, the radio shifted to a heavier track—low growl of bass, crackling guitars, and a voice soaked in anger and defiance—raw and ready to set fire to every expectation.

"We need to start a band," he said suddenly, the words spilling out before he fully realized he was going to say them.

Indy raised an eyebrow in intrigued surprise. "A band?"

"Yeah," Anthem said, his voice gaining momentum as the idea crystallized. "Remember, I was musing over the idea weeks ago. Now sounds like a great time to see it through. But not just any band—a Sound Weaver band. We take all of this..." he gestured broadly. His hands glowed faintly as his powers resonated with his excitement. "Everything we've been hiding, all the power we've been keeping in the shadows, and put it out there for everyone to see. A group of Sound Weavers, playing music that's magic—literal magic. We show the world exactly who we are."

From the back of the van, Solstice stirred. He leaned forward, elbows on knees, clicking his drumsticks together in a slow, thoughtful rhythm. "You're suggesting we paint targets on our backs? Bold plan...I like it."

---

1. Track 18 – The Warning – Hell You Call A Dream

"Targets they already painted," Anthem said, his tone cooling. "We're just choosing what kind of devils we get to be."

Solstice sat forward. "Devils?"

Anthem turned to face them both. "The CEA wants to cast us as monsters. Demons. Fine. If that's the story they want to tell... then let's own it. Let's be the devils in the hell they created. *Devils by Design.*"

Indy's eyes lit up first, a smile tugging at the corner of her lips. "That's... actually really good."

Solstice tilted his head, nodding slowly. "Intentional rebellion. Not born bad. Made dangerous." He smirked. "I've heard worse."

"Exactly," Anthem said. "We're not evil—we're inconvenient. We're what happens when people refuse to be muted. They tried to design a world without us. Now we show them we were designed to survive it."

Indy leaned back, letting the name settling. "*Devils by Design.* Damn, that's going to look great on a poster."

Anthem's fingers drummed against the steering wheel, the rhythm quickening without thought. Ideas surged like a rising tide—names, stages, songs not yet written. For the first time in forever, the future didn't feel like a burden. "We'll gather the best Sound Weavers, and we'll make something unforgettable. This is our chance, Indy. Our chance to lead this renaissance."

"You're right. Together, we could lead the Sound Weavers into a new era, one filled with harmony and the raw power of creation." Indy replied.

And just like that, something shifted. The road ahead no longer felt like a desperate sprint—it felt like a march. Anthem glanced at Indy and Solstice, and for the first time in a long time, the path ahead was clear, brightly lit by their declaration.

No longer rebels in the dark.

They were *Devils by Design.*

The three of them sat in silence for a moment, the weight of their decision hanging in the air like the final note of a powerful performance. Outside, the lights of Crucible City twinkled in the darkness, and for the first time in days, Anthem felt like he could finally see the road ahead. The *Riff Runner* had always been a symbol of his journey, of freedom and self-discovery. Now, it would be the vehicle that carried him into this new era.

Anthem turned the key in the ignition. The van rumbled to life beneath them, its engine crackling like an opening chord. The headlights cut through the night, illuminating a winding street that stretched beyond what they could see.

He didn't know what battles still waited. What enemies would rise. What sacrifices might come next. But he knew who he was. And more importantly, he knew the sound he wanted to leave behind.

And it wouldn't be silenced.

391

Anthem's Journey Will Continue...

ABOUT ME

Thanks again for reading The Sound Weaver Saga. I can't express enough, how grateful I am for anyone to read these words I strung together.

But here is a little about me. I currently live in Denver, Colorado, where I spend an alarming amount of time lost in fictional worlds.

A proud movie buff, television addict, comic book hoarder, and self-declared book snob, I believe that no story is too big, too weird, or too ridiculous to be told. I like to write stories that I like to read. That ranges across genres, happily swinging between themes like friendship, power, identity, and survival — sometimes all in the same afternoon.

I write because creating something out of nothing feels like the closest thing to real magic (and because shouting ideas into the void wasn't paying the bills).

And lastly, when I'm not writing, I'm probably debating who is the G.O.A.T. of professional wrestling. (John Cena)

Stay connected (he promises he's not *that* weird):

Linktree: https://linktr.ee/sterlingstone

Instagram: @sterlingstonewrites